THE PERFUME
COLLECTOR

Also by Kathleen Tessaro

KATHLEEN TESSARO

THE PERFUME COLLECTOR

The Perfume Collector
Copyright © 2013 by Kathleen Tessaro.
All rights reserved.

Published by HarperCollins Publishers Ltd

First published in Canada by HarperCollins Publishers Ltd in
an original trade paperback edition: 2013
First Harper Perennial trade paperback edition: 2014
This mass market edition: 2017

HarperCollins books may be purchased for educational, business,
or sales promotional use through our Special Markets Department.

HarperCollins Publishers Ltd
2 Bloor Street East, 20th Floor
Toronto, Ontario, Canada
M4W 1A8

www.harpercollins.ca

Library and Archives Canada Cataloguing in Publication
information is available upon request.

ISBN 978-1-44345-454-4

Printed and bound in the United States

LSC/H 9 8 7 6 5 4 3 2 1

For my son Eddie
Always, evermore . . . and then some

Acknowledgements

I would like to thank the following people: my agents Jonny Geller and Jennifer Joel, my editors Katie Espiner, Maya Ziv and Lorissa Sengara, as well as Cassie Browne, Jaime Frost, Louisa Joyner and Katherine Beitner. I'm especially grateful for the notes and encouragement of Jo Rodgers, the support of my husband Gregory Liberi and the editorial comments of my friend and mentor, Jill Robinson.

Paris, Winter 1954

Eva d'Orsey sat at the kitchen table, listening to the ticking clock, a copy of *Le Figaro* in front of her. This was the sound of time, moving away from her.

Taking another drag from a cigarette, she looked out of the window, into the cold misty morning. Paris was waking now, the grey dawn, streaked with orange, seeping slowly into a navy sky. She'd been up for hours, since four. Sleep had inched away from her these past years as the pain increased, shooting up along the left side of her body.

The doctor had given up on her months ago. His diagnosis: she was not a good patient; arrogant, refused to follow directions. The cirrhosis was spreading rapidly now, pitting her liver like a sponge. For him it was simple: she had to stop drinking.

'You're not even trying,' he'd reprimanded her at the last appointment.

3

She was buttoning her blouse, on top of the examination table. 'I'm having difficulty sleeping.'

'Well, I'm not surprised,' he sighed. 'Your liver is completely inflamed.'

She caught his eye. 'I need something to help me.'

Shaking his head, he crossed to his desk; scribbled out a prescription. 'I shouldn't even give you these, you know. Take only one, they're very strong,' he warned, handing her the script.

'Thank you.'

Still, he couldn't resist one last try. 'Why don't you at least cut down on smoking?'

Why indeed?

Exhaling, Eva stubbed the Gitanes cigarette out in the ashtray. They were common – too strong. Unladylike. But that suited her. She could only taste strong flavours now. Cheap chocolate, coarse pâté, black coffee. What she ate didn't matter anyway; she had no appetite left.

There was something naïve, sweetly arrogant about the doctor's assumption that everyone wanted to live forever.

Picking up a pen, she traced a ring of even circles along the border of the newspaper.

There were still a few more details to be arranged. She'd been to the lawyer weeks ago, a diligent, rather aloof young man. And she'd left the box with the

4

sour-faced concierge, Madame Assange, for safe keeping. But last night, when she couldn't sleep, another idea occurred to her. There was the passage, from London to Paris. The idea of an aeroplane intrigued her. It was extravagant and unnecessary. But there were a few things a person should experience in life; air travel was definitely one of them. She smiled to herself, imagining the approach to Paris, the miles of cold, blue sea and then the first sighting of the city.

She winced. Pain again, knife stabs, followed by numbness down the side of her body.

She thought about the bottle of cognac. She didn't want to drink during the day. After 6 p.m. was her new rule. At least that's what she planned. But her hands were shaking now; her stomach lurched.

No. She would run a bath. Dress. And go to 7.30 Mass at Église de la Madeleine. Of all the churches in Paris, this was her favourite. There, Mary Magdalene, that wayward, difficult daughter of the Church, ascended regally into heaven on the arms of angels all day, every day.

Mass was like grand opera, a magic show with the most expensive props in town. And faith, a sleight of hand trick, in which one was both the magician and the audience; the deceiver and the deceived. Still, who could resist a good magic trick?

Folding over the paper, Eva pushed out her chair and stood up.

She would wear her best navy suit, sit in the front pew with the faithful. Together they'd listen to the young priest, Father Paul, struggle to make sense of the scripture, try with all his considerable intellect to apply it to the present day. He didn't always succeed. He didn't know how to justify the inconsistencies; hadn't yet realized that they themselves were the mystery. Still, his mental adroitness pleased her, almost as much as it pleased him. Frequently he was reduced to searching through layers of various possible Hebrew translations for an unexpected verb form to finally shed light on some vast spiritual contradiction. But his heroism in trying wasn't lost on her. And she valued those who tried, especially those whose struggles were public and obvious.

Of course he didn't see it that way. Only a few years out of seminary, he imagined he was imparting spiritual sustenance and guidance to his flock. What he didn't understand was that his elderly parishioners, mostly women, were there for him, rather than the other way around. Father Paul was at the start of life. His glassy convictions needed protection. They waited patiently until he too succumbed to the unbearable unevenness of God's will, the sureness of his grace, the darkness of his mercy.

6

These thoughts calmed her. Her mind was off, whirring again on a familiar track: the paradoxes of faith and doubt. Like a worn piece of fabric, made soft by much handling, comforting to the touch.

Mass and then, yes, the travel agent.

Taking the ashtray to the sink, she emptied it, rinsed it out. Below, in the alleyway, something moved . . . a looming shadow – shifting, cutting. Black wings beating, wheeling as one, until they filled the entire wall opposite, blotting out the pale rays of the winter sun.

Suddenly another memory took hold. A breathless, stumbling terror; the smell of green fields and damp woodland – and a massive flock of ravens, reeling across the open sky, wings glistening like ebony, beaks like razors – crying, shrieking.

Eva grasped the counter, pressed her eyes closed. The ashtray dropped, clattering into the porcelain sink.

It shattered.

'Damn!'

Eva peered warily out the window, her heart still pounding. The shadow was gone. A flock of common city pigeons most likely.

Picking up the pieces, she lined them up on the counter top. It was an old, inexpensive object. But it reminded her of another time, when life was full of beginnings.

The clock ticked loudly.

She wavered only a moment.

Reaching for a glass, Eva took down the bottle of cheap cognac and poured with unsteady hands, gulping it down. Instantly the alcohol warmed her, radiating out through her limbs; taking the edge off.

That doctor understood nothing.

He didn't know what it was like to live between memory and regret with nothing to numb it.

Pouring another, Eva ran her finger over the rough edge of the broken porcelain.

She would glue it.

Bathe.

Wear her navy suit.

Tilting her head back, she took another swallow.

It didn't matter anymore if the cracks showed.

London, Spring 1955

Grace Munroe woke up with a start, gasping for breath.

She'd been running, stumbling, over uneven ground, in a thick, dense forest; searching, calling out. But the harder she ran the more impenetrable the woodland became. Vines grew, twisting beneath her feet, branches whipped against her face, arms and legs. And there was the panicky feeling that time was running out. She was chasing someone or something. But it was always just ahead, out of reach. Suddenly she lost her footing, tumbling head over heels into a deep, rocky ravine.

Heart pounding in her chest, Grace took a moment, blinking in the dusky half-light, to realize that she was in her own bedroom, lying on top of her bed.

It was a dream.

Only a dream.

Reaching across, she turned on the bedside lamp, falling back against the pillows. Her heart was still galloping, hands trembling. It was an old nightmare, from her childhood. She thought she'd grown out of it. But now, after years, it was back.

How long had she been asleep anyway? She looked across at the alarm clock. Nearly 6.30. Damn.

She'd only meant to take fifteen minutes. But it had been nearly an hour.

Mallory would be here any minute and she still had to dress. Grace didn't want to go tonight, only she'd promised her friend.

Going to the window overlooking Woburn Square below, Grace pulled back the heavy curtains.

It was late afternoon in April, the time of year when the daylight hours stretched eagerly towards summer and the early evening light was a delicate Wedgwood blue, gilded with the promise of future warmth. The plane trees lining the square bore the very beginnings of tender, bright green buds on their branches that in the summer would form a thick emerald canopy. Only now they were just twigs, shaking violently with each gust of icy wind.

The central garden had been dug and planted with produce during the war; its railings had been melted down and had yet to be restored. The buildings that survived in the area were blackened by smoke and pitted from shrapnel.

There was a sense of quickening in the air, the change of seasons, of hope tempered by the impending nightfall. Outside, the birds sang, green shoots of hyacinth and narcissus swayed in the wind. Warm in the sun, freezing in the shade, it was a season of extremes.

Grace had a fondness for the sharpness of this time of year; for the muted, shifting light that played tricks on her eyes. It was a time of mysterious, yet dramatic metamorphosis. One minute there was nothing but storms and rain; a moment later a field of daffodils appeared, exploding triumphantly into a fanfare of colour.

Grace pressed her fingertips against the cold glass of the window. This was not, as her husband Roger put it, their real house. He had more ambitious plans for something grander, closer to Belgravia. But Grace liked it here; being in the centre of Bloomsbury, close to London University and King's College, it reminded her of Oxford, where she'd lived with her uncle until only a few years ago. It was filled with activity; businesses and offices, and students rushing to class. In the street below, a current of office workers, wrapped in raincoats, heads bent against the wind, moved in a steady stream towards the Underground station after work.

Grace leaned her head against the window frame.

It must be nice to have a job. A neatly arranged desk. A well-organized filing cabinet. And most of all, purpose.

Now that she was married, her days had a weary open-endedness about them; she floated like a balloon from one social obligation to another.

Roger took each engagement very seriously. 'Did you speak to anyone at the Conservative Ladies Club luncheon? Whom did you sit next to? Tell me who was there.'

He was uncannily skilled at dissecting hidden meaning behind every interaction.

'They put you at the first table, near the front. That's good. Make certain you write to Mona Riley and thank her for the invitation. Perhaps you could arrange an informal dinner? Or better yet, invite her for tea somewhere and see if you can wangle a dinner party out of her. It would be better if they asked us first. One doesn't want to seem eager.'

He was counting on her to grease the wheels, only Grace wasn't much of a social mechanic. And she lacked any pleasure in the game.

Still, she needed to hurry, she reminded herself, if she didn't want to keep Mallory waiting.

Opening the bedroom door, she called down the steps to the housekeeper, who was cleaning downstairs. 'Mrs Deller!'

'Yes?' came a voice from the kitchen, two flights below.

'Would you mind terribly bringing me a cup of tea, please?'

'Yes, ma'am.'

Grace hurried into the bathroom, splashed her face with cold water and dabbed it dry, examining her features in the mirror. She really should make more of an effort – buy some blue eyeshadow and black liquid eyeliner; learn to pencil in her eyebrows with the bold, stylized make-up that was all the rage. Instead, she patted her nose and cheeks with a bit of face powder and applied a fresh coat of red lipstick. Her hair was long, just below her shoulders. Without bothering to brush it out, and with the deftness of much practice, she arranged it into a chignon, pinning it back with hairpins. Downstairs the doorbell rang.

'Damn!'

Of all the times for Mallory to actually be on time!

Flinging open the wardrobe doors, Grace grabbed a blue shantung silk cocktail dress and tossed it on the bed. She stepped out of her tweed skirt and pulled her blouse up over her head without undoing the buttons.

Where were the matching navy shoes?

She scanned the bottom of the wardrobe. Bending

down, she felt the heel of her stocking begin to ladder up the back of her calf.

'Oh, bugger!'

Unfastening her suspenders, she could hear Mrs Deller answering the door; the soft inflections of women's voices as she took Mallory's coat. And then the steps of the old Georgian staircase creaking in protest as Mallory made her way upstairs.

Grace yanked a fresh pair of stockings from her chest of drawers and sat down on the edge of the bed to put them on.

There was a knock. 'It's only me. Are you decent?'

'If you consider a petticoat decent.'

Mallory poked her head round the door. Her deep auburn hair was arranged in low curls and a string of pearls set off her pale skin. 'Haven't you changed yet? It's already started, Grace!'

Grace hooked the tops of her stockings and stood up. 'Isn't it fashionable to be late?'

'Since when are you concerned with what's fashionable?'

Grace pivoted round. 'Are my seams straight?'

'Yes. Here.' Mallory handed her the cup of tea she was carrying. 'Your housekeeper asked me to give you this.'

'Thank you.' Grace took a sip as Mallory rustled across the room in her full-skirted evening dress, perching delicately on the edge of the armchair, so as not to crease the fabric.

'What have you been doing all afternoon, anyway?' Mallory chided.

'Oh, nothing.' Grace didn't like to admit to sleeping during the day; it felt like the thin edge of the wedge. 'And what about you? What did you do?'

'I've only just got back from the hairdresser's an hour ago.' Mallory turned her head, showcasing both her lovely profile and the result of their handiwork. 'I swear, Mr Hugo is the only person in London I'll let touch my hair. You should go to him. He's a miracle worker. Have you got a spare ciggie?'

'Just there.' Grace nodded to a silver cigarette box on the table. She took another gulp of tea and put it down on the dresser.

Mallory took one out. 'What are you wearing tonight?'

'The blue taffeta.'

'Old faithful!' Mallory smiled, shaking her head. 'We have to take you shopping, my dear. There are such beautiful things out at the moment.'

At thirty, Mallory was only three years older than Grace but already established on the London social scene as one of the fashionable young women. Married to Grace's cousin, Geoffrey, she tried to take Grace under her wing. However, Grace proved

15

frustratingly immune to her instruction.

'You don't like this dress?' Grace asked.

Mallory shrugged. 'It's perfectly fine.'

Grace held it up again. 'What's wrong with it?'

'It's just, oh, I don't know. You know what Vanessa's like. Everything's always cutting edge, up to the minute. The very latest look of 1956 . . .'

'Which is remarkable because it's only 1955, Mal.'

'That's exactly what I mean! She's ahead of her time.'

'Yes, but I don't have to compete with Vanessa, do I? We can't all be trendsetters. That woman has far too much time on her hands and far too much money.'

'Perhaps, but nobody wants to miss one of her parties, do they? You need to start entertaining properly too. Tonight will be a good opportunity to steal some names from Vanessa's guest list. I've got a little notebook and pencil in my handbag if you need it.'

'Oh God!' Grace shuddered. 'I can't bear the thought of it!'

'Honestly!' Mallory rolled her eyes. 'What did you do up in Oxford for entertainment anyway?'

'My uncle is a don. We had people round for cauliflower cheese and played bridge.'

'How ghastly!' Mallory laughed. 'You're going to have to get over this aversion to speaking to other people if you want to be an asset to your husband. He's not going to be promoted on his good looks

16

alone.' She smiled. 'You haven't got a light, have you? Do you like this?' She stood up, twirling round, showing off the full skirt of the deep red off-the-shoulder dress she was wearing. 'It's new. From Simpson's.'

'Very fetching.' Grace stepped into her navy dress. 'There's a lighter in there, isn't there?'

Mallory rifled round in the cigarette box. 'Not that I can see. Here.' She popped the cigarette into the corner of her perfectly rouged mouth. 'Let me do you up.'

Grace stood in front of her while Mallory zipped up the back of her dress. 'Roger must've taken it. We're always losing lighters. That one's my favourite though. I'll kill him if he's lost it.'

Mallory tugged at a good two inches of fabric that should have been fitted closely to Grace's waist. 'This is too big. You've lost weight again.' There was an accusatory tone in her voice.

Grace crossed to her dressing table, opened a drawer and took out a box of matches. She tossed them to Mallory, who caught them midair, with the hidden athletic reflexes of a childhood tomboy. 'Light me one too, will you?'

'With pleasure. After all, you are my date tonight.'

'Thank you for that.' Grace caught her eye in the mirror and winked, as she put a pair of pearl clips on. It wasn't lost on her that Mal was actually trying

17

to help her. 'It was good of you to invite me.'

'We can't have you wasting away while Roger's out of town.' Mallory lit two cigarettes and passed one to Grace. 'Besides, it's not often I get to ditch my husband for someone who actually listens to what I say. He can't bear Vanessa anyway, thinks she's a bad influence.'

'Is she?'

'Of course.' Mallory picked up a pamphlet lying on top of a stack of books on the table. 'What's this?'

'Nothing.' Grace wished she'd had the foresight to put them away now. 'Just a schedule of classes.'

'The Oxford and County Secretarial College?' Mallory flipped through; it naturally fell open to the pages Grace had already dog-eared. 'Advanced Typing and Office Management? Bookkeeping?' She made a face. 'What's all this about?'

'You never know,' Grace slipped on the navy pumps, 'it might be quite helpful. Roger may well open his own offices one day. I could be a valuable asset to him; organize his appointments, type letters . . .'

'But Grace, you *have* a job,' Mallory pointed out. 'You're his wife.'

'That's not a job, Mal.'

Mallory flashed her a look. 'Really? I wonder if you've read the fine print on your marriage certificate.

18

It's up to you to create a home, a family, a vision of where you all fit in the world and where you're going. Think about it – the children's schools, where you spend the weekends, your entire social circle – it's all down to you.' She put on an exaggerated accent. 'Oh, the Munroes? Of course I know them! Isn't she wonderful? Her son is at Harrow with our eldest. And I love what she's done with the house, don't you?' Mallory took another drag, tossing the leaflet down. 'Believe me, Ducky, you have a job. Besides, this place is in Oxford. How many times do I have to remind you that you live in London now?'

'Yes, but the courses only last a few months.'

'A few months? Are you mad? What's Roger supposed to do while you're gone?' Mallory exhaled. 'Honestly, you should learn something useful in your spare time.'

'Like what?'

'I don't know . . .' The whole idea of self-improvement was alien to her. 'Flower arranging. Or the harp, perhaps.'

'The harp? What's useful about a harp?'

Mallory thought a moment. 'It's soothing. Isn't it? And you get to stroke something between your legs in public!'

'Good God, you're depraved!' Grace laughed. 'I'll

tell you what's soothing — rearranging a filing cabinet, ordering new stationery or getting the books to balance.'

'Grace . . .' Mallory threw her hands up in despair. 'Do you listen to anything I say? Honestly, you're not in Oxford now. And I'll tell you a little secret,' she dropped her voice to a stage whisper, 'men don't like clever wives, they like charming ones!'

'No!' Grace gasped in pretend shock. 'You don't think I'm charming?'

Mallory rolled her eyes. 'You're delightful. I'm only saying—'

'I understand,' Grace cut her off. Mallory wasn't about to be persuaded. Every time they met, she had new suggestions for enhancing her homemaking skills; talents she clearly felt Grace was lacking. Why should tonight be any different?

Mallory checked her lipstick in her compact mirror. 'When's Roger coming home anyway?'

'In a week. Maybe sooner.'

'He's been away on business a long time. You must miss him.'

Grace said nothing.

'When he's home, you'll forget all that nonsense. Now, have you got a belt you can wear?' She rustled up behind her. 'Really! Didn't anyone explain to you that you're meant to gain weight in the first few years of marriage? How am I meant to become the spoiling godmother if you don't get down to the business of fattening up?'

Something changed in Grace's eyes. Inhaling hard, she turned away. 'I don't think I have a belt,' she said quietly, looking through the dresses hanging in her wardrobe.

Mallory stared at Grace's slim back.

She'd obviously hit a nerve.

'Here,' Mallory reached across, tugging a cummerbund of black velvet from another evening gown. 'This one will do just fine,' she said, fitting it round Grace's waist.

Grace looked small tonight, even younger than usual. She reminded Mallory of a little girl dressing up in her mother's clothes. It was the hairstyle, so conservative and staid; it would've suited an older woman but on Grace it only accentuated her youth. It made her eyes look even larger than normal; they were a very clear grey-green colour, wide set and almond-shaped.

'Do you think this is all right?' Grace examined her reflection in the mirror, tense.

It wasn't like Grace to care too much what others thought. Suddenly Mallory realized it was one of the things that secretly she'd admired about her friend, despite their constant sparring.

21

'It's perfect,' she assured her. 'Now let's go or we shall miss the whole thing.'

Coming down the stairs, Grace paused to check the second post on the hall table.

'Oh look!' She held up an envelope. 'I've got airmail! From France. How exciting!' She tore it open. 'Who do I know in France?'

'Is it from your uncle?' Mallory pulled her coat on.

'No, he's in America, lecturing.' Grace unfolded the letter, began reading.

Mallory waited; tapped her foot impatiently. 'We must go.' She took out her car keys. 'What is it anyway?'

'This doesn't make sense.'

'Is it in French?'

'No. No, it's in English.' Grace sat down on the hall chair. 'There's an aeroplane ticket.'

'An aeroplane ticket? For where?'

'To Paris.' Grace looked up, handing her the letter. 'This is a mistake. Some sort of very bizarre mistake.'

Mallory took it.

It was typed on the kind of heavy, good quality paper that signaled official correspondence. In the corner she noted the name and address of a law firm in central Paris: Frank, Levin et Beaumont.

Dear Mrs Munroe,

Please accept our sincere sympathies for your recent loss. Our firm is handling the estate of the deceased Madame Eva d'Orsey, and it is our duty to inform you that you are named as the chief beneficiary in her will. We request your presence at our offices at your earliest convenience, so that we may go through the details of your inheritance.

Again, we apologize for this intrusion on your time of grief and look forward to being of service to you in the near future.

Yours sincerely,

Edouard A. Tissot, Esquire

'Oh!' Mallory looked up. 'I'm so sorry. I had no idea you'd recently lost someone, Grace.'

Grace's face was unchanging. 'Neither had I.'

'I beg your pardon?'

'Mallory, I've never met any Eva d'Orsey. I have no idea who this woman is.'

<hr />

Vanessa Maxwell knew how to throw a party. It was her greatest contribution and would doubtless be her lasting legacy to those who had known, if not loved her, long after she was gone.

The first rule was that they were almost always held on the spur of the moment. Unlike some hostesses who sent out invitations a month in advance, Vanessa understood that the success of the entire venture depended upon the delicate relationship between anticipation and fulfilment; too long a wait between one and the other resulted only in indifference and boredom. And any event that didn't demand the frantic re-juggling of previous commitments, a trail of white lies and the testing of long-held personal loyalties wasn't worth attending.

Secondly, she was ruthless about whom she invited. She almost never returned an invitation with one of her own. In fact, she was famous for picking people she'd only just met, pairing them up in unlikely, possibly incendiary ways. She tossed elder statesmen next to starlets, seated royalty across from working-class playwrights; once she sent her chauffeur to the Florida Club only to return with an entire jazz ensemble plucked off stage and half a dozen dancers from an all-male burlesque review in Soho to 'liven things up a bit'.

Lastly, her events were held in rooms far too small, far too bright. People rubbed up against one another, jostled for space, occasionally landed in one another's laps. While any other hostess would lull her guests into a coma with soft lights and deep comfortable sofas, Vanessa demanded that everyone, regardless of age or position, wedge themselves into a cramped pub in Shepherd Market, around the slippery border of a public swimming pool or onto the balcony of a private club. People shouted to be heard, grabbed at the drinks floating by on silver trays, eavesdropped shamelessly on intimate conversations as they allowed their hands to wander, brushing up against the warm limbs of strangers.

There was an air of danger to her gatherings; the frisson of mischief. At her most famous dinner party she hired a sprinkling of actors to pose as staff and one as an unfortunate guest who was then dramatically poisoned during the first course. It was then up to the remaining guests to solve the mystery before the police arrived or they themselves were eliminated through one heinous end or another.

It was just this kind of daring enterprise that had catapulted her and, by default, her husband, businessman and tobacconist Phillip Maxwell, to the top of the London social scene.

Grace had never been invited to one of Vanessa's parties before; to say they didn't travel in the same circles was putting it kindly. Grace's husband Roger knew Phillip Maxwell professionally and had known Vanessa before either of them were married. But Grace, coming from Oxford, was still an outsider.

Mallory, however, had been twice before; a distinction she both relished and pretended not to notice. She'd been the first to fall into the water at the famous midnight pool party and charmed everyone with the nonchalance with which she proceeded to wear her sopping wet gown, transparent and clinging to her admirable figure, for the rest of the evening.

Tonight, however, was a relatively simple affair by comparison. As loyal members of the Tory Party, the Maxwells were hosting a campaign fundraiser aimed at securing Anthony Eden as prime minister. Eden, appointed Churchill's natural successor upon his resignation, had called a general election for 26 May and his pledge that 'Peace comes first, always,' struck a chord with a nation weary from sacrifice and loss.

To highlight this dawning age of prosperity, Vanessa had organized an impromptu 'Summer Fete' in the Orangery of Kensington Palace, with traditional entertainment and food, including a coconut shy, dunk tank, horseshoes, egg-and-spoon races, jugglers and even pony rides, while vats of Pimm's, strawberry ice, caviar tarts and champagne made the rounds. The only difference was that the tickets were purchased in pounds rather than pennies, and the stalls were manned by famous faces from the stage and screen.

As soon as they entered it was clear from the crush of bodies that most of fashionable London was in attendance. A large banner with the slogan 'United for Peace and Progress' hung across the entrance. People were shouting and waving to one another across a sea of faces; smoke clouds hung thick and heavy; the constant throbbing tempo of a brass band could be heard pulsing like a heartbeat beneath the general roar.

Holding each other's hands, the two girls slipped through the crowds.

'Can you see her?' Grace scanned the long gallery.

'She's over there!' Mallory shouted back, waving to a small, dark-haired woman, surrounded by people on the other side of the room.

She dragged Grace through the throng.

'Vanessa!'

Vanessa turned round. Dressed in a gauzy evening gown of layered black chiffon, she had sharp, even features and rather small, deep brown eyes. Although not very tall, she was so delicate and perfectly proportioned that despite her unremarkable face she could only be described as exquisite. Next to her, other women appeared suddenly bedraggled and bovine. Her manner was relaxed; almost bored, as if she weren't greeting her guests so much as auditioning them. And every detail of her person was flawlessly finished – from the smooth centre-parting of her hair drawn back behind her ears to reveal a pair of magnificent emerald clips, to her long, slender fingers, accented with creamy, pale polish, the precise translucent shade of the small cluster of rosebuds that adorned her waist. Vanessa smiled, taking a long, slow drag of her cigarette. 'Welcome, ladies! I hope you're feeling lucky. There's a tombola that includes a ladies' gold watch from Asprey and the tickets are going like hot cakes. That new comedian Benny Hill is hosting the auction.'

'The one from the television?' Mallory's eyes widened.

'The very same. And let me tell you, he's nothing like that in real life!'

'How did you manage it?'

'The same way I manage anything – through sheer unrelenting gall.' She turned to Grace, looking at her steadily from beneath hooded lids. 'I don't believe we've had the pleasure.'

'Oh, I want you to meet my friend, Grace Munroe. Roger's wife.'

'Hello,' Grace held out her hand. 'And thank you for having me. This is simply . . . well . . . incredible!'

Vanessa received Grace's fingertips with a squeeze, tilting her head to one side, 'So, you're Roger's wife. We were all wondering where he'd disappeared to.' Taking another deep drag, she regarded Grace with frank curiosity, as if she were a rare specimen on display in a museum. 'You're related to Lord Royce, aren't you?'

'He's my second cousin on my mother's side. He inherited the title when my grandfather died.'

'I see.' Vanessa exhaled, a long thin stream of smoke shooting from her nose. 'You're quite pretty, aren't you?'

Grace blushed a little, feeling suddenly gauche; like a child who'd been trotted out before bedtime to entertain older relatives with their good manners. 'Thank you.'

'And where is your husband tonight?' Vanessa asked.

'In Scotland. On business.'

'How terrible for you. Or,' she arched an eyebrow, 'perhaps lucky. I know I'd be euphoric if Phillip went away.'

'You've done a wonderful job.' Grace shifted the conversation away from herself. 'I'm sure the fund-raiser will be a grand success.'

'I do my best. Wander round,' Vanessa suggested with a wave of her hand, turning back to greet some other guests. 'And buy lots of tickets, girls. It's for the good of Britain.' She flashed Grace a little smile. 'So nice to meet you. Really.'

'Let's get a drink,' Mallory decided, heading for the refreshments table. 'And I don't mind telling you, I have designs on that gold watch.'

Grace put a hand on Mallory's arm. 'How did Vanessa know about my family?'

'I don't know. I suppose it's common knowledge. Why?'

'Nothing.' Grace frowned. 'Only there's a family rumour my cousin is going to be forced to sell the estate soon. Roger's quite upset about it. But those old places simply burn money and there's so much debt.'

Mallory gave her hand a squeeze. 'Don't think about that tonight, darling. It's probably just a coincidence that she brought it up.'

Grace hadn't expected to enjoy herself but the evening was surprisingly entertaining. Vanessa's cattle car policy meant that conversation was immediate and the carnival games created a raucous sense of competitive camaraderie. Mallory lost almost five pounds on the coconut shy before finally landing an up-and-coming Rank starlet in the dunk tank, to the extreme delight of all the men nearby. Grace excelled at horseshoes, eventually being outplayed by the Duchess of Kent. Neither of the girls won the gold watch. Grace discovered a few familiar faces amidst the throng and both she and Mallory devoured several caviar tarts washed down with champagne.

Then Mallory spotted the Mr Memory stall, manned by Phillip Maxwell himself in a top hat and tails, and became even more excited.

'Look! We used to play this game all the time as children.' She grabbed Grace's arm and dragged her across the hall. 'I'm an expert at this. Come on. I'll go against you, one on one.'

'I've never played.' Grace stared at the row of increasingly larger trays lined up on the stall counter. Each was covered with a cloth. 'What do you do?'

'It's the easiest thing in the world, ladies!' Phillip Maxwell tipped his hat, giving them an exaggerated bow. 'Each tray has upwards of fifteen objects on it. I remove the cloth for a minute, cover it again, and you have another minute to record as many objects as you can remember. The person who's able to remember the most objects correctly is the winner.'

'That's all?' It sounded straightforward enough. 'All right, Mal. You're on.'

Phillip Maxwell handed them each a pencil and a piece of paper. 'Now, you can't begin writing your answers until the tray has been completely re-covered, understand? Ready, steady, go!'

He lifted the cloth, timing the minute with a stopwatch, then replaced it.

Mallory began furiously jotting down her list.

Grace, however, didn't move.

'Time!' Maxwell called. 'Pass me your papers!'

Mallory handed hers across then looked at Grace. 'But you haven't written anything.'

Grace smiled. 'I don't need to.'

'Oh really? And why is that?'

'I remember,' Grace said.

Maxwell and Mallory exchanged a look.

'Well, go on then!' Mallory crossed her arms in front of her chest. 'Prove it!'

Grace took a deep breath. 'One thimble; four needles of various sizes stuck into a pincushion in the shape of a green tomato; a small red rubber ball; a box of Bromo; two shillings, one heads side up, one tails; a glass ring, emerald cut; a letter opener with an ivory handle; a letter addressed to the leader of the Labour Party, unopened; a tortoiseshell comb; a leather hunting flask; a bill of sale from Ogden's bookshop in Bloomsbury for two books, totalling one pound, two shillings; a folded road map for Dorset; a used packet of Chesterfields; a token from a fairground ride; a china salt shaker in the shape of a duck; a nail file; and a teaspoon with the letters "VM" engraved on the handle.'

Mallory blinked. She turned to Maxwell, who examined the contents of the tray.

'My God, that's uncanny!' he said, looking back up.

'How can you do that?' Mallory asked.

Grace shook her head, her cheeks colouring. 'I don't know. It's a rather useless talent, actually.'

'Go on,' Mallory pointed to the next larger tray.

'Do that one.'

Again, the tray was uncovered for a minute and then re-covered.

Grace flashed Mallory a smile. 'Do I get another drink for this?'

'Absolutely!'

'A small black leather notebook and a gold pencil; a ball of twine; two horn buttons probably from a sweater . . .' Again, Grace proceeded to reel off another twenty objects, in great detail, with eerie accuracy.

By now a small crowd had gathered around them.

'What's she doing?'

'She doesn't even need to write them down!'

'She's cheating!' someone shouted out.

'Impossible!' Mallory turned on them. 'She's never even played the game before.'

'I don't believe it,' someone else chimed in. 'This is a set-up.'

'Have you hired her, Maxwell? Is this a joke?'

'Absolutely not,' he assured them. 'Everything's on the up and up.'

'Like your candidates?'

A roar of laughter.

The crowd continued to swell.

'Make her do another one!'

'Make it harder this time!'

Grace reached out for Mallory's hand. 'Come on, let's go,' she whispered.

'We can't go now. You've been accused of cheating. It will look like you're guilty. Besides, you're winning,' she added with a grin.

Phillip Maxwell was enjoying the high drama of the occasion too.

'Fine,' he agreed, tipping the contents of one of the trays out on the counter. 'We shall give this young woman a real challenge!' He whispered in the ear of one of the waiters, who hurried away, returning moments later with an evening bag ornamented with black jet beads.

Maxwell held it up with a flourish. 'My wife Vanessa's handbag, ladies and gentlemen! Who knows what mysteries lurk in its dark depths!'

Laughter.

'There is no possible way that this girl could know the contents – not even I know the contents and, quite frankly, I'm not certain I want to!'

More laughter and a smattering of applause.

'And just to up the stakes, this time I'll uncover the tray for only half a minute! Now, turn around,' he instructed Grace, who did as she was told, turning to face the crowd of people who had gathered behind her. She could hear Maxwell emptying the handbag, arranging the objects on the tray.

Finally he gave her the go-ahead.

Mallory took her by the shoulders. 'Are you ready?'

Grace nodded.

Mallory turned her round and Maxwell unveiled the tray. After only thirty seconds he covered it again.

'Your time starts – now!' he said, looking at his stopwatch.

Grace concentrated. 'A linen handkerchief with the letters "VM" embroidered in one corner in white silk thread; a green enamel and gold powder compact; a tube of Hiver lipstick; an alligator change purse; a small tin of Wilson's headache pills; a silver cigarette case; a torn Cadbury's wrapper with half a piece of chocolate; an empty matchbox from the Carlisle Hotel; a ticket stub for the seven-twenty showing at the Regent Cinema in Edinburgh; a latchkey; a mother-of-pearl and gold cigarette lighter . . .'

She stopped, her face suddenly draining of colour.

'A mother-of-pearl and gold cigarette lighter,' she repeated slowly, 'with the words "Always and Evermore" engraved on the side.'

The crowd burst into a round of enthusiastic applause.

'It's amazing!' Maxwell raved. 'Absolutely incredible! How could you even see what was engraved on that lighter?'

But Grace didn't seem to hear him. 'I'm sorry, you said this is your wife's handbag?'

'The very same,' he beamed back at her. 'Another round of applause for our champion, ladies and gentlemen! I'll be renaming this stall *Mrs* Memory from now on!'

Cheers and applause.

Unseen hands clapped Grace on the back as she pushed her way through the crowds, desperately searching for the exit.

'Well done.'

'Very impressive.'

'What a clever girl!'

Head pounding, palms sweating, she felt unreal, as if she were moving through the distorted landscape of a dream; her mind shrinking in on itself, focusing down to a single terrible point.

It couldn't be true.

It couldn't.

She could see the door now. It was only a few steps away.

'Well, you certainly showed them!' Mallory caught up with her. 'Where are you going?' She took her arm. 'Hold on a moment, I'm going to buy you a drink . . . Grace, what's wrong?'

'Let go of me.' Grace pulled away. She made it through the doors and just managed to get clear of the pavement before she was sick.

'Good God! What's all this? A case of nerves?' Mallory dug around in her evening bag and handed her a handkerchief. 'Easy does it. And mind you don't get it on your shoes.' She stepped back gingerly. 'Or mine.'

When Grace had finished, she wiped her mouth, sinking onto the front steps.

'Do you think it was something you ate?' Mallory sat down next to her.

'No.'

'Maybe you had too much champagne? Perhaps it was the tarts. Oh dear,' she frowned. 'I had them too.'

'Mal . . .' The words stuck in Grace's throat. 'That's my lighter.'

'I'm sorry?'

'It belonged to my father. It's one of the only things I have of his.'

'What lighter? What are you talking about?'

'The lighter on the tray.'

It took Mallory a minute to place it. 'Really? What's it doing in Vanessa's handbag?'

Grace looked across at her. 'There was a match-box as well. From the Carlisle Hotel.'

Mallory stared at her blankly.

'The Carlisle Hotel is in Scotland, Mal. So is the Regent Cinema.' Her voice tightened. 'Along with my husband.'

'You mean . . . oh.' Mallory finally got it. 'Oh. I see.'

Grace rested her head against her knees.

It was a beautiful, crisp night. Inside, the band played, laughter soared, the party reached a glittering frenzy.

Outside, they sat in silence.

After a while, Mallory stood up. 'Come on, darling. It's cold. I'll drive you home.'

Grace got up too. 'I want it back.'

'What?'

'The lighter.'

Mallory stared at her in horror. 'Grace, be sensible! Let it go!'

'It was my father's.' Grace's voice was steely. Mallory had never seen her so determined. 'It's the only thing I have left of his.' She opened the door. 'I want it back.'

Mallory stopped her, barring the way with her arm. 'Then I'll get it. Do you understand? Let me deal with it. You've had a terrible shock and you can only make matters worse for yourself. But right now, darling,' she took Grace firmly by the shoulders, 'I'm taking you home.'

'I wish you'd let me go with you.'

Three days later, Mallory was standing in the front hallway at Woburn Square again, this time watching as Grace buttoned up her mackintosh and adjusted her hat in the mirror.

'I'll be fine.' Grace pulled on her gloves.

Mallory looked worried. 'I'm not so sure. Besides, my French is better than yours.'

'A cat's French is better than mine.' Grace smiled. 'Anyway, I appreciate you driving me to the airport.'

Grace opened the door and stepped outside, into the misty early morning fog. Mallory followed, taking the suitcase. She fitted it into the boot while Grace locked up the house. Then both girls climbed into Mallory's car, a blue Aston Martin DB2.

'Have you even spoken to him?' Mallory asked.

'Not really. I told him I had some unexpected business to attend to in France.'

'And that was all?'

'Yes. I didn't go into the details.' Then she added quietly, 'And he didn't ask.'

'Humm.' Mallory took in this final bit of information.

Matters were worse than she'd suspected.

She started the engine. 'I don't like you going on your own.' Lurching into traffic, she pulled out directly in front of a slow-moving milk float. 'It's all so sudden. And, well, you've had a dreadful shock. Tell me again what they said when you rang the lawyers in Paris.'

Grace sighed. They'd already been over this half a dozen times.

'I spoke to a man named Tissot. I told him I thought there must be a mistake, that they'd clearly sent the letter to the wrong person. But he was insistent. He said he was certain the information was correct and that I should examine the will and see for myself.'

'And that's it?'

'That's it.'

'Perhaps he didn't understand you.'

'No, he understood. His English was quite good.' Grace shifted. 'By the way,' she tried to sound casual, 'were you able to get it?'

'It's in my handbag.'

'Do you mind?'

'Go ahead.'

Grace opened Mallory's handbag and took out the mother-of-pearl lighter. She wanted not to ask the question but couldn't help herself. 'What did Vanessa say when you asked for it back?'

Mallory concentrated on the road. 'Nothing. She just gave it to me.'

'Nothing?' This wasn't at all what Grace had expected. 'Well, what did you say?'

Mallory made a sharp turn, narrowly avoiding hitting the back of a number 19 bus. Bracing herself, she took a deep breath. 'I told her that I believed she had something that didn't belong to her and that I would appreciate it if I could have it back, on behalf of the original owner.'

'Oh.'

Grace had imagined something more heated; for sides to be taken, honour defended. The polite civility of Mallory's interchange felt like a slap in the face.

Mallory sensed this. But she didn't want to tell Grace the truth; that Vanessa had barely even acknowledged the request at all. In fact, her non-chalance had been nothing short of magnificent.

She'd merely raised a black eyebrow. 'Oh? And what might that be?' she'd asked coolly.

It was Mallory who'd been embarrassed, unable to meet her gaze. 'A lighter,' she'd mumbled. 'With mother-of-pearl on it.'

Vanessa had obligingly searched through her handbag, handing the lighter over with an easy, open smile. 'One hardly knows where one picks these things up!'

That was it.

No guilty looks, no pretend surprise. If anything,

Mallory was the one left feeling apologetic for taking up her time.

It only struck her later that Vanessa didn't bother to ask to whom the lighter belonged.

She didn't have to.

Still, Grace's disappointment hit a nerve. Mallory knew she'd been unable to rise to the occasion. And to her shame, part of her had even been secretly impressed with Vanessa's subtle blend of poise and audacity.

'What did you want me to say?' Mallory's voice was brittle.

Grace looked out of the window. 'I don't know.'

She was being unfair to Mallory. She'd got the lighter back, after all.

Grace slipped it into the pocket of her coat, where she often kept it; within easy reach. It had already begun to wear a hole in the silk lining.

'It was bloody awkward, I can tell you. We were at the Royal Horticultural Society Spring Luncheon,' Mallory added, as if that made her efforts more heroic. 'Do me a favour. Light me a cigarette, will you?'

Grace lit two.

They smoked for a while.

Mallory turned on the radio, moving from one station to the next, then turned it off again.

The tension remained.

Soon she reverted to her favourite subject. 'So, what are you going to do about Roger anyway?'

'I don't know.'

'Bloody fool!' Mallory exhaled. It was easier to talk about his failings than hers; they were, after all, so glaring. 'Men are so stupid, you just want to strangle them.'

Grace said nothing.

'What was he thinking of?' She was building up momentum now. 'Or was he thinking at all? I doubt it. How could he do this to you?'

Grace turned the lighter over and over again in her pocket, feeling the reassuring weight of it in her hand. 'It's not entirely his fault, I suppose,' she said quietly.

'Not his fault?' Mallory turned to look at her. 'What on earth are you talking about?'

Grace paused, shifted uneasily. 'There are other factors, Mal. Things you don't know about.'

'What factors? You can't possibly be defending him.'

'I'm not. Not really.'

'It sounds like you are.'

'It's just . . . well, the thing is . . .' Grace stopped. She longed to confide in someone. And sitting here, side by side with Mallory in the car, felt safe; she wouldn't have to look directly at her . . . she could just say it. 'Our marriage has been difficult for some time.'

43

Mallory looked at her. 'What are you talking about?'

Grace avoided her gaze. 'The truth is, I'm something of a disappointment to Roger.'

'A disappointment?' Mallory felt her temper soar. 'He's the one who's a disappointment! Why, there was a time when you could do no wrong – he used to worship you!'

Mallory's use of the past tense stung Grace's ears – used to.

She took another drag for courage. 'I became pregnant, Mal. When we were first married.'

'What? You never told me.'

'I didn't tell anyone. The truth is, I got pregnant before the wedding.'

'Oh.' She blinked at Grace in surprise, as if seeing her for the first time. She didn't seem the type – so controlled and naïve.

'And then I lost it,' Grace added numbly.

'Why didn't you ever tell me? I could've helped you.'

'Because it was over before it had really begun. Four months in, I woke up in terrible pain. There was blood . . . everywhere. It was a dreadful night.'

'I'm so sorry, darling. But you know,' Mallory added gently, 'that's not uncommon with the first try. Sometimes it takes a few goes before you last full term.'

'Yes, but there won't be any more tries,' Grace

44

said quietly. 'There was an infection; it scarred me. I can't have children.'

'Are you sure?'

'Yes.'

'But have you been to see a doctor?' Mallory pressed.

'I've been to see three.'

There was silence.

Grace rolled down the window; she wanted fresh air on her face.

'Sometime afterwards,' she went on, 'Roger took me out to dinner. He booked the same restaurant he proposed in. All the regular staff were there, shaking his hand, welcoming us back. Alfonse, the maître d', took us to our favourite table, the one where Roger had got down on one knee two years earlier. Do you remember that?'

Mallory nodded. 'He gave you a diamond ring the likes of which I have yet to see again.'

'Yes. Well, we sat down, ordered champagne cocktails and rib roast. It had been a long time since we'd been out together, just the two of us. We raised our glasses to toast one another and Roger looked at me and shook his head. He had this strange, empty expression on his face. "You'll never be the same, will you?" he said. "You'll never be the same lovely girl I married." I didn't understand. I thought he was

45

making some bad joke. But he wasn't. He took a drink and said, "So, now what are we going to do?"'

Mallory looked across at her, stunned.

'I suppose in his mind, that was the end. He hasn't been with me, you know, slept with me, since.'

'But what happened wasn't your fault, Grace!'

Grace wiped a tear away with her gloved fingertip. 'It doesn't make any difference, Mal. I'm broken, defective. I can't give him what he wants. Now he regrets that he married me at all.'

It began to rain, a fine misty shower, sending rivulets snaking down the windows as they wove through the London morning traffic.

Mallory turned on the windscreen wipers.

She was out of her depth. Any difficulties in her marriage had been swiftly negotiated with extra cocktails and placating trips to the jewellers.

But from the very beginning, everything about Grace and Roger's romance had been extreme; the vivid Technicolor version of everyone else's black-and-white lives. From their first meeting at the Grosvenor Square Ball, Roger had been almost frighteningly in love with her. Grace was new to London, unaffected and artlessly charming. His attentions were obsessive, extending to lavish gifts and very public displays of adoration. There was the surprise birthday party he'd thrown her at Scott's, after only

46

a few months of knowing her, complete with a pearl necklace and fifty of his closest friends. Mallory remembered being slightly jealous; wondering why Geoffrey couldn't make more of an effort.

And Grace had been dazzled. By the time their engagement was announced, it was already a foregone conclusion.

It struck her as strange that such violent affections could be reduced to utter indifference.

Mallory tried to keep her voice light and calm, as if she were talking to a child or an invalid. 'Perhaps it's just a stage. Maybe he simply needs to adjust. Get used to the idea.'

'I think he *has* adjusted, Mal. And he's apparently doing very well without me.'

Grace's confidences appeared to have cost her; she leaned her head against the window.

'I have dreams . . .' she said after a while. 'Nightmares. I'm running in a wood, looking for something or someone. But no matter how fast I run, I cannot find it. Sometimes I think it's just ahead of me, and then it disappears again. Then I start to fall, into some black, hideous abyss and I wake up. I used to have them all the time when I was a child. And now I only have them when something's wrong, terribly wrong.' She looked across at Mallory. 'I had that dream again the night of the party.'

'Grace—'

'It's hopeless, Mal.' Grace sighed, cutting her off before she could continue. She wasn't in the mood to be placated. 'I used to think it would get better, that over time he would see me again the way he used to. But the opposite is true. It's only become worse.' She stared blankly out of the window, at the grey fog settling in thick filmy layers across Hyde Park. 'I suppose it was only a matter of time before something happened.'

Mallory didn't know what to say. She thought about the leaflet for the Secretarial College in Oxford. How Grace had been searching for a purpose; a way to be useful. And then she recalled, to her shame, how she'd dismissed the idea out of hand.

They drove along, down past Holland Park Underground station and into Shepherd's Bush. London was a Turner watercolour this morning; rendered in dreamy, shifting blues and dusky greens, wet, melting, only ever half finished.

Mallory tossed her cigarette butt out of the window and looked across at Grace; at the deep frown line that cut down the centre of her brow; at her lips, tightly pursed.

She wanted to apologize; to reach out and hold Grace's hand and reassure her. But she didn't know how. If only she'd had the gumption to wrestle

Vanessa to the ground on behalf of her friend.

Instead, she did what her mother used to do; one of the only signs of affection that ever passed between them. Mallory took a fresh handkerchief out of her coat pocket. It smelled faintly of Yardley *Lily of the Valley* toilet water, the perfume that haunted the bedrooms of her childhood. She pressed it into Grace's hand.

'Take this, darling. Just in case.'

Folding it over, Grace slipped it into her handbag. 'Thank you.'

'Who knows?' Mallory forced a smile, trying to remain positive. 'Perhaps a change of scenery will do you a world of good.'

'May I help you find your seat, madam?'

The air hostess was attractive and smiling, with a model's figure. Her soft brunette hair was tucked into a neat pillbox hat and her lipstick matched exactly the shade of her smart red uniform.

'Yes, please.' Grace glanced around uneasily, taking in the layout of the main cabin, the other passengers already comfortably seated, reading magazines and chatting.

The hostess looked at her ticket. 'You're just here,

on the left. Allow me to hang up your coat.'

'Thank you.'

Sitting down, Grace peered out of the odd little window, at the ground staff piling the luggage into the hold, at the row of shining silver planes parked like enormous long motor cars, one after the other, in a line. She felt almost queasy with the combination of nerves and excitement.

The hostess was back. 'Is this your first trip to Paris?'

'Yes. And I've never been on an aeroplane before.'

'It's perfectly safe,' the girl reassured her. 'May I bring you a glass of champagne to help you relax?'

'Are you sure? I mean, won't it spill?'

The hostess laughed. 'It's not like that. You'll see. The whole thing is much smoother than you imagine. Sit back and try not to think too much. We'll be there in no time.'

Grace watched as she slipped into the narrow galley, which appeared to be little more than a series of metal boxes and drawers. Soon the distinctive pop of a champagne cork could be heard. A little while later, she moved easily down the aisle with a tray, handing out glasses like a hostess at a dinner party.

And it began to feel like a party, with laughing and drinking, people chatting across the aisle to one another. The pilot, handsome in his uniform, paused

50

before climbing into the cockpit to welcome them all aboard, even joking about how strange it felt to fly across the English Channel without being shot at, which got a spontaneous round of applause.

Then the doors were shut. The engines started and the whole plane shuddered and trembled. They rumbled along the runway, building up speed.

Grace looked out of the window trying to discern the moment when the wheels left the ground. And then, without her really feeling it, they were airborne, climbing at a steep angle before banking to the left.

London, with its little winding rows of identical brick houses, rendered in a thousand shades of grey, receded rapidly as they flew into the dark, wet fog. Then, quite suddenly, a sparkling blue strip of horizon appeared, high above the thick cloud cover; a golden place removed from the blanket of bad weather below.

Leaning back, Grace took a sip of the cold champagne and, opening her handbag, took out the letter.

She'd read it many times since it first arrived but she still had the compulsion to reread it, as if this time she would finally spot something she'd missed.

Madame Eva d'Orsey.

Eva d'Orsey.

The name meant nothing to her.

But there was a kind of poetry in it, a soft, lilting rhythm that captured her imagination.

Perhaps she'd been a friend of her parents. A fellow writer like her mother or a colleague of her father's.

Or maybe she would travel all the way to Paris just to discover that in fact the whole thing had been nothing but a misunderstanding after all.

In any case, England had disappeared now entirely from view. And only a vast, empty canopy of sky lay ahead.

New York City, 1927

Mrs Ronald, the Head of Housekeeping, leaned back in her chair and sighed. 'This is very unusual. We normally go through an agency. This is not how it's done at all, Mr Dorsey. Not at all.'

Antoine d'Orsey, the Senior Sous-chef, stood very still but said nothing, staring patiently at the space between his feet on the floor. He was making an awkward request and, in his experience, the most effective way to get what he wanted was to simply wait it out. Years of marriage had taught him that; say what you want and then hold your ground. Also, after working at the Hotel (as the Warwick was known to the staff who ran it) since it opened, he was familiar enough with Mrs Ronald to know that her tough exterior masked a sentimental disposition, along with a keen, practical mind. It was well known that she was short of staff and the summer season was only beginning. In the end, she needed his help too.

Not that she was willing to admit as much. 'Does she even speak any English?'

'Yes, of course.' He shifted slightly. 'You see, my wife has taken a job with a family in Westchester. There is nowhere else for her to go.'

Mrs Ronald considered this, sucking hard on her back teeth. She felt for Antoine. She knew him to be hard working, quiet, stubborn; perhaps a little too fastidious. His nickname was 'Escargot' because the Head Chef claimed he moved at a snail's pace. However, he was always one of the first people to arrive and one of the last to leave; a cornerstone of the kitchen staff.

Sighing again, she surveyed the young girl who stood in front of her.

Small and thin, she had dark hair that hung lankly to her shoulders. Her face was more unfortunate than pretty, with wide-set, oddly coloured eyes that curved upwards like a cat's and a rather long, narrow nose. They were aquiline features, with a sensual, curving mouth that struck Mrs Ronald as somehow obscene; far too large for her face. She was dressed very plainly, in a simple navy skirt and white blouse, the inexpensive fabrics worn from use but neatly pressed. She kept her eyes on the floor.

Mrs Ronald turned back to Antoine. 'She doesn't look old enough.'

'She's fourteen,' he said. 'She's just small for her age. She's already been working for two years – she has references from a family in Brooklyn.'

'And why did she leave their employ?'

'They were from Austria and were only here for a short time.'

He nodded to her and the girl took an envelope out of her pocket and handed it to Mrs Ronald.

'Eva,' Mrs Ronald read aloud, her lip curling. 'That's an odd name. Eva Dorsey.' She managed to make it sound ugly.

Antoine was straining to correct her, only it did no good. Mostly he was used to his family name being butchered, flattened out to its nearest American counterpart. Today, however, it grated.

'She's my wife's sister's child. Both her parents are dead now. I gave her my family name when we came over.'

There was hardness in his voice. He resented his niece's history and there was a lot of it he avoided recounting to people like Mrs Ronald. But the last thing he wanted was anyone mistaking Eva for his own child.

She was a quiet girl, conscientious and obedient, but he mistrusted her instinctively. Her mother had been pregnant out of wedlock and died of tuberculosis. Eva was invariably cut from the same cloth; an unwelcome drain on both his time and his resources.

Mrs Ronald raised an eyebrow. 'I see you worked as a lady's maid. That might be useful.' She handed the letter back to her. 'We have several female guests who fancy themselves as ladies, though nothing could be further from the truth. Come here,' she ordered. 'Let's see your hair.'

Eva bent her head down while Mrs Ronald searched her scalp. 'No sign of lice. Good. Show me your hands.'

Eva did as she was told.

'She's clean,' Antoine assured her. 'My wife is very strict about that. And in good health.'

Mrs Ronald crossed her arms in front of her chest. 'Still, it's hard graft. I'm not convinced you could handle the work.' (She didn't like to give in too easily.) 'Do you have anything to say for yourself?'

Eva paused, looking from one to the other. 'I think, ma'am, that you know best. However, I would be grateful for the opportunity to try.'

The girl was smart and polite. And she knew how to address a superior.

Mrs Ronald nodded. 'I appreciate your confidence in my judgement.'

Antoine's shoulders relaxed.

'I will take her on trial,' Mrs Ronald decided, looking

across at him. 'I can't promise beyond that. Now,' she made a quick notation in the ledger in front of her, 'there are things you need to know about working here. Be warned, Miss Dorsey. The Warwick is different from any other hotel in New York City. And with good reason. Mr Hearst built this hotel at the same time he built the Ziegfeld Theatre. The stars from the Follies depend on us; above all, they want somewhere comfortable and discreet to stay. We are their home away from home. Everything you see, everyone you encounter, stays here, within these walls. Do you understand?'

Eva nodded.

'Many of these people are dancers, performers; they behave like cattle sometimes, believe me. However, they are still Mr Hearst's guests. Whatever a client wants, he or she gets. And we do things here in the old-fashioned way – your presence is felt, not seen. You're here to be part of the woodwork. That means no face powder, no jewellery, no lip rouge; caps must be worn at all times. If a guest notices you, especially a male, you've failed in your duties.'

She stood up, taking a heavy set of keys from her pocket, and unlocked a closet on the far side of the office, hanging with spare uniforms. 'I expect you to be early rather than late, to anticipate your guests' needs rather than waiting to be called, and above all, you must be polite.' She rummaged through, searching for the correct size as she continued, 'We take a very serious view of stealing. Everyone is always prosecuted. No exceptions.' She held up a grey cotton uniform. 'This is going to be too big but I'm afraid it will have to do. Can you sew?'

'Yes, ma'am.'

'Then take it in. Not too tight, mind you.' She locked the closet again. 'And if I hear that you've spoken to the press or to a gossip columnist, you can expect to pack your bags immediately. Do you understand?'

Eva nodded.

'Each chambermaid is responsible for cleaning and maintaining fifteen rooms. However, when you're on duty, you're entirely at the clients' command. No request is to be denied if at all possible. We have standards here, much higher, much more obliging than other establishments.'

She turned to Antoine. 'I suppose she'll need accommodation.'

'Well, if it's not too much—'

'She'll have to share,' Mrs Ronald cut him off. 'And I want it understood that there are to be no guests, male or female, at any time in this hotel. Have I made myself clear?'

Again, Eva nodded.

'If you'd like to get your things, you can start this afternoon.'

'These are my things, ma'am.'

Mrs Ronald looked down. There was a small parcel, wrapped in brown paper, by the girl's feet.

'I see. Then I'll ring for one of the girls to come down and show you your room. Mrs Crane will instruct you in your duties. That will be all.'

'Thank you, ma'am.'

She left the office.

Antoine hesitated a moment by the door.

'I appreciate this,' he said.

'Yes, well,' Mrs Ronald moved back behind her desk, 'mind she makes you proud, Mr Dorsey. I'd have no pleasure in firing her but I'd have no problem doing it either.'

***

He went out into the hallway, where Eva was waiting.

She watched as he took a hand-rolled cigarette out of his shirt pocket, and lit it. He looked at her hard, as if she'd already done something wrong.

Eva lowered her eyes, concentrating on the floor. Where other people only saw different-coloured tiles, she saw comforting patterns and equations.

There were twenty-nine black tiles to every eighty-seven white. Three white to every one black. A whole hidden world of order and symmetry appeared if you only looked closely enough.

'If you have any trouble, you're on your own. Do you understand? You're old enough to answer for yourself from now on.'

'Yes, sir.'

Then he turned and walked away, towards the lower kitchen, disappearing into the long maze of corridors that ran underneath the main hotel.

Eva exhaled for what felt like the first time in hours.

The weight that had been pressing into the centre of her chest all morning was finally beginning to ease. She folded her uniform on top of the small parcel of her belongings and waited with her back pressed against the wall.

The only thing she'd had all morning was coffee, black and strong. Her uncle ate at work and now that her aunt had gone, there was no reason, in his mind, to keep food in the apartment or, in fact, an apartment at all. Her stomach knotted and growled.

She didn't want to share a room with a stranger. She wasn't even certain she wanted a job as a chambermaid. But what she wanted didn't matter.

Eva pressed her eyes together.

There had been 778 tiles on the floor of Mrs

Ronald's office. 426 grey and 352 white. If you multiplied them together you got 149,952. If you subtracted 352 from 426 you ended up with 74 and if you added 4 plus 2 plus 6 you got 12 and if you added 3 plus 5 plus 2 you got 10 and if you divided 12 into 778 . . .

'Already asleep on the job, eh?

She flicked her eyes open to see a blonde-haired girl standing in front of her, also a maid, only her uniform fitted. Hand on her hip, the girl had somehow contrived to position her cap at a fetching angle, just between two of the blonde kiss curls that adorned her wide forehead. There was a neatness and a compactness about her; a sureness in the swagger of her movements.

'I'm Sis, short for Cecily.' She thrust a hand out and pumped Eva's palm hard. 'I'm from Virginia, in case you hadn't noticed. Looks like we'll be sharing together. I knew my luck couldn't hold out forever. Had the room all to myself for nearly a week. Anyway,' she sighed. 'I guess I'm meant to show you around. Follow me.'

She led Eva down the long hallway and up a back staircase. When they got to the first floor she stopped. 'Ever been in the front lobby?'

Eva shook her head, too nervous to speak. Already she was in awe of Sis; of her Southern drawl and her easy, careless attitude. She was afraid to speak in case Sis didn't like her accent. It had happened to her in the house in Brooklyn, where the Scottish cook insisted on referring to her as 'the Foreigner' even though their employers spoke German and her own Glaswegian accent was only barely comprehensible.

'Ever even seen it?' Sis asked.

Again, Eva shook her head.

'Figures. You have the look of someone who's spent her entire life going round to the back service entrance. Come on.' Sis pushed through the door at the top, and they peered out into the West Lobby.

By hotel standards it was modest, intimate. But if it wasn't the largest or grandest hotel lobby in New York, it certainly was one of the most glamorous.

The marble floors shone beneath the oriental carpets, banks of settees were piled with velvet and silk pillows, and the bevelled mirrors which lined the walls reflected the beautiful profiles of the off-duty chorus girls parading through on their way to the bar.

Carefully chosen for the perfection of their figures, they were all the same height, with long shapely legs. Their laughter was punctuated by the clicking of their high-heeled shoes and the swishing of their daringly short skirts. A piano was playing and someone was singing.

A bellhop wove through the pockets of guests

with a silver salver. 'Madame Arpeggio,' he called loudly. 'Madame Arpeggio.' The air smelled of brass polish, cigar smoke and the lush, overripe sweetness of fresh-cut tiger lilies.

Eva watched as a small, round woman dressed entirely in black, her head crowned with a velvet turban fastened with a large ruby brooch, entered with a pair of enormous shaggy grey Irish wolfhounds. Their black leather collars were studded with pearls.

Instantly one of the doormen brought them water in china bowls, which they lapped loudly, creating puddles on the marble floor, while their mistress paused to light a cigarette and check her messages at reception.

'Who's that?' Eva was so fascinated, she forgot about her resolution not to speak.

'No one really.' Sis sniffed. 'Some filthy Prussian countess. Never bathes and doesn't take those dogs out nearly as much as she ought to. Her room smells like a zoo. They've already changed the carpet once.'

The girls watched as she turned, and proceeded at a regal pace towards the elevator.

'Thing is,' Sis confided, 'all the important people here look ordinary and the really fancy ones are usually broke or on the make. I'll tell you, you're in an upside-down world now,' she said, shaking her head. 'Takes a while, but you'll get used to it.'

Eva shared a room with Sis in the attic eaves of the building; it had a basin in one corner, a shallow closet and two narrow single beds. The window looked into the light well of the tall building opposite and the alleyway below. There was no view of the sky.

Not that it mattered. Both girls were up at six and eating in the lower kitchen, which also served as a staff canteen, by six-thirty. Then they stood in line waiting for Mrs Ronald to inspect their uniforms and appearance.

Eva had successfully managed to take her uniform in; however, the gauzy white apron and cap were still too big, bordering on ridiculous. It was a fine line between hiring girls who would not excite notice among the guests and making sure that they matched Mrs Ronald's inner vision of the overall chic of the establishment. So Eva was assigned the less desirable lower floors, in the hopes that she would grow another few inches over the summer.

After inspecting the girls' hair and nails, Mrs Ronald briefed them as to which guests were check-ing in and which were checking out that day, along with any special preferences.

These included the actress who required black

velvet curtains hung in her suite so that she could sleep during the day and whose room must only be serviced at night, when she was on stage at the Zeigfeld Follies a block away. And the movie producer who had a horror of anything which had been used by other people; his bed, mattress and bedclothes had to be replaced, new each time he came and the sheets were to be washed separately from those of the other guests, a duty which he only trusted Mrs Ronald to perform (but which she regularly passed off to one of the other girls).

Then there were the more common requests: extra ice buckets, satin sheets, special requests for certain types of flowers – hothouse roses and gardenias were the most popular. Some guests requested that there be no paintings or artwork in their rooms while others couldn't bear certain colours and had them banished from sight. Imported foods were provided at vast expense – chocolates from Paris, fresh pineapples from Mexico, black tea from India, and thick, long Cuban cigars. Extra pianos were delivered almost daily, as were exotic pets, new automobiles and hunting guns; and police guarded vans carrying jewellery, which was stored in the vaulted hotel safe.

Dance floors were installed so that stage stars could practise their routines, furniture removed, massage tables and exercise equipment set up. One week the entire Grand Ballroom was turned into a championship boxing ring when Jack Dempsey was fighting Jack Sharkey at the Yankee Stadium.

Guests frequently brought their own staff as well. Extra valets and ladies' maids hovered on the edges of the lobby, unsure of their place outside the dominion of their homeland. Not quite guests and yet not quite servants when their employers departed for the day, they were often both suspicious of and intoxicated by their new-found freedom.

The city itself had a dangerous effect on their normally restrained personalities. More than once they lost not only their heads, but their positions as well.

There was the valet who was found to be posing as his employer, the Prince of Wales, who ran up enormous gambling debts in Harlem before being discovered *in flagrante* with a black prostitute in his master's bed. And the lady's maid who had never tasted alcohol before and yielded to temptation, only to wake up somewhere near the waterfront next to an Italian dock worker who politely informed her, in broken English, that they were married and he would like to claim his conjugal rights.

Eva was assigned to learn her duties from Rita Crane, an older woman of indeterminate age and one of the world's most unsuccessful secret drinkers. Rita kept a flask in the depths of her laundry cart, an old rubbing alcohol bottle filled with gin in her locker and a vial of morphine in her handbag that her doctor prescribed for her ever deteriorating nerves. Every morning she showed up, hands shaking, arms covered in bruises. Eva wondered if she'd been beaten with a stick but of course, couldn't ask.

Rita had probably once been a beauty. But too much drinking, too many ex-husbands and a fondness for good old-fashioned English cuisine had left her quite round; her bust large like the prow of a ship tapering to two hefty legs, ribboned with varicose veins. Her features were lost in the soft folds of her white skin, and her eyes had a curious downward slant which made them seem automatically sad. Her lips were so thin as to be nothing more than an idea for a mouth. Rita moved as if resentful of gravity; as though the whole idea of a physical body caused her untold inconvenience. On the whole she was like a creature raised underwater, without the benefit of light for which eyes were optional and a spine a positive luxury.

There was a violence to Rita's scrubbing; a furious zeal to her bed making and a positive rage to her dusting which left Eva in no doubt that she was not only capable of murder but most likely experienced in it as well. Her last husband had died eleven years ago. Now she was married to her job. She hated and resented it, uttering a constant stream of pro-fanities under her breath, the way a nun recites a rosary. Yet she was fiercely committed to performing each task to her own exacting standards. Over the years Rita had tailored her expectations of life and others accordingly – anticipating the worst at every turn and managing to find the damp, dark potential in any cloudless sky.

For an entire two weeks, Rita supervised every move Eva made; correcting her toilet-bowl cleaning technique, insisting that she sweep each carpet in perfectly straight vertical lines and then again hori-zontally, chastising her for the lack of artistry with which she arranged the linen hand towels, all the while attacking her youth, personal appearance and general foreignness as she felt appropriate.

Eva soon learned that when Rita was drunk she was much easier to handle. In fact, in the canteen after her shift she could be almost funny.

Back in Lille, Eva had a grandfather who was a drinker. When her grandmother needed him to be sober for an important event, she always treated him to his own personal supply of chocolates. 'The sugar calms him,' she used to say.

Eva couldn't afford chocolates but she began to make Rita cups of very sugary tea throughout the day. Rita in turn grumbled and complained but drank them just the same. While it didn't make her pleasant, at least it kept her from being downright vicious.

By the time Eva ended her training period, she had mastered all the arts of domestic service, including the proper display of hand towels.

Rita had gained seven pounds.

***

Soon Eva adapted to the regular rhythm of hotel life. In the evenings the girls laundered and ironed their clothes, mended and gossiped. There was a radio in the pantry of the lower kitchen that the staff crowded round, listening to the Silvertown Cord Orchestra or the comedy antics of Amos 'n' Andy. Drinking was out of the question; Mrs Ronald was very strict about that. And the only dancing they did was with each other. A tall, lanky black girl named Wallace was the recognized Charleston expert and willing to teach anyone for the price of a Coca-Cola, even though chances to use their new-found skills were next to nil. On Saturday evenings, they went to confession at St Boniface. On Sunday mornings, early, they went to Mass.

There were occasional treats – matinée performances tucked into the balcony at the Strand theatre, followed by a sandwich at the Riker's Drug Store counter. Sometimes, they went to stare at the lights of Times Square, waiting to see the crowds leaving the theatres and discuss what the fashionable women were wearing.

Other times, they strolled across Central Park to Fifth Avenue, walking down past the grand department stores but never daring to go inside. There were places in the East End, small shops run by immigrants where fabric could be purchased, shoes traded, coats and jewellery pawned.

Sis took Eva to the public library and showed her how to get a card. Every week, Eva read her way through the works of Charles Dickens, Jane Austen, Anthony Trollope, Henry James and Elizabeth Gaskell. She dreamed of heroines from modest backgrounds attracting unprecedented attentions, soaring tales of love across social divides and sudden unexpected reversals of fortunes. In these pages, anything was possible, even for a girl like her.

'The trouble with you is, you're a romantic,' Sis pronounced one Sunday afternoon, as they all sat knitting by the radio in the kitchen. 'That's not going to get you anywhere. You need to be practical. Romantics get their hearts broken too easily.'

'That's true,' Rita agreed for once, resting her swollen feet on an empty vegetable crate. 'You need a man with a good solid job who doesn't drink or gamble. One that won't hit you or the kids too much and that goes to church. None of my husbands ever made it to Mass. Let that be a lesson to you,' she warned. 'Truth is they were never sober enough to make it out of bed on a Sunday morning.'

Sis considered. 'Maybe my Charlie knows someone.'

She was already engaged to a young doorman from the Iroquois Hotel and was the supreme social architect of the backstairs staff. Sis treated marriage as a coup; a strategic overthrow of the natural male instincts which must be systematically attacked and maintained through military ruthlessness and fortitude.

At seventeen, she'd already vetted and refused more men than the rest of them combined. With her first month's earnings she'd invested in a bolt of real lace from Ireland for her wedding dress. Sis knew which neighbourhood she wanted to live in, right down to what houses she would accept and had long decided on the names and professions of her future children (all of them boys). Despite her modest circumstances, she'd amassed a considerable collection of housewares, china and linens, stored in a trunk underneath her bed that she referred to as her 'hope chest'.

Charlie was only a few years older than Sis and

had yet to receive so much as a kiss from her. But Sis already managed his money and his career; she had him working extra shifts and taking an evening class in accounting with a view to heading up reception some day.

And he was in awe of her. Sometimes he came to meet them in the park or after a movie (Sis wouldn't let him sit next to her in the dark in case he got the wrong idea), and Eva could see the mixture of fear and pride in his face when he was around her.

'Pick a man with an overbearing mother,' Sis advised. 'Charlie's mum is a widow with seven kids to feed and only a Bible to keep her warm. Charlie feels guilty from the moment he wakes up in the morning and what's more, he's used to taking orders from a woman.'

Eva nodded.

She never argued with Sis's advice. It wasn't sensible if you wanted a quiet evening.

'Good God!' Rita laughed, jerking her head towards Eva. 'You've got your work cut out with that one! She'll be a lot tougher to shift than you, Sis.'

Everyone turned to Eva.

She felt her cheeks colour.

'She's not done growing yet, is all!' Sis shot back. 'Besides, you managed to get a few husbands and you're not exactly the Queen of Sheba!'

Still, when the conversation changed, Eva got up and went outside.

It was true: she was too thin, her face too long; her features seemed stretched out like a cartoon character from the Sunday papers.

Sis was tall and blonde, like a smiling Gibson Girl in an advertising poster.

Eva was short and dark and foreign-looking.

She wandered out into the back alleyway, sitting alone on the back steps. The warm humid air of New York clung to the night, unwilling to relinquish its suffocating hold. And yet to Eva, the city had an underlying hum of possibility; a constant forward motion that promised, no matter what, that change was on its way.

In every book she'd ever read, the heroine was subject to self-doubt and unjust criticism. And in every case, it only served to harden their resolve. Besides, what did Rita know? If Eva wanted a life scrubbing toilets, she could follow Rita's advice. But she didn't. She wanted something more.

She wasn't certain what, exactly, or how she would get it. But for right now, she didn't need to think about that. She could simply sit, basking in the glow of not-so-distant stars, which must be somewhere, blinking behind the thick layer of cloud that masked the evening sky.

Paris, Spring, 1955

The offices of Frank, Levin et Beaumont were located on the Rue de Rivoli, on the upper floors of one of the galleried arcades. Grace had the last appointment of the afternoon, and, after a somewhat confusing conversation with the secretary in her halting French, had been shown into Monsieur Tissot's chambers, which occupied a corner, with two windows overlooking the north wing of the Musée du Louvre.

Grace sat, still in her overcoat, her handbag firmly anchored on her lap. It felt unreal to be here, like an overly vivid, slightly alarming dream.

She wasn't used to travelling on her own. Mallory had insisted that she stay at the Hôtel Raphael, where she'd been with her mother before the war. Located near the Champs-Élysées, it was discreet and quietly grand; much nicer than anything Grace would have chosen for herself. Her room wasn't terribly large but it had high ceilings and was decorated in soft pink and the palest eau-de-Nil, feminine candyfloss colours mirrored in the silk taffeta swags and thick, embroidered bedspread. There was even a chandelier above her bed. Lying on her back last night, she'd stared at it, amazed. Clearly the French expected something rather more interesting to occur here than the English did.

There was a small balcony, barely a few feet wide. Grace opened the doors and stepped outside, gazing over the wide tree-lined street below.

The city seemed extravagantly, shamelessly beautiful. In London, entire blocks had been levelled in the war; whole neighborhoods gone. The landscape was punctuated by gaping concrete wounds and piles of charred rubble; grotesque monuments to once great structures. But here, the pavements were smooth and even, the skyline intact. Whatever damage the occupation had done, Paris had put it behind her.

Even the air smelled more refined; not full of damp, oily coal but clear, fragrant with continental sunlight and warmth.

The coffee at breakfast had been shockingly strong, the croissant flaky and buttery – more like a biscuit or a cake. How decadent that people ate them every day! It was only the potential shame at being caught that prevented Grace from jamming an extra one into her handbag.

Later that afternoon, walking across the Jardin des Tuileries to her appointment, a kind of giddiness came over her, accompanied by a sudden realization: no one knew her here. Her anonymity both thrilled and disorientated her.

The concierge had given her a street map, but she found herself unable to concentrate on the neat little labelled lines when the city itself surrounded her. She'd always heard that Paris was elegant but had struggled to imagine how. She'd assumed it would be rigid; the demanding intolerance of perfection. But, being here, she was struck by the easy naturalness of everything. From the tall, slender trees, their leaves rustling high above her, to the chalky gravel that crunched beneath her feet or the classically proportioned buildings that rose, uniformly constructed from the same blonde stone, it was all orchestrated to hold the light. The entire city was enveloped in a halo of glowing softness.

The French were fluent in the language of beauty, just as she'd been told. But it was a more subtly encompassing comprehension than she'd anticipated. In fact, it made sense. Who wouldn't construct the corners of buildings to curve gently rather than meet in a point if they had the means and inclination? And who wouldn't match all the roof tiles in the city radius to create a harmonious landscape of sloping shades of bluey-grey, augmented with squat terracotta chimney pots? Anything else seemed careless.

Likewise, while the men and women were no more naturally attractive than their English counterparts, they dressed with an assurance and attention to detail that would have been considered the height of arrogance in England. Here, maintaining a certain chic was apparently nothing less than a civic duty.

Even now, in the lawyers' chambers, there was a unity and precision in the colours, shapes and sizes of the furniture, as if an editor had walked through earlier, removing any distractions.

The door opened and two men walked in.

The first one was an elderly gentleman with stiff, formal bearing and a neat white moustache. A younger man stood respectfully behind him.

'Madame Munroe?' The elderly gentleman greeted her unsmilingly, with a curt nod of his head. 'I am Henri Levin,' he announced in heavily accented English. 'This is my firm. And this is Edouard Tissot, my associate. He will look after you. I trust his service will be satisfactory.'

With that he gave a brisk little bow, turned on his heel and left.

Grace didn't know quite what to make of this abrupt introduction.

'Please forgive him.' Monsieur Tissot stepped

forward. He looked to be somewhere in his mid-thirties; tall and slender, a feature highlighted by his traditional pinstriped suit. His dark hair matched his black eyes; his expression was both reserved and intelligent. 'He's not used to speaking English,' he explained, his voice lowering discreetly. 'He's terrified you will ask him something he won't understand.'

'Oh, I see,' she said, nodding.

He held out his hand. 'Allow me to welcome you to Paris, madame.'

'Thank you.' Grace extended her own, expecting him to shake it.

However, instead he held it lightly, his lips hovering just above the white flesh of her wrist, before releasing it.

It was both a quietly formal and yet intimate gesture; he hadn't actually touched his lips to her skin. But still her skin tingled where they might have been.

'And let me begin,' Monsieur Tissot continued, 'by saying that I am very sorry for your loss. Please allow me to assist you in any way possible during your stay.'

'Thank you very much,' Grace murmured, averting her eyes. She'd decided in advance it was best to say little or nothing until she knew more. Instead, she moved the subject on to safer ground. 'Your English is very accomplished, Monsieur Tissot.'

'Thank you.' He acknowledged the compliment with a nod. 'That's precisely why I was chosen to meet with you.' Taking a seat behind his desk, he searched through a stack of legal files. 'I'm sorry to make you come all this way, Madame Munroe. However, the terms of the will are quite specific. And of course there are a great many signatures required and other details to attend to.' He pulled the correct file out, scanning the documents enclosed. 'Here we are. The inheritance comprises largely the likely proceeds from the sale of a property, as well as a portfolio of stocks which are currently managed by the stockbroking firm of Lancelot et Delp.'

She must've misheard him. 'Pardon me, did you say a property?'

'Yes. An apartment. Or a flat, as you English say. The deceased was living in it up to the point of her death and therefore unable to liquidate the funds earlier. We've had the property assessed and I can assure you, it's quite valuable.' He took some official-looking papers out and arranged them on the desk. 'Madame d'Orsey had a power of attorney prepared, so that we could oversee the sale on your behalf. I only await your signature in order to proceed.' He looked up. 'I'm making the assumption, perhaps mistakenly, that you would prefer to have us deal with this matter rather than handle it yourself.'

Grace leaned forward to look at the papers, only the words made no sense. 'They're in French. Aren't they?'

'Ah! Yes,' he admitted, shaking his head. 'I apologize. I would be happy to go through them with you. Or if you prefer, you may have your English lawyer approve them. I can arrange to have them translated—'

'I'm sorry,' Grace interrupted, 'but I'm not entirely certain I understand. Would you mind explaining everything to me again? Slowly?'

'Yes, of course. Maybe I'm not being very clear. You see, according to the terms of the will, you're to have the entire proceeds, minus the transaction fees, of the purchase price of Madame d'Orsey's property holdings. We're planning to accept bids from several different leading estate agents and then, with your permission of course, we'll be able to market it. In addition, a portfolio of stocks also comes into your possession. However, they are being managed elsewhere.'

Grace's mouth was open but she was unable to close it. 'I've inherited stocks and a . . . an apartment? In Paris?'

'Well,' Monsieur Tissot paused, 'not quite. The will specifies that you are to receive the proceeds of the sale of the property. It's my understanding that Madame d'Orsey wanted you to have the funds, rather than the property itself. It was always her intention to provide you with a lump sum for your personal use.'

'A lump sum? For my use?' It was unnerving to imagine a stranger planning her future in such detail; even a benevolent stranger.

'Yes, and quite a considerable one at that.'

'But surely she didn't intend for the money to go to me, directly?'

'On the contrary, that's precisely what she intended. My understanding was that she wanted you to have financial independence. *Le droit de choisir* was how she put it. The right to choose.'

Grace felt light headed; her hands were tingling with pins and needles. 'But not for me, personally. What I mean to say is, am I not inheriting this by default, as it were?'

'Default?' He frowned.

'Yes, I mean, surely this was originally meant for someone else, wasn't it?'

'Madame, you are the named recipient in the will.'

'Are you sure?'

Monsieur Tissot's frown deepened.

Grace tried to swallow but her mouth felt dry, as if her tongue was made of felt. Financial independence. A lump sum. 'May I trouble you, Monsieur Tissot, for a glass of water, please?'

'Of course.' He went to the door and said something to the secretary.

A moment later, he handed her a glass. 'Are you quite all right? Your cheeks are white. Perhaps you should lie down, Madame Munroe.'

Grace took a sip. 'I'm a little tired, that's all. I'm not used to travelling by myself and this, this has come as something of a shock to me.'

'Of course.'

'Did . . .?' She stopped; started again. 'I'm sorry, did you know her? Madame d'Orsey?' She tried to sound casual.

'I drew up the will with her. But that was all. She was quite a strong personality. It's a shame that she died so young.' His face shadowed with concern. 'Are you sure you wouldn't like some time alone? I would be more than happy to leave the room.'

'No, thank you. I feel better now.' She put the glass down, forced herself to look him in the eye. 'Monsieur Tissot, are you quite certain . . . Is it at all possible that you have the wrong Grace Munroe?'

Monsieur Tissot regarded her warily. 'Why would you ask that?'

'Are you certain,' she repeated, 'that I am the right woman?'

He reached again for the file, taking out an envelope. He handed it to her. 'Is this you?'

Grace opened it. There was an old newspaper photograph cut out from the society section of *The Times*. It showed Grace and two other young debutantes in long white strapless ball gowns, standing on the massive sweeping marble staircase at Grosvenor House. The caption underneath read, 'Miss Grace Maudley, Lady Sophia Hapswood and Miss Daphne Sherbourne attend the Grosvenor House Ball'. There was also a piece of paper, folded. Grace opened it. It was written in a woman's handwriting, flowing, slanted letters.

Grace Jane Munroe (née Maudley)

39 Woburn Square

London, NW1

Born: 30 May 1928

Only child of Jonathan and Catherine

Maudley of The Great Hall, West Chal-

low, Oxfordshire, England

Grace stared at it.

The words seemed to float, blurring together on the page.

'Madame Munroe?'

Suddenly the room was too hot; too close. The papers slipped through her fingers, drifting to the floor.

'Would you be so kind as to call me a taxi?' she heard herself say. 'I think perhaps I'm a little unwell after all.'

<hr />

Monsieur Tissot drove her back to her hotel. They didn't bother to talk. Instead, Grace stared out of the window at the winding narrow streets and the people, so much more vivid than in London, pushing in and out of shops and businesses. They seemed to be removed from her by more than just language. French people leading French lives. Why was it that anything you couldn't readily understand became mysterious and glamorous?

When they pulled up at her hotel, her hand was already on the door handle, pushing it open. 'Thank you.'

'Madame Munroe.' Monsieur Tissot turned off the ignition and faced her. 'I don't mean to be intrusive, however, I'm curious. What was your relationship to Madame d'Orsey?'

'Well, Monsieur Tissot . . .' Grace stiffened, assuming her loftiest tone. 'I'm . . . I'm not really certain that it's any of your business.'

He was disturbingly immune to her rudeness, looking at her with a distinctly French mixture of amusement and indulgence. 'Of that I'm certain.'

She reached again for the door handle.

'You've never met her,' he guessed.

Grace glared at him. 'That's preposterous!'

'It *is* preposterous. However I'm right, aren't I?'

She frowned, pursing her lips tightly together. She should have taken a cab.

Easing back in his seat, he continued, 'I've overseen countless will readings. Never before have I witnessed a beneficiary as perplexed as you are. Is it true, Madame Munroe?'

Grace hesitated. 'In a manner of speaking.'

'So,' he crossed his arms in front of his chest, 'you've received an inheritance from a woman you've never met. Is that correct?'

'Yes.'

'A woman, if I'm right, you've never even heard of.'

She flashed him a look. 'How did you know that?'

'Am I right?' he asked again, ignoring her question.

'Yes.'

'Well then,' he shrugged, 'why didn't you say so?'

85

'I . . . I don't know,' she faltered. In her panic, she'd imagined more dramatic consequences – possibly a trip to the local police station or the British Embassy. 'I wasn't sure what would happen.'

'Nothing can happen. The inheritance is yours, regardless of whether you knew her or not. You've done nothing wrong.'

'It feels as if I'm stealing,' she admitted, loosening her grip on the door handle.

'It is unusual.'

'Yes. But she had my name and address; that photograph from the newspaper.'

'Is she a friend of the family?'

'I suppose she might have known my parents before they died. Still, what kind of person gives her money to a complete stranger? And what kind of stranger just takes it?'

'I don't know.' The whole idea appeared to interest rather than disturb him.

'Did she ever explain the bequest to you?'

'No. I only met her once, when she composed the will. She came through another client of ours, Jacques Hiver.'

'Hiver?' Grace repeated, trying to place the name. 'Where have I seen that name before?'

'In every chemist's window in the city. He's the owner of one of the biggest cosmetics companies in France.'

'Yes, of course!'

Hiver rouge – the advertisement featured a drawing of a beautiful dark-haired woman, blindfolded with a black silk scarf, wearing the deepest shade of red lipstick. Underneath it read simply, *Embrasse-moi* – kiss me. She'd noticed it because the image seemed so daring; not at all the type of poster one would ever see in England.

'So,' she tried to fit the pieces together, 'Madame d'Orsey was his wife?'

'Well, no . . .' He looked at her sideways. 'He passed away earlier this year. His wife is still alive. You see, we didn't handle Monsieur Hiver's – how do you put it? – legitimate affairs. He had another, much bigger firm for that. We dealt with those matters that required a more delicate legal approach.'

'In what way delicate?'

'I believe she was his mistress.'

'Oh!'

Grace stared at the cobbled street in front of her. Her first inclination was to judge. And yet it wasn't so easy, when you were on the receiving end of such generosity.

They sat a moment.

'Did she give you any indication . . . any clue when she drew up the will, as to why she was giving the money to me?'

He shook his head. 'The question never arose. She had the information I showed you, which she handed to me as soon as we began. I don't recall that we ever discussed any personal aspects of the will. She came fully prepared. I remember being very impressed with how clearly she'd outlined her wishes and how straightforward everything was. Her main concern seemed to be that the assets should be liquidized as quickly as possible. And that you should receive the bequest in person. On your own.'

'Really?' That was an odd caveat.

He nodded. 'If you'd come with someone else, I was to ask that they wait outside.'

'I see.' It sent a chill through her to think of the care and planning this stranger had expended on her behalf.

It began to rain a little, a soft misting that settled silently on the windscreen.

'What did she look like?' she asked quietly.

'Very striking, with dark hair. She must have only been in her early forties and she was quite attractive. But one could see that she seemed to be in some sort of pain, and I think it wore on her; it showed in her face.'

Grace continued to stare at the cobblestones, now damp and glistening in the flickering lamplight, as the afternoon drew to a close. 'I have no idea of what to do.'

'But there's no need for you to do anything. I can assure you, the will is perfectly legal and binding. Once you sign the papers, you can simply take the proceeds and return to London.'

'But how?' Couldn't he see how impossible that was? 'I couldn't live my life without even knowing who she was or why she gave it to me. It would drive me mad!'

'Think of it like winning a lottery,' he suggested.

'I don't believe in gambling, Monsieur Tissot. To me, chance isn't random. The universe is bound by unseen threads. We have only to untangle them a little to see a pattern unfold.' She turned to face him. 'Are you certain there hasn't been a mistake?'

He straightened, clearly irritated at the inference. 'I can assure you, I'm not in the habit of making mistakes. And I have no evidence that Eva d'Orsey did either. On the contrary, all the information she has provided has been correct so far.'

Grace sighed, running her hand across her eyes. There were no answers, only more questions. Now her head was beginning to ache. 'I'm completely at a loss. I honestly have no idea of where to begin.'

He thought a moment.

He'd been instructed by the senior partners to deal with this case as quickly and discreetly as possible.

They were eager to prevent any scandal that might impact on the remaining Hiver family members. But he hadn't expected Madame Munroe to be quite so baffled by the situation. And he found her reluctance to simply accept the bequest intriguing. Her insistence to know more hinted at some measure of character; a quality he found increasingly rare these days. And so, despite his instructions, Monsieur Tissot made an unorthodox decision. 'Well, then.' He turned on the ignition. 'You need help,' he said matter-of-factly.

'Where are we going?'

'Madame Munroe, I'd like to be of assistance but I can't do anything until I've had my supper.' He pulled out. 'There's a bistro round the corner.'

She looked at him in surprise. 'And you're taking me with you?'

'Do you have plans?'

'I . . . No.'

'Then it seems the kindest thing to do.' And for the first time he smiled; a rather surprising, angular grin, punctuated by two dimples. 'I cannot solve your mystery, but at least I can feed you.'

Monsieur Tissot took Grace to a café with a bistro on one side and a more formal restaurant on the other. The staff seemed to know him there and quickly seated them at a corner table, where they sat, side by side, looking out onto the rest of the room. Grace hadn't dined alone with a man who wasn't her husband since her marriage. But perhaps because of the circumstances, or the strangeness of the country, it was easier than she imagined. Monsieur Tissot didn't seem to require or expect conversation. Instead they sat, watching the other diners – a fascinating occupation in itself.

Grace surveyed the menu. 'I think I'll have the *ragout de cou d'agneau*,' she decided, closing it.

'The lamb's neck stew? Excellent choice.'

'Lamb's neck?' She picked up the menu again.

He grinned. 'Shall I order for both of us?'

'Well . . .' She scanned the entrées again, searching for something familiar. 'I'm afraid I don't have a very sophisticated palate. By French standards, that is.'

'Well then,' he leaned back, stretching out his long legs, 'tell me what you like to eat at home and I will advise you.'

'Well, I suppose I eat a great deal of . . . toast.'

'Toast?' He cocked his head, as if perhaps he hadn't heard her correctly. 'I'm sorry. Out of choice?'

'The thing is, I'm not used to anything too . . . too French.'

'You are in Paris, madame.'

'Yes, but you know what I mean, don't you? Dishes with too much flavour?'

'How can anything possibly have too much flavour?'

'What I mean is too many strong flavours, like onions and garlic . . .'

They gazed at each other across a great cultural divide.

Grace gave up; put the menu down. 'Yes. I trust you.'

The waiter came up and Monsieur Tissot ordered for both of them – *salade mixte*, *poule au pot*, and a bottle of *vin rouge*.

He poured her a glass, passing the bread. And she realized that she was very hungry. Lunch had passed and she'd forgotten about it. She tore off a piece of baguette; it was both crusty and soft, still warm in the centre. It was amazing how something so simple, so basic could be this delicious. And so completely different from its counterpart in England.

'Who is this woman?' Grace wondered aloud, devouring the bread. 'That's the question. And why on earth is she giving me this money?'

'Of course,' he nodded. 'But what I'd like to know is – what do you propose to do with it?'

She hadn't considered that, perhaps because she didn't really believe the money belonged to her.

'I'm not sure.' She took a sip of wine.

'You could buy a new house, travel, collect art, invest . . .'

'Perhaps.' She wasn't familiar with making financial decisions. 'I suppose the best thing would be to discuss it with a professional lawyer.'

He folded his hands in front of him. 'I'm a lawyer.'

'Well, yes, but I need one versed in English law.'

'Yes but they can only advise you. What would you like to do with it?' he pressed.

Grace thought a moment. 'Live, Monsieur Tissot. I'd like to live in great comfort. And peace.' And then she added, quite to her surprise, 'With no one to tell me what to do or how to do it.'

He raised his glass. 'An admirable aspiration!'

'Are you making fun of me?'

'No, I'm quite serious. People take for granted what is in fact an art. To live well, to live comfortably by one's own standards takes a certain maturity of spirit, exceptional character, truly refined taste, and—'

'And money.' She tore off another piece of bread. 'It helps.'

She looked at him sideways. Perhaps it was being in Paris or the bizarre situation but she felt free to ask, 'Do you live by your own standards?'

He thought a moment. 'I believe it's a privilege,

madam. One that's earned through a certain amount of courage and adversity.'

She laughed, shook her head. 'You haven't answered my question.'

'Sometimes,' he smiled. 'Sometimes I do and other times I do what's expected of me.'

It was an oddly frank thing to say; one that, nevertheless, Grace understood. Only she'd never heard anyone say it out loud. He looked away, moving the subject back to safer territory. 'And where would you live this life of comfort?'

'I don't know. Maybe by the sea. But wherever it is, they would make this bread.'

'And your husband? What does he make of all this?'

He caught her off guard. It was the first time in hours she'd even thought of Roger. And now, to her surprise, she wasn't certain what to say. 'My husband?'

'Yes. What does he think?'

Looking down, she brushed a few crumbs carefully off the tablecloth, 'I don't know. The truth is, I haven't had the opportunity to discuss it with him.'

'I see.' He looked as if he didn't entirely believe this. 'Well, he's bound to have some ideas of his own.'

'Yes, that's for certain.'

There was a polite silence.

'There are some magnificent coastlines in the

South of France,' Monsieur Tissot said after a while.

'Yes,' Grace agreed, grateful he wasn't pursuing the subject of her husband. 'I've never been but that's what I've been told.'

The chicken was served in a thick red clay pot with a lid, simmered with vegetables and small new potatoes. Warm and succulent, the meat fell from the bone. It was a simple dish yet filled with subtle layers of flavour. It struck her as lavish and exotic. When Monsieur Tissot explained that it was essentially peasant fare, she was amazed.

'Chicken in a pot,' he explained, with a little shrug. 'You said you wanted something plain.'

'It's delicious.'

Customers came and went, some for supper, some just for coffee. The small café was the centre of its own little universe, swirling with its own local population. Everyone seemed to know each other, and to have passionate views they never even considered keeping to themselves. They spoke freely, tossing unsolicited advice and opinions across tables. A family came in, several married couples, a pair of quite nicely dressed elderly women, a pile of young men on their way to a club, a single old man reading the paper, a couple of middle-aged women . . . They watched and ate and, to Grace's delight, Monsieur Tissot would occasionally interpret for her.

He nodded in the direction of the two women, now sitting tête-à-tête. 'They've been to the cinema,' his voice was low. 'This one says she didn't like the mother. And the leading man was too fat but had a nice face.'

'What film was it?'

'Humm,' he strained to hear. '*Marty*? Apparently they both cried at the end. And now they're having a drink to make themselves feel better.'

'Oh, yes! I want to see that. I've heard it's quite good.'

'And over there.' He pointed to an elderly couple involved in a heated discussion – he was shaking his head and she was folding her napkin, planting it firmly on the table, preparing to walk out. 'He says he thinks the veal is fine. She knows it's got too many capers and not enough lemon.'

Grace couldn't believe it. 'They're fighting like that about food?'

He nodded.

'That would never happen in England.'

'I know,' he smiled.

Afterwards, since the rain had stopped, he walked her the short distance back to the hotel.

She stopped outside. 'Monsieur Tissot, am I correct in assuming from what you've said that you have access to Madame d'Orsey's apartment?'

96

'Yes, of course.'

'And that it's not been sold yet?'

'No.'

'I see.' Grace folded her arms across her chest. 'Then I would like to see it, please.'

He hesitated. 'My instructions were to ensure you were in receipt of the proceeds from the sale. I don't believe it was ever Madame d'Orsey's intention that you should visit the property.'

'Perhaps,' Grace countered, 'but without my signature on the power of attorney, there will be no sale. Am I right?'

'Yeees . . .' he said slowly. 'That's true.'

'And this is a situation which requires a delicate legal approach.'

His eyes narrowed 'You're quite tenacious, aren't you?'

'And I believe you're stalling.'

Rocking back on his heels, Monsieur Tissot pushed his hands deep into his pockets. She was more resourceful than he'd given her credit for. And she was also intelligent and amusing in a very particular English way. He could easily show her the apartment and still complete this business quickly. 'Very well, Madame Munroe. What time tomorrow would you like me to collect you?'

New York, 1927

Almost every night there was some sort of party at the Hotel. Many started in the bar then worked their way up into the rooms. But often there were simply outbreaks of dancing and drunkenness which flared up, taking over whole floors without warning like a kind of impromptu orgy. Doors would be propped open, and guests who formerly hadn't even been on nodding terms gathered in hallways, collecting in doorways, laughing and shouting, music and smoke filling the air. Illegal liquor appeared, bottles were passed; more ice and glasses were in constant demand. Within the hour, cars pulled up outside, from the opposite end of town or the suburbs, laden with fresh recruits; girls piled on each other's laps, shrieking with delight and young men wearing evening jackets, as if they'd been permanently on call for just such an occasion. Racing past the doorman, they followed the noise like bloodhounds tracking a scent, fearful of missing 'the best bits'.

The chorus girls were famous for these ongoing revelries; interrupted only briefly by bouts of sobriety and the occasional comatose slumber. The entire cast of the Follies seemed to be condemned to the Sisyphean fate of forever reeling from room to room, floor to floor, searching for the next cocktail, the next dance partner, the next eruption of intensity. The following morning, or more often late in the afternoon, survivors could be found wandering bleary-eyed round the corridors and lobby; girls without shoes and missing their handbags, men clutching car keys, with only the vaguest memory of where they might have parked, politely enquiring as to where they were before heading off again.

Cleaning up after these affairs was far less glamorous. It wasn't unusual to discover that someone had relieved themselves on the balcony, in a potted palm or an ice bucket; stray stockings and missing undergarments were wound about bedposts, jammed into dumb waiters and stuffed between sofa cushions; pools of vomit attracted flies and cockroaches and, along with blood and lipstick, required intense bouts of scrubbing to remove from the carpet. Almost once a week a body would turn up somewhere, sometimes quite dead looking, but usually in a state of extreme intoxication; a person no one knew or remembered, who was eventually carted off by the police to the local hospital.

At the same time, movie and Broadway stars were apt to manifest like sudden, dazzling apparitions. Douglas Fairbanks, Will Rogers, John Gilbert and W. C. Fields frequently charmed young women in the bar, while Ruth Etting, Marion Davies and Fanny Brice could be glimpsed, wrapped in furs, gliding through the lobby before disappearing into chauffeur-driven cars.

The air itself crackled with undercurrents of possibility. Fame, intoxication, sudden sexual encounters – both welcome and unwelcome – simply materialized, as unstoppable and unpredictable as the weather.

And in the summer time, it only got worse.

***

'Mr Waxman has tried to commit suicide again,' Sis sighed, when they were folding linens one stifling Tuesday morning.

'What do you mean, again?'

'He does it every once in a while. Gets too drunk, starts hollering and then goes out on the ledge and stands around a while. He's gonna have to leave. They already asked him to leave once but they're gonna have to get the police to do it this time.'

'Why does he do it?'

'Question is, why *doesn't* he do it? I mean, if you're

gonna jump, jump! It's all this in-and-out business that's so upsetting. He's meant to be writing some movie or something and every once in a while he just has to get out there and make a fuss. "There's nothing to live for! This is it! There is no God! Nothing can save you!" Last year everyone panicked. This year they just let him go on and after a while he climbed back in and ran himself a bath.'

'Doesn't he know suicide is a sin?'

'So's standing around on a ledge upsetting everyone. Besides, Mr Waxman's a Jew. They can do what they like.'

'Who knows.' Eva rearranged a row of fresh sheets. 'Maybe he has a point.'

Sis glared at her. It was far too hot already, making everyone more irritable. 'What's wrong with you?'

'I don't know. I'm just saying . . .

'Oh, honestly!' Sis shook out a bath towel with an imperious snap. 'God has better things to do than float Mr Waxman down from the eleventh floor. And I'm not gonna let some crazy man dictate to me about the nature of the divine.' Then she stopped. 'Hey, heathen, where'd you get those shoes?'

'Do you like them?' Eva showcased the sophisticated t-bar design with a twirling dance move. They were only slightly too big around the heel.

'Sure. But where'd you get them?'

'Gino gave them to me. Said his sister outgrew them.'

'You mean Pots and Pans?'

Eva nodded. Gino was a dish washer in the kitchen.

Sis put her hands on her hips. 'And he gave you shoes? What's his sister doing with a pair of shoes like that anyhow?'

'I don't know,' Eva shrugged. Why was Sis making such a thing of it? 'I thought it was nice of him.'

'Humm,' Sis frowned.

'What's that supposed to mean?'

'Nobody ever gives anything away for free.'

'You're a cynic.'

'And you're too young to be wearing high-heeled shoes. He has designs on you.'

Eva wrinkled her nose. 'He's an old man! Besides, they're hardly worn.'

Sis moved the stack of towels Eva had just arranged to the opposite side of the cupboard. 'Old or not, he's a man. Give 'em back or you'll find yourself living in a two-room apartment in Brooklyn with his entire family.'

'No, I won't.'

'Honey, to my knowledge, he doesn't even have a sister.'

Eva's heart sank. 'He doesn't?'

Sis shook her head. 'Say they don't fit you and give 'em back. Say your aunt is going to get you a new pair. You can't be too careful.' Sis turned out the light and closed the linen closet door. 'Mr Waxman's not the only crazy person around here.'

Eva looked wistfully down at her feet. They'd been without a doubt the most exciting thing she'd ever worn in her life. Then she thought of Pots and Pans; his balding head and the way the spit gathered in the side of his mouth, forming a little pocket of foam when he spoke. 'I guess you're right.'

'Of course I am.' Sis headed down the hallway. 'And whatever you do, don't talk to Mr Lambert in 313.'

'Why not?' Eva ran to catch up with her, which was more difficult than she thought in the new red shoes.

'He's a Dangerous Man. You know Otto, from reception?'

'The one with the red moustache?'

'That's the one. He has it on good authority that Mr Lambert is a communist. Do you know what that is?'

'Not really.'

Sis turned on her. 'Oh, they're just the worst! For example, they believe in common property. Do you know what that means? What I have would belong to you too and vice versa. Isn't that barbaric?'

Eva thought about Sis's bolt of Irish lace. 'I guess so.'

'Otto says he believes in blacks marrying whites,

white people not marrying at all, everyone living in communes and the entire overthrow of democracy.'

Eva tried to imagine a black man marrying a white woman. What colour would their children be?

'And real communists, the ones in Russia, have no religion at all. It's outlawed. There's not a church for thousands of miles!'

'What do they do on Sunday mornings?'

'Nothing. No God, no heaven, no hell. I mean, that's just asking for trouble.' She sighed deeply. 'He's a Fallen Man, my friend. Forsaken. He only stays here because they won't let him back into the Continental on account of the oyster incident.'

Eva's eyes widened. 'What's the oyster incident?'

'Believe me,' Sis waggled a finger in Eva's face, 'you don't want to know! But I'll tell you this, the young lady involved was very offended.'

They'd reached the end of the corridor, where the service trolleys were kept.

'You may have to clean his room,' Sis continued, 'but don't talk to him. And don't let him tell you about any of his ideas.'

'OK.' Eva pulled out her cart and adjusted her cap again, which kept falling down about her ears.

A jumper in room 1129 and an Enemy of the State in 313.

She was definitely going to need extra towels.

For the first week, Eva hardly saw Mr Lambert. Then one day she noticed him locking his room, heading down the hallway.

He was distracted; head down, in a hurry. He looked like any other middle-aged man; of average height, not fat or too slim, brown hair. His gait was awkward, as if one leg faltered, but it appeared not to bother him.

She stared hard.

He didn't look fallen. Or did he?

'Good morning, Mr Lambert.'

She didn't know quite why she did it. And she said it softly, under her breath.

He hadn't heard her.

So she said it again, a little louder.

'Good morning, Mr Lambert.'

(Sis was going to kill her.)

Stopping, he turned and looked straight at her. He didn't have the eager enthusiasm of an American but seemed to weigh up whether he would speak or not.

'Good morning.' His voice was low and cultured and he tipped his hat, ever so slightly, before heading down the hallway again.

Eva watched, terrified and thrilled, as he turned the corner.

He had eyes so blue they were almost navy and a thin dark moustache just like John Gilbert. Sis had neglected to mention he was handsome.

Eva let herself into his room.

There was that particular stillness which pervades after a flurry of activity; a palpable sense of energy settling. She walked into the bathroom; the air was still damp and humid, smelling of soap, warm flesh and aftershave.

Picking up the wet towels from the floor, she washed the dark hairs from the drain, wiped everything down, arranged his shaving kit and toothbrush at right angles on either side of the sink. Eva collected his laundry, retrieved stray socks from under the armchairs, and smoothed the rumpled sheets of his bed where he'd lain only twenty minutes before, propped up on one arm, reading the morning newspaper and drinking coffee. Was it her imagination or were they still almost warm?

She felt a closeness to him she didn't feel for any of the other guests. A proximity that mimicked intimacy.

There were extra glasses in his room, one smeared in lipstick marks, a cheap waxy shade of bright pink. What kind of man wanted to look at that on a girl's face?

Eva put the glasses in her cart and took out fresh ones. But as she dusted and hoovered, she spotted nothing more damning – no strange leaflets with slogans calling for the overthrow of Western civilisation, no foreign newspapers or telegrams in other languages; not even the odd book in Russian.

Eva opened the window to let air in and turned round. The room was clean.

Still, she lingered just a bit longer than she needed to.

According to Sis, men were both stupid and dangerous, in much the same way that poison ivy is one of God's worst ideas and all too easy to catch. But there was clearly a world of difference between Pots and Pans's high-heeled shoes and the refined corruptions of Mr Lambert.

Fallen women were common; all you had to do was have sex before you were married to qualify. But for a man to fall required much more – a deliberate turning away from God, a conscious decision. Such decisions were rare. Religious sloppiness was easy. Rejection required moral and intellectual convictions.

For this reason, along with the way he tipped his hat and the unnatural blueness of his eyes, Eva decided that Mr Lambert was worthy of respect.

Paris, Spring, 1955

There was a chill in the air as they got out of Monsieur Tissot's tiny red Citroën and walked across the park in the centre of the Place des Vosges, the oldest residential square in Paris. It was a vast, elegant enterprise, a triumph of early civic planning with an aesthetic unity rarely seen in a public structure. Imposing brick buildings bordered the central park on all sides, built over galleries which housed shops and restaurants.

Grace surveyed the symmetrically arranged park with its formal fountains, rows of thick, boxy yew trees and neat gravel paths. 'This is very posh.'

'Very posh indeed. It was first built in the early 1600s.'

'I had no idea it would be so grand. It must be expensive.'

'I believe the apartment was a gift.'

'From whom?'

'I understand that it's been in the Hiver family for years.'

'Is that usual?' It struck Grace as particularly brazen to have the two worlds so closely intertwined. 'I mean, to give a mistress a family property?'

'The rich make their own rules.'

'It isn't at all what I was expecting.' She bit her lower lip uncertainly.

Monsieur Tissot looked across at her. 'Were you hoping for a garret?'

'I don't know . . . I suppose so.'

'We don't have to go in, if you'd rather not.'

'I know.' Pushing her hands deeper into her coat pockets, Grace slipped her fingers round her father's old lighter for comfort. 'But I want to.'

Monsieur Tissot led her through the galleries and into a narrow passageway with a wrought-iron gate. Pushing it open, they walked into a courtyard beyond, a kind of rectangular-shaped, cobblestone space with a small fountain in the middle. Ivy wound, reaching its long tendrils, thick and deep green, up the side of the building, which was classical in proportions, the red brick augmented by ivory stone. Large French windows, leading to balconies, looked out onto the courtyard from the first and second floors. Above, shutters covered the windows on the higher floors. The flagstone steps, with their curving wrought-iron handrail, were worn away in the centre from centuries of use. And the front door was stripped oak, two massive arched panels with gleaming brass knobs.

'I'll talk to the concierge. She has a set of keys.' Monsieur Tissot walked round to a side passage and knocked on the concierge's door. Grace waited, standing a little apart, out of sight. After a few minutes, he returned.

'We're in luck. The apartment is empty. It was cleared a few days ago. I explained that you were Madame d'Orsey's heir and she was very obliging.'

He unlocked the outer door and Grace followed him in through the front entrance. A high spiral staircase wound above them.

A gust of wind sent a few dry leaves spinning round their feet. Grace pulled her coat around her. She had the uncomfortable feeling of trespassing. But it was too late now; her feet were already in motion, following Monsieur Tissot up to the first floor. He unlocked the door, swung it open.

'After you.'

'Thank you.' Grace pulled her shoulders back, trying to appear more confident than she felt. 'But I think I'd like to go in alone, if that's all right with you.'

'Certainly. I'll be downstairs if you need me.'

Grace waited until he'd gone. Then, taking a deep breath, she walked inside.

Her heels clicked on the smooth surface of the parquet floor in the entranceway, echoing throughout the empty flat. It led into a large, formal drawing room, with three sets of French windows opening onto a balcony overlooking the square below. It was an enormous room, easily thirty-five feet in length, with high ceilings and detailed moulding. The sheer scale of it was breathtaking. An imposing black marble mantelpiece dominated; above, a glass chandelier sparkled. Grace could make out, from the faded markings on the toile wallpaper, the outlines where clusters of paintings had hung; the shadows where chair backs and tables had once stood against the walls.

No, this wasn't what she'd imagined at all. Perhaps not a garret but something much more modest in size, discreet. But this was a vast reception room, capable of entertaining on a grand scale. It seemed not just extravagant but somehow audacious to keep a mistress in such opulent style.

She moved into the room beyond.

Here was the bedroom, smaller, yet still luxurious in its proportions. As soon as she entered, the smell of perfume hit her. Not flowery or whimsical but sophisticated, strong. Like a hand reaching out across the impossible distance to pierce the veil that separated them, it pressed hard against her solar plexus, stopping her in her tracks. It had a metallic sharpness, almost intrusive in its originality.

The hairs on the back of Grace's neck rose. This woman was real, not some soft, benevolent, fairy godmother from a children's story. Grace was on her territory now.

A carved double wooden bed frame stood in the centre of the room. It was a *lit bateau* style frame, with an intricate inlaid-wood design on the headboard, the only piece of furniture left in the whole apartment.

Grace looked up.

The ceiling was painted a very pale blue, illuminated with an inner golden light. It mimicked, very cleverly, the delicate shades of a summer's sky.

This is where Madame d'Orsey entertained her lover, practised her art.

The thought sent a chill through Grace's spine. She couldn't help but think of Vanessa; her ghost seemed to drift soundlessly through these rooms, self-possessed, unapologetic, padding across the wooden floor in bare feet and pearls.

Love was an art, a game teased out and manipulated by skilled players.

A game Grace didn't know how to play.

Turning away, she peered into the bathroom, with its roll-top bath and mysterious, low bidet. The cabinets were open and empty; the plumbing reassuringly

112

noisy, the cistern tank of the toilet filling and refilling again and again.

She went through to the kitchen.

It was tiny. The smallest, most ordinary room in the whole apartment, with a green Formica counter top and a deep, square butler's sink. There was a simple built-in table with benches against one wall, with an ashtray and a morning paper on it.

Grace sat down. This room was dark, warm and womblike, the ceiling low. A cheap plastic clock ticked above the oven. The newspaper, *Le Figaro*, had been refolded after it had been read. She turned it over, looking at the date. It was more than a month old. Along the bottom of the page was a series of even circles, drawn in pen – the idle doodles of an otherwise engaged mind.

She traced her finger lightly across the rim of the ashtray. It was an inexpensive design, reminiscent of the styles of the 1920s; a simple square in heavy pottery china. It had been broken and then glued back together. But it wasn't the kind of object that seemed worth saving. She turned it over. Just visible in the lower right-hand corner was the faded inscription, Riker's Drug Store, New York City.

The other rooms felt unreal, like part of a stage set. But this room was intimate, quiet. The mysterious Madame d'Orsey had sat here, listening to the ticking clock, the dull hum of the refrigerator; smoking, reading the paper. A middle-aged woman, a woman whose face, as Monsieur Tissot had put it, was changed by pain.

Grace stared at the broken ashtray.

Le droit de choisir.

The phrase repeated itself again and again in her mind.

No one had ever advocated her independence before. The entire success of her marriage, her whole career as a woman, depended largely upon her cheerful, uncomplicated dependence, first on her family and then on her husband. But now this stranger was challenging her; asking her to make choices, take responsibility.

Why?

It supposed an intimacy; expectations. But Grace didn't even know her, let alone approve of Eva d'Orsey.

Opening her handbag she took out a crumpled pack of Chesterfields and lit one.

Pretty girls didn't lead independent lives; didn't Eva d'Orsey know that? Their triumphs were measured in the swiftness with which they moved from one pair of waiting arms to another. It was the less fortunate girls – the 'sensible' and 'clever' ones – who had to face the world on their own. (When she was young, if the word 'intelligent' was used when describing a girl, it was always a criticism; nothing signalled more completely the hopelessness of their future situation than the label of 'clever'.)

Exhaling slowly, Grace watched the smoke gather just above her head.

And yet their handicap bought them freedom – just the sort of liberty and responsibility this unknown woman was demanding of her now.

Leaning her chin in her palm, Grace opened the newspaper.

If she were truly the beneficiary, why did it feel as if Madame d'Orsey were taking something away from her rather than giving it?

Turning the pages, she tried to string together the few words she recognized. There was a sale at the Galeries Lafayette, with the promise of a new season of architecturally engineered girdles and brassieres outlined in bold drawings . . . a photograph of some sort of sporting disaster involving a young man and a racing car . . . obituaries . . . classified ads . . . here was something circled in black pen . . .

Avis de saisie vente de boutique, 23 Rue Christine, Saint-Germain, Paris.

Boutique . . . that meant shop, didn't it? *Avis de saisie vente* . . . Her French wasn't good enough to make out the rest.

Grace stared out of the window above the sink, at the shadow of the sun creeping across the wall opposite.

The little kitchen was soothing, familiar in its domesticity. The clock ticked; here the city felt removed.

I don't know what I'm doing, she thought, pulling the cracked ashtray closer, taking another drag. I'm completely out of my depth.

Le droit de choisir.

But the right to choose what?

Grace wasn't used to making choices on her own; wasn't certain she liked it. How would she know if she'd made the right ones?

Sighing, she flicked a bit of ash off the end of her cigarette.

There was a knock at the door.

Grace started, hurrying to stub out her cigarette in the ashtray.

'Monsieur Tissot? Monsieur Tissot, is that you?' She stood up.

There was no reply.

'Hello?'

Again, another knock.

Grace went into the front hallway. Listened. If she did nothing, maybe they'd go away.

But they didn't; the knocking continued.

Grace opened the door. 'Oh, hello!' She smiled in relief.

A young girl was standing on the landing, holding a cardboard box. She was maybe thirteen or fourteen, with even brown plaits and a serious face.

'May I help you?'

'*Bonjour, madame. Parlez-vous français?*' she asked, pronouncing each word with exaggerated clarity.

'*Ah, well, oui . . . un peu . . . mais je ne parle pas très bien . . .*'

'I speak some English.' (Obviously the answer to the girl's question was 'no'.) 'The man downstairs said you were, ah, the heir? Is this true?'

'Ah, yes. I suppose I am.'

'Yes, um, my mother, she wanted you to have this.' The girl handed her the box.

'I'm sorry, who is your mother?'

'*Pardon.*' The girl was looking down at her shoes. 'She is the concierge, Madame Assange. She says this is for you.'

'Really?'

'You're English, yes?'

'Yes.'

'And this is you, yes?' She pointed to the top of the box.

Scrawled across one corner was her name: Grace Munroe.

Grace felt her skin go cold. It was written in the same, strong slanted hand she'd seen on the paper in Monsieur Tissot's office. 'Yes.' She nodded, 'That's me.'

Grace opened the lid.

Inside was a collection of half a dozen small china figurines, wrapped in newspaper; delicate frolicking shepherdesses with white faces and flowered gowns, the kind of inexpensive, sentimental bric-a-brac she abhorred.

'Madame d'Orsey gave them to Maman for you, to keep safe. She didn't want Monsieur Migret to have them.'

'Who is Monsieur Migret?'

'Monsieur Migret owns . . . ah . . . *l'antiquaire* . . . *Il vend* . . . he sells *les bibelots* . . . um . . . *les deuxième main* . . .' the girl pointed to her hand.

'A second-hand shop?' Grace guessed. (She'd always been good at charades.)

'Yes,' the girl nodded. 'Second-hand. He clears the house when someone dies.'

'And he cleared this apartment?'

'Yes.' The girl turned to go.

'Wait,' Grace stopped her. 'This Monsieur Migret, do you know where his business is?'

'He has a shop . . . um . . . on Rue Saint-Claude.'

'Rue Saint-Claude,' Grace repeated, committing it to memory. 'Is that close?'

'A few streets away.'

'Thank you.' Grace took another step forward. 'Do you think, perhaps, I could meet your mother? I would like to thank her and to speak to her, about Madame d'Orsey.'

The girl hesitated, her face suddenly guarded. 'My mother does not speak English, madame.'

'Yes, but maybe you could help me,' Grace suggested, with a smile. 'You could sit between us. Or Monsieur Tissot, the man you met downstairs, he would help.'

The girl's brow furrowed. 'She does not like gossip.'

'But this wouldn't be gossip. I just have a few questions about what Madame d'Orsey was like.'

'Yes, well . . .' The girl inched away from the door. 'I will let her know. She is very busy though.'

She started back down the steps.

'Did you know her?' Grace called after her.

The girl turned. 'Madame d'Orsey?'

'Yes.'

She thought a moment. 'She gave me a doll once for my birthday. I was five. It was very pretty – with blonde curls made from real hair and a china face. The nicest one I have ever owned.'

'So she was a friend of the family?'

The girl looked at her blankly. 'Oh no, madame. My mother would not let me keep it.'

'Why not?'

The girl shifted. 'You will have to ask her, madame.'

Grace watched as she slipped into the shadows of the hallway and down the stairs. Far below, she heard urgent, muted voices, speaking in French. Then a door closed and there was silence.

New York, 1927

The proper way to enter a guest's room is to knock, three times. First, you knock. Next, you knock again, loudly, calling out, 'Maid service.' Last, you unlock the door and pause. 'Maid service,' you say, knocking one more time. And still, you are likely to walk in on quite a few situations, the least disturbing of which is a guest emerging from the bath.

It was amazing how many people did hear you call out but didn't seem to mind. Eva had noticed that as soon as she put on her uniform, she became invisible. And in situations which would have been considered improper if she were wearing normal clothes, she suddenly disappeared.

This was the procedure Eva followed when delivering extra towels to room 313.

There was no reply.

The bathroom door was slightly ajar and she could hear the taps running.

'Maid service,' she called out again. 'I'll leave your extra towels on the bed, sir.'

'Thank you.'

She put them down.

There were some cards spread out on the table; in several rows, stacked in groups. Eva had seen plenty of people playing solitaire but she'd never seen a game like this one. But already, she thought she recognized some sort of pattern.

She moved closer.

It wasn't obvious.

It was more than just suits . . .

'So.' Mr Lambert was standing in the bathroom doorway, wearing nothing but a bath towel, dabbing shaving foam from his jaw. 'What would you do next?'

Startled, Eva grabbed the towels. 'Sorry, sir.' She headed for the door.

He leaned against the bathroom door frame. 'Aren't you forgetting something?'

She stared at him. The towel was wrapped round his waist; he was well built, dark curls against the tawny skin of his chest.

He smiled.

'Oh!' She felt herself blushing and handed him the towels. 'Pardon me, sir.'

'You're the girl who said hello to me in the hallway, aren't you?'

'I . . . yes.'

He nodded to the card game. 'The way you were looking at that, I thought maybe you were trying to figure it out. Not many people can, you know.'

It sounded like a challenge.

'Go on,' he grinned, 'tell me what you see.'

She looked again at the cards. 'They're prime numbers, aren't they? Or superior suits, whichever comes first.'

'That's right,' he nodded. 'Don't tell me you've played it before.'

'No, sir. Cards are a bad idea.'

'Most things are. But if you don't play, then how did you figure it out?'

'I'm pretty good with numbers.'

'Really?' His eyes narrowed. 'How do you know you're good at numbers?'

She felt suddenly defensive, out of her depth. 'I'm sorry. I was mistaken.'

Mr Lambert went to the dresser, lit a cigarette. 'Do you think I'm going to hurt you or get you into trouble?'

'You're asking a lot of questions.'

Mr Lambert smiled. 'I'm bored. That's hardly a crime, is it?'

She shook her head.

'So,' he sat on the edge of the bed, 'are you going

123

to answer me or not?'

'I used to work for a family in Brooklyn. The man, he was a professor. He used to work on problems all day long in his study and sometimes, well, he'd leave puzzles on the blackboard.'

'What kind of puzzles?'

'I'm not certain what you'd call them. Number problems. They had patterns and sequences. Some of the numbers were already there and I would try to fill in the blanks.'

'What made him think that a maid could do that? I used to live with household servants and I tell you, most of them could barely make change.'

'Oh no, sir! I didn't fill them in on the blackboard,' she corrected him. 'I did it in my head. You see, one day I accidentally erased something when I was cleaning. I wiped away a problem that he was working on. Except I didn't know it at the time. His wife became furious. Only, I was able to copy it out again, the same way. So I got to keep my job. But he never knew about it. It was between her and me.'

'Really?' His interest was peaked. 'Do you still remember it?'

'Uh . . . maybe.'

Going over to the desk, he handed her a pen and a piece of paper. 'Go on then.'

Eva frowned, concentrating. Then she started to

write, covering the entire page.

Mr Lambert stared at it. 'How is it that you can recall such a complicated equation? Are you trained in mathematics?'

'I don't need to recall the equation, sir. I see it. It's like a picture in my brain. All I have to do is look at it in my head and then write down what I see.'

He thought for a moment, taking this in. Then asked, 'Why did you leave?'

'I'm sorry?'

'Why aren't you working for them now?'

'They moved. Went back to Austria. But his wife, well, she didn't like me much anyway.'

'I should think not. Well,' he took a deep drag, crossing his legs, 'isn't that a useful talent?'

'Not for a girl, sir.'

'And how did you do on the puzzles that he left on the blackboard?'

She thought a moment. 'I think I did well on them, sir. Sometimes I figured them out before he did.'

Mr Lambert pointed to the cards on the table again. 'So which one would you play over here?'

Eva could feel her heart racing. She pointed to a club. 'That one, sir.'

'Well done. And after that?'

'I'd move the nine over there.'

'Why?'

'That's the highest card left.'

'How can you tell?'

It seemed obvious to her. 'Well, because of what's on the table. There are only fifty-two cards. Isn't that right?'

'How long were you here?'

'Not long, sir.'

'Did you touch anything?'

She shook her head.

'But you can tell how many cards have been played and how many are left even though you don't know the game?'

She nodded.

'Well now, let's see . . .' Crossing, he sat down and began turning the cards over. After he'd turned them all over, he looked up, smiling. 'Looks like you were right. But you don't play cards.'

'No, sir. My uncle used to play cards until he lost an awful lot of money he didn't have. After that cards weren't allowed in the house.'

'Well, that happens. But you don't play?'

'You keep asking me that.'

'Yes, I keep asking.' Leaning back against the table, he crossed his arms in front of his chest. 'What an interesting ability you have.'

A minute passed.

He cocked his head to one side. It was hard to tell if he were smiling or not. His lips curved but there was nothing, no warmth in his eyes.

'Are you a communist?' she finally blurted out, unable to bear the silence anymore.

'Why? Are you?'

'Me? I don't believe in anything.'

'Well, that makes two of us.'

That wasn't quite what she meant.

'Are you . . . I mean,' she was almost too embarrassed to ask, 'is it true that you're titled, sir?'

He made a face. 'Where did you hear that?'

'My friend told me. She says that in England you're Lord Lambert but you don't like to use it.'

'She's right. I prefer Mr Lambert. Besides, just between you and me, I haven't got the means to back it up.' He smiled. 'Lately I've been thinking of changing it to Mr Mutton . . . what do you think?'

Eva suppressed a giggle.

'If you're going to have an alias you might as well have fun.'

'But why do you need an alias?'

He shrugged. 'As much as I don't give a damn what anyone thinks of me, I still want to keep the shame I bring on my family to a minimum. I'm not fond of many of them but the ones I do like, I like very much.

Do you know what I am?' He grinned. 'I'm what's known as a scoundrel, my dear. Or in more eloquent terms, a son of a bitch.'

'Oh, sir! You shouldn't say such things about your own mother.'

He flicked a bit of ash in the ashtray. 'If you only knew her. She's the one who disinherited me. But that's another story entirely.' He pointed his cigarette at her. 'I'm bad luck. I've been given every opportunity and squandered it. I lack self-control, moral-fibre, character – "The expense of spirit in a waste of shame!"' He looked over at her, staring at him, wide-eyed. 'Shakespeare, my child. If you're going to rant, do it in iambic pentameter. What's wrong?'

'Please, sir . . .' It wasn't her place, but she carried on regardless, 'please don't say those things about yourself.'

Mr Lambert, frowned, his eyes softening. 'What's your name?'

'Eva, sir.'

He bowed his head a little. 'Very nice to make your acquaintance, Eva.' Opening a drawer, he took out a new pack of cards and handed it to her. 'Here. I think you'd better have these.'

She wasn't meant to take gifts. 'Are you sure?'

'Absolutely.'

'Thank you, sir.'

Eva left, walking in a daze, back out into the hall-way. Her heart was thumping, her palms sweating. She was having trouble catching her breath, as though she'd been running.

Sis came round the corner carrying a breakfast tray. 'What's wrong with you?'

Eva jammed the cards into her apron pocket. 'What do you mean?'

'Your face is all red.'

Eva pressed her hands to her cheeks. They felt hot. 'I'm fine.'

'Here.' Sis took the glass of iced water from the tray. 'Have some. You look sick.'

'No. I'm fine.'

'You better not throw up on the carpet.'

'There's nothing wrong with me.'

'Suit yourself,' Sis shrugged, continuing down the hall. 'But you look like a beet.'

<hr />

Eva sat alone on the fire escape that wound round the back of the building, holding the pack of cards. They were beautiful, with bees on them.

She never showed anyone what she could do with numbers. It was secret; something private that she did, to calm herself, to take her mind away from anything that made her anxious, or to ease her boredom. And the puzzles were her own guilty pleasure; the only form of entertainment she'd had in that sombre, silent house. In fact, she couldn't recall a time when numbers hadn't appeared like vivid colourful shapes, carving through the chaos in her mind, bringing order.

It felt strange to think that now Mr Lambert knew, of all people. But he hadn't ridiculed her or teased her. Instead he'd given her a gift.

It was wrong to keep them. Against the rules. What would Sis say if she knew?

That she was being corrupted; that it was the beginning of a rapid descent into depravity.

Eva thought of the family she'd worked for in Brooklyn. The way the Professor's wife used to follow her around, checking her work. How ferocious she was about every little detail and the way she used to stare at Eva, when she didn't think anyone was looking, as if she hated her. Frau Brohemer had lost her baby son shortly after they arrived in America, from pneumonia, presumably contracted on the journey. It had made her bitter and mean.

The Hotel was much better than that. She should be grateful for what she had and leave well enough alone.

But Mr Lambert was only being kind to her. What was wrong with kindness? She just wanted to see the cards, to look at them for a few minutes.

Eva broke the seal on the box and fanned them out.

Already the numbers and suits were arranging themselves in intricate patterns in her head and she felt a warm, familiar surge of contentment in her chest.

After a few minutes, she knew she was never going to give them back.

———— ❧ ————

Eva didn't see Mr Lambert for the next few days but she carried the pack of cards with her at all times, in the pocket of her uniform apron. She was afraid to leave them in the room she shared with Sis but she also wanted them close. He had given them to her.

When she finally did see him again, he was escorting a laughing blonde to his room, whispering in her ear.

Eva froze at the other end of the corridor, standing rigid in the hallway with her bucket and mop.

They swayed and reeled, clutching one another and giggling; sharing a private joke.

Mr Lambert unlocked his door, arm round the blonde's waist, and pushed it open.

She in turn threw her arms round his neck, tilting her face towards his as they fell inside.

The door shut.

The Laughing Blonde was wearing the same unfortunate shade of lipstick that Eva had found on the glasses.

Wrapping her fingers round the cards in her pocket, Eva stared at the closed door.

Men were like that, she told herself. They liked cheap-looking girls that laughed too easily, too loud.

He probably didn't even notice her hideous rouged lips.

But then again, he probably hadn't given her anything either.

The next morning the blonde was gone. Mr Lambert was having coffee and reading the paper, lingering over his breakfast tray when Eva knocked.

'Good morning, sir,' she said brightly.

He turned over another page. 'Good morning.'

Silence stretched out before them.

'I . . . I wanted to thank you for the playing cards, sir.'

'You're welcome.'

She hovered behind his chair.

'It was very nice of you,' she added.

Mr Lambert took a sip of his coffee. 'I'm a nice man, the nicest you'll ever meet. Also, I need more lavatory paper.'

'Yes, sir.' She stood stupidly, unsure of what to do

next. She wanted him to talk to her more, the way he had the other day, but she didn't know how to start the conversation.

'Besides,' he folded his paper, put it down, 'I thought you said cards were a bad idea. Root of all evil. I'm surprised you kept them.'

'Well, I . . .' She was suddenly wrong-footed. 'Why did you give them to me if you didn't think I should have them?'

He shrugged, lit a cigarette. 'Innocence, like virginity, is more fun to lose than to keep.'

'Both are quite expensive, sir.'

'Well!' he laughed. 'Aren't you full of clever observations? Have you played at all?'

'Only by myself.'

He exhaled, forcing a stream of smoke through his nose like a bull. 'That's not going to get you anywhere. Sit down.'

Tucking his cigarette into the corner of his mouth, he took a deck of cards from his jacket pocket and began to shuffle. 'I'm going to teach you a game called Twenty-one.'

She watched in fascination as the cards flashed between his fingers. She'd never met anyone who carried a deck of cards with them everywhere.

Except herself, she realized, with a flush of excitement.

'Is it a good game?'

'What do you mean?'

'I mean, is it a gambling game?'

'Now there's a question. Let's see – you can place a bet on whether it's going to rain tomorrow or not. If you're inclined to gamble, everything's a gambling game. But the definition of gambling means taking a chance. Now, if I'm right about you, your talent for numbers means that chance, or risk, is considerably reduced. So in fact, you're not gambling at all. You're simply proceeding with what you believe to be true, which is like faith, really – the spiritual dimension of this exercise is one we'll touch on another time.'

'Will we?'

'Don't interrupt. So you see, you can play the same game I do. However, I can be gambling because I know very little and therefore am taking a huge risk – this is hypothetical, of course. I want to stress to you that I'm extremely proficient in what I do . . .'

'And what is that, sir?'

'I am a connoisseur of chance, a pioneer of probability, little girl. And, as I was saying, I can be gambling because I know only a little. You, on the other hand, with your unique gift, can be simply playing out a rather complicated equation whose conclusion only you can see. So, "no" and "yes" and "sometimes" are the answers to your question.' He had done dealing. 'Here are the rules. We're playing with one deck for the purpose of this demonstration but normally it's six. I want to break you in slowly.'

She stared at his handsome face. 'Why are you showing me this?'

He looked up at her as if it were obvious. 'Some day it will be useful to you. And remember what I said, it's only a gamble if you don't know what you're doing.'

So Mr Lambert taught her how to play Twenty-one. The next day he schooled her in the rudiments of poker. And she was frighteningly, thrillingly quick to learn. There was a disarming calm about her; she simply proceeded, first to learn the games, then to beat him. Hand after hand, with no sign of nerves.

It was easy for her; she knew what was going to happen.

Eva had never been clever at anything. And she wanted to please Mr Lambert.

She focused on the cards he discarded, the number of cards played; holding the facts to one side in her brain. She seemed to see in her mind's eye all the various possibilities and combinations of scenarios at once. Then another card was played and they narrowed. Before long she could see pretty much the whole game in her head and then it was only a matter of what order cards were being played rather than what they would be. And when this happened, Mr Lambert became excited. His eyes lit up and he regarded her as if she were delightful and amazing.

Eva had never actually seen the expression directed at her before, but from all she'd read and been told, Mr Lambert looked at her as if he loved her.

∽

And then the Laughing Blonde came back.

Only she wasn't laughing anymore.

She was hungover, smoking a cigarette, picking the crusts off a slice of cold toast.

She appeared one morning, without any warning, when Eva knocked on the door to service Mr Lambert's room.

Worse, her suitcase was in the corner.

Eva stared at that suitcase in silent desperation. The woman was one thing. The case was another.

The Blonde blinked at her through puffy, red eyes. 'Yeah?' She had lines across her forehead, hollows in her cheeks. She wasn't nearly as pretty in the daylight.

'I'm sorry, madam,' Eva spoke stiffly, trying her best not to betray her feelings. 'I'm here to service the room. Would you like me to come back?'

136

The Blonde shrugged, took another bite of toast, tossed it back on the plate. 'Sure. Though I guess I'd better get dressed,' she sighed, 'if we're going to make the noon train.'

'Train?' The word slipped out before Eva could stop it.

The Blonde stood up, pulling the robe sash tighter around her waist. She was so thin, it looked like it would cut her in two. 'Yeah. Niagara Falls.' She smiled to herself, flicking ash into her coffee cup, where it fizzled in the remains. 'Very romantic, wouldn't you say?'

Eva felt all hope drain away. 'I'm sorry to disturb you. I'll come back later, ma'am.'

As she pulled the door shut behind her, Eva could hear the Blonde singing softly to herself . . . 'It Had to Be You'.

Halfway down the hall, she realized she was crying.

Paris, Spring, 1955

The shop on Rue Saint-Claude was, like most second-hand shops, stacked indiscriminately from floor to ceiling with all manner of furniture and objects: lamps, appliances, cushions, curtains, vases, pictures, books. Wooden chairs dangled from hooks on the ceiling along with chandeliers and drying racks; every available space had not just one but at least five unrelated objects crowded onto its surface. A small bell jangled when they opened the front door. It smelled of mildew, damp fabric and dust.

Grace squeezed past the entrance, and Monsieur Tissot trailed in after her. This was not going according to his plan. They should be back in the office now, not foraging among garbage. 'Explain to me again why we're here, madame?'

'The concierge's daughter said this man cleared Eva d'Orsey's apartment.'

'Yes, but what does that have to do with us?' He

sidestepped a wooden crate, filled with nothing but old doorknobs. 'Are you looking for something? What do you hope to find?'

'I don't know. Whatever I can. An address book and a complete set of personal diaries would be useful.'

'An address book?' He looked at her incredulously.

'I'm teasing. What I mean is, there may be something here, some clue about who Madame d'Orsey was – something personal.'

He cast round at the chaos. 'Here?'

'You never know.' Grace continued to push her way through. She picked up a small metal object that looked like a sugar sifter but turned out to be some early eighteenth-century magnifying glass. It was badly rusted and the glass was broken. 'Besides, Monsieur Tissot, you didn't need to come with me. I'm sure you have more pressing business to attend to.'

'You are my business, Madame Munroe.' He brushed a patch of dust from the elbow of his suit jacket; a gift from a set of moth-eaten velvet curtains. 'I'm your lawyer.'

'My lawyer?' Grace put down the glass. 'I'm sorry but I thought you were Madame d'Orsey's lawyer.'

'Yes, but her interests are now your interests. Until the sale of the property is complete, my obligations remain unfulfilled. Unless of course,' he added, 'you would prefer that I no longer represented you.'

'I see.' Grace hadn't anticipated this. 'Doesn't this go somewhat beyond your brief?'

'I've never had a client in your situation before. Especially one that requires additional proof in order to proceed.' He folded his arms across his chest, looking at her squarely. 'So we are both beyond our brief, don't you think?'

'I suppose, though I certainly don't want to monopolize your time, Monsieur Tissot. I don't want you to feel you must chaperone me the entire day.'

'Yes, but I cannot allow you to wander all over Paris without an escort,' he pointed out. 'Your French alone, madame, would get you arrested.'

'Actually,' Grace straightened, 'I thought it was improving.'

'You're wrong.'

'Well then, what do you propose?' she challenged, crossing her arms too. 'I hope you understand, I cannot simply accept a large sum of money without knowing where or why it's come to me. I have to have some answers.'

'And what if there are no answers?'

She held her ground. 'Then at least I will have asked the questions.'

Monsieur Tissot sighed, running his hand across

his eyes. She was surprisingly stubborn. Not a lot of people argued with him, ever. And he wasn't used to capitulating. But he judged the fastest way forward was to let her have her way for an hour more. And, in truth, part of him respected the fact that she wouldn't let go of her principle.

'Fine,' he decided, 'then I will help you. As I said, your interests are my interests.' Suddenly scrunching up his face, he sneezed violently, three times in quick succession. '*Mon dieu!* The dust in here. *Allô! Bonjour!*' he called out.

A small middle-aged man poked his head up from behind a wall of soft furnishings. He had thick glasses and a sharp pointed nose underneath a worn leather cap. '*Oui? Qu'est-ce que vous cherchez?*'

'Please tell him that I'm looking for anything to do with Madame d'Orsey,' Grace said.

Monsieur Tissot explained but before he'd even finished, the man interrupted him.

'He says,' Monsieur Tissot translated, 'that most of the furniture went very quickly. He had people waiting for it, bidding against one another.'

'Are you telling me there's nothing left?'

Monsieur Tissot quizzed the man again. But he just shook his head, waving his hand dismissively.

'He says he could hardly even unload it from his truck.'

Grace looked at him in disbelief. 'Is that normal?'

Before he could answer, the man began to talk again, very rapidly, hands waving emphatically. Whatever he was saying, he felt strongly about it.

'Apparently, she had a reputation,' Monsieur Tissot elaborated.

'Really?' Grace didn't like the sound of that. 'What kind of reputation?'

'Everyone knew her. Or rather,' he corrected himself, 'everyone knew *of* her.'

Grace bristled, suddenly defensive on this stranger's behalf. 'And what precisely does that mean?'

Monsieur Migret didn't answer but instead spat on the floor and narrowed his eyes, suspiciously.

'What about the bed?' Grace persisted. 'Why did he leave that behind?'

Again, Monsieur Tissot asked and the man shook his head.

'Apparently the bed wasn't his to sell,' Monsieur Tissot explained. 'It's an antique, belonging to the Hiver family. The new owner is to collect it himself.'

'Arnaud Hiver,' Monsieur Migret interjected, with a low, sneering chuckle. '*Le souvenir de son père!*'

'A memento from his father,' Monsieur Tissot offered quietly, under his breath.

Grace glared at Monsieur Migret. She didn't like him at all. But to Monsieur Tissot she whispered, 'Is that customary? To leave such a thing to one's son?'

Monsieur Tissot shrugged. 'I'm unfamiliar with the customs of having a mistress, a son or an antique bed, madame.'

The man stepped forward. '*J'ai quelques plaques, des bagages, quelques lampes* . . .' He pointed to a table in the corner piled with odds and ends.

'There are just a few things left – over there on the table.'

Grace headed eagerly to the table and Monsieur Tissot followed.

There were a pair of matching chinoiserie black lacquer lamps, a stack of blue-and-white china plates, a couple of large leather cases . . . Grace bent down, rifling through a box of books, all of them in French, while Monsieur Tissot dug half-heartedly through a box of table linens. She'd joked about the address book and journals but still she'd hoped to find something more revealing. However, the novels looked like rather mundane romantic popular fiction. There were no hidden notes inside; no telling inscriptions; no underlined passages.

Monsieur Tissot picked up an old leather satchel. 'This isn't half bad, actually. It reminds me of something I had as a student.'

Grace got up again and began combing through another crate of kitchenwares. Serving spoons, mismatched cutlery . . . nothing.

She sifted through a box of art and exhibition catalogues. Then she rifled through a pile of old shoes; opened handbags, turning them upside down. That was it. In a matter of minutes they'd been through what was left.

And there was nothing, nothing at all specific or even remotely intimate.

Monsieur Tissot was still examining the leather bag, testing the latch. How like a man to be fascinated by the obscure.

Grace looked round the shop again, her frustration mounting. The whole idea of a second-hand shop had captured her imagination. Now, she was childishly disappointed. 'Let's go,' she decided grimly. 'There's nothing here.'

'I wonder how much he wants for it.' Monsieur Tissot turned the bag over.

First she had to drag him in here and now she couldn't get him out. She was losing patience. 'The strap is broken. And I don't like that man, he's rude. Please, Monsieur Tissot, you were right. This was a waste of time. Let's get out of here.'

The latch snapped open. 'There's something in here.'

He took out what looked to be a delicately made blouse. Only it wasn't.

Grace bent in closer. 'What is that?'

'I believe it's a dress.' He held it up. 'A very small dress.'

It was a child's pinafore, cut from white linen, now yellowed with age, finished off with smocking and tiny embroidered yellow flowers. He laid it on the table.

'That's odd.'

'Maybe it belonged to someone else.' Monsieur Tissot checked the inside of the bag again. 'It's empty.'

Grace ran her fingers lightly across the yoke of the dress. It wasn't a manufactured garment, but handmade. The delicate silk thread still gleamed, highlighting the exquisite detail and skill of the handiwork involved. It was a true labour of love; even the tiny leaves of the blooms were rendered in varying shades of contrasting greens.

'I used to have a pocket kerchief with little embroidered flowers like this when I was small,' she recalled.

'Little girls have flowers over everything. Don't they?'

'These are little daffodils – narcissus. They bloom in the springtime. The English call them paperwhites.' As she said it, she felt her cheeks flush, suddenly embarrassed. 'I suppose it's just a coincidence but

145

they've always been my favourite flowers. Someone's gone to a lot of effort. Embroidery like this takes real skill to make. I haven't seen anything like it in a very long time.'

'Look here.' Monsieur Tissot held up the battered leather luggage tag. 'I suppose it did belong to someone else after all.'

Scrawled across a faded, yellowed label was a different address.

M. A. Valmont
23 Rue Christine, Paris

Grace frowned, concentrating. 'I know that address. I've seen it before, in Eva's apartment!'

'And . . .?'

She looked up. 'Do you know where that is? Rue Christine? Is it far?' He was staring at her. 'I mean, not that I expect you to take me or anything like that . . .' she fumbled.

It was his own fault. He should never have shown her the apartment in the first place.

'Well, madame,' Monsieur Tissot put the bag back down on the table, brushed the dust from his hands. 'I suppose there's only one way to find out.'

Rue Christine was located on one of the narrow winding streets down by the Seine on the Left Bank. Monsieur Tissot pulled up and turned off the ignition. 'This is it, madame. Number 23.'

Grace's heart sank. 'Are you certain?'

'Quite certain.'

They were parked in front of an abandoned building, its doors and windows boarded up. A torn black awning flapped wildly in the spring wind.

'Oh dear.' Grace scrutinized the bleak exterior, her face falling. 'Well, I suppose you were right.' She conceded. 'That's it then. A wild goose chase.'

A moment earlier she was full of hopeful anticipation. Now she sat back, dejected. Apparently the matter was much more important to her than he'd realized.

And for the second time in two days, Monsieur Tissot found himself doing something he almost never did – taking impulsive action.

'Let's see about that.' He opened the door and climbed out.

Grace followed him. 'What are you doing?'

'I thought you wanted answers, Madame Munroe,' he called over his shoulder, heading to the front door.

'I do. But this place is deserted!'

He peered between the boarded-up windows. 'It looks like some sort of shop.'

'A shop?' Grace came up next to him, squinted to see through the dirty glass. 'What kind of a shop?'

'I'm not sure. Let's find out.' Monsieur Tissot stepped back and prised off the large board nailed across the front door.

'What are you doing?' Grace hissed, panicking.

'I'm conducting a thorough investigation on your behalf.' Leaning in hard with his shoulder, he pushed. The door handle was jammed.

'Well, stop it this instant!' She looked around quickly to see if anyone had spotted them. 'I don't want you to! This is against the law, isn't it?'

'It's all a matter of intent. You don't intend to steal anything, do you?' He pushed again, harder. The rotting wood of the door frame splintered and the door gave way, groaning as it opened. '*Voilà!*' he smiled, triumphant.

'You're mad!'

'You're welcome.'

Gingerly, they both stepped inside.

Ahead of her in the cool darkness, Grace could just make out the dim outlines of a shop counter, high shelves lining the walls. It smelled of damp, of cold, stale air and mildew. Wind whistled in through the shattered corner of one of the windows.

Monsieur Tissot jiggled the light switch to no avail. 'There's no electricity.' He pulled back the heavy velvet curtains that hung across the front windows and light flooded in.

'My goodness!' Grace gasped.

Even in its state of extreme neglect, the room dazzled; walls of glass and mirrors reflecting light so that Grace was blinded for a moment. As her eyes adjusted, she could see that the space had been designed as a series of bold contrasts. The dark wood counter was a rich warm mahogany. The floor was covered in black-and-white marble tiles. A tiered crystal chandelier, thick with dust and filmy cobwebs, hung from a heavy black silk cord in the centre of the ceiling. And the shelves were filled with rows and rows of slim glass flacons, cloudy grey with dirt.

In the curve of the bay window a pair of salon chairs stood, covered in black velvet, faded and rotting, and an ottoman in leopard skin. Grace reached down to touch the smooth fur. It was real.

Silvery-white silk taffeta lined the walls, now badly water damaged and falling away in strips. The ceiling was fitted with an enormous mirror, cut from a single piece of glass, now shattered in one corner, long cracks reaching out like fingers from the central wound. Somewhere in the back recesses, water dripped; leaking, into a bucket long overfilled.

On the counter were a number of shapely glass bottles, in various sizes, with crystal stoppers.

'This isn't like any shop I've ever seen,' Grace said. 'It's more like a nightclub. But it's in a dreadful state – like it's been ransacked.'

'It clearly hasn't been open in years but it may have been plundered by the Nazis. They weren't known for their manners. Also, we've been having strikes lately. There has been some violence.'

Grace pushed aside a curtain, peering into the back room. 'What do you think it was? Some kind of chemist?'

'I'm not sure.' Monsieur Tissot reached up and took down one of the bottles. She watched as he removed the stopper; a rich floral fragrance escaped.

Raising an eyebrow, he looked across at her. 'I think we're in a perfumery.'

Grace stared in amazement at the walls crowded with hundreds, even thousands of tiny bottles. 'You mean, these are all filled with scent?'

The sheer number was astonishing.

'I have to admit, this isn't like any perfumery I've ever seen.' Monsieur Tissot reached up, fitting the flacon back on the shelf. 'A traditional perfumery has just a few categories, like florals, orientals, greens and citrus . . . maybe a dozen bottles for each . . .'

Grace looked across at him. 'How do you know so much about perfume?'

'It's common knowledge. I know what everyone

knows,' he insisted. 'Every man alive has bought perfume at one time or another.'

'My husband has never bought me perfume.'

'Your husband isn't French. Besides, all women love perfume.'

'All women except me.'

'Madame Munroe,' he sighed, shaking his head, 'you are an exercise in perversity!'

'That's not quite a compliment, is it?' she pointed out.

'What have you got against perfume?'

'I don't know. I suppose I never found anything that didn't seem too . . . too loud.'

'You mean strong,' he corrected her.

'No, loud. And I hate to be contradicted, monsieur.'

'As do I.'

'I wanted something that whispered, not shouted. I gave up a long time ago.'

'Well, if you were interested in perfume, this would have been the place to come, I can guarantee you that. Look, you probably cannot read these headings, with your appalling French, but allow me to translate.' He pointed to a section. 'There are entire scent collections listed under sun, sea, air, earth – they're referenced and cross–referenced . . . some under ages.' He indicated another shelf. 'This row is devoted to women between the ages of thirty to thirty-five and then over here, for forty-seven to forty-nine.'

Grace moved closer, fascinated. Each vial had handwritten notations on a small card underneath. She pointed to one. 'What does this say?'

'"Diminishes",' he read, moving on to the next one. '"Wears well". Look at this one! "Caution! Overstays its welcome".' He snorted. 'I've sat next to women in the theatre wearing that one. And there's more.' He gestured to other clusters of vials. '"Romantic", "Realist", "Vain", "Sophisticate", "Sensualist", "Timid". "Extreme", "Calm", "Nervous", "Talkative", "Bright", "Soft" . . . and here are the names of gods and goddesses – "Aphrodite", "Artemis", "Narcissus", "Hera".'

'How could anyone come up with all of this?' she wondered. 'It's more like a laboratory or a wizard's workshop.'

She took down one of the vials from the self. *Jasmin de la Mer*, the label said. Opening it, she sniffed the cork. Its contents had long since evaporated, leaving a slightly grainy amber residue at the bottom of the bottle. But there was a ghost of the intensely white bloom, undercut by a coolness, an almost metallic airiness, slicing through the depth and lushness that lingered still.

It was disturbing how quickly the scent transported her; she felt a fleeting sense of euphoria and vastness completely unrelated to her surroundings. It was as though someone was playing a trick on her. It was a long way from the staid, single-note fragrances she was used to – Penhaligon's talcum powder and spray, with a dainty little drawing of a bluebell on the label.

Monsieur Tissot leaned over and smelled it too. 'Remarkable!'

She put the lid back on. 'Is this a collection? I don't recognize any of the names. Not that I'm an expert, but there are no familiar perfume brands here. But . . . but,' she turned, gazing at the thousands of bottles, 'that's impossible, isn't it? A person would have to be completely obsessed to create such a comprehensive library of scent!'

They continued to pick their way through the derelict surroundings.

There was a slender black lacquer oriental cabinet to one side. With some difficulty, Grace managed to open its doors. Inside was shelf upon shelf filled with easily several hundred much more elaborate perfume bottles. Each had a specific name on it: commissions. Underneath each bottle was a card and notation. Others were clearly works in progress, distinguished only by numbers. Grace reached up to the top shelf. There were stacks of ledgers, leather-bound journals filled, when she opened them, with clients' details, dates and long lists of ingredients, presumably formulations for scent.

'Look at this!' she called excitedly.

Monsieur Tissot came, leaning over her shoulder to read what was written.

Certain pages were devoted each to a single client. For example, in 1932 Mademoiselle Dallois commissioned a perfume. There was a list next to her name. Grace tried to make out the words. '"Pink roses", "clean hair" . . .' She pointed to the next line. 'What's that?'

'"Papa's pipe. And cake"!' he read. 'My God, this sounds like a child!'

Grace scanned the hundreds of bottles. 'Do you think it's here?'

'What?'

'Mademoiselle Dallois's perfume.'

She stood on her tiptoes, reaching further on the shelf to the bottles at the back.

Had someone managed to create a fragrance equivalent to cake and pink roses?

'Here, let me,' Monsieur Tissot offered.

Something fell to the floor – a faded, yellowed note card.

Grace bent to pick it up when suddenly there was a sharp crack on the counter behind them.

They both whirled round.

'*Dehors! Sortez!*' It was an elderly woman, tall and very thin, dressed in a rather old-fashioned black wool dress that hung from her gaunt frame, a walking stick poised like a weapon in the air between them. '*Sortez!*'

'I'm . . . I'm so, so sorry.' Grace backed away, stumbling into Monsieur Tissot, who steadied her.

A small terrier ran into the room, yapping wildly around its owner's feet.

'*Je ne crois pas!*' the old woman asserted, waving the walking stick menacingly, taking another step forward.

'*Doucement! Doucement!*' Monsieur Tissot intervened. '*C'est ma faute! Ne vous en faites pas!*'

'*Qu'est-ce que vous faites?*' the old woman turned on him, fiercely. '*Allez-vous en! C'est mon accueil! Balayeur de rue!*'

'She thinks we're thieves,' Monsieur Tissot translated, inserting himself between them.

'Maybe because we're acting like thieves. *Pardon*, madame,' Grace pleaded. '*Nous cherchez l'information à Madame d'Orsey!*'

'*Pardon? Que voulez-vous?*'

'*Nous . . . nous cherchons . . .*' Grace couldn't think fast enough. 'We need your help, madame,' she blurted out.

The old woman eyed her suspiciously. 'Why? What do you want?'

'You speak English!' Grace gasped in relief.

'*Pardon*,' Monsieur Tissot stepped forward. 'I am Edouard Tissot and this is Madame Munroe, from London. I'm a lawyer, madame, representing the estate of the late Eva d'Orsey.'

'What?' The old woman's expression changed.

'I'm a lawyer. For the estate of Eva d'Orsey,' he repeated.

Grace took a tentative step forward. 'Did you know her?'

But the woman seemed not to hear her. 'Eva . . . Eva d'Orsey is dead?'

'*Oui, madame*,' Monsieur Tissot said softly.

'Eva . . .'

The information seemed to strike her like a physical blow. For a moment it looked as though she might lose her balance. 'Get out of here.'

She said it so quietly that at first Grace thought she'd misheard her.

'I'm sorry?'

'Get out!' the old woman shouted, raising her stick again. 'Get out! You're not the first people to come breaking in here, trying to plunder and steal.'

'What people? What are you talking about?' Monsieur Tissot wanted to know.

'I've seen them, in their big black cars. Liars, all of you! Now leave!' She cracked the stick on the counter again, this time dangerously close. 'Get out of my damned sight!'

They turned and stumbled out of the building, into the bright afternoon of the street outside.

Heart pounding, Grace turned round to look at the shopfront again.

The dog continued to bark. The front door slammed behind them but not before she caught a glimpse of the old woman's face, her features angular and gaunt; large round black eyes, staring into nothing.

The torn awning fluttered and flapped, tossed by gusts of cold spring wind, the faded gold outline of the name of the shop just barely visible: *Recherchez-moi*.

Look for me.

New York, 1927

The woman in room 512 was Russian and known by the name of Madame Zed. She was what the French would describe as *jolie laide*; with an oval, rather long face and dark, heavy-lidded eyes. Her mouth was small, with a tendency to smile on only one side, when she smiled at all. But mostly she sat and drank, smoking long black cigarettes and talking in either Russian or French to a small coterie of devoted followers who came to visit her at the Hotel each day. Sis said many of them were Russian aristocracy, displaced by the Revolution. They travelled from country to country, hotel to hotel, searching for anyone who remembered who they used to be.

An inner gravity dominated Madame Zed. Her voice was low and resonant, pulling in those around her like an undertow. Her figure was very tall, rail straight and angular but she had a way of moving which was fluid and eminently watchable, and she knew how to dress simply so that these movements were emphasized. There was in her, for all her physical failings, an ambiguous, otherworldly sensuality. When her black eyes took you in, her capacity to stare unblinking, without any emotion, was both shocking and mesmerizing.

She'd come directly from Paris and shared a suite of rooms with her assistant, a young man named Valmont. Slightly built, he had brooding features and large, serious brown eyes. He stood in her shadow, listening, nodding in agreement, laughing in appreciation of her wit, managing her appointments, overseeing her preferences. The door was always left open between their rooms in case she wanted something.

One of his many duties was to ensure that the curtains of her room were drawn at all times and the rotary fan turned on high. Madame Zed was incredibly sensitive to smells. Almost everything offended her refined sensibility. This meant she was also incredibly picky about what sorts of cleaning supplies were used. Before Eva could start, Valmont would smell them, his upper lip curling in a pantomime performance of revulsion. 'For you, it is nothing. But for her, it's crucial. She has to spend all night with these foul odours!'

Eva had never heard of anything so ridiculous. 'Bleach is the only way to remove a soap ring completely from the bath. Wouldn't she rather know that the room was really clean? The smell of the bleach lets you know that it's clean.'

He looked at her as if she were something foul, stuck to the bottom of his shoe. 'When I need your advice, I'll ask. And don't speak to me with that tone again.'

Eva turned away. She hated being ordered about by a boy only a few years older than herself. '*Je peux dire ce que je veux*,' she grumbled, head down.

'What did you say?'

'I said, no one else in the hotel complains.'

'No one else in the hotel is a master perfumer! And I don't know who taught you to *parler français* but you have the accent of a peasant.'

He had nerve.

'I *am* French!' she retorted. 'My family is from the South.'

'Of what? New Jersey? You cannot come in here with that revolting-smelling liquid.'

'Then what do you suggest?'

Valmont folded his arms across his chest. 'What do you suggest, sir?'

Eva gritted her teeth. 'What do you suggest, sir?'

'I suggest that you solve the problem.'

'Trade with me,' Eva begged Sis that night in bed. 'I'll do anything for you if you just take over that one room for me.'

'Are you crazy?' Sis snorted. 'I have enough trouble on my floor as it is. I've got some batty old duchess who keeps wanting me to tuck her into bed each night. Must be ninety-three if she's a day. Calls me Nanny and asks me to sing her to sleep. Do I look like a nanny?'

'I'll take her. Please, Sis!'

'No. And don't ask again. Face it, you can't give that one away, honey. You're just going to have to make do until they check out. Everyone's got at least a few a year. And I'll tell you something for nothing, it could be worse.' She rolled over onto her side, her back to Eva. 'It could always be much worse.'

✦

Eva was so desperate she even searched out her uncle in the kitchens for advice. It was between services and most of the staff were eating an early supper; the kitchens were empty with the exception of one of the pastry chefs, who was crushing lemon halves, squeezing out the juice, for *tarte au citron*. The entire kitchen was filled with the bright, refreshing aroma of lemons.

Eva watched as he tossed the used halves into a bucket at his feet.

'Pardon me,' she asked after a while, pointing to the lemon rinds, 'are you using those?'

He looked up, surprised. 'I'm sorry?'

She looked around the kitchen. 'What do you think goes with lemon juice?'

'Lemon juice? Sugar,' he laughed. 'Lots of it!'

'No, not to eat.' She picked up a bunch of fresh mint from a crate of produce, held it to her nose. 'To smell.'

In the end, she concocted a solution of lemon juice, a few judicious drops of pressed rosemary oil and large quantities of baking soda mixed into a thick, abrasive paste. When she returned later that afternoon to scrub the bathroom, even she had to admit that the bracing, herbal aroma imparted an invigorating satisfaction to her efforts.

'Not bad.'

Eva turned around to see Valmont standing in the doorway, leaning against the frame with his hands in his pockets. 'Though a little lavender would have been a nice touch.'

She got up from her hands and knees. 'You're wrong.'

His eyes narrowed. 'I'm sorry, what did you say?'

She held her ground. 'Lavender wouldn't be an improvement.'

'You're arguing with me?' He laughed, incredulously. 'What qualifies you to correct me?'

She picked up her bucket. 'Nothing. I'm just right.'

'I'll have you know that Madame Zed is a world renowned perfumer and I am her only apprentice!'

Eva took a deep breath. 'Yes, but we all have noses.'

Suddenly they were interrupted by a deep, throaty laugh.

'Bravo!' Madame Zed walked forward from the half-light of the bedroom behind them, clapping her hands. 'This little maid has seen through you, Valmont! She knows your downfall – you always add another note, complicate things. She's right, you see. Simple is cleaner, more elegant.'

Valmont scowled at his feet. 'Yes, madame,' he muttered.

'There is nothing more difficult than simplicity,' Madame added, turning her back on them. 'And therefore, nothing more refined.'

Valmont ceased to harangue Eva after that and the next morning, Eva noticed that Madame had placed a small white rose in a water glass near the sink.

She took it as a sign of approval.

163

As time went on, Eva grew to respect and even admire the eccentricities of Madame Zed. For example, rather than adapt to her surroundings, she transformed them. Madame Zed's rooms were layered in personal history, as if their occupants had lived there for years rather than weeks; she created a mysterious and exotic atmosphere out of a few select additions. Embroidered silk shawls were thrown across armchairs, brocade and velvet cushions tossed in soft, inviting piles on the floor, like an oriental harem. White orchids with waxy petals gave off a hypnotic scent and collections of pastel, sugary French confections were dotted about the room on silver dishes. Steamer trunks, papered with tags from all over the world, were lined up against the far wall, bursting with long flowing gowns in rich colours and strangely asymmetrical tunics. The thick curtains let in only the dimmest fraction of light so that even during the day, her quarters had a smoky decadence about them, like a world suspended in a permanent night.

Eva had almost finished in Madame Zed's room one afternoon, when she noticed a circular black flacon with a gold stopper on her dressing table. It had a solid, pleasing roundness that made her want to pick it up, feel the weight of it in her hands.

Eva knew it was wrong to disturb a guest's belongings but the black bottle was too intriguing.

She lifted it up.

My Sin, the label read, in gold lettering.

Very carefully she opened it, holding the gold stopper to her nose. Up wafted the intense floral top notes of narcissus and freesia, warming to a dark, almost animal muskiness. It was intoxicatingly beautiful and, at the same time, dangerous, with jarring hidden depths.

It was a smell she recognized, aspired to; the hypnotic veil of sensuality that clung to the skin, the clothes, even permeated the sheets of every chorus girl, socialite and movie star that graced the lobby of the Hotel.

Closing her eyes, she inhaled again.

'I suppose that means you like it.' Standing in the doorway was Madame Zed, wrapped in a dark lace shawl, her face half hidden in shadow. She was smoking a cigarette, in a long mother-of-pearl holder.

Eva put the bottle down. 'I apologize, madam. I'm so sorry.'

'Careful! That's the only one I have. Otherwise, I shall have to buy it. Can you imagine, buying your own creation?' And she chuckled a little, crossing the room to put the stopper back on.

'I'm terribly sorry.'

Madame Zed gave only the ghost of a shrug. 'It's no matter. I myself cannot resist smelling other people's perfumes. In five minutes, I can dissect their entire palate. But this,' she pointed to the black bottle, 'this you like?'

Eva felt her face grow hot with embarrassment. 'I've never smelled anything like it. It's so . . . so,' she struggled to find the words, 'so full of different things.'

Madame Zed inhaled, looking at her closely through those heavily lidded black eyes. 'Complex,' she said at last. 'It's a complex perfume.'

'Yes. One minute it's pretty and floral and the next, it's full of spice and heat and . . . I don't know how to put it . . .'

'Sex.' Madame interjected. 'It was always about sex, right from the start.'

'Oh.' Eva's eyes widened.

'Why not? Everyone wants it.' Madame Zed settled into an armchair. 'I suppose that's why it's so popular. Of course, I had to make it stronger than I would've liked.'

'You made it?'

She nodded. 'That is my profession. I am a "nose", as they say. I've been mixing perfumes since I was your age. Though now, I've finished.'

'But why?'

'To be honest,' she flicked a bit of ash off her long cigarette, 'I cannot bear that everyone smells alike. It's vulgar. And that,' she nodded to the bottle of *My*

166

Sin on the dressing table, 'already all of Paris smells like it and most of New York. There is something wrong, deeply wrong, about an entire room of women who all smell the same.'

'But to be able to create something like this is like . . . like being an artist or a magician!'

Madame Zed laughed. 'You're very young.'

'I wouldn't mind smelling like that.'

'Oh now, really!' Madame protested. 'Think of a man, dancing with a beautiful young girl, in a crowded ballroom. He presses his nose into her soft hair and inhales. Then, two minutes later, he's dancing with another girl who smells exactly the same. What's the point? Perfume should tell a story – the story of who you are, who you might be, perhaps even of who you fear becoming . . . all of these things are possible. It's a very intimate element of a woman, just like her signature or the sound of her voice. And it conveys feelings and states of being that have no name, no language. Its very ambiguity makes it truer than words because, unlike words, it can't be manipulated or misunderstood. You see, it's not the perfume itself that isn't worthy – it's an original, one of the finest of the decade. But I'm tired of making off-the-peg dreams. I want a challenge worthy of my art.'

'The name, madam . . .' Eva could hardly say it out loud without blushing.

'*My Sin*.' Madame Zed said the words slowly, her black eyes unblinking. 'What about it?'

Eva hesitated. 'It's just . . . well . . . what does it mean? What sin?'

Madame was silent for a moment, looking past Eva, or rather through her, as if she were transparent. Finally she spoke. 'Do you know what sin means?'

'To do something wrong?'

Madame shook her head. 'That's one meaning. But there's another, from the Greek, *hamartia*, which translates, "to miss the mark". That's the meaning I prefer.'

'To miss the mark,' Eva repeated, committing it to memory.

'Yes,' Madame continued. 'We try and fail, like archers who aim for the target but fall short of the mark.' Eva watched as she removed the lace shawl. 'When you are older and have swum out into the stream of life, you'll see – there are no "good" people, little girl. We're all trying and failing, trying too hard and failing too often. Remember that. We shouldn't judge too harshly, in the end, the sins of others.'

'No, madam. Of course not.'

Eva wasn't sure she'd answered her question.

But the older woman sank down into the armchair, stretching her legs out on the ottoman. She took another drag of her cigarette. Her voice softened to almost a whisper. 'Sometimes I think the only things we have in common with one another are our shortcomings.'

Eva stood enthralled.

Exhaling a long stream of smoke, Madame closed her eyes and her head lolled to one side.

Eva waited for her to continue.

Madame's hand relaxed.

The cigarette fell to the floor.

Eva rushed to put it out before it burned a hole in the carpet.

Then Madame began to snore, so loudly that Valmont came in.

'Oh. It's you,' he said, jamming his hands sullenly into his pockets. 'I should've known.'

Eva planted her hands on her hips. 'What's that supposed to mean?'

He ignored her question. 'Jesus! She's been to Chinatown again. Help me get her onto the bed,' he ordered, lifting Madame up under her arms.

Begrudgingly, Eva grabbed her legs. 'Goodness!' she gasped. 'She weighs a lot for someone so skinny!'

Together they hauled her onto the bed. Madame didn't even so much as miss a beat in her snoring and rolled over heavily onto her side.

'I've never heard anyone so loud.'

'It is a bit much,' Valmont admitted. 'It goes right through the door at night. I sleep with about four pillows on my head. She'll be passed out for the rest of the day now.'

'She doesn't smell drunk.'

He rolled his eyes. 'Don't you know anything? Opium,' he explained. 'She's been smoking opium.'

'Oh.' Eva stared in awe at the sleeping woman. An opium den. How dreadful, low and exciting.

'We're going to Morocco soon and it will only get worse.'

'Morocco? What are you going to do there?'

'We're buying ingredients. They have, among other things, one of the finest jasmine harvests in all the world. Normally we buy them through a third party but I'm sure if we go there ourselves we'll discover not only purer absolutes for a better price, but I have a feeling we'll also stumble across some rare indigenous ingredients we haven't encountered yet in Europe. And that's what we're looking for – a new palette, something truly original.'

Eva smiled to herself, gathering her duster from the dressing table.

'Why are you sneering at me?' he demanded.

'I'm not sneering.'

'Yes, you are.'

'You always talk like you're in charge,' she pointed out.

'Well, I do have influence. She values my opinion.

She's one of the world's greatest perfumers and I am, after all, her only apprentice.'

'So you keep saying – over and over again. Besides, I thought you were her secretary.'

'I'm more than that. You see,' he followed her into the bathroom, leaned against the doorway, 'you can't go to school to learn the art of the perfumer. You have to possess a natural, God-given talent and then the secrets of the profession must be passed on by a master. I have been an apprentice to Madame since I was nine.'

'Nine? How old are you now?'

'Eighteen.'

She snorted. 'Are you a slow learner?'

'It's an art!' He glared at her. 'It takes years just to memorize the various ingredients. It isn't just about mixing notes together but about developing a palette, a comprehension of scent and how it works. Do you have any idea of how difficult it is to create a fragrance that develops properly on the human skin and lasts?'

Eva folded her arms defensively across her chest. 'So how did Madame know you had talent in the first place?'

'I suppose she could just tell.' This girl really asked the most presumptuous questions. 'Actually, even when I was small I could dissect smells, take them apart and decipher their precise ingredients.

There is a story that Madame discovered me one day standing in the neighbour's garden, standing over a rosemary bush. Apparently I was so lost in concentration, I couldn't hear my name being called. It was by far the nicest-smelling thing in the whole village,' he recalled.

'And your parents just gave you to her?'

'No! Of course not!' he snapped.

'I'm only asking!' she snapped back. 'Did they pay her?'

'They don't have that kind of money. My parents came from Prussia. They'd escaped, during the Revolution, with nothing but what they could carry. My father was a cantor.'

'A what?'

'A cantor,' he repeated, his cheeks colouring a little. 'It's a singer of religious songs in the Jewish temple.'

'Oh.' She'd never actually spoken to anyone Jewish.

'It's a sacred profession – a vocation really – that's been passed down through generations,' he continued. 'I suppose they thought I might follow my father one day. But my parents couldn't afford to keep all of us – my brothers and sisters are younger than me. And cantors don't make much money. For a while I lived with some neighbours down the street.

I suppose they were nice enough. Tailors. I used to press the garments, deliver orders and clean the work room to earn my keep.'

'How old were you?'

'I'm not sure . . . six or seven. And then Madame came along, looking for an assistant – someone she could train. Her offer was a rare opportunity.'

'Still, it's quite young.' Eva's voice softened. 'Did you ever seen them again – your parents?'

He shook his head.

'You must miss them.'

'Oh, I don't know. I never really think about it.'

Eva wasn't fooled. 'My mother died when I was born, back in Lille,' she said. 'My aunt and uncle brought me here. But they didn't really want me. It's funny, isn't it? How you can miss someone you've never known.'

'I suppose.'

Eva adjusted the tin bucket and mop on the side of her cart. 'I sometimes wonder what it would've been like if my mother had lived. If she would've cared for me at all.'

Her words touched him.

He also wondered if his parents ever thought of him; if they'd found it easy to let him go. Even now, there was no contact between them. He'd never known if it was because they'd preferred it that way or because they'd been too ashamed to try. He preferred to believe the latter.

'I guess it's better not really knowing for certain,' she added, with a wry smile. 'This way I get to imagine what I want. And we must take our comfort where we can, don't you think?'

He nodded.

He was reminded of the terror of leaving his parents, his village, even his brothers and sisters whose very existence guaranteed his expulsion from the family. And of the strange, dark figure of Madame Zed, who had taken his small hand firmly in her own and led him away to the station.

'We have something in common,' she informed him. They were sitting alone together in the cold, second-class compartment as the train pulled away.

He had tried not to speak; he was afraid of crying if he opened his mouth. But he managed to ask, 'What's that?'

'We are both exiles,' she said, fixing him with her steady black eyes.

And then, as the train wove through the countryside, she told him the story of how her family were arrested and executed one bright September afternoon at their estate outside St Petersburg, during the Red Terror. And how her old nurse, a devout woman with little care for her own life, had smuggled her out hidden in a hay wagon, wearing a kitchen maid's clothing and clutching a knife hidden under her coat.

By the time she'd related the details of her journey from St Petersburg to Odessa, penniless and starving, of the unexpected kindness of the naval officers who gave her sanctuary on a British ship to Constantinople, and of her subsequent journey from Malta to Marseille, they were halfway to Paris. The lamps glowed softly in the compartment. It was warmer now; tea and cakes were served from a trolley and Madame had covered him with her own thick woollen travel blanket.

She looked out of the window, at the sun setting behind them, her long, sharp features outlined in shadow against the glass. 'You will see. We will make our fortune, you and I, and no one, ever again, will be able to tell us where or how to live. Or die.'

Neither of them had ever spoken about their pasts again.

Now, Valmont watched as Eva gathered her cleaning supplies together.

She was an odd girl.

She reminded him of the fresh lemons she'd used for the cleaner but with less rosemary, more bergamot: abrasive, sharp edged but with unexpected softness too.

And without saying anything, he held the door open for her as she pushed her cart out into the hallway.

Paris, Spring, 1955

'Well,' Monsieur Tissot was trying to be philosophical, 'that didn't go perhaps as well as we might have liked.'

They had crossed the street to the embankment, near a little gravel playground. Small children were running between the trees, playing with a football. And they were recovering from what could only be classified as pure folly on his part.

'Who was that woman?' Grace was certain her heart would never slow back to normal. 'She appeared out of nowhere!'

'She must live above the shop. The owner perhaps? She certainly spoke as if she owned it.'

'She knew Eva d'Orsey, that much is certain. Did you understand what else she was talking about? That business about men in a black car, breaking in?'

'No. To be honest, she seems quite mad. Probably suffering from senility.'

'Do you think?' The old woman didn't strike her as mad; she seemed more frightened than anything. And there was the way she'd reacted to the news of Eva d'Orsey's death. It was more than just shock . . . what was it? Anger? Regret?

They continued to walk across the park, without any real purpose or destination, more to steady their nerves than anything else.

Monsieur Tissot turned the collar up on his suit jacket, pulling it tight against the wind. He was a grown man, a respected professional and yet he'd just spent the afternoon being chased out of a derelict building by a pensioner. This was hardly his finest hour. But he felt relaxed, even exhilarated. 'I suppose we aren't much good at playing detective.'

'It was your idea,' she reminded him. 'Is that a hobby of yours – breaking and entering?'

'Men are forced to resort to ridiculous displays of bravado in front of women.'

She stopped. 'So, it's my fault?'

She was standing with her arms crossed. Her hair had come loose from her chignon and the wind tossed it, so that it danced around her face. She was looking at him hard with those strange clear eyes.

'Without question.'

'Just for being female?'

There was a kind of magnificence to the way, even harried and disheveled, she refused to let him have the last word. Slipping his hands in his pockets, he gave a little shrug. 'You're not just a female, Madame Munroe. A man might do a great deal more to impress you.'

That seemed to startle her.

Feeling her cheeks suddenly flushing, Grace quickly turned away, carried on walking. 'It was incredible though, wasn't it?' she said, changing the subject. 'I cannot get over how many different kinds of perfumes there were. Do you think they were all created by a single person? Or that they're some sort of collection?'

'It's impossible to say. Besides, I thought you hated perfume.'

'I didn't say I hated it. I'm just not fond of smelling like a florist's stall.'

'That's right,' he agreed with a smile. 'No one wants to be too loud, do they?'

She turned on him. 'You know, Monsieur Tissot, I do believe you're making fun of me.'

'Pardon me, madame.' He gave a little mock bow. 'But the English strike me as amusing. Things that smell loud, flavours that taste too much . . .'

'Yes, well, I'm not simply representative of my country. I can assure you my . . . my eccentricities are entirely my own!'

178

'It wasn't my intention to offend,' he said, more serious now.

She gave a little shake of her head, suddenly embarrassed. 'I'm what is known as a queer duck back home.'

'Really?' He gave her a look. 'A duck?'

'A bit of an oddball,' she tried to explain. 'Never mind. It's all right. I'm used to it.'

But he stopped anyway. 'In what way an oddball?'

'Oh, I don't know.' She looked out over the Seine, at the tourist boats floating across the choppy water. Instinctively, she reached again for the lighter in her pocket, slipping it round and round between her fingers. 'I suppose I've always been a bit peculiar. I'm picky about things I'm not supposed to care about and lazy about the things that matter.'

'And what are the things that matter?'

Grace was unused to confiding in men, especially one as provoking as Monsieur Tissot. But for once he was quiet, looking at her with genuine interest. 'Well,' she thought a moment, 'for example, I don't care what I'm wearing or what I'm going to serve guests for supper but I become obsessed with working out the probability of the train being on time.'

'And are your predictions accurate?'

'More often than not.'

'And why do these matters concern you?'

'I'm not sure,' she admitted. 'I like figuring things out. Not dull things, like where to seat so-and-so at a dinner party but larger, more abstract things. Only to me, they don't seem abstract. They seem very practical and relevant.'

'In what way?'

'Oh, I don't know.' It wasn't a subject she'd ever discussed with anyone before. 'Well, for example, I often wonder about the bombs in the war. Why does a bomb fall out of the sky and land right here, on this house, and on no other? My mother died during the Blitz, so I suppose I have a morbid curiosity. But you see, if you knew the weight and density of the bomb, how fast the plane was flying, its elevation, the direction and strength of the wind – it wouldn't be a mystery; you could figure it out. Nothing would be random or accidental anymore.'

'And you don't believe in chance, do you?' he reminded her.

'No, no I don't.'

'But then tell me, where exactly does that leave God in your equation?'

'Where God has always been; somewhere between the weight of the bomb and the house.'

He laughed. 'You're not a duck, you're an owl – an intellectual!'

'Oh, I don't know about that,' she smiled shyly. And then, almost without thinking, she asked, 'Do you believe in God?'

It had been drilled into her head since childhood that politics and religion were not suitable topics for polite conversation. But Grace found herself hungry to discuss real things; subjects that weighed on her in private but that she couldn't speak about with Roger, Mallory or indeed, anyone else in her set.

He looked across at her, surprised. 'Yes,' he said after a moment. 'I believe in a God I don't understand and don't necessarily agree with. The force between the plane and the bomb,' he added.

They carried on walking.

After a while, Monsieur Tissot spoke. 'I like that shop.'

'Yes. I do too.'

'I like the name. Did you see it?'

'*Recherchez-moi?*'

Yes, but under that. *L'apothicaire des Sens.*'

'The apothecary of . . .'

'The senses.'

'I see. Yes, it's evocative, isn't it?'

'You English have a saying. "Come to your senses."'

'Yes.'

'What do you think it means?'

'It means to be reasonable, sensible.' She looked across at him. 'Doesn't it?'

'Maybe.' His eyes caught the afternoon light; flickering amber, flecked with green.

'What else could it mean?'

'Perhaps it's an invitation. Maybe we need to literally come to our senses, to return to our sense of taste, touch, sight, smell, hearing and find sustenance in them, inspiration. Life is, after all, a sensual experience. Our senses have the power to truly transport us but also to ground us. Make us human.'

She stared at him in amazement. 'I'm afraid, Monsieur Tissot, that you're something of a philosopher – and a sensualist.'

Looking down, he kicked the gravel with his feet. 'I can assure you, nothing could be further from the truth.'

'Well, you're a mass of contradictions. One minute you're an analytical lawyer, the next you're climbing through windows and advocating the complete overthrow of reason.'

'Reason is entirely overrated, unless, of course I'm the one doing the reasoning. And may I remind you, we went in through the door.' He indicated a bench behind them. 'Shall we?'

They sat down, side by side, facing outward onto a narrow strip of parkland.

'It seems we've reached a dead end in our enquiries, Monsieur Tissot,' Grace said, resting her elbows on her knees.

'Perhaps. But there's still the appointment at Lancelot et Delp. I'll be very interested to find out more about those stocks.'

'Yes, but what shall we do now?'

He should have pointed out to her that there was nothing else to do; that there were papers waiting to be signed in the office. But this English girl was interesting; he found himself waiting for her to speak again, to hear the workings of her mind. His own wit was put to the test with her, like a dog being run off in a park. And it felt good, to be stretched.

'I think we should wait,' he decided.

'For what?'

'I don't know.' Leaning back, he stretched out his long legs; taking in the spring clouds racing across the sky and the sweet sharpness of the late afternoon air. 'But if you don't know what to do, then it's best to do nothing.'

'Is that your professional advice?'

Turning his face towards the sun, he closed his eyes. 'Absolutely.'

Easing back in her seat, Grace watched the children in the playground opposite, coats off, faces flushed, laughing hysterically with pleasure. They were so vividly alive, completely immersed in the game. She tried to recall a time when she'd been that way and realized she couldn't remember when that had been. She'd lost the knack of forgetting herself. Instead she seemed to look down on herself throughout the day, scrutinizing, judging; finding herself wanting.

'Madame Munroe . . .'

Grace glanced across at Monsieur Tissot; at his profile with the aquiline nose and full lips, at the dark fringe of his lashes. 'Yes?'

Without opening his eyes, he said. 'You do know what matters.'

'Do I?'

'One cannot underestimate the importance of a train being on time. Or leave to chance the space between the plane and the bomb.'

Grace smiled to herself. Closing her eyes, she turned her face to the sun too. 'Yes, that's what I thought.'

New York, 1927

New York was engulfed in a heatwave. By the middle of July, the combination of blazing sun and torpid humidity had risen to such levels it became impossible to walk even a few blocks without dripping with sweat. All around the Hotel, guests holed up in darkened rooms, ordering ice packs for their headaches, extra fans; lying naked on top of their beds, too limp even to touch one another, or submerged in long cool baths drinking pitchers of iced tea and sugary lemonade, laced with illegal gin.

This left Eva and the rest of the housekeeping staff with the unenviable task of trying to service the rooms while the guests were still in them.

Mrs Ronald made no concession for the hot weather; the girls were expected to wear their full uniforms, including their thick black stockings. 'We have standards, girls!' she reminded them daily. 'Neatness begins with your appearance.'

It might not have been so bad if they were able to clean the rooms in the early morning, but as no one in the hotel roused themselves until mid-afternoon, the girls found themselves wrestling with dirty linens and scrubbing floors at the hottest hours of the day.

'If you feel you're going to faint, then excuse yourself and do so in the privacy of the back hallway,' Mrs Ronald reminded them. 'It's extremely awkward to have to deal with an unconscious girl. And be aware of your eyes – keep them low. Guests should never be forced to look at you directly, do you understand? You're invisible, a pair of unseen hands.'

Unfortunately, this ideal was harder to live up to in real life.

Madame Zed was lounging one afternoon in one of her loose diaphanous creations, drinking cold black tea and smoking copiously. She appeared to be recovering from the rigorous exertions of the night before, and sat, very still, curled into the lap of an armchair, eyes closed, as if she could meditate the temperatures down by sheer force of will.

Eva went about changing the bed sheets as unobtrusively as she could, her uniform clinging to her damp underarms, her hair plastered with sweat to her forehead under her starched cap. She felt drowsy with lethargy, as if she were moving through water, fighting to finish the smallest task.

Finally, Madame opened her eyes. 'What is your name?'

'Eva, madam.'

'Eva, will you please fetch Valmont for me? I cannot bring myself to move. I'm simply paralysed.'

'Yes, madam.'

Eva trudged across to the interconnecting door, which was closed. She tried to open it. 'It's locked, madam.'

'Then open it!' Madame sighed, rolling her eyes to the gods in an exaggerated gesture of utter despair. 'My head is splitting in two! I need him.'

Eva took out her pass key and unlocked the door. Then she knocked several times. There was no answer, so finally she gently pushed it open.

The room had only one window and, with the curtains drawn, was surprisingly dark. As her eyes adjusted to the lack of light, Eva could just make out the outline of Valmont, curled on his side on the bed. He was sleeping naked, with just his top sheet wound around his waist. His torso was pale, thin.

Eva took a few tentative steps forward. In the hazy blackness, the air pressed in around her, sultry with sweat and sleep. Everything seemed unreal, suspended in a dream-like state.

Carefully, she leaned over him. 'Pssstt! Sir! Wake up!'

He shifted, rolling over onto his back.

She tried again.

Bending closer, she gave his shoulder a shake. 'Sir!'

His eyes opened, blinking to focus.

'I'm sorry, it's only Madame wants you,' she explained in a whisper. 'She says . . .'

Suddenly he grabbed her wrist. 'Hush!' And, still in a fog of sleep, he pulled her close.

Eva pitched forward, into his arms.

Valmont inhaled.

At first her natural scent seemed straightforward, simple; the slightly acrid, almost creamy aroma of a child's damp skin. But underneath that, a rich, musky element seeped through, unfolding slowly; widening and expanding to a profound, primitive animalistic essence. The sheer range and complexity of her odour was astonishing. The effect, intensely arousing. It was the most compelling, deeply sensual thing Valmont had ever encountered.

Eva pushed him away, horrified. 'What are you doing?'

'You smell . . .' he murmured.

'Yes, thank you!' She scrambled to her feet. 'I hardly need you to tell me that!' she hissed. 'Madame wants to see you . . .'

'No, you don't understand.' He reached for her

again; short sharp intakes now, savouring the notes, rolling them round on his olfactory palette. 'It's unique. Completely unique.'

'Get off!' Eva swatted him.

Suddenly something shifted in the bed; a body. The person next to him stretched out and rolled over onto their stomach.

It was another man.

Eva recoiled. Stumbling backward, she blundered towards the interconnecting door.

'Well?' Madame opened her eyes. 'You appear to be alone,' she observed flatly.

Reeling, Eva focused at the floor. 'He is asleep, madam.'

'Well then, wake him!' Madame gasped in exasperation, running her hand wearily across her eyes. 'I need him!'

This was dreadful, truly dreadful.

Eva tried to stall her. 'He's not dressed, madam. I can help you. Would you like me to fetch you something from the drug store?'

With another heavy sigh, Madame forced herself up from her chair and marched into Valmont's room. Eva hovered in the doorway, watching in shameful fascination.

Madame stopped; she stood in the darkness a moment. Then she turned back on her heel.

And with more moans and sighs, she dug through one of her handbags until she pulled out some loose coins. She shoved them into Eva's hand. 'I need aspirin. And some Woolcott's, please. I have the most blinding headache known to mankind.'

Eva stared at her. Had Madame seen what she'd seen? Did she have any comprehension of what a mortal sin it was?

It was as if her thoughts could be heard aloud.

Madame turned to her. 'You know,' she began, 'there are many stages in a man's life. Young men especially are very easily excitable. They need more variety, more experiences than girls. Do you understand?'

'Yes, madam,' she lied.

'These little dalliances are merely preludes to the real interludes. They fade over time. Of course,' she added, returning back to her chair, 'I do worry about Andre. Gossip is the plague of the idle and insecure. I'm relying upon your discretion.'

'Yes, madam. Of course.'

'Then we shall speak no more about it. And do close that door.' She pressed her eyes closed again. 'I suppose we never should have opened it in the first place.'

Andre Valmont lay on his back, fully awake now, staring into the darkness. Beside him the boy he'd met in the club in Harlem snored softly.

He closed his eyes.

He could see her smell; it glowed against the backs of his eyelids, pure shimmering gold to deep undulating amber. And he could taste each note; savour the melting progression on his tongue, the shocking, perfect combination of contrasts, underpinned by a creamy, intensely carnal core of raw sexuality. He wanted to bury himself deep in her flesh; to consume each molecule of her, one breath at a time.

And that wasn't the way he normally felt about girls.

He pulled the sheet back. He was stiff; erect to an almost painful degree. Spitting into the palm of his hand, he closed his eyes again.

He imagined peeling off her uniform, each layer of clothing saturated more densely with her warm sweat, until there was nothing between them but skin; emanating, covering them both with the shimmering dark dew of her incredible odour . . . he trembled, ecstasy surging, shuddering through him.

Here at last was a story he understood. A song of youth; of burgeoning, ripe sexuality; of frustration and longing . . . of a nymph and a femme fatal, both trapped in the body of an graceless young girl . . .

a mythic parable that could only really be captured in perfume.

And above all, her natural odour radiated. As though it were issuing from the top of a high peak. In its velvet glow, the dim landscape of his creative gifts finally came into focus.

Valmont got up, washed himself; lit a cigarette. Then he woke up the boy from Harlem and sent him home.

He had work to do.

Paris, Spring, 1955

Two days later, Grace found herself standing in the foyer of the offices of Lancelot et Delp, located in a strikingly modern concrete building near Les Halles. They had a sparse, marble lobby with floor-to-ceiling windows, manned by a desk of young women wearing telephone operator headphones. Monsieur Tissot confirmed their appointment and soon afterwards a young man bolted from one of the ten lifts at the centre of the lobby to greet them.

He was wearing a modern narrow-cut suit with a thin, bright yellow tie and thick-framed black glasses. His hair, a mass of dark curls, stuck straight up in the air. As he bounded over to them, hand already outstretched, it struck Grace that he reminded her of a human exclamation mark, with the same emphatic energy.

'Good afternoon! Welcome! I'm Albert Dubois.' He pumped both their hands hard. 'Pleasure to meet you! Would you like coffee? Tea? Have you been here before?' All the while he was speaking, he ushered them to the lifts, heedless of any answers.

'How lovely that you speak English,' Grace commented, as they stepped inside and the doors closed.

'Oh, I also speak German, Spanish, Portuguese and a bit of Japanese. The one that always trips me up is American!' he laughed, pushing his glasses further back on his nose.

'Japanese!' Monsieur Tissot looked at him as if he were mad. 'Whatever for?'

'I'm telling you, they're picking themselves up – they're going to be a force to be reckoned with soon.'

'I seriously doubt it,' Monsieur Tissot disagreed.

The lift opened again and they stepped out, pushing through a pair of glass double doors.

The din hit Grace first; the sound of a hundred voices all speaking at once. Row after row of desks stretched to the end of the huge office, each desk with at least two phones; young men in shirtsleeves were shouting across to one another and there was a large board mounted on the far wall, where more young men ran from one end to another, making constant adjustments to the numbers.

'Sorry about this,' Monsieur Dubois filtered them off to a private side office and offered them a seat. 'New York has just opened so things are heating up.

So.' He sat down across from them at his desk and took out a file. 'You're here about the d'Orsey stocks, is that right? Oh, so sorry for your loss,' he added, looking at Grace.

'Thank you,' she murmured, trying not to catch Monsieur Tissot's eye.

'Well, I have to say,' he smiled as he opened the file, 'one of my all-time favourite clients, Eva d'Orsey. What a nose she had for this game!'

'What do you mean?' Monsieur Tissot sat forward, interested.

Monsieur Dubois sifted through the papers in front of him. 'She came to me about five or six years ago with a handful of Hiver stocks. A gift, she said. She knew nothing about the stock market and wanted someone to advise her. Fine. I made a few conservative recommendations – commodities, gold, bonds, things like that. But before I knew it, she was calling me with suggestions. Did I know that Citroën was building a new suspension braking device? Was I aware that Goodyear were expanding in Mexico? What did I think of the new American rock 'n' roll dance craze?'

'Really?' Monsieur Tissot laughed incredulously.

'She was quite extraordinary. She understood the numbers, did research.' He passed Grace a report from the top of the file. 'She took that handful of cosmetics stocks and finessed it into a valuable long-term investment portfolio.'

Grace looked down the long list of company names – United States Steel, EMI, Standard Oil, Firestone, Citroën, Le Monde, Amoco . . . somewhere near the bottom she noticed Hiver. And next to each entry, there was a monetary value in francs. Her mind was swimming; drowning in information. 'I'm sorry, but what does this all mean, Monsieur Dubois?'

He nodded to the file. 'This portfolio was Madame d'Orsey's sole means of income. And she was very savvy – with every excess profit, she bought more stocks. What this means,' he explained with a gleam in his eye, 'is that you're quite a wealthy woman, Mrs Munroe.'

<hr>

Grace turned to Monsieur Tissot as they left the offices of Lancelot et Delp. 'This is mad! Some sort of bizarre mistake.' She felt giddy, slightly light-headed from the news. 'I'll wake up any minute now – the real Grace Munroe will suddenly appear, probably from Australia or something, and I'll be sent packing back to London.'

'You *are* the real Grace Munroe. You're just in shock.' He offered her his arm as they crossed to where the car was parked on the other side of the street. 'You need to eat something.'

She shook her head, smiling. 'You know, food isn't the answer to everything.'

'Spoken like a true Englishwoman.' He opened up the car door. 'I know the perfect place.'

'You cannot keep taking me out to eat,' she protested. 'It's too . . . too extravagant.'

'Calm yourself: I wasn't suggesting Maxim's,' he said. 'But this is a cause for celebration. And, as I'm the only person you know in Paris, I'm afraid you're stuck with me.'

They drove back into the city and he pulled up in front of Fouquet, on the Champs-Élysées.

Grace looked up at the sky as they climbed out of the car. The clouds had grown dark and heavy; the temperature was dropping. 'Do you mind if we sit outside?'

'Not at all,'

They dined under the distinctive red awning and before she could stop him, Monsieur Tissot ordered them both oysters and champagne.

'Have you ever had oysters before?' he asked as the waiter set a platter down in front of them.

She bit her lower lip. 'No.' They were a great deal wetter and more raw than she'd imagined. This went far beyond the confines of her normal luncheon of tea and toast.

'Don't be frightened. They're not nearly as difficult as they seem,'

'I'm not frightened.'

'You're terrified.' He poured the champagne. 'And your lip is curling.'

'They look like something one would avoid stepping on in the street.'

'Don't be bourgeois.'

'Bourgeois!' Her eyes narrowed. 'Well, then, explain this to me – how is one meant to eat them without looking foolish?'

'Simple.' He demonstrated, taking one. 'You just let it slide down.'

She watched in horror. 'You don't chew?'

'No. I like a squirt of lemon, that's all.' Taking a slice, he squeezed the fresh juice onto them.

'But what if I choke?'

'Then I'll move to another table. Go on,' he dared. 'Tilt your head back and relax your throat!'

Taking off her gloves, Grace picked one up warily. 'You're doing this on purpose, aren't you? Playing "Torment the English Girl".'

'Trust me, if I wanted to torment you, there are cheaper ways.'

'Fine.' Closing her eyes, she braced herself; swallowed. 'Oh my goodness!' she gasped, wide-eyed.

'Now,' he handed her a glass, 'have a sip of champagne – quickly.'

The crisp, icy bubbles exploded against the back of her palate. 'Oh, yes,' she laughed, surprised. 'That is good!'

'Bravo! To the English Heiress!' he toasted.

'To the Impostor!' she toasted back. 'How many of these am I allowed to eat?'

'As many as you like. As long as you don't eat these six, which are mine and completely off-limits.'

'Spoilsport.'

He sat back and lit a cigarette, watching as she squeezed the lemon carefully on each one and devoured them.

'Do you feel better now?' he asked after a while.

'Yes, thank you, I do.'

He smiled, exhaled.

'Actually,' she went on, 'I feel like a sheet of paper that someone's torn into tiny pieces and thrown to the wind. But the wind in Paris is rather nice.' Grace downed another oyster. It was sinful, how delicious they were. 'See, you can't call me bourgeois now.'

'I could,' he corrected her, taking a drink, 'but it would be inaccurate.'

'*Mon Dieu!* Have you always been so pedantic?'

'Always. And please don't speak French – it's nails across a chalkboard.'

'I suppose splitting hairs is quite useful in your profession.' She sat back, opened her handbag and took out a pack of Chesterfields. Leaning across the table, he gave her a light. As she inhaled, the thick acrid smoke mixed with the salty brine of the oysters and the cool, moist air – an unexpected, earthy combination. She took another sip of champagne. 'So, is the law your life, Monsieur Tissot?'

'Not entirely.'

'Do you spend much time with your family?'

He shook his head. 'I'm a bachelor.'

'Oh!' The shock in her voice was unmistakable. For some reason she'd naturally assumed he was married.

He caught this, and, looking down, smiled. 'Not everyone is suited to a domestic life,' he pointed out.

'No, of course not,' she agreed quickly. 'I've often wondered if I'm not one of them.'

'Also, I've never had the luck of finding anyone who could tolerate my glittering personality.'

She laughed. 'They must be dazzled by the light. You should provide sunglasses.'

'Actually,' he flicked a bit of ash into the ashtray. 'I like to repair things in my spare time.'

'Really?' She was relieved the subject had changed. 'Like what?'

'Bicycles, toys, clocks. I managed to fix a revolver once but nearly blew my ear off in the process.' He made a whistling noise. 'It went right past. Gave me the shock of my life. I have a garage behind my building. There's a work table, tools, all manner of spare parts hanging from the ceiling.' Looking down, he smiled to himself. 'I'm very popular with the children on my street. Also, I play the guitar.'

'Are you any good?'

He picked up another oyster. 'I'm an exceptional artist. Trapped in the body of man with no musical ability.' He tilted his head back and swallowed. 'But I don't let that stop me.'

'I don't envy your neighbours.' She smiled

'Neither do I. And you, do you have children, madame?'

Grace shook her head. 'No. No I don't.'

A barely perceptible shadow passed across her eyes. Taking another drag, she looked away, into the busy avenue crowded with traffic and passersby. He could sense, by her silence, this wasn't a topic she wanted to continue.

'The description of your workshop reminds me of my father,' she said, after a minute or two. 'He loved making things.'

'Making requires more vision. I'm a fixer. For me the challenge comes in spotting the flaw and eliminating it.' He refilled their glasses. 'Is your father still alive?'

'No, he died of a heart attack when I was very young.'

'I'm sorry.'

There was a low growl of thunder, a flash of lightning and the skies erupted in a sudden downpour, emptying the streets of people; sending them scattering. Beyond the shelter of the awning, pedestrians rushed past, heads bowed, ducking into doorways and crowding onto the front steps of buildings for refuge. Most of the café customers moved to tables inside.

They alone remained.

Grace leaned forward, resting her chin in her elbow, watching the rain pour from the red awning in a sheer, translucent veil. On the other side, Paris became a distant, muted place. 'It's kind of you to bring me here. I'm very grateful for your consideration.'

It wasn't often that he was accused of being thoughtful.

'My pleasure, madame. Your business is nearly at a conclusion. And you've had the best possible results,' he reminded her gently.

'Yes, I suppose you're right,' she agreed.

'When you've signed all the papers, we can begin marketing the apartment. Then you're free to return to England.'

'Yes.'

Closing her eyes, Grace breathed in. The air was a delicate cocktail of things foreign and familiar; both damply green and faintly musty; as sea-soaked as the oysters, as crisply refreshing as the champagne. She took another drag. 'Do you mind very much if we just sit here for a while?'

'Not at all.'

'I don't know why,' she confessed, 'but I've always loved the smell of rain.'

'*Bonjour, madame.*'

'*Bonjour,*' Grace nodded to the doorman standing at attention as she passed into the lobby.

She stopped by the concierge's desk. 'Excuse me, are there any messages for Madame Munroe?'

'Ah, let me see,' the concierge riffled through the papers in front of him. 'There it is!' He held up a telegram triumphantly and then presented it to her with a little bow. 'For you, madame.'

Grace could feel her mouth go dry with nerves. At last. 'Thank you.'

On her way to the lift, she eagerly tore open the envelope: *DARLING STOP WHAT NEWS STOP MALLORY.*

Her heart sank.

Mallory had the decency to contact her before her own husband did.

It had been at least a week now since she'd informed him, with perfunctory politeness, of her planned trip to Paris. A week without so much as a letter or a phone call.

Wadding the telegram up, Grace went to shove it into her coat pocket but there was something already in there. She took it out. It was the card she'd found on the floor of the shop when she and Monsieur Tissot were startled by the old woman. She must've put it in her pocket by accident, without thinking.

Grace examined it for the first time.

It was written in stylized, energetic script and the card itself was watermarked and yellowed with age. She turned it over; it was covered on both sides by dense writing. *Ma chérie, Quelle idée merveilleuse pour un parfum!* the correspondence began, but beyond that her French failed and she needed help.

She had a French dictionary in her room.

The lift doors opened and she stepped on.

At least an exercise in translation might take her mind off the echoing silence from across the Channel.

New York, 1927

'Andre, hand me that book, will you please? We must go to a bookshop today or we shall be forced to read what's in the ship's library, which will be appalling.'

Valmont passed Madame Zed a novel from her bedside table. They were in the midst of packing – the ship for Lisbon left in the morning – and they had enlisted Eva's help; she hauled a pile of garments out of the closet and laid them on the bed, ready to fold in layers of tissue paper.

But instead, Madame stared at her, appalled. 'What are you doing?'

'Packing, ma'am.'

'No, no, no, no, no! Those clothes are old. They reek of last year's thoughts and aspirations. Absolutely not! Stop immediately!'

Eva looked to Valmont, who rolled his eyes, stepping in to intervene. 'So what exactly do you want us to do with them?'

'I don't care what you do with them! We are creatures of fashion and fashion is about change. About the new and exciting. We cannot be married to the past like this. No.' She turned her back on the pile. 'Just looking at them makes me weak with indifference.'

'Fine,' Valmont sighed, 'but you will need something to wear. Or will we simply be spending all our time in the cabin?'

Madame draped herself across the arm of the sofa, picking at a tray of French confections. 'Well, that's an excellent point. As it happens I've met the cleverest little man in Chinatown who has the most beguiling selection of Chinese silk you can imagine and is most industrious with a sewing machine. I've ordered an entirely new wardrobe.' She popped a pink sugared bonbon into her mouth and smiled, that characteristic one-sided grin. 'Paris will be agog when we return! There is nothing like it to be had in the whole of Europe! Picture yards and yards of flowing silk, matched with embroidered fitted jackets with stiff mandarin collars, exotic bell-shaped sleeves, all in jewel colours that will make you weep from longing. I'm going to have some Arabian slippers made as soon as we come into port. The only thing is, you need to collect them, Andre. He doesn't speak a word of English and never sets foot out of Chinatown. His name is Mr Wu.'

'Mr Wu,' Valmont repeated, flatly. Eva got the impression there were many Mr Wu's all over the world, and that Madame always managed to engage their services. 'And how will I find this Mr Wu?'

'Oh, that's easy! His shop is in a basement. Somewhere between a grocery and an apothecary.'

'Easy?' Valmont ran his hand over his eyes. 'A basement. In Chinatown.'

'But you will know the apothecary because there are two great stone dragons with their tongues sticking out by the entrance and huge blue porcelain jars of herbs in the windows. Of course all the signs are in Chinese so giving you a name is of absolutely no use.' She stood up. 'I have every confidence in you, my boy. But do hurry. We're running out of time and there's still so much to do.'

'Do I need to pay him?'

Madame paused, her brow wrinkling. 'Now there's a question. You know, I can't recall. It seems I spent quite a long time there one afternoon. We drank vast quantities of green tea, had a very vivid conversation neither of us understood; measurements were taken, fabric was discussed. I must have had my purse with me . . .' she mused, looking about the room. 'Have you seen it since?'

'I'll take cash along anyway,' Valmont decided, going into his room to retrieve his jacket and hat.

'Now,' she turned to Eva and waved at the pile of signature voluminous creations lumped together on the bed, 'do me a favour and remove all these. I can't bear to have them in my sight!'

Eva stared at the yards and yards of beautiful fabric. 'What do you want me to do with them, ma'am?'

'Burn them! Drown them! Do whatever one does to stray cats with no home. One must never be sentimental about leaving the past behind.'

'Do you, I mean, would you mind terribly if . . .'

'Take them!' Madame cut her off. 'As long as I don't have to see them, I don't care what becomes of them.'

When he came back, Valmont was holding a small glass vial. He handed it to Eva. 'Here.'

She looked up at him in surprise. 'What's this?'

He shoved his hands into his pockets. 'Why don't you sniff it and see.'

Eva lifted the lid off. The fragrance rising up was at first green, mossy and coolly fresh. Then, gradually, it warmed to a sweeter, subtly musky base. It was a perfume balanced precariously between unfolding layers of pure white flowers, spring green herbs and something darker, more knowing.

'Where did you get this?'

'I made it.'

'You . . .?' She stared at him in disbelief.

His cheeks coloured a little. 'I told you I could make perfume,' he said, turning away from her, adjusting his hat in the mirror.

'But this is . . . it's beautiful!'

'You didn't believe me, did you?'

'No. Not at all.'

'Well,' he tried to appear nonchalant, 'you can have it if you like.'

'You can't give this to me,' she protested, putting the stopper in the vial and handing it back to him.

'Don't you like it?'

'Yes, of course. But you mustn't waste it.'

'Waste it? What were you going to do? Pour it around the room?'

'No, of course not. I don't mean to be ungrateful—'

'Then don't be,' he cut her off, pushing it back into her hand as he headed for the door. 'Now you'll know better than to doubt me,' he added, on his way out.

Madame glanced sideways at Eva as she lit another cigarette. 'He's trying to impress you, you know.'

'Me, ma'am?'

'Yes, you.' She laughed. 'Men aren't as complicated as they seem. They simply want to be admired by everyone. Also,' she nodded to the vial in Eva's hand, 'that's good. The first really good perfume he's ever made. Who would've thought he'd find inspiration in the heat of New York City? Oh, damn. Look, he's forgotten his key again.' She pressed it into Eva's hand. 'Do run after him, will you? I don't know where I'll be when he gets back.'

Eva hurried down the hallway and caught up with Valmont just as he was about to get in the elevator.

'Wait!' she called. 'You forgot your key.'

He stopped, the elevator doors closed. They were alone in the corridor.

'I've been meaning to say something to you,' he began, looking down at his feet.

She wasn't sure she wanted to hear it. 'Yes?'

'Well, the thing is . . .' he hesitated, frowning, 'I just wanted to say you were probably right about the lavender.'

'I'm sorry?'

'You remember, the lavender in the cleaning solution you made?'

Had he really been thinking about that all this time? 'I didn't put any lavender in.'

'Yes, but that's what I meant. To not put it in. There were a number of notes one could've concentrated on, all equally interesting,' he continued, assuming his familiar, lofty tone, 'and, although I might well have used lavender to great effect, I appreciate that your . . . your . . .' he searched the air around him for the right word, 'your resolution of the problem had merit.'

'Thank you.' She was unsure of what she was actually thanking him for.

'It seems you have an appreciation for scents.'

'I guess.'

'So, did you try it? I've never made a perfume for anyone specific before,' he suddenly admitted. 'Have you put any on?'

She nodded shyly. 'Just a little.'

'May I?' He held out his hand.

Eva extended her arm. Valmont took it, pressing the white skin of her wrist to his lips.

The effect was beyond what he could have imagined. His perfume highlighted her youthful freshness and yet blended naturally with her rich, musky undertones. It 'finished' her, gave her a polished elegance, joining the fractured sides of her together. It was astonishing how she added so much to his composition; how the very fact of her fuelled his imagination. And he felt an inner quickening. Already his mind was whirring with half a dozen refinements and variations.

Eva watched him. The expression on his face was familiar; it was the same look of transcendence and ecstasy she saw every week on the stone faces of the martyred saints in St Boniface, that teetered precariously between pleasure and pain. It frightened her.

She pulled away. 'Why did you make this for me?'

Valmont stared at her in astonishment. It was impossible to put into words the way her natural scent had inspired him; driven him, in fact, to devise a fragrance that would match the complexity of her skin.

'I had to,' he said.

'What do you mean, "had to"? You don't even like me.' She took a step forward. 'Do you?'

The elevator doors opened and closed again.

Neither of them moved.

'You don't understand,' his expression was reverent, almost sad. 'You're extraordinary.'

Paris, Spring, 1955

Pushing his wire glasses further back on his nose, the man behind the counter frowned, turning the card over to read the other side.

'Where did you get this?'

Grace was reluctant to tell him the truth. 'I found it. Quite by accident.'

She was standing inside the Guerlain boutique on 68 Champs-Élysées, speaking to master perfumer Jacob Androski, one of the assistants to the legendary Jacques Guerlain. Dressed in a white lab coat over his suit and tie, he'd been summoned from the workshop by one of the sales assistants to help her. He was examining the card that she'd found on the floor of the shop; the one she'd inadvertently put in her pocket.

'You found it?'

His tone made her blush.

'It was in an abandoned shop, a perfumer, on the Left Bank.' She tried to answer without giving too many details. 'I . . . had some business there . . . to see the property . . .' She stopped herself, mid-lie. 'The place was called *Recherchez-moi*. Do you know it?'

He looked at her strangely. 'Of course. But it's been closed ever since the war. Andre Valmont owned it.'

'Valmont?'

'Yes. Andre Valmont was a perfumer; one of the finest in all Paris.' He turned the card over again.

Grace leaned closer, across the counter between them. 'You see, I tried to translate it on my own but I couldn't work it out. I'm afraid my French dictionary didn't help much – even the words I could find I didn't really understand in context. But I know it has to do with a perfume and some sort of a recipe . . .?'

'It's not a recipe, but a formula. It's technical in nature – a correspondence between two professional perfumers. In fact, it's a shopping list of really quite expensive perfume ingredients. See this,' he pointed to the second line. 'Oudh – that's a very rich, intense oil taken from the heart of the aquiver tree. And there's jonquil, also narcissus from Morocco. These are extremely rare and very difficult flowers to extract,' he explained. 'It requires an astonishing number of them to arrive at even a single gramme of absolute.'

'Absolute?'

'Yes. An absolute is the purest form of essential

oil and therefore extremely costly,' he explained. 'In fact, it looks as though no expense was spared on these ingredients. Neroli from Tunisia, Bulgarian tuberose, vanilla from Madagascar. But here,' he frowned, 'these are very odd requests indeed.'

'In what way odd?'

'They want hair.'

Grace wondered if she'd heard him correctly. 'Did you say hair?'

'Yes.' He translated, '"Am struggling to find any variety of hair that yields the warmth and depth you describe. Perhaps blonde will work. Though I believe you will be impressed with the accord of wet lambswool."'

'Wet lambswool?'

'That's what it says.'

'I'm sorry,' Grace was struggling to keep up, 'but can you explain, what's an accord?'

'Of course,' he smiled apologetically. 'An accord is a mixture of two or more ingredients which produce a new scent, quite different from any of its individual parts. You see, a great perfume may include several fresh, new accords. They are like small scent compositions, inside a larger, more far-reaching canvas. The complexity and juxtaposition of the accords involved makes the difference between a truly revolutionary perfume and a merely pleasant-smelling scent.'

'But why would anyone want hair in their perfume? Or wet lambswool?'

'It's not inconceivable. Not every smell in perfume is floral or pretty. In fact, a perfume would have very little staying power if that were true. Musk, for example, is extremely common. Almost every modern formulation has it in one form or another and yet it's incredibly strong, gamey – an acidic, sexual scent that comes from the musk gland of a Himalayan deer. Civet from the civet cat smells like faecal material and pure oudh is unbelievable – it's an infection of the aquiver tree in India. In response to the fungus the tree creates an incredible dense amber resin that smells of mould, sweet decaying wood, vivid green notes. Most people hate it when they first encounter it and yet it seeds itself in your imagination – becomes addictive. These darker notes are like a heart, pumping at the centre of a great fragrance.'

'I had no idea.'

He leaned forward. 'One of my favourite ingredients is ambergris. Have you ever heard of it? Do you know where it comes from?'

She shook her head.

'It's coughed up by the sperm whale when it devours cuttlefish. It's a greenish, revolting mass that floats on the surface of the ocean, ripening in the sun and rain until it's washed ashore. And yet, from these humble beginnings, develops the most

216

indescribable scent. It literally expands on the skin – creates a vista in the senses.'

'How extraordinary. But how were these ingredients discovered?'

'God only knows! Perhaps one of the most instinctive things to do when you encounter something new is to pick it up and smell it. Though I don't like to dwell on the discovery of the civet cat too long. You see, most people assume perfume is made only from crushed flower petals but nothing could be further from the truth. All these ingredients give weight, dimension and contrast. Without them, the result is shallow and one-dimensional. But,' he held up the card again, 'hair has a very subtle, elusive, earthy quality. Extremely difficult to capture.'

Grace looked at him closely. 'Have you ever tried to capture it?'

'Oh, yes. Many times,' he admitted, a little self-consciously. 'It's one of the first things you notice, that you smell, during an embrace. The warmth of your lover's hair.'

She felt her cheeks colour a little and looked away. 'I hadn't thought of it like that.'

He reread the card. 'It appeared to be a specific request. The same with the lambswool.' He paused. 'As though someone was creating accords of an experience. Or a memory.'

Grace had never heard of such a thing. 'Is that possible?'

'Oh, yes.' His face was quite serious. 'Though not very common. It's something of a connoisseur's obsession.' Lowering his voice, he indicated the beautifully dressed women who strolled in a leisurely manner from one counter to another around them, like rare, exquisite creatures, meant only for show. 'Most customers want to smell like those they aspire to become, not who they were in the past. But perfumers are always attempting to capture scents that remind us of certain places, people, moments. It's the great challenge, to capture not only a true scent but one that recalls an entire experience.'

'Can that even be done?' It sounded more like alchemy than perfume.

'Occasionally. Here,' he gestured for her to follow him, 'let me show you something.'

He led her behind the glass counter and into a private storeroom behind the main shop. Taking out a set of keys from his pocket, he unlocked a narrow door into a dark, cool room where he selected a bottle.

'Close your eyes,' he instructed, taking the lid off. Then he dabbed a drop of it onto her wrist.

Grace shut her eyes and inhaled.

Suddenly, she wasn't indoors any more or even in Paris. But outside her parents' home in rural Oxfordshire, on the low sloping hill facing the house. It was late afternoon, the sky heavy with thick white-grey clouds; the lights in the house windows glowing brightly, like flame. The air tasted of ice.

She opened her eyes, stared at him, her mind reaching to grasp at a certain feeling . . . a specific time and place. 'I know that smell! But how do I know it?'

He grinned, delighted. 'Snow.'

'Snow! Of course.' She pressed her wrist to her nose. 'But how can you do that?'

'It's one of my own,' he said proudly. 'It's taken me years to perfect it. You see, nothing is more immediate, more complete than the sense of smell. In an instant, it has the power to transport you. Your olfactory sense connects not to the memory itself, but to the emotion you felt when that memory was made. To recreate a scent memory is one of the most challenging, eloquent pursuits possible. It's poetry, in its most immediate form.'

Grace looked at him with wonder. 'I was a child, on the hill outside my parents' house.'

He nodded. 'Scent memory is incredibly personal, a very private experience. My own memory couldn't be more different. Hungry, running across a frozen field. Dawn breaking.' His expression shifted, he seemed to recede before her, slipping into another place. 'Then the snow.'

Monsieur Androski replaced the lid.

Grace caught sight of the label: *La Pologne*, 1942. Poland.

The winter after the invasion.

She watched as he replaced the bottle in the store-room and locked the door.

They walked back out into the boutique, golden with light, soft-spoken sales assistants, the air thick with the hypnotic floral blends that Guerlain had become famous for.

He handed the card back to her. 'Whatever she was working on, it was not meant to be an ordinary commercial perfume.'

'She?' Grace asked. 'What makes you say "she"?'

He pointed to the signature at the bottom. '"M. Zed". It can only be Madame Zed. Do you know who she was?'

'I'm sorry. No.'

'She was a very well-known perfumer in the early 1900s. Russian, I believe. There was a rumour that she was some sort of escaped aristocracy from the Russian Revolution. She became the house nose for Lanvin and created maybe fourteen or fifteen per-fumes for them. And then suddenly, at the height of her success, she disappeared. Of course her most dis-tinctive creation is world famous – *Mon Péché*.'

'*Mon Péché?*'

'*My Sin*. Really, a very modern formula and unique

for its time. Still one of my personal favourites. She completely withdrew from the perfume world after that. However, she did have an apprentice – a young man.' He caught her eye. 'Eventually he opened his own boutique near Saint-Germain.'

'Andre Valmont?' she guessed.

'Exactly.' He sighed. 'I wonder what they were working on. I would have loved to have smelled it. Madame Zed had a very unique palate. Somewhat abrasive, challenging. But ultimately quite elegant. As for Valmont,' he paused, searching for the right words, 'he was nothing short of a genius. His library of accords and absolutes, the complexity and variation of his formulations, were nothing short of astounding.'

'Did you know him?'

He shook his head. 'Sadly, no. But I went to his shop once, shortly after my arrival in Paris. I shall never forget it. If Guerlain is a cathedral, Valmont's shop was a pantheon, a pagan shrine to everything possible – nothing edited, nothing denied. Floor-to-ceiling shelves, glittering mirrors, lush fabrics. It was tiny, exclusive, terribly chic. There was a woman, perhaps the most extraordinary creature I've ever seen, who presided over the whole thing. You could not, for love nor money, get an appointment with Valmont himself. But this apparition would sit with you, talking, bringing down one bottle after another until you were drunk with scent!'

'Why didn't he open up again after the war?'

He face grew sombre. 'Andre Valmont was Jewish. He did not survive the war, madame.'

'Oh.' She frowned.

'He was not a conventional perfumer,' he added. 'And he died very young. Who knows what creations he might have made in another ten or twenty years? It's a terrible loss to the profession.'

Grace held out her hand. 'Thank you, for your considerable time and expertise.'

He shook her hand. 'My pleasure, Madame Munroe. Let me know if you discover anything more. I am, and always will be, an admirer of his work.'

Grace headed out of the tranquillity of the boutique and on to the bustling pavement of the Champs-Élysées.

The sky was bright, the air balmy and mild.

She raised her wrist and inhaled.

And suddenly she was back in time again, on that late November afternoon, dense with mist and fog, standing on the ridge beyond the garden gate.

She could see her mother coming out of the house, waving eagerly to her to come in. And her father hurrying up the path that ran along the side of the house, head down, distracted. He was carrying something – notes – walking away. He wasn't coming in to tea.

A sick, painful longing filled her entire chest.

That was one of the last times she ever saw him alive.

New York, 1927

Miss Waverley was miraculously made. She had gleaming mahogany hair, cut into a sharp, sleek bob and eyes that were the colour of dark chocolate – huge doe eyes framed by black lashes. Her skin was ivory and her proportions amazing; a thin tapered waist, high full breasts, shapely legs. She walked with such casual sensuality that it was impossible not to stare at her. And she was a woman who was used to being stared at.

Miss Waverley was well known at the Hotel. She was a regular guest, although not a paying customer herself. She just appeared, rather as an intriguing footnote to the travel arrangements of some of their wealthier male clients. They would request an adjoining room to their own suite or sometimes, if discretion were a serious consideration, another suite on the next floor up. During the time that they visited, Miss Waverley adorned the Hotel like a rare, exquisite flower, only occasionally accompanying her benefactor out in public. She never rose before 11 a.m., at which time she had a standing order for strong coffee, a bowl of ice cubes and lemon slices, and half a grapefruit. No one knew what she did with the ice. Half an hour later, no matter what the day, a hairdresser, masseuse and manicurist arrived to attend to her in her room. She emerged, two hours later, a shimmering apparition of dewy youth, as graceful and artlessly arranged as a field of wild flowers.

She had a smooth, low voice and a naughty, shocking sense of humour. Laughter followed in her wake; she collected admirers, both male and female, simply walking across the lobby. She had a certain knack for including everyone in her own private jokes, bending in conspiratorially to say something wickedly off-colour to one of the old stone-faced dowagers waiting for a cab. The next moment, they'd both be giggling uncontrollably and Miss Waverley would be offering to have her chauffeur take the old dear wherever she was meant to be going.

If she dined downstairs in the restaurant, service to the other tables would inevitably stagnate while the staff jostled for a view from the kitchen doors to see what she was wearing.

'Is she a movie star?' Eva wondered, the first time she saw her.

'She wishes!' Rita snorted. 'She's a prostitute. Gets

treated better than the Queen, though. Just goes to show, doesn't it? What the world's coming to.'

Eva couldn't believe it. Prostitutes were women in cheap garments, standing in the shadows at the wrong end of town. 'Really, Rita,' she admonished, 'you shouldn't spread gossip.'

'It's not gossip. It's a known fact. And watch who you're calling a liar!' Rita trotted off, chin in the air, affronted and superior.

Miss Waverley stayed in room 321 for ten days at the end of July. She'd come at the bequest of Senator Henry Clayton Grimsby of the Boston Grimsbys. However, Senator Grimsby was also travelling with his teenage daughter and son. Therefore, Miss Waverley had a corner room not too far, not too close. And, due to the fact that it was the Grimsby children's first trip to New York, a little more time to herself.

Eva was only allowed to service her room after 3 p.m. And she looked forward to it as a child anticipates its birthday. At 3.00 precisely, Eva unlocked Miss Waverley's door and stepped inside a world of glamour and luxury.

The wardrobes were bulging with packages from dress designers and hat makers. Beautiful gowns lay tossed onto the backs of chairs from the night before. Tissue-thin stockings were bunched on the floor; filmy underthings of satin and lace, too sheer, too delicate to even imagine wearing, lay crumpled on the bed. Eva moved slowly, carefully, savouring each moment, hanging the clothes, making the bed, pulling back the thick curtains to let in the blazing afternoon sun. The air smelled of some exotic, rich perfume and stale cigarette smoke. There were full ashtrays on the side of the bath; half-finished glasses of champagne left on the balcony.

Everything about Miss Waverley fascinated Eva. And she refused to believe that someone so sophisticated and charming stooped to the moral depths Rita described. It was most likely that she'd misunderstood; after all, Rita was far too eager to believe the worst of everyone.

Eva's favourite bit was cleaning the dressing table. Here was the front line of female alchemy. Eva owned an old hairbrush she'd had since childhood and a small box of wiry hairpins to secure her hat – those constituted her only toiletries. But Miss Waverley's dressing table was covered in mysterious jars, bottles and compacts; gold lipstick cases, round face-powder puffs, tins of pink rouge, black squares of eyeliner and a large perfume atomizer. She dusted and rearranged them, wondering how they were all put to use.

Eva liked to imagine this was her room she was cleaning; that she'd been up all night dancing with Mr Lambert and that these were her golden shoes on the balcony, their half-empty glasses of champagne. Here she was, hanging her beaded dresses, ready for their next evening out; these were her expensive nightgowns she was folding.

She pressed her cheek to the cool, smooth silk. This is what sophistication felt like, what it felt like to be a grown-up woman.

'It's handmade. I had four fittings on the bodice alone. You wouldn't believe what I had to do to get that.'

Eva's eyes shot open.

In the doorway stood Miss Waverley.

Dressed in a tailored black-and-white summer dress and a large rimmed black sun hat, hand on her hip, she looked like some exquisite, if angry, apparition.

Eva dropped the nightgown.

'Easy does it! Do you have any idea of what that cost?'

'No, ma'am.'

Miss Waverley tossed her gloves and handbag on the bed. 'Pick it up. And mind you don't rip it.' Taking off her hat, she gave her head a shake and her hair fell automatically back into place. 'Did you steal anything?'

'No, ma'am. I wouldn't dream of it! I'm so sorry, ma'am.'

'Wouldn't dream of it, huh?' She looked at Eva hard. 'Just a bit curious, I suppose.'

'I apologize, ma'am.'

Taking out a silver cigarette case, she lit one. 'How old are you anyway?'

'Fourteen.'

She inhaled deeply. 'I was curious at your age. Got me into a lot of trouble.' She walked over to the window.

'Maybe I should come back, ma'am. Clean the room later.'

'No, no. Later won't be a good time.' She took another drag. 'Later is never a good time. Do it now.'

She went out onto the balcony, where she sat smoking, looking out over the skyline, while Eva finished the room.

～～

One day Miss Waverley's regular hairdresser, masseuse and manicurist failed to show up. Her breakfast tray sat, untouched, outside her door. Then, somewhere just after noon, she rang for more towels. Eva delivered them, knocking repeatedly on the door before eventually using her pass key.

'Hello?' She stepped into the bedroom. The curtains were still drawn and the bed sheets were in a tangle. There were vases of flowers, heavily scented and beginning to rot in the cloudy, stagnant water.

'Hello, housekeeping?' Eva almost tripped over a pair of shoes.

'In here.' The voice that came from the bathroom was weak, hoarse.

'Shall I leave the towels outside?'

'No.' There was a pause. 'I need help.'

Eva slowly pushed the bathroom door open. Miss Waverley was doubled over in the bathtub, but there was no water. She was wearing a pale pink silk nightgown. From the waist down it was bright red.

She raised her head. Without make-up, her face looked childishly small and washed out. Her eyes were bloodshot, swollen. 'I need a doctor,' she told Eva. 'You must not call reception. I need a doctor who will come up the back stairs, do you understand?'

Eva wasn't sure she did, but she nodded and put the towels down on the basin.

Racing out of the room and into the hallway, she spotted Rita trundling down the corridor towards her, pushing her cart.

'There's a problem!' Eva rushed up to her. 'Miss Waverley, she's sick. Very sick.'

'Jesus! Keep your voice down, will you?' Rita winced. She was nursing a hangover.

'But what should I do?'

'Do?' She looked at her as if she were insane. 'What's it got to do with you?'

229

'But she's ill!'

'The woman deserves what she gets. Close the door and get on with your business, that's what I say.' Rita sniffed, giving her trolley a shove.

Eva ran down to the front lobby and over to Alfonse, the doorman, who was still on duty from the night shift. He was the man who could get you what you needed when you needed it, without any questions. At least, that's what she'd heard.

'There's a problem,' she panted. 'I need a doctor.'

He didn't even bother to look up from his paper. 'See reception.'

'No, the kind who can come and go through the back entrance.'

He looked up, eyes narrowed, then put the paper down. 'Staff or guest?'

'A guest.'

He picked up the phone. 'What room?'

She told him. Then she went back to Miss Waverley.

Eva knocked softly. 'It's me.'

She was still in the bathtub, eyes closed. 'Is the doctor coming?'

'Yes.'

'Get me a drink, will you?'

Eva had never seen so much blood. It ran in thick dark rivulets into the drain, pooled in eddies around her pale feet. 'Shouldn't we . . . I mean, shouldn't you . . .'

'Just get me a drink.'

Eva went to the next room and poured her a whisky. She came back in. 'Here.'

'Thank you.' Miss Waverley's hand was shaking. She took a sip, wincing, and handed it back to her. 'Don't be frightened. It looks much worse than it is. Does he know what room to go to?'

'Yes.'

'Thank you.' She closed her eyes again, lay her head on her knees. 'You can go now.'

Eva laid her hand across Miss Waverley's damp forehead. 'You're hot.'

'So I am.'

Eva turned on the water and washed the blood away. Then she took a washcloth and very gently doused Miss Waverley with lukewarm water. It ran over her slim frame, down through her shoulder blades, over her chest. The silk gown clung to her.

The phone rang.

Eva got up.

Miss Waverley looked at her, sudden panic on her face. 'He mustn't know,' was all she said.

Eva picked up the receiver by the bed. 'Miss Waverley's room.'

The person on the other end hesitated. Finally a man's voice said, 'Is she there?'

'I'm sorry, sir. Miss Waverley is indisposed. May I take a message?'

'Who are you?'

'Housekeeping, sir.'

'No. No. Tell her I'll . . . no, no message.'

He hung up.

When she went back into the bathroom, Miss Waverley was resting her head against her arms. 'You're clever,' she murmured, without looking up. 'You're a clever girl.'

Soon the doctor arrived, a rather shabby-looking man with a worn black case. While he examined Miss Waverley, Eva tidied the room, changing the sheets and hanging up her clothes. After a while he came out and handed Eva a bottle of thick black liquid.

'I presume she has no husband.' It was a statement rather than a question.

'Not that I know of, sir.'

He sighed, rubbed his eyes. 'She doesn't want to go to the hospital. But she'll need this for the pain. And she needs to eat something and drink lots of fluids. Give her anything – just so long as she rests and takes it easy. Do you understand?'

She nodded. 'What's wrong with her?'

He put on his hat. 'She's having a miscarriage. Quite a good idea to sit in the bath actually. Here.' He handed her a bill. 'Call me again if her temperature rises or the pain gets too bad.'

Then he left, going down to the far end of the hallway to use the service staircase.

Eva came back several times to check on Miss Waverley in between her duties. By early evening, she was in bed resting and Eva had managed to get her to eat some ice cream, drowned in Coca-Cola.

She sat in the corner of the room as Miss Waverley drifted in and out of sleep, her face drawn, lips colourless, tense with pain. The man hadn't rung again.

A little before nine, Miss Waverley woke and sat up in bed.

'You're still here.' Reaching across to the nightstand, she groped for her cigarettes. Lighting one, she leaned back against the pillows and took a deep drag.

'You need to eat something.'

'Where's that medicine?'

'Here.'

After she'd taken some, washed down by whisky, she looked across at Eva. 'Why did you stay?'

'You needed help.'

'Where are you from?'

'France. The countryside, near Lille.'

Miss Waverley exhaled, a stream of smoke drifting up slowly to the ceiling. 'Farmland?'

'Yes,' Eva nodded. 'My grandparents had a small dairy farm.'

'I came from Minnesota. I can still smell the cow shit. I'd rather die than go back.'

'Really? I thought maybe you were from New York.'

She laughed, like a hard little cough. 'Well, we don't have to tell everyone, do we? Are your parents alive?'

'No.'

'I'm sorry for you. You have to make your own way then, don't you?'

It had never occurred to Eva that there was another way. 'Yes. I suppose so.'

The woman tilted her head. 'There aren't many professions a girl with no background can go into.'

'No, ma'am.'

Miss Waverley's face tensed. Stubbing out her cigarette, she looked exhausted again. 'You can go now. I'll be fine. Turn out the light, please. No one needs to know about this, understand?'

The next day, Miss Waverley's normal morning appointments resumed.

And when Eva went to service her room that afternoon, she was out.

———— ❧ ————

After that, Eva took it upon herself to visit Miss Waverley almost every afternoon. She often entertained at odd hours, with black jazz musicians from Harlem, exotic dancers and nightclub performers. There were buckets of champagne and bottles of gin, and there was music playing constantly. Both she and her guests treated Eva like a cross between a pet and a little sister; calling her Lulu for no particular reason other than it made them laugh, teaching her how to dance, sending her on endless errands for cigarettes, magazines and chocolates. But she didn't mind. In fact, she loved feeling that she was a part, no matter how peripheral, of Miss Waverley's glamorous set.

Sometimes there was no one else and Eva and Miss Waverley would spend the time alone. Eva guessed that she didn't like being on her own much;

she sensed that, left by herself, Miss Waverley's mood could be changeable and even morbid. She needed the reassurance of company. So she would amuse herself by trying on different outfits for her evening engagements and Eva would help her to select her jewellery and accessories. Other times, Miss Waverley would sun herself, lying naked on a silk robe on the balcony while Eva ironed her clothes.

Miss Waverley had no shame of her body but treated it rather like a weapon, meant to disarm those around her. She held her head high, her shoulders back, hips swaying as she sauntered lazily from one room to the next. And she was physically fascinating; her breasts were high and full, with pink swollen nipples. Her pubic hair curled in thick dark tendrils. She teased Eva, winking as she walked by, 'You know, you really shouldn't stare,' which made Eva blush. Only she couldn't help staring. Eva couldn't tell if she was in fact perfect, or simply gave the impression of perfection. And Eva was shocked and yet mesmerized by the overwhelming undertow of eroticism that surrounded her. Eva's own body was just forming, tiny buds of breasts and a pale hint of hair around her groin, of which she was inexplicably both ashamed and frightened. She avoided looking at herself in the mirror. But Miss Waverley was like some wonderful goddess, meant to be openly adored.

One day when it was too hot to sunbathe, Miss Waverley amused herself by making up Eva's face and teaching her how to apply thick coats of black eyeliner and red lipstick.

'Your face is like a blank canvas. First you smooth it out with powder, then you paint a dark frame around your eyes. There is no need to try to make it look natural. It's better when you exaggerate. Timidity is deadly. In anything. Always be bold. Look at you!' She stood back, admiring her handiwork. 'See how you're transformed?'

Eva stared at her reflection. It wasn't her at all but some exotic intruder, using her body, her features. She couldn't take her eyes off herself, she looked so different, so much older.

'You just don't know how to make the most of yourself, that's all,' Miss Waverley said. 'A diamond in the rough. That's what we call it.' Then she frowned, holding up a mass of Eva's hair. 'But this is getting in the way. And it's not very modern looking. You need to cut it.'

'Cut it?'

'Absolutely!' Opening a drawer, she pulled out a pair of scissors. 'Sit down.'

'But . . .'

'I'll make it look like mine. Don't you want to look like me?'

'Yes.' More than anything, Eva thought.

'Well, then.'

Miss Waverley pulled up a chair and sat Eva in front of the mirror. 'Be still,' she commanded, pouring herself a drink. She downed it in one.

Eva watched nervously as she chopped off a huge section. 'Do you cut your own hair?'

'Are you mad?' Miss Waverley snorted. Another pile of locks fell to the floor. 'Look at that! You have a neck.'

Eva closed her eyes. It was probably best not to look.

Forty minutes later, she stood side by side with Miss Waverley in front of the mirror. Miss Waverley wrapped an arm around her shoulder.

'What do you think?'

'I guess it takes a while to get used to it.'

'We look like sisters. I've never had a little sister before.'

And it was true. Eva was shorter, but they had the same delicate build, and now the same sleek dark bob.

Eva blinked, heart pounding. 'Do you think?'

'Sure. I know, let's put a dress on you, shall we?'

She helped Eva out of her uniform, then stopped.

'Good God, is this really your underwear?' She cringed at Eva's dingy pair of cotton shorts and threadbare camisole. Eva felt her face go hot from shame. 'They're dreadful! You need new ones.'

Miss Waverley tugged one of her dresses over Eva's head. The smooth jersey fell over Eva's figure, draping it in gentle curves. It felt cool and silky against her skin. Miss Waverley stood behind her, pulling in the waistline so that it appeared to fit perfectly in the reflection. 'You look like a film star!'

Eva stared at herself, fascinated.

'Do you know what this dress is for?' Miss Waverley whispered.

Eva shook her head.

'Seduction!'

The word disturbed Eva; it was laden with the murky enticements of sin, dangerous moral ambiguity and the certain promise of future remorse. But even worse than that was the implication of mysterious skills that remained beyond her comprehension. 'I wouldn't know how to seduce anyone,' she murmured.

Miss Waverley raised an eyebrow. 'If you're old enough to want a man, then you're old enough to seduce him. It's easy. Seduction is nothing more than knowing that you want someone and then showing them, very gradually, very deliberately, that you do. It's the way you do it – reveal, tease, ignore, take it back – that makes it seduction.'

'But how do you know when to reveal, when to take away?'

'Simple. You think about what you would like and then do it to them.'

She made it sound so obvious.

'Do you know how much this dress cost?' Miss Waverley continued. 'More than you make in a year. But look,' she gestured to the wardrobe, its doors open, overflowing. 'I have more than I know what to do with. Of course, a girl has to be smart. Did you know I used to work in a canning factory sticking labels onto tins of bromide?'

It didn't seem possible. 'What happened?'

'I had a little conversation with my boss one evening. See, the truth is, most girls don't understand men, don't know what they want.'

'What do they want?'

'Well . . .' Miss Waverley seemed about to say something for a moment but then changed her mind. 'If you really want to know about it, I'll tell you some day. But trust me, it's not complicated. Now, hang that, will you? And be a good girl and clean this up,' she pointed to the mess of hair on the floor. 'I'll buy you some new underthings in just your size. When I come back.'

'You're leaving?'

But Miss Waverley didn't bother to answer.

240

Instead she poured herself another drink, went into the bathroom and shut the door.

———— ∽ ————

'What in the Lord's name did you do to your hair?' asked Sis in horror, down in the laundry room.

Eva pulled her cap further down on her head. 'I didn't do it. Miss Waverley did.'

'Oh my goodness!' Sis grabbed Eva by the shoulders and turned her round. 'She cut it all off!' She ran her fingers through the blunt edge at the back of Eva's neck. 'It's gone!'

'I know. But it will be easier to keep clean,' she added, trying to sound reasonable. Suddenly Sis's grip felt like cement on her shoulder. She moved away.

'That's one way of looking at it,' Sis said grimly, handing her another pile of wet linen. 'That woman's trouble.'

'No, she isn't. She's just being nice.' Eva took the sheets, feeding them in between the heavy rollers of the laundry press. 'Besides, you think everyone's trouble.'

'I know all I need to know. And I'm right. What do you do with her anyway?'

'Nothing.' Eva concentrated on forcing the sheets through rather than on Sis's face. 'I help her get dressed, iron clothes.'

'Why did you let her cut your hair?'

'I look older. That's good, isn't it?'

'But why do you want to look older? That's what I want to know.'

A taut silence stretched out between them. Sis yanked the pressed sheets out of the other end.

'She lies about with no clothes on,' Sis said after a while, unable to leave the subject alone. 'Everyone knows she does it.'

Eva rolled her eyes. 'She's sunbathing. In the privacy of her own room.'

'There's nothing private about a balcony in the middle of New York City.'

'It's all the rage, among fashionable people.'

'If you want to look like a farmhand. Fashionable my eye! She has a reputation, you know.'

'She's good to me.'

'Who do you think pays her bills?'

Eva tried to take the high ground. 'Not everything in this world is black or white, Sis.'

'Sure it is.' Sis eyed her harshly. 'The sooner you figure that out, the easier life goes for you. Good, bad, right, wrong. You wanna live in the grey area, you're gonna find out you don't know your ass from your elbow.' She lifted another pile of sheets. 'And mark my words, grey turns to black pretty damn fast.'

Paris, Spring, 1955

Grace had luncheon on her own, sitting at an outdoor table in a café in the sun. Turning over in her mind what Monsieur Androski had told her, she thought about perfume and its connection to memory.

Monsieur Tissot had teased her about her sensitivity to taste and smell and he wasn't the only one. Part of her seemed to have always known what Monsieur Androski had clarified; that certain smells were the custodians of memory. And once they were unleashed, their effect was instantaneous, like switching on a light – flooding the senses far too quickly and completely. They had the power to transport and overwhelm. For that reason, one needed to be wary of them.

There were blocks of time in her memory that simply didn't exist. In fact, she had very little recollection of anything before the age of eight. Perhaps it wouldn't have been unusual except that Grace's memory in everything else was exceptional.

It was as if she were inwardly holding her breath, afraid to inhale life fully.

Around her the tables were filling with people, tourists planning their next stop over a coffee, businessmen meeting for luncheon, well-heeled women taking a break from their sprees, leaning in to gossip with one another, shopping bags piled at their feet.

It was such a simple yet satisfying pleasure to dine out of doors in the sunshine. Taking a sip of her citron pressé, Grace relished the refreshing contrast of sweet syrup and lemon juice. And she found herself thinking of Monsieur Tissot's philosophy: come to your senses.

Yield to them.

Had she ever entirely yielded to anything? The word implied a suppleness of spirit; an inherently optimistic predisposition she'd never fully entertained.

After luncheon, Grace began to walk, aimlessly at first, with only the vaguest sense of direction. She had no agenda. But Paris was much easier to navigate than she had imagined. London had sprung up wildly, everything thrown on top of everything else. But Paris had been designed. Here, historical landmarks appeared graciously; evenly spaced for maximum aesthetic impact. One had only to follow from one to another to reach any destination, including the Left Bank.

And weather that in England would have been blustery and punctuated with freezing rain showers was refreshingly breezy and fresh. The wind pushed the clouds across the sky at enormous speed but the sun remained high and warm. Before long Grace found herself back on the narrow winding little side street near the embankment – Rue Christine.

In front of her, on the corner, was Andre Valmont's abandoned shop.

It was as if she couldn't keep away from it; her curiosity was too strong. And now that she'd spoken with Monsieur Androski, it was even stronger.

From across the street, she watched as a workman finished nailing new boards across the windows and door of the corner shop; repairing the damage she and Monsieur Tissot had done. Head down, Grace walked on, past the front door, around to the back, looking to see if there might be a private entrance. And she found one, a discreet, faded red door in an alleyway behind the building.

Grace looked up. There was a light on in the second-floor window.

Perhaps Monsieur Tissot was right; maybe the old woman did live in the flat above the shop.

Gathering her courage, Grace knocked on the red door. Sure enough, a dog sprang to life upstairs, yapping excitedly, its toenails clicking against the floorboards as it scurried between the feet of its owner down the steps.

'*Oui?*' a voice called through the locked door.

Grace took a deep breath. 'Madame, I'd like to speak to you if I may. I'm Grace Munroe, the woman . . . the woman who was in your shop.'

She waited, listening.

Silence.

Minutes passed with no movement on either side.

Finally, Grace heard a bolt slide across and the door eased open a crack.

The old woman eyed her suspiciously. 'I should phone the police. You have no right to be here.'

Grace proceeded delicately. 'I'm truly sorry that we gave you a fright. It was wrong to break in like that. My lawyer and I believed that the shop was abandoned. We had no idea you were living above.'

'Fine,' she dismissed her, waving her away. 'Consider yourself absolved.'

She was beginning to close the door when Grace took the card out of her coat pocket and offered it to her. 'I found this on the floor of the shop. When you surprised us, I accidentally put it into my pocket. Does it by any chance belong to you?'

The old woman stared at it before taking it, turning it over slowly in her hand. 'What do you and that lawyer have to do with Eva d'Orsey?' she asked.

'I'm her heir.'

'Her heir?' She looked surprised.

246

'Yes.'

She opened her mouth to say something, then stopped. 'Did you read this?' she asked, after a moment, holding up the card.

Grace nodded. 'Yes, I did.'

She handed it back to Grace. 'I don't care what happens to it now.'

Again, she began to shut the door but Grace held it open with her hand. 'Pardon me, but are you by any chance Madame Zed? The famous perfumer, Madame Zed?'

'How do you know that name?'

'Are you she?'

'What business is it of yours? Why do you want to know?'

'Well, the thing is,' Grace explained quickly, struck yet again by the absurdity of her situation, 'I'd like to ask you some questions, if I may. You see, I never met Eva d'Orsey. She's a complete stranger to me and I know nothing about her.'

Madame Zed paused, taking this in. 'You're English, aren't you?'

'Yes, madame.'

'And when were you born?'

'I'm sorry?'

'How old are you?' she pressed.

'I was born on 30 May 1928. Why?'

'In London?'

'No, in Oxfordshire. Or rather, just outside.' The woman was looking at her as if she expected more. 'My parents died when I was young. After that, I was brought up by my uncle who is Professor of Medieval Literature at Balliol.'

'An English girl,' Madame repeated.

'Yes.'

'And how did you find me? Who told you to come here?'

'No one. I saw it in a newspaper, in Eva d'Orsey's apartment. She'd circled something, with this address.'

'A notification . . . of repossession,' Madame deduced. 'I'm surprised she noticed. Well, then,' she stepped back, opened the door wider. 'Yes, I think perhaps you'd better come inside.'

<hr />

Madame Zed's apartment was in stark contrast to the decadent aesthetics of the shop downstairs. The high narrow windows were simply shuttered against walls of soft bluey-grey. The furniture was sparse, arranged on a bare wooden floor and in the angular geometric art deco style. A large collection of cubist paintings, interspersed with old master portraits and landscapes, crowded the walls. In one corner, an antique harpsichord dominated, its keys worn and yellowed. Piles of sheet music were stacked high underneath it.

It was an apartment of extremes – classic, modern – and undeniably sophisticated. Almost no concessions had been made to convention. It wasn't a social setting but rather a sanctuary.

It was such a different world from the one Grace was familiar with. She'd lived her life in English heritage houses, with chintz fabric, Queen Anne furniture, paintings of long-dead family members – all with their noses and eyes in the right places. She was unused to a home that didn't cheerfully sport a traditional public face. It seemed to her a luxurious disregard.

Madame Zed brought in a bottle of cognac and some glasses. 'I'm afraid it's not very ladylike, however I prefer this to tea.'

'You have such a wonderful home,' Grace admired.

'I *used* to have a wonderful home,' Madame corrected her, pouring out two drinks. 'It's outdated. But I'm old now. I have neither the strength nor the means to redo it.'

'Outdated! On the contrary, I think it's extremely modern.'

She handed her a drink. 'All my life I've been a creature of fashion. Fashion, like life, is all about change. About embracing the new and the unknown. This look is old. I'm stuck.'

'Where I come from, everything is stuck.'

'And that,' Madame raised her glass, 'is why no one travels halfway across the world to buy a dress in London.'

Touché, Grace thought with a smile.

'I understand that you're a perfumer, is that right? That you created some very memorable scents.'

Madame Zed gave a little shrug. 'I've enjoyed some success in my time.'

'Do you still make perfume?'

'No. Not in many years. A lifetime ago.' She settled into a chair across from her. 'But now, tell me how you came here?'

'Well, actually, there's very little to tell. I live in London. I'm married. I lead a perfectly average life,' she admitted. 'Then one day, I received a letter from Madame d'Orsey's lawyer, Monsieur Tissot, informing me that I was the sole beneficiary of her will. I was certain there had been a mistake. But Monsieur Tissot insisted. So I arrived in Paris a few days ago to see for myself.' She put her glass down. 'As bizarre as it sounds, apparently I've received an inheritance from a woman I know nothing about. The entire situation is absurd!'

Madame raised a hand to stop her. 'I'm sorry,

but what precisely is your inheritance, if you don't mind me asking?'

'According to the will, my inheritance is to be the proceeds of the sale of an apartment, in the Place des Vosges. Do you know it?'

'Oh.' Madame Zed frowned; shifted. 'I see. Nothing else?'

'Well, there are some stocks.' Grace sat forward. 'The lawyer – I'm sure he thinks that I should just take the money and leave. But I can't. I'm looking for someone who knew Eva d'Orsey, for some clue to my connection to her.'

Grace waited, hoping that Madame Zed would willingly fill in the gaps, but instead she took a sip of her cognac, her features unreadable. She seemed hesitant, even reluctant to offer any information.

Still, Grace remembered the way the old woman had reacted when she'd heard of Eva's death. She tried again. 'You knew her, didn't you?'

'Yes. Yes, I knew her.' However, instead of explaining, Madame fell silent, drifting into her own thoughts.

'What was she like?' Grace prompted.

'Eva?' Madame's black eyes held the distance, as if she were looking inward, into her own memory. 'Eva was the most genuinely original, singularly elegant woman I think I have ever known. She was also very

251

troubled. Desperate even. I knew her a long time. The truth was we both had certain expectations of each other. In the end, I suppose they were too high.'

'What kind of expectations? What do you mean, desperate?'

Madame looked across at Grace. 'It's a complicated history, Mrs Munroe. I'm not entirely certain even I understand it.'

Her evasiveness was frustrating.

'I just want to know something about her.' Grace felt as though she was begging; perhaps she was. 'I know nothing!'

Madame considered a moment. 'What if knowing more meant that your life would change?'

'How?'

But Madame Zed didn't elaborate. Instead she stared at Grace, as if trying to measure her resolve.

'Hasn't my life already changed?' Grace pointed out. 'The only difference is, right now I don't understand why.'

'Very well,' Madame agreed finally.

Then, to Grace's surprise, the old woman got up and left the room.

When she returned, she was holding three very different bottles of perfume, which she put down on the table between them. Two were in fine hand-blown glass flacons with crystal stoppers. The first was elegant, a slim, simple rectangular shape; the second was a multifaceted crystal creation that threw rainbows of light around the room. Each had a gold-embossed printed label. One read *La Première* and the other said *Auréole Noire*.

The last one was nothing more than a plain, generic chemist's vial, sealed with a cork stopper. A yellowed, peeling label read *Choses Perdus*.

Grace looked up. 'What's this?'

Madame sat down again in the chair opposite. 'Once upon a time, I was a perfumer, Mrs Munroe. Now I'm reduced to a custodian, a collector of the past. I can't write or paint or compose . . . my language is scent – the vocabulary of feeling and memory. So forgive me if the story I'm about to tell is illustrated in a slightly unconventional way.' She gestured, indicating the perfumes. 'Here is a history. A love letter, in fact.'

Grace stared at the three bottles again. 'In perfume?'

She nodded. 'Only these perfumes weren't created by me. They were the work of my only apprentice, Andre Valmont, an extraordinarily talented young man.'

'The shop below was his, wasn't it?'

'That's right. His, mine . . . and to a certain extent, Eva's. You see, Eva d'Orsey was his muse, his greatest source of inspiration. She gave him vision. And he gave her clarity, focus.'

Grace sat forward, eager to hear more. 'A muse? So, was she beautiful?'

'Not when I first met her. Then she was just a girl – awkward, unformed.'

'Really?'

Madame smiled indulgently. 'Most people assume that a muse is a creature of perfect beauty, poise and grace. Like the creatures from Greek mythology. They're wrong. In fact, there should be a marked absence of perfection in a muse – a gaping hole between what she is and what she might be. The ideal muse is a woman whose rough edges and contradictions drive you to fill in the blanks of her character. She is the irritant to your creativity. A remarkable possibility, waiting to be formed.'

Madame picked up the bottle marked *La Première*. Very gently she eased the stopper off and held her nose above the bottle. Eyes closed, she inhaled.

She passed the bottle to Grace.

Gingerly, Grace smelled it too.

It was a heady, overwhelming veil of scent. At first it developed almost hypnotically into a floral, fruit bouquet; languid and sensual with a musky, almost dusty depth. But then a sharpness emerged, beautiful, icy, unexpected. There was something almost over-whelming about the lush complexity of the formulation, the sheer unbridled eroticism which came across in wave after wave of contrasting notes.

'This is floral, earthy, and there's the clean overlay of aldehydic waxiness and soft flowers,' Madame explained. 'And then, underneath, a whiff of more feral, impolite essences. Under the clean, innocent exterior there's a carnal presence. It's not without ulterior motive.'

Grace stared hopelessly. Here was a language she definitely didn't understand. 'I'm sorry?'

Madame Zed looked across at her. 'This, Mrs Munroe, is the scent of intoxication and desire. The perfume of seduction.'

New York, 1927

It was nearing the end of August when Eva saw Miss Waverley again. She was strolling down the hallway on the arm of a dark-haired man with a very thin moustache as Eva was coming out of the linen closet on the third floor.

'Oh, hello!' Miss Waverley smiled gaily, as if Eva were an old friend.

'You're back!' Eva beamed in turn, ridiculously thrilled at the sight of her.

Miss Waverley laughed and pulled the long chinchilla wrap she was wearing up on her shoulders. 'I told you I would be.'

The gentleman tipped his hat at her.

Miss Waverley squeezed his arm. 'This is Mr Wiener. And this, my dear,' she said, turning to him, 'is the little maid I told you about.'

Miss Waverley had been talking about her; had remembered her. Eva's whole chest swelled with pride.

'Charmed,' he nodded. He had a German accent and intent, almost entirely black eyes.

'So, you're still here,' Miss Waverley said.

'Yes.'

Mr Wiener lit a cigarette. 'Does it suit you?'

'Pardon me, sir?'

'This type of work?'

They were both looking at her very seriously, waiting for a response.

'It suits me very well, sir.'

'You have no ambition?'

'I don't know what you mean, sir.'

'Really? Tell me, you don't want to be in the movies like everyone else in the world?'

'Don't tease her,' Miss Waverley chided. 'She doesn't know what you're talking about. Josef is a film director,' she explained Eva. 'And a world-class cynic.'

'So.' He had a way of staring directly into her eyes that made her uneasy. 'You are the only girl in New York who doesn't want to be a film star, is that right?'

'I don't think I can act, sir.'

He laughed. 'That has never stopped anyone else! Everyone wants something. Go on, tell me your dream.'

'Me?' She looked to Miss Waverley, who just smiled at her. 'I don't think I have any dreams, sir.'

'Really? That's a shame. Because I might just be

inclined to give some of them to you.' He tipped his hat again and they continued on.

Tossing the chinchilla over her shoulder, Miss Waverley caught Eva's eye and gave her a wink. 'Do come and see me later,' she called. 'I have a present for you. But come after midnight. I'll be out until then.'

It was half past midnight when Eva knocked on Miss Waverley's door.

She opened it, wrapped in her dressing gown, and smiled. 'I thought maybe you weren't coming.'

The room was dark, just a few candles and a record playing. It was a hot night. The balcony doors were open. Eva could just make out the dark outline of a man, smoking in one of the chairs.

'Oh.' She backed away slightly. 'You have company, miss.'

'Oh, don't mind him.' Miss Waverley took her by the hand and closed the door. 'He won't trouble us.' Then she walked over to the dressing table and poured Eva a drink. 'Here. Want one? It's about time you learned how to handle whisky.'

Eva looked at the outline of the man; at the glowing embers of his cigarette. Then she looked back at Miss Waverley, smiling at her in her scarlet silk dressing gown.

Eva took the glass, sat on the edge of the bed. She already knew how to drink whisky; she'd watched her uncle do it. She tossed the entire shot straight into the back of her throat, where it burned, searing down the centre of her. She held out the glass again and Miss Waverley laughed.

'Well, look at you! So many hidden talents,' she said, filling it again. Then she took a little package from the top of her wardrobe wrapped in pink tissue paper, tied with a white ribbon.

She laid it on the bed. 'Here. Open it.'

Eva ran her fingers over the paper. She felt anxious; slightly woozy from the whisky. She tugged at the ribbon and the layers of paper floated to the side. Inside there was a tiny shell-pink demi bra and tap pants with embroidered lace silk stockings. They were extremely delicate and exquisitely made, with tiny bluebells hand-stitched along the borders.

'They're beautiful.'

'Go on,' Miss Waverley urged, 'aren't you going to try them on?' She leaned back in the armchair, propping her feet up on the ottoman. 'I want to see if they fit.'

Eva stood up; a reeling wave of light-headedness washed over her. She took the lingerie into the bathroom. The whisky had hit her hard; her hands seemed miles away from her body, her fingers tingling. She looked at her reflection in the mirror.

She didn't want to change, but she didn't want to seem rude either. Besides, they had played dress-up before.

Eva finished her drink. Then she put on the panties and bra, the silk stockings.

When she opened the door, Miss Waverley was waiting. She had changed the record. It was a slow song. The candles glimmered.

'You look just perfect. Like a real lady.'

The man had got up and was standing in the shadows, by the doorway.

'Now put some lipstick on. Just like I showed you.'

'I'm not sure I want to.' Her voice sounded small and far away.

Miss Waverley took a step closer. 'Of course you do.' Her voice lowered to a whisper. 'He wants to take us with him. To California. We're going to live in a big white house in the hills and each of us will have a car and there will be maids and housekeepers and a screen test for both of us!' She smiled, her eyes burning with excitement. 'This, my dear, is what opportunity looks like.'

'You mean you want me to go with you?' Eva couldn't believe what she was hearing.

'Of course! Do this right and we'll end up in California, making movies. You'll never have to pick up another dustpan and brush in your life.' She pointed to the dressing table. There was a tube of red lipstick, its cap already off, waiting. 'Go on.'

Eva reached for the lipstick, her hand trembling.

'Here.' Miss Waverley helped her to apply a slow smear of blood red. She stood behind her in the mirror. 'You want to be with me, don't you?'

Eva nodded.

'Good. Just do what I do.' Then, louder, she said, 'Now, we look like sisters, don't we?' She ran her hands over Eva's shoulders, slowly down her arms. 'I like that idea, don't you?'

Eva looked past Miss Waverley's reflection, at the man smoking by the balcony door, staring. The embers of his cigarette glowed hot as he inhaled hard. Her legs felt rubbery, her head dizzy. 'I think I'd better go. I'm not well.'

'Really?' Miss Waverley's grip tightened on her arms. 'I think someone deserves a thank-you, don't you?'

'Thank you, ma'am.'

'Such a good girl.' Miss Waverley's dark eyes showed in the flickering light.

Suddenly Eva couldn't speak. It was as if her mouth could move but she'd forgotten how to form words. Her limbs felt numb and heavy.

The man stepped out of the shadows. There was the distinctive thin moustache, the penetrating black eyes.

'Only,' Miss Waverley tilted her head, smiling softly at her in the mirror, 'I'm not the person who paid for them.'

~∾~

'Get up.' Someone was shaking her, gently at first and then more firmly. 'Come on. It's time to get up!'

Eva tried to open her eyes, but her lids were so heavy. Sleep pulled at her, tugging her under.

More shaking; harder this time. 'Do you want to lose your job? Get up!'

Eva recognized that voice; the same voice that had scolded and berated her non-stop for two weeks. It was Rita.

She forced her eyes open. Rita was standing over her, hands on hips. It was daylight and Eva was lying in a bed; the wrong bed, not her narrow little cot but a wide soft mattress with piles of pillows. Her whole body hurt and her head throbbed. She tried to move, to sit up. The room started spinning. 'I don't feel well,' she gagged.

'Jesus Christ!' Rita grabbed the waste-paper basket and then hauled Eva up with one powerful arm. 'Be

262

sick in here. And mind you don't splatter!'

Eva threw up in the basket and Rita wiped her face with a wet washcloth. Then Eva sank down again, into the pillows. She heard Rita running the bath.

Her breathing slowed and she closed her eyes, slipping back down underneath the black waves of sleep.

'Oh no, you don't.' Rita shook her arm again. 'You've got to get up. Here,' she handed her three aspirin and a shot of whisky from her rubbing alcohol bottle.

Eva tried to push them away. 'Please, no!'

'Don't answer back. You take them or you won't be able to walk across the floor let alone up the steps.'

Eva did as she was told. 'What time is it?' She had no idea how long she'd slept; if it had been a few hours or a whole day.

'Just after nine in the bloody morning.' Rita hoisted Eva up. The beautiful silk lingerie was twisted, torn and stained. The silk stockings ruined. 'Good God! Look at the state of you!' Rita peeled off the shredded stockings. 'Don't tell me this is what you've been wasting your wages on.'

'Where is she? When did she say she would be back?'

'Who?' Rita shot her a look. 'You mean that whore? Oh, you'll never see her again, missy. I told you she was no good but you didn't want to listen, did you?'

263

'But she's coming back for me. She said she would take me with her.'

Rita shook her head. 'She's checked out. First thing this morning with that Hun. That's the only reason I'm cleaning this early. And what happens? I open the door and find you spread out on the bed like a corpse.'

'No.' Tears ran down Eva's cheeks and chin. 'I'm . . . I'm ruined!'

'Well, if you want to swim with the sharks you're going to get bit.' Rita sighed. 'And there's no need to be dramatic. You're not the first girl in the world to make a mistake. Now, get up.'

Rita undressed Eva and put her into the bath. Then she rolled up the sleeves of her uniform and bathed her, as gently as a baby.

***

'She's sick, ma'am.'

Mrs Ronald narrowed her eyes and searched Sis's face. 'Really. What kind of sick?'

'She's throwing up, ma'am. Some sort of fever, I think.'

'I hope this isn't the result of any alcoholic drink, Cecily?'

'No, ma'am. I think, although I couldn't say for

264

certain, that she's got some sort of influenza.'

'Influenza,' Mrs Ronald repeated, sucking hard on her back teeth.

'Or maybe she ate something that didn't agree with her.'

'Isn't that interesting. Especially as you all eat in the canteen together. I've had no other reports.'

'With all due respect, ma'am, she *is* foreign. They eat things no one else would touch.'

Mrs Ronald sighed. It was almost impossible to tell when Sis was lying; she was clever. It served her right for hiring a clever girl in the first place.

'I'd be happy, ma'am, to clean her rooms in addition to my own,' Sis offered.

Mrs Ronald leaned back in her chair, folding her hands together in her lap. 'Would you now? Perhaps we should call a doctor for Miss Dorsey?'

Sis didn't flinch. 'As I said, ma'am, I can't say for certain, but to me it looks like something that may well pass in a couple of days.'

'That's a lot of work, even if it is only a couple of days.'

Sis straightened. 'She'd do the same for me, ma'am.'

'Would she?'

For the first time, Sis dared to look Mrs Ronald in the eye. 'Yes, ma'am, I believe she would.'

It was almost the end of October when Mr Lambert finally returned.

Eva caught a glimpse of him as he was riding the elevator one morning. She was dusting the light fixtures in the hallway when the doors opened and another patron got off. They were about to close again when he recognized her. 'Oh, hello, it's you!' He jammed his hand between the doors and bounded off. 'What have you done to your hair?'

His suit was badly in need of a press, his collar grey and frayed, but his eyes were just as blue as she'd remembered; his smile instantly disarming. She made herself concentrate on dusting.

'So, you're still here.' His voice was low, conspiratorial.

'Yes. I'm still here.' Then she added, against her better judgement, 'Did you enjoy Niagara Falls, sir?'

'Niagara Falls?' His brow furrowed as if he had no idea of what she was talking about. 'I can't say I did. Place with all the water, isn't it?'

And the Laughing Blonde, she thought. But instead she just nodded. 'That's what they say.'

'Yes, well, it's been a busy summer. I've been all over the East Coast so it's hard to remember.'

'Must be.' She moved a little further down the hallway.

'Well, here's the thing,' he said, strolling up behind her, hands in his pockets. 'I've been thinking of you quite a lot. Of your many admirable qualities.'

She glanced at him sideways. 'Have you?'

'And I have a small favour to ask of you. Well, a proposition really. You know,' he leaned casually against the wall, 'I'd like to discuss it with you sometime, only not here. It's a private matter. Nothing one would talk about in a public hallway. You understand.'

'Of course, sir.'

'I'm in room 701. So, what do you say?' He smiled charmingly. 'Come and see me, say, in an hour?'

'I'm not sure I have time,' she said quietly.

'Of course. Well, I mean. You know where I am, so you can come when you like.'

She continued to avoid his eyes; gave a little shrug. 'I'll think about it, sir.'

Mr Lambert blinked, as if suddenly seeing her for the first time. She'd changed. Her face was different; there was a shift in her demeanour and tone. He opened his mouth to say something, then stopped.

The little maid was off, heading down the hallway.

He stood, more than a little surprised, watching as she walked away.

Two days later, at the end of her shift, Sis came down to Eva's floor with a message.

'I've got someone asking after you,' she informed her, hand on hip.

'Who?'

Sis leaned up against the counter, watching as Eva washed out dirty glasses in the tiny room-service kitchen. 'Mr Lambert, of all people.'

Eva kept her eyes down. 'Really.'

'Humm. Why's he asking after you?'

'I don't know,' she shrugged. 'He was on my floor for a while. Maybe he misses the way I change the sheets.'

'Maybe he does.'

Eva looked up. 'What's that supposed to mean?'

'Evidently, you've caught his eye.'

'I doubt it. Actually,' she gave Sis a look, 'I believe he favours blondes.' Eva scrubbed the glasses hard, running them under hot water.

'That haircut makes you look fast. I'm only saying this as your friend. You've filled out, your hair's as short as a chorus girl's and now I've got grown men asking me where you are. What am I supposed to think?'

'You're supposed to think more of me.'

Sis frowned, bit her lower lip. 'When are you going to come to confession again? You haven't been for ages.'

Eva wiped down the counter. 'I've nothing to confess.'

'What about Mass?'

'No, thank you.'

'Do you want to end up in hell?'

Eva folded up the towel. 'Is it any different from this?'

Sis opened her mouth but didn't know what to say. She tried another tack.

'Has he . . . I mean,' she lowered her voice, 'did he try to touch you? That's happened to me. Men get grabby when they're away from home. And they seem to think you're included in the price of the room.'

'He's never laid a finger on me.'

Sis sighed, shook her head. 'Well, he wants to see you.'

Eva took off her apron, turned off the lights. 'Thank you.'

'Well?' Sis followed her out into the hallway. 'Are you going to go?'

'I don't know. I'm certainly not going now.'

'But what if he complains? What if Mrs Ronald hears about it?'

Eva stopped. 'I don't understand. What do you want me to do? Go or not go?'

'I don't know! If you don't go you could get in trouble. But I mean, why? Why is he asking for you?'

'How do I know? People are strange.' Eva headed down the hall towards the back stairs. 'Why did that old woman want you to sing her to sleep?'

Sis caught up with her up. 'I told you he was a communist, didn't I?'

'Yes.'

'Leave the door open. Do you hear me? Go, but make sure you leave the door open. That way, if he makes a lunge for you, you have an exit.'

'I told you, I may not even go.'

Sis sighed heavily as they climbed up the stairs. Eva could hear the tears begin to catch in her throat. 'You used to tell me everything.'

'There's nothing to tell.'

'Just like that night, huh?'

'I don't want to talk about it.'

'Why won't you tell me?'

Eva turned on her. 'Because I can't! I'll make it up to you, I promise.'

'I don't want you to make it up to me! I want you to talk to me.' She stopped. 'I don't know what happened to you that night, but if you can't even tell me then there's a pretty good chance you shouldn't be doing it at all!'

Sis turned on her heel and stormed back down

the staircase, the door slamming again at the bottom.

Sinking down on the steps, Eva cradled her head in her hands. Suddenly a wave of nausea washed over her. She was going to be sick again.

It had begun out of nowhere. Eva woke up when the sky was still dark, her head spinning, retching for no reason. And then the sickness was gone, only to return again the next morning. And Sis was right, she had filled out. All of a sudden her breasts were painfully tender and full.

Curling into a ball, she rested her head on her arms. She needed to be still a moment. Very still. Until the nausea passed.

She hated herself.

All around her doors were closing.

Life in the grey area had become very dark indeed.

It was not permitted for staff to go through the main corridors once they were off duty. Eva's heart pounded as she made her way down the hallway towards room 701. She walked slowly, pushing her shoulders down and her chin up. She hesitated a moment when she reached his door and then knocked.

'Come in,' he called.

She opened the door and stepped inside. 'You wanted to see me.'

Mr Lambert was standing by the window with a drink in his hand. He turned. She was wearing street clothes, a dress, and carrying a handbag and a hat. Her dark hair gleamed, smooth and satiny in the glowing light of the evening sunset.

'Where are you going?' It had never occurred to him that she might have a life outside the hotel.

'I'm on my way out.' The statement was both vague and final.

He took a few steps forward. He almost didn't recognize her. Her face looked older; a casual, knowing expression had replaced the eagerness. And with her new haircut, her features had a symmetry and boldness he'd never noticed before.

'You wanted to see me,' she said again.

He was staring at her. 'Yes.'

She waited, looking him calmly in the eye.

In her uniform, she was his servant. But now, even in the simple black dress she'd made from one of Madame Zed's curious cast-off tunics, she was suddenly his equal. She could feel him taking her in, adjusting himself to this new reality of her.

'You're very quiet,' she said, after a while. 'Perhaps you've forgotten what it was that you needed to say.'

She had her hand on the doorknob. 'Good evening, Mr Lambert.'

'Stay.'

'Pardon me?'

'Stay.'

'Is that an order?'

'A request. Please.' He pulled out a chair.

She hesitated, then sat down on the edge of the seat.

He poured her a drink.

She took it, holding it, untouched, on her lap.

He sat down across from her. 'I, umm . . . I wanted to talk you about . . .'

She crossed her legs, her stockings gleaming in the light, and suddenly he was unable to concentrate clearly.

'Yes?' she prompted.

'Well, it seems to me,' he tried again, 'that we used to have a pretty good time playing cards.'

'Yes, Mr Lambert.'

'And that you had a great deal of talent. A talent one wouldn't normally expect from a young . . .' (he was going to say 'girl' but changed his mind) 'a young woman. And well . . . there's quite a number of ways to enterprise on a talent like that . . .'

She tilted her head to one side. 'Are there?'

He felt his stomach tighten and his pulse quicken;

he hadn't anticipated this at all. Only a short time ago if he'd so much as looked in her direction, she blushed. Now she seemed almost bored by him.

'Yes.' He took another drink. 'I know how to make the most of those skills.'

The darkness gathered softly around them.

'Not many people can do what you do,' he continued.

'Can you, Mr Lambert?'

'I'm sorry?'

'Can you do what I can do?'

He blinked. The distance between them seemed to have shrunk though neither of them had moved.

'No,' he admitted, finally. 'No, I can't. I've met people who could count cards, who were fast and clever. But I've never met anyone who could see the game the way you do in your head.'

'So,' she put her drink down, 'how can I help you?'

Just like that the entire conversation turned.

'You don't understand.' He laughed awkwardly. 'I know how to help you.'

'I'm not sure I need help, Mr Lambert.' She got up. 'But thank you all the same.'

He stood too, cutting her off before she reached the door. 'I'm offering you a chance out of here!'

'Are you?' She looked up at him with those strangely feline eyes. 'As what?'

His face hardened. How did she get to be so unflappable? 'Don't play me, kid!'

'Then don't play me,' she countered smoothly. 'And I'm not a kid.'

'Aren't you?'

'No. Not anymore.'

He grabbed her by the wrist. She winced but didn't pull away. He turned her arm over; there were three burn marks across her forearm, seared holes in the flesh, red raw, evenly spaced. He looked at her in horror. 'What happened to you?'

'What happens to everyone.'

'Does it hurt?'

Her mouth softened into the ghost of a smile. 'Only when you touch it.'

He let go.

She was right; she wasn't a kid anymore. Someone had stolen the last vestiges of innocence from her and replaced them with this unnerving self-posses-sion instead.

'If you want something, Mr Lambert, say it.'

He took a step closer. She smelled both coolly reserved and somehow earthy and narcotic. 'Come with me.'

He saw her lips part slightly, her cheeks flush. 'Why?'

'I can teach you.'

She said nothing, leaned back against the door frame.

He came closer still. He could feel the warmth of her, the heat of her gently curving body; smell the musky sweetness of her hair. 'We can make a lot of money.'

She laughed.

And suddenly he realized that he'd been ambushed, overthrown by this odd little creature with the thrilling mind, green eyes and shape-shifting body. She had an effect on him he'd never suspected; it was in motion, already under way, a dangerous, teasing undertow.

'Come with me. So that I can finish teaching you what I began. So that we can make a great deal of money in beautiful cities all around the world. But most of all,' he ran his finger along her cheek, 'because I hate to drink alone.'

Paris, Spring, 1955

Madame Zed reached again for her glass of cognac but it was empty. Grace pushed the bottle across to her.

'So Eva went with him? This Mr Lambert?'

She nodded.

Something inside Grace's chest flared; a deep sense of indignation. 'But she was just a child! You do realize that, don't you? Whoever this man is, this Lambert, what he did was a crime.'

Madame merely looked at her, head tilted thoughtfully to one side. 'One is never sure, in the end, of who seduces whom. A young woman on the cusp of her sexual awakening is a powerful creature. She's often unused to, even unaware of, the tremendous power she holds and is easily intoxicated by it.'

Grace couldn't believe her ears. 'Are you defending him?'

Madame Zed shrugged. 'I'm not defending any-one. Or condemning anyone.' She looked at Grace thoughtfully. 'Are you a prude, Mrs Munroe?'

'A prude? Well, no. I don't think so,' Grace fumbled, offended.

'I only ask because this is not a fairy tale, my dear.' Taking out a long black cigarette holder, Madame Zed fitted a cigarette into it and lit it. She looked across at Grace, staring at her from beneath her heavily lidded dark eyes. 'You came to me. You wanted to know more. But I can't change the story to put you at ease.'

'No. I don't want you to do that,' Grace relented. 'I just suppose it's a bit shocking that she would go off with a . . . a grown man like Lambert.'

Madame exhaled. 'Lambert took her to Europe, introduced her into society, gave her an education of sorts. Some of us, no matter how hard we try, aren't meant to lead ordinary lives. Fate finds us. Gives us a shove.' She drew the holder to her lips and inhaled slowly. 'Fate has given you a little push, hasn't it?'

'Me?'

Madame nodded. 'Here you are, in a foreign city, with a strange legacy.' She exhaled through her nose. 'Perhaps, Madame Munroe, you weren't meant for a mundane life either. Perhaps you're considerably more exciting than you realize.'

'Me? Oh no, I'm as dull as ditchwater.'

'Really?' Madame tilted her head to one side. 'Tell me, where did you grow up again?'

'In Oxfordshire. A small village called West Challow.'

'And you lost your family in the war?'

'My mother died in the Blitz. But my father died before the war, of a heart attack.'

'Yes, I remember now,' she nodded to herself. 'You told me that. And what was she like, your mother?'

'My mother?' Grace frowned, laughing a little. She hadn't expected to be the topic of conversation between them. 'Well, let's see . . .' She tried to concentrate. 'She was small, very energetic and had that kind of deep auburn hair I've always wanted myself but wasn't lucky enough to inherit.' She smiled to herself. 'She seemed very beautiful and charming to me. She was also the author of several rather badly written romantic novels published under the pen name Irene Worthing.'

'Really?' Madame seemed fascinated. 'How extraordinary. Have you read them?'

'Of course. A thousand times.'

'What about your father?'

'It's difficult for me to remember him at all, to be honest. He was a botanist. He came back a hero from the Great War . . . he was quite deaf from all the shelling and had suffered terribly from mustard gas poisoning. He was unable to be comfortable for any period of time.'

'Do you miss them?'

Grace looked across at her. It was an odd thing to ask.

'It's been so long,' she said after while. 'At least, I think I miss the idea of them. I have to admit that I've forgotten almost everything about them or it's been distorted. For example, my mother used to smell a certain way – of rose water perhaps, or of soap, I can't remember which. I don't know if she smelled like that all the time or just once.' She paused. 'We lived on my mother's family estate. But we didn't live in the Great Hall – we had a smaller, separate house on the grounds where my father could work on his research as a botanist. He was always brooding, distracted. He didn't speak much because of his hearing. I think he was actually extremely shy. He drew a lot, took notes. He preferred to make things.'

Madame inhaled slowly. 'Like what?'

'He made a three-storey house for the hens that was heated by a row of light bulbs under a wire mesh floor in the winter and that was always perfectly snug.'

'How funny!'

'Yes,' Grace smiled. 'And he built my mother a series of rotating pantry shelves and a wringer for the laundry that was operated by using a pedal on the floor rather than a handle so her arms wouldn't grow tired.'

'Did she like that?'

'Well, she wasn't very domestic – not much of a cook. She was more involved with her writing. Besides, we always had help for the housekeeping duties. They must have liked his inventions. But my father liked solving problems, I think, and my mother let him. I don't think . . . I'm sorry.' Suddenly Grace found it hard to concentrate on what she was trying to say. 'I think something's burning, isn't it?'

'What?'

'Have you got something in the oven? Your supper? I think it must be burning.'

'Oh, *merde*! Not again!' Crushing her cigarette into the ashtray, Madame got up and hurried to the kitchen. Grace could hear her muttering and cursing, the banging of pots and pans, the sound of running water.

When she didn't return after a few minutes, Grace ventured into the hallway. The smell of charred pastry crust filled the corridor. 'Can you save it?' she asked, doubtfully.

'It's nothing.' Madame opened the kitchen window to clear the smoke out. 'Nothing that can't be made again another time. I have always abhorred cooking. But every once in a while I try.'

'I'm a dreadful cook. Far too easily distracted. I suppose I get that from my mother.'

Madame gave her a curious look. 'Perhaps you do. But you must forgive me,' she began ushering Grace towards the door, 'it's late. And as you can see, I have some cleaning to do.' She held the door open for her. 'Come again. Maybe tomorrow. And we will talk some more.'

～～～

Grace lit a cigarette on the pavement outside the deserted perfume shop on Rue Christine and began walking back to her hotel through the quiet, dimly lit streets, recounting Madame's words. One sentence echoed in her mind, replaying itself over and over.

'A young woman on the cusp of her sexual awakening is a powerful creature.'

She took a deep drag. Here in this strange city, the net of her memory loosened. She too had been intoxicated by her awakening sexuality.

It had happened just as Madame had noted; early on; after her mother's death when she was thirteen or so. She'd only recently gone to live with her uncle in Oxford. He had no experience with children; suddenly she found she had the run of the house. He was always working and she was left more and more to her own devices, treated as an adult rather than a child. Grace remembered feeling such a tangle of opposing emotions – the aching loss of her mother, fear, and at the same time a new confidence and terrible, thrilling freedom. But underneath all that, there was an unfamiliar, overwhelming desire to be touched. Her body had grown languid, easily aroused. And overnight it had transformed from the narrow shapeless body of a child to that of a young woman, with a slimmer waist, swelling breasts, curving hips.

She began attracting attention. Clandestine looks and mysterious tensions suddenly corseted her days; unspoken invitations tugged at her awareness. Her uncle, always on the periphery, receded even further, maintaining a respectful distance from her transformation. But his colleagues gazed upon her with new eyes and suddenly she too had moved a little slower, a little more deliberately, teasing out their interest without knowing why; simply because all of a sudden she could.

She was fascinated and repulsed in equal measures by the sudden increase in male attention. She learned to cover her desire with a steely surface of indifference, playing the tensions off one another.

It had been an effective strategy, surprisingly sophisticated for one so young.

Near the banks of the Seine, tucked beneath

bridges, in the shadows, Grace glimpsed the outlines of couples, bodies entwined, stealing embraces.

She crossed over the river, the black water rushing beneath her like a sheet of moving glass, the lights from the shore reflected in its smooth surface.

There had been a student of her uncle's, a young man in his early twenties named Theo Lund; lanky, serious, with large, round blue eyes. He was shy, studious, socially awkward. From a modest background, he didn't mix much, but was instead dedicated to earning his degree.

He came to the house every week, while working on his thesis, for private tutorials.

And she made a point of being the one to answer the door, showing him into her uncle's study. She took care with her dress, her hair; lingering, allowing him to make conversation with her. And her answers to his questions were always evasive, teasing. Week after week, she felt his interest and admiration grow.

In private, she dreamed of his hands on her skin; of the pressure of his mouth on hers. She yearned for a physical pleasure she couldn't quite imagine, didn't understand.

Then she'd offered to show him the garden one late spring evening, with the magnolia tress in full bloom.

He'd followed her into the grove, talking too fast,

too much. The trees had formed a canopy of rich blooms, waxy petals of deep pink, exploding with colour and perfume. She'd stood, quite still, while he admired them, looking everywhere but at her. And then finally he stopped. His hands shook a little as he reached for her.

She had met him more than halfway, tilting her face up, wrapping her arms around his neck. Tentative, tight-lipped kisses became urgent, hands travelled . . .

'Grace!' Her uncle's voice cracked like a whip. 'What are you doing?'

He was standing at the end of the path, rigid with indignation.

Even after all these years, her whole body still withered with mortification at the thought of it.

She never saw Theo Lund again. Was unsure if he ever graduated or not.

It was odd now, looking back . . . she'd been only a girl then. But her lasting impression was that he'd been the vulnerable one, the one whose innocence had been lost and led astray.

And then later, there was Roger.

That night after her birthday party at Scott's, she was meant to be staying with Mallory but instead she and Roger had taken a room in a small hotel in Mayfair. She'd wanted to make love, couldn't wait to be alone with him.

Once the door was locked, she went to him immediately.

'You're like a wild animal,' he teased, extracting himself to make them both drinks. 'Take it easy!'

'But I don't want to take it easy.'

Later, in bed, he manoeuvred her from one position to another; he had more experience and enjoyed instructing her. However, her willingness, her talent as a student, threw him.

'Have you done this before?' he accused.

'No, but I want to please you.'

'Relax,' he said firmly, pushing her arms down by her side. 'Let me.'

But by relax, he meant, 'Be still.'

Grace had unladylike appetites; aggressive lusts. And a grasping emptiness in her soul. She should be ashamed of herself. It was painful to her, in the same way that certain high-pitched noises are unbearable to the ears, to even acknowledge this part of her nature.

Climbing the steps to the hotel, Grace paused, taking a long look at Paris, in all its shimmering, enigmatic elegance, wearing the night as a beautiful woman wears diamonds.

Madame Zed was right; one is not always sure who seduces whom.

Back in the rich, warm glow of the hotel lobby, piano music played, soft and melodious; the scent of white hyacinths, massed together in great brass urns near the front desk, perfumed the air with a sharp green sweetness. And the vast marble foyer echoed with conversation, laughter and the clinking of glasses.

It was cocktail hour.

'Madame Munroe!' The concierge bustled out from behind his desk. 'You have a message, madame. A gentleman, Monsieur Tissot, has telephoned for you today.' He handed her a slip of paper. 'Here is his number. And also your husband has rung.'

'My husband?'

'Yes, madame. He has asked if you might be so good as to return his call.' He handed her a second slip. 'He is staying at his London club. This is the number.'

Her heart lifted. 'Thank you. Thank you very much.'

<hr/>

Upstairs in her room, Grace lit a cigarette and stood smoking by the window, looking out over the city skyline.

Every day she'd expected something; a letter or flowers, perhaps?

As the days dragged out, her hope withered.

But sure enough, in his own time, here it was.

Closing her eyes, Grace took another drag, gathering her nerve.

Mallory must've given him the name of the hotel.

She hated the thought of a strained, long-distance conversation. But perhaps it was for the best. He could apologize and they could move on with their lives, though the idea of him explaining his behavior; of being vulnerable in any way, made her cringe inwardly. They simply needed to get past this episode. And she told herself she could bear anything as long as he didn't go into details; she didn't want to imagine the affair any more vividly than she already had.

As long as Roger understood that it was over, forever, they could carry on.

Resolved, Grace stubbed out her cigarette and picked up the receiver.

'Yes, I'd like to place a trunk call please, to the East India Club in St James's.' She waited, gnawing on her fingernails while the operator connected her, eventually being transferred via the club switchboard to his room.

'Hello? Hello?' Roger's voice crackled on the other end of the line. He sounded as if he were speaking through a tin can, and very far away.

Automatically, Grace's spine stiffened. 'Hello? Hello, Roger . . . it's me.'

'Who? I'm sorry? Who is this?'

'It's Grace,' she said, louder. Who was he expecting?

'Oh. Yes, of course.' There was silence. 'How are you?'

'I'm . . . I'm in Paris,' she said stupidly, unable to think of anything else to say.

'Yes, so I gather. I've spoken to Mallory.'

'Really.'

'And how was the trip?'

'The trip? Fine. It's a nice hotel.'

'Good.'

More silence.

Her mind raced, tripping over itself for something, anything, to fill in the void. She could tell him about the will, explain the extraordinary inheritance of Madame d'Orsey . . . but she didn't. His transgression was the matter at hand. However, she couldn't help but notice, with a sense of growing misgiving, that he hadn't even asked as to the nature of her business.

'And you?' she fumbled. 'Are you well?'

'Well,' he paused, 'as well as can be expected. I can't say I was thrilled to return from Scotland to an empty house.' He sounded petulant, put-upon. 'There wasn't a single thing to eat, Grace.'

It was amazing how he managed to twist things, to imply that he was being stoic in the face of her abandonment. She could hear him shifting, changing position. 'How are you bearing up? Can you stomach the food?'

Grace's skin went cold. Was this it? Was he just going to make pleasant conversation and pretend that nothing had happened? 'It's quite good really,' she answered numbly. 'I like it.'

'You either love or hate it. Too much garlic for my taste. But it's worse in Rome.'

'Yes. Yes, that's what they say.'

Pause.

'Well, good. I just wanted to ring and see if you were all right. After all,' his words assumed a pointed tone, 'you left so abruptly. Also I wanted to know when you planned to return home. People have been asking after you. I can't put them off forever.'

Grace blinked, amazed by his dexterity.

He'd simply sidestepped the entire thing. As far as he was concerned, she was the one leaving him in the lurch. And suddenly it struck her, clearly, that he had no intention of ever acknowledging his affair.

And he expected her to behave in the same way.

Grace sat down hard on the edge of the bed, took a deep breath. 'What about Vanessa?'

'Excuse me?'

'Vanessa.' Grace's heart was beating so hard, she felt as though she was going to be sick. 'What about her?'

It took her a moment to realize that the sound she

was hearing was laughter. 'What are you talking about? What has Vanessa Maxwell got to do with anything?'

Vanessa Maxwell. He said her full name, as if he wasn't familiar enough to call her by her first name alone.

The shock of it was like iced water seeping through her veins.

'Are you . . . are you having an affair?' She forced the words out of her mouth.

'An affair? What are you talking about? With whom?'

Grace couldn't bring herself to say anything more.

'Grace? Grace! What's got into you?' he demanded.

She reached for her cigarettes; her hand was shaking. 'You deny it.'

'Deny what? There's nothing to deny.'

He had the power to dissolve reality. Suddenly she was falling, with nothing to hold on to.

'I think you've lost your mind,' he said coldly.

'I need to go now. It's late.'

'You could at least do me the courtesy of letting me know when you plan to return.'

'I . . . I don't know. I need time.'

'Time for what? For more ridiculous accusations?'

'This call is costing a fortune. I really must go. Goodbye.'

She hung up abruptly, managed with some difficulty to light another cigarette.

The hopelessness of her situation pressed in around her, as thick and dark as the evening shadows that filled the room.

How could she make him give up a mistress who didn't exist?

———— ❧ ————

The telephone was ringing. Grace struggled to lift her head off the pillow but it felt as though it was made of marble. And the telephone didn't sound right. It had a short, high ring; sharp and fast.

She opened her eyes. Blazing morning sunlight filled the room, blinding her.

Good God, what was that? A chandelier dangled precariously overhead. For a moment she thought it might fall. Then she remembered.

The telephone was a French telephone.

She was in Paris.

Slowly, Grace propped herself up on her elbows. She was still wearing her blouse and skirt from yesterday, now badly creased. She must've cried herself to sleep last night on top of the bedcovers.

Finally the ringing stopped.

Sinking down, she groped on the bedside table for her cigarettes. The packet was empty.

'Damn it!'

She swung her legs out, the parquet floor cold beneath her feet. She made her way to the telephone and dialled the front desk.

'Hello? Hello . . . I mean, *bonjour*, yes . . . this is Mrs Munroe. I need some aspirin, please. Yes, aspirin. And some toast and coffee. As soon as possible, please.'

Shuffling into the bathroom, Grace turned on the bathwater, then caught sight of herself in the mirror. Her eyes were swollen and bloodshot from crying, her nose red; half of her hair was standing straight up and the other lay flat, pressed against her head.

Sinking down on the side of the bath, she trailed her fingers in the warm water. Perhaps she should just go back to bed; crawl under the covers and never come out. Who would know the difference or care?

There was a knock on the door. It was too soon for room service.

Turning off the tap, Grace yanked a dressing gown over her wrinkled clothes and answered it.

'*Bonjour!*' Mallory struck a pose in the doorway. She was wearing a chic little day suit of brilliant blue wool and a new red hat, no doubt purchased for the occasion.

'Mal!' Grace blinked at her in surprise. 'My God! What are you doing here?'

Laughing, Mallory gave her a hug. 'I've been ring-ing your room for ages but you never answer your phone. You're not the only one who can get on an aeroplane, you know!' Then she stood back. 'My God, Grace. What's happened to you? Are you ill?'

The waiter delivered the aspirin and placed the large silver dining tray on a table by the window, pouring out two cups of strong hot coffee.

'Let me see if I've got this right.' Mallory had settled herself in the corner of the settee and kicked her shoes off, pulling her feet underneath her. 'So, you're saying you've inherited a flat and some stocks and shares? And you still have no idea who this woman is?'

Grace perched on the end of her bed. 'That's about it. The only one who seems to have any information about her is this Madame Zed.'

'The perfumer.' Mallory poured crème into her cup and stirred.

'Yes. Otherwise, I'm rather lost. Oh,' she frowned, suddenly remembering, 'except for these.'

She'd almost completely forgotten about the china figures. Pulling the cardboard box out from under the bed, Grace took out each of the six figures, unwrapped them and placed them in a line on the writing desk.

Mallory made a face. 'Oh dear.' She picked one up – a white-skinned shepherdess running through a field of small yellow flowers. 'Where did you get these?'

'Apparently, they were left for me by Eva d'Orsey. The concierge had them and when I visited the flat, her daughter brought them up for me in that box.'

Mallory turned the figure round. 'This woman leaves you a beautiful flat, shares of who knows what value and *these*?' She put the figure down. 'They're not even originals – they're mass-reproduced replicas. They've got no maker's mark, nothing. Of all the things you've told me, darling, that's the oddest.'

Grace poured herself a second cup of coffee. 'Perhaps they have some sentimental value.'

Mallory shrugged. 'The entire affair is quite frankly unbelievable.' She took a sip. 'But I can't wait to spend some time with you,' she smiled. 'And to see Paris again!'

'How long are you staying?'

'As long as I can. I persuaded Geoffrey that you were in dire straits and my services were required immediately and indefinitely. As far as he's concerned, that gives him free reign to stay at his club, drink too much and lose at cards, which is fine by me. And be warned: I plan to make the most of my shore leave. The hotel is arranging a room for me right now.'

Grace flopped back onto the bed, propping a stack of pillows behind her head. 'Oh, I am glad you're here, Mal.' She sighed. 'I can't tell you how strange this whole thing is. The lawyer tries to be helpful but he has no more information about her than I do. It's as if she never really existed.'

'You said she was someone's mistress?' Mallory perused the breakfast tray. She selected a piece of toast and spread it generously with butter.

'Jacques Hiver. The cosmetics giant.'

'There we go!' Mallory waved her toast. 'He probably kept her hidden, perhaps he had political ambitions. Look, do you have any cousins you could speak to? Aunts or uncles? Someone's bound to know something. Could she have been a friend of your parents or even of your grandparents?'

Grace shook her head. 'It's possible. But right now my uncle is on a lecture tour in America so there's no one else to ask. He hasn't been in touch for weeks.'

'So, any other news?' Mallory looked across at Grace significantly. 'Have you spoken to Roger?'

Grace sighed. 'If one can call it that. He simply pretends that the affair never happened, that I'm making it all up. He even has the nerve to act as if he barely knows Vanessa. I feel like Alice, tumbling down a rabbit hole!'

Mallory considered carefully. 'Did he ring you or the other way round?'

'I had a message. I rang him back.'

'Then he's noticed your absence.'

'Oh, he's noticed that I've gone. He just won't acknowledge why.'

Mallory crunched into her toast thoughtfully. 'He knows why. You can't expect a man like Roger to own up to anything. But you have the upper hand, you just need to know how to make the most of it.'

'Make the most of it?' How like Mallory to find an opportunity in even the direst marital impasse. 'He won't even speak to me about it, Mal.'

'Of course not. But that doesn't mean you don't have the upper hand. He won't want a scandal, Grace. It could ruin his career.'

'I don't think he cares about that.'

'Don't be fooled. He's full of bravado but that's all it is. And, with all due respect, darling, he's no golden boy. He needs a good reputation to survive. If you play your cards right, you could end up at an advantage.'

'What advantage? What advantage is there being in a . . . a . . .' A cuckold sounded too medieval, 'a loveless marriage' like some cheap romance novel.

Mallory took another bite of toast. 'He'll be in your debt.'

'So you're suggesting I put up with it? Regardless?'

'I'm trying to think about your best interests, Grace. Really, what other options are there?'

'I don't know. I could divorce him, couldn't I?'

'Oh my Lord! Talk about cutting your nose off to spite your face! What will that accomplish?'

Grace frowned at her. 'What are you saying – that I'm too old to remarry?'

'Of course not! But whom will you remarry? How will you meet anyone worth knowing if you're divorced? It's not as if you'll be invited to the same parties on your own. In fact, you won't be invited anywhere.' She jammed a pillow into a more comfortable position underneath her elbow. 'Face it, a woman has to be very rich indeed to change husbands the way one changes clothes and get away with it.'

Grace felt overwhelmed by Mal's harsh assessment. 'Well, I may not even want to remarry.'

'What are you going to do? Race back to Oxford and become some lonely eccentric, with ugly shoes, mad hair and a library card? You need to walk every scenario through, in detail, right to the very end. At the moment you may want to run away but will you want it in five years time? One can't simply waltz into a whole new life. Doors will close, Grace. Doors that will never reopen.' Mallory looked across at her. 'One doesn't want to act in haste.'

'I thought you hated Roger.'

'I do! The man's an ass. For Christ's sake, I'm trying to be level-headed!'

'So, you're advocating that I . . . what?'

'I'm advocating that you weigh up your options carefully. A repentant husband can be a very useful thing.'

Grace felt her throat tighten. 'I don't care about that.'

'Darling, don't be naïve.'

'Can't we talk about something else?'

Mallory sighed. 'Of course.'

They sat a moment in silence.

Finally Mallory sat up. 'Let's plan our attack for the day, shall we? I'm warning you, I intend to go shopping and drain every last penny from my current account. I suggest that you do the same.'

'Roger would kill me.'

'Roger will countersign anything you do now.'

Grace shot her a look. 'I thought we'd agreed to talk of something else.'

'Fine.' Mallory took out a small notebook from her handbag and flipped it open. 'I've got the names and addresses of several boutiques, a beauty salon that promises to reduce your waist by two inches in an hour, the furrier Josephine Wexley uses . . .' She pursed her lips, concentrating. 'But I think the only place to start is at the Galeries Lafayette,' she decided, snapping the notebook shut. 'After all, I want to break you in slowly. Now,' she stood up, brushing the crumbs off her skirt and slipping her shoes back on, 'get in the bath before I wash you myself. Your hair looks like a piece of avant-garde art and I don't mean that in a good way. I'm going to check on my room. And when I come back, I expect you to be scrubbed, scented and ready to spend.'

Grace nodded. 'Done.'

Turning to adjust her lipstick in the mirror, Mallory caught Grace's eye. 'I really do only want to help,' she said softly.

'I know. But I wish with all my heart this wasn't my life right now.'

'Fine.' Mallory turned to face her. 'Then for the next few days, it won't be. I promise, I won't bring it up again.'

<hr />

Just after breakfast, the two of them headed to Galeries Lafayette on Boulevard Haussmann. Although not a keen shopper, Grace enjoyed the comfort of being with Mallory again. And she couldn't help but be in awe of the dramatic golden-domed interior of the place; floor after floor of spiralling boutiques that sent Mallory into a series of delighted squeals as soon as they arrived.

Mallory darted from one counter to another with the focused determination of a pirate looting an exotic port, and Grace trailed behind her, carrying her ever-increasing bags. Normally, a day spent shopping would've sent her running. But for once the crowds didn't irritate her, possibly because it took real concentration for her to pick up anyone else's conversation; she felt protected by her own foreignness. And Mallory's gusto was such that she barely noticed that Grace was lagging behind. They moved with methodical speed from hats to gloves to scarves to lingerie and so on up the winding floors, Mallory debating the merits of each purchase in an ongoing conversation of her own.

'Too coy?' she asked, adjusting the veil of a tiny 'fascinator' hat, featuring a cluster of enormous black silk roses. 'Or simply bizarre?'

Before Grace could answer, Mallory replaced it with an even more extreme version featuring three rather obscene organza calla lilies. She examined her reflection. 'Don't you find that the line between something being ravishing and revolting is dangerously close? Sometimes something is so ugly, it becomes amazing. Which do you think this is?'

Grace shook her head. 'Not sure. What would you wear it with?'

'What wouldn't I wear it with!' Mallory turned to inspect her profile. 'Do you think those fuzzy yellow stamens are just the tinsiest bit suggestive?'

'Only if you have a lewd imagination.'

Mallory shot her a look. 'So I'll take that as a yes. Oh, Gracie,' she sighed. 'I'm in two minds about this one. If one's going to make a statement, one might as well have fuzzy stamens, don't you think?'

'What statement are you trying to make, Mal?'

They caught each other's eye and laughed.

'You'll see.' Mallory took the hat off. 'We'll get back to London and fuzzy stamens will be all the rage and I'll have you to blame for missing the boat!'

'I'm not stopping you. Buy two – three if you like!'

On the next floor up, they spent almost an hour in the lingerie department.

'Gracie, look.' Mallory ran her hand through the sheer silky chiffon of a delicately embroidered night-dress. 'Oh, what heaven! Geoffrey doesn't deserve it but I do.'

The saleswoman at the lingerie counter was only too pleased to help each of them to select several pairs of beautiful silk stockings, and advise them on the newest designs of cantilevered girdles and bras-sieres. 'These are essentials,' Mallory insisted, piling another two satin slips on the counter for the sales-woman to ring up.

'You said that about the gloves and the hats too.'

'And I'm right.' Mallory thrust her chin in the air. 'One cannot go about the business of being a woman without the proper equipment.'

Eventually, after they'd had a restorative lunch of salade niçoise and black coffee in the rooftop restaurant, they made it as far as the women's dress department. There they browsed slowly through the collections, in a kind of awed, reverent silence. The exaggerated full skirts, crinoline petticoats and impossibly nipped-in waists of the Paris fashions were more daringly tailored than those in England; fashioned from yards of luxurious moiré silk, faille and taffeta in bold, saturated colours. It was the kind of excessive abundance of lavish beauty that London had been missing since the war.

'I think I'm going to faint!' Mallory whispered to her, holding up a marine blue chiffon evening dress.

Gingerly, Grace felt the gauzy fabric.

It was beautiful.

Mallory's eyes began to well up. 'I have to try it on,' she sighed, shaking her head hopelessly. 'I have to try them all on!'

And with the help of a seasoned shop assistant, Mallory piled five or six dresses into a changing room.

Grace continued to walk through the racks on her own. She wished she could be like Mallory and shop with enthusiasm.

Certainly her clothes were dull and dated. What's more, she didn't even like them. Yet the wide skirts, embellished with beads and rich embroidery, all in bright peacock colours for the upcoming summer season, seemed almost garish.

Pausing, Grace looked helplessly at her reflection. It was always like this: she meant to change her wardrobe, take herself in hand, but as soon as she arrived in a shop, she lost her nerve. She was back on the bus, on her way home, before she'd so much as tried anything on.

She was just about to head back to check on Mallory when an older shop assistant spotted her wavering amidst a sea of taffeta and net. '*Comment puis-je vous aider?*' she enquired with a polite smile.

'*J'ai besoin d'une robe,*' Grace blurted out, instantly regretting that she'd spoken at all.

'*Alors!*' The woman spread her arms wide, as if to say, 'Here we are.'

'*Oui, ou je sais . . . non,*' Grace struggled, her limited French failing her, '*une robe simple . . .*'

'*Simple?*'

'*Oui,* ah, *simple, noir . . .*'

The assistant tapped her finger on her lips, looking Grace up and down. Then suddenly she smiled. '*Voilà! Avec votre sèche, je sais que la chose!*'

Grace didn't understand. She watched as the woman bustled into the back room.

After a few minutes she came out with a very sculptured, simply cut black dress, which she held up proudly. '*Elle est nouvelle. C'est Balenciaga!*'

'*Balenciaga?*' Grace had never heard of this designer.

'*C'est très nouveau, très chic!*' the woman assured her.

And indeed, the dress was unlike anything Grace had ever seen before: architectural in shape, stark, restrained. It was the polar opposite of the elaborate gowns all around her.

'May I try it on?'

'*Oui!*' the assistant agreed with a nod.

Holding the dress solemnly before her, she led Grace across the department to a fitting room on the other side. '*Attention!*' she waved to the other assistants as they passed. '*La Balenciaga!*'

Soon three or four of them were gathered in their wake.

The fitting room was easily the size of her bedroom in London and far more glamorous, with a plush chaise longue and pinkish walls. The saleswoman hung the dress on a rail and closed the fitting-room curtain with a flourish.

As soon as Grace pulled the dress over her hips, she knew this was no ordinary design. And when she stepped out of the fitting room, the staff were waiting, greeting her with sighs of appreciation and soft flutters of applause. '*C'est parfait!*' her assistant declared. '*Ce n'est pas une robe – c'est le destin!*'

'*Pardon?*' Grace flushed, shy yet delighted by all the attention.

'This is not a dress,' a younger assistant offered, 'it is destiny!'

'My God, Grace!' Mallory emerged from a neighbouring fitting room, dressed in a floaty canary-yellow ball gown, and looked Grace up and down. 'Where did you get that?' She turned to the saleswoman. 'Does it come in other colours?'

'*Non. Elle est unique.*'

'Shame.' Mallory put her hands on her hips. 'Then again, so is my friend.'

The dress did cost the most extraordinary amount of money. More money than Grace had ever spent on anything in her life. But what woman turns her back on destiny?

Exhilarated and exhausted, the girls made their way downstairs, past the accessories department, through to handbags and finally into the make-up department on their way out in search of a taxi.

Grace paused before a counter with rows of perfume bottles on display. One bottle in particular caught her eye. It was perfectly round, filled with deep amber liquid, ornamented with a gold stopper.

It was a bottle she was familiar with but had never really looked at.

Grace stopped, picked it up.

'Oh, I love that one,' said Mallory. '*My Sin*. My mother used to wear it.' She held out her arm. 'Here. Give me a squirt – for old times' sake.'

Grace sprayed a little on Mallory's wrist. 'It's strong.'

'I know. Mummy only ever wore it on special occasions.' Lifting her wrist, she sniffed. 'Used to give me a headache, now that I think of it.'

'It's one of Madame Zed's perfumes.'

Mallory looked at her, impressed. 'Really?'

There was a picture, rendered in gold leaf on the glass – an abstract image of a mother, arms out-stretched, bending to embrace her child. 'Jeanne Lanvin' was printed underneath. The two figures formed a single, seamless golden arch of affection.

A young sales girl came up. '*Puis-je vous aider madame?*'

'*Ah, oui, je pense . . .*'

'Are you English?' the girl smiled.

'Yes.' Grace pointed to the picture on the label. 'This is an unusual trademark. Do you know what it means? Where it comes from?'

'That is the symbol of Lanvin. The . . . ah,' the girl thought a moment, her brow wrinkling, 'how do you say it? Tag? You see,' she leaned closer, pointing to the delicate outline on the glass, 'Jeanne Lanvin loved her daughter, Marie-Blanche, very much. The most important person in her life. They say this trademark is from a picture of them before a ball. Now it's the symbol for Lanvin. It's very unique, wouldn't you say?'

'Yes,' Grace agreed. 'Yes, it is.'

'I was thinking of getting a new perfume,' Mallory said. 'Can you recommend something different? Something I wouldn't be able to find in London?'

'You know what I like,' the girl said, picking up another bottle – a narrow slim black rectangle with a tall golden stopper. 'This one is by Hiver, *Ce Soir*. It's an unusual scent, very compelling.'

'Tonight,' Mallory translated the name and advertising slogan. '"Some chances only come once." Oh!' She gave Grace a look. 'That sounds a bit thrilling!'

'There's nothing else like it.' The girl sprayed a little onto her own wrist and held it across for Mallory to smell. 'Here.'

Intrigued, Grace bent forward too.

The layers of fragrance that unfolded were soft at first, darkly sensual layers of wild violet, amber, cedar, and bark . . . dry mossy woodland smells which then, very gradually, stealthily, gave way to raw musky richness; they had an intensity, a slightly damp, earthy density that was mesmerizing . . . and there was something else there too . . . sharp, almost acrid, yet hauntingly familiar . . .

'I never thought I'd say this,' Mallory frowned, 'but I think there's something almost obscene about it.' She lifted the bottle to her nose and inhaled. 'Then again, it's rather more-ish, isn't it? How much is it?'

'Well, that depends,' the girl explained. 'There is the original perfume, which is the one you're holding, and then there's a newer formulation. I'm afraid the original is quite costly.'

'Why are there two formulations?' Grace asked.

'Well, you see, *Ce Soir* was first made during the war, when the Hiver factories were taken over by the Nazis. Hiver commissioned this fragrance from a private perfume house, which produced it by hand. During the occupation, it was very exclusive, almost impossible to get. Now it is the most popular fragrance Hiver sells. I have a bottle. It's very unusual, very refined.' The girl leaned in. 'They say Hiver gave in to the Germans too easily. That the war was too comfortable for him. But no one can resist this perfume. However, apparently the perfumer who made it never sold Hiver the formula. This is common, for perfumers alone to know all the ingredients. Hiver has tried to recreate it but they cannot get it right. No one wants the newer version. I cannot sell it.'

'Oh, then I must have a bottle!' Mallory opened her handbag and took out her purse.

'But you said this was their most popular fragrance.' Grace picked up the bottle. 'If Hiver can't reproduce it, then they'll have a crisis on their hands.'

'Precisely,' the girl agreed. 'When Jacques Hiver died, the company suffered. But you see, while there are many lovely perfumes, there are only a few great ones.'

'In that case, we'll both have one.' Mallory pulled a stack of French francs from her purse.

'Mal . . . where did you get all that?'

'Coutts, silly. I ordered them in advance. I've been planning this trip since the day I drove you to the airport. And I want to treat you,' she insisted. 'A woman who buys her own perfume is a sorry creature.'

'You just bought yourself a bottle.'

'I'm the exception to every rule,' she smiled. 'Especially my own.'

Grace watched as the assistant wrapped up their purchases.

'Why would someone create a perfume for a company like Hiver and then not sell them the formula?' she wondered. 'Surely it would be in their best interests financially to do so.'

'Maybe it wasn't about money,' Mallory said.

'It's a business. What other motivation could they possibly have?'

'Who knows?' Mallory tucked the bag with her latest acquisition over her arm, with all her other bags. 'Perhaps it was out of sheer spite.'

<hr />

The woman's name was Paulette and she spoke no English at all.

Not that it would have mattered. From the moment Grace and Mallory appeared in the famous Carita beauty salon on Rue du Faubourg St-Honoré for their scheduled appointments the next day, their fate was clearly out of their hands.

The salon itself was a sparkling white monastery of beauty, featuring staff of both sexes, neatly dressed in white uniforms that looked like scientists' lab coats over their suits and dresses. And indeed, the whole ethos of the salon was 'the science of beauty'; a solemn pursuit, a long way from the local hairdresser's Grace was used to. The salon not only styled hair but offered a range of beauty treatments neither of the girls had ever even heard of – including *le drainage*, a procedure involving half a day, a vast quantity of various creams and lotions and what looked like a small vacuum cleaner.

After a brief review of the schedule, the receptionist whisked Grace into one changing room and Mallory into another, where each was given a clean white gown to put over her street clothes and then introduced to her stylist. While Mallory babbled away to hers in unbroken French, Grace sat silent as the woman walked slowly around her.

Fiercely groomed and compact, Paulette regarded Grace with aloof curiosity, as if she were something between an unsightly stain on the floor and an exotic pet.

Grace, in turn, smiled nervously and laughed, then gestured to her head, doing a little mime performance meant to illustrate the way she normally liked to style her hair.

Paulette watched with a blank expression.

When Grace had finished, she opened a drawer and took out a pair of razor-sharp scissors.

'*Coupez les cheveaux.*'

Grace stared at the scissors in horror. 'Off? You mean, cut it off?'

'*Absolument.*' Paulette took down Grace's long hair from the knot on top of her head and began brushing it out. 'Off.'

It was decided.

Paulette was a singularly focused woman. After she'd cut at least six inches from Grace's hair, she applied a lather of colour and popped her under a hair dryer. Then she began filing Grace's fingernails. Without further consultation, she finished them off with a coat of deep red lacquer. Then she rinsed Grace's head, and, having towel dried it, she took her by the shoulders and placed her in front of one of the many salon mirrors.

'*Voilà!*' she declared, proudly.

Grace stared back at herself, amazed. Her hair shone, a tousled glossy black bob. Suddenly her features appeared delicate and pixieish, her skin white, her eyes clear and vividly green. It was as if someone had flipped a switch and she was illuminated, only from within.

Paulette bustled her into the next room where she wound her hair into curlers and popped her under another hair dryer. The final effect was softer, more feminine, yet still striking.

An hour and a half later, Grace met Mallory again in the salon foyer.

Mallory froze in astonishment. 'Grace! Is that you?' she gasped. 'Why, there was a sophisticated woman lurking underneath that woolly Oxford jumper this whole time!'

'Thank you, I think.' Grace laughed.

'Well,' Mallory pivoted round. '*Et moi?* What do you think? Am I not transformed?'

Mallory's hair looked like a slightly pouffy version of what Mr Hugo usually did for her.

'Wonderful,' Grace smiled.

'It's miles better, isn't it?' Mallory admired herself again in the mirror. 'I'm going to have one of those drainage treatments tomorrow. I've arranged supper for us with the Prescotts who are in Paris until next Thursday. Daphne's always whippet thin – and now I know why. I'm just going to get my coat.'

While Grace waited, she spotted the silent Paulette hovering by the door.

Digging through her handbag for a suitable tip, Grace handed her a note (either far too much or far too little) which Paulette slid into her white uniform pocket without so much as a glance. Then, taking a deep breath, Paulette placed a hand on Grace's shoulder. '*Vous ne savez pas qui vous êtes.*'

'*Pardon?*'

Paulette tried again. '*Vous êtes belle.*' Her tone was firm.

It took Grace a moment to realize it wasn't a compliment, but a reproach.

'*Comprenez-vous?*' Paulette eyed her sternly.

Grace nodded, afraid to argue.

Paulette shook her head and sighed. In her world Grace had failed to meet the responsibility of her own beauty. This was not just a waste but a sin.

'*Belle.*' She repeated the word, as a warning against future infractions.

By the time they got back to the hotel, both girls were exhausted. 'Let's meet in the lobby for a drink before supper,' Mallory suggested. 'But now I need a lie down!'

Upstairs, Grace closed her bedroom door, kicked off her shoes and lit a cigarette.

Then she reached for her French phrasebook, trying to remember exactly what Paulette had said. '*Vous ne savez pas qui vous êtes . . .*'

Tucking the cigarette into the side of her mouth, she sat down on the edge of the bed and flipped through the pages.

Vous ne savez pas qui vous êtes.

Savez . . . from *savoir . . .*

. . . to know . . .

Exhaling, Grace closed the book. She collapsed backward into the soft pillows and closed her eyes.

You don't know who you are.

***

At breakfast the next morning, Grace was drinking her coffee alone when Monsieur Tissot suddenly appeared in the dining room. He scanned the faces. She waved to him and he came over.

'You are avoiding me, Madame Munroe,' he announced, pulling out the chair opposite her. 'May I?'

She gave a little nod.

'And you have changed your hair.' He sat down. 'Is this part of your plan to elude me?'

'And good morning to you.' She signalled to the waiter to bring another cup. 'Yes, I think of you constantly and every single thing I do is born out of a desire to thwart you. Coffee?'

'Yes, please. I've been leaving messages for you which the concierge assures me he's delivered.'

'It's reassuring, isn't it? To know they take their obligations so seriously.' The waiter brought another cup and she poured him some coffee. 'Cream?'

'No, thank you.'

She passed it to him.

'They're not the only ones who take their jobs seriously, madame. One can't be too careful with heiresses roaming about the streets of Paris.'

'You read too many cheap novels, Monsieur Tissot. Your sense of the dramatic is overdeveloped.'

'Except in this novel the heroine is difficult to track down.'

'The truth is,' she explained, 'a friend of mine has joined me from London, quite unexpectedly. I've been caught up with her the past few days.'

'I'm pleased to hear it. However, I'm here with news. I've had an offer on the apartment.'

She frowned. 'But how? Have you been advertising it already?'

'No. The offer comes from an unexpected source. Madame Jacques Hiver.'

'Jacques Hiver's widow?'

He nodded. 'Her lawyers contacted me two days ago. She would like to purchase the property before it goes on the market publicly. And she's willing to pay twice its estimated value in order to complete the transaction quickly.'

'Twice its value! But why? Doesn't it strike you as in particularly poor taste to want to purchase the apartment your husband's mistress lived in?'

'I'm not sure what her interests are. However, she would like to meet you.'

'Meet me?' Grace put her cup down. 'Oh, I don't think so!'

He leaned back. 'What do you think is going to happen?'

'I don't know . . . what if she rails at me for her husband's affair?'

He looked at her quizzically. 'And why would she do that? What have you got to do with it? Her offer seems entirely above board. However, it's up to you. I felt it was important that you be aware of these developments and have time to consider them. It is, after all, a great deal of money.'

'Of course. I'm grateful, Monsieur Tissot, that you took the time to inform me. And I apologize for not keeping in touch.'

He smiled, taking another sip of coffee. 'So, what else have you been doing besides avoiding my calls? Did you make any enquiries? Or find anything else out about Madame d'Orsey?'

'Well, as a matter of fact, I have been to see the old woman who lives above the perfume shop again. She's a perfumer herself. And she knew Eva d'Orsey quite well.'

Monsieur Tissot's face turned serious. 'You shouldn't go there by yourself. She seems quite mad.'

'I've only spoken to her once.'

'Well, I should come with you next time, if there's going to be a next time. I don't like the idea of you going there on your own.'

'I can't take you everywhere I go,' she laughed.

'And why not?'

'People will talk.'

'You're in Paris. People began talking when you got off the plane.'

'I didn't wish to waste your time – you're a busy man.'

'Who's wasting whose time?' Mallory had come down to breakfast and was standing between them, looking from one to the other.

Immediately, Monsieur Tissot was on his feet, offering his hand to Mallory. 'Edouard Tissot, madame. At your service.'

'And how very lovely to meet you, Monsieur Tissot.' She smiled her most charming smile.

'This is my dear friend, Mrs Hayes,' Grace introduced them. 'Monsieur Tissot is my lawyer here in Paris, acting on behalf of Eva d'Orsey's interests,' she explained.

He shot her a look. 'And your interests as well,' he corrected her.

'And how are matters proceeding, Monsieur Tissot?' Mallory took a seat, as a waiter brought her a cup. 'Please, sit down and join us.'

But he remained standing. 'There have been several new developments. However, I don't wish to intrude upon your time together.'

'I would love to see this apartment.' Mallory looked across at Grace. 'I find it all so exciting!'

'It would be my pleasure to arrange another viewing. Let me know when it's convenient.'

Folding her napkin, Grace stood too. 'I'll walk you out.' She turned to Mallory. 'Darling, order some tea, will you? I'll be right back.'

'Think about the meeting with Madame Hiver,' Monsieur Tissot advised, as they made their way through the dining room. 'I would give it serious consideration. Twice the asking price is a great deal of money. By the way,' he glanced at her sideways, as they strolled into the front lobby, 'your new hair-style is very fetching.'

Grace felt the heat rise to her cheeks. 'Yes, but it failed to throw you off the scent. Perhaps I will have to become a redhead next.'

'You aren't going to lose me that easily.'

They'd reached the main entrance.

'I forgot,' she held out her hand, 'you're a dedicated professional. You won't rest until that flat is sold.'

He took her hand. 'That's certainly part of it.'

He gave her fingers a squeeze, then released her. 'I will be in contact when I've arranged the meeting. And I would be grateful if in future you would be so kind as to return my calls.'

With a little bow, he left.

Grace headed back into the dining room and sat down.

Mallory bit into a croissant. 'Well, he's certainly very attentive,' she said with a smile.

'He's just doing his job.'

She arched an eyebrow. 'Really?'

'So, what are your plans for today?'

'Well, I'm practically almost completely at your disposal. Only I've got a luncheon arranged with Tippi Miller who's on her way back from Nice and is only here for two nights. She's staying at the Ritz and I know she'd love to see you,' she added hopefully.

'God save me from Tippi Miller!' Grace groaned, filling her cup again. 'She's a terrible gossip. No sooner is someone's back turned than she's sticking a knife in it. What are you thinking of, Mal?'

'She rang me. Besides,' she added with a little shrug, 'everyone becomes a friend when you're in a foreign country.' She leaned forward. 'She's been up and down the French Riviera for a month and yes, she will be choking with gossip and I want to hear it all first-hand. She's already told me she only just avoided being named in a divorce suit, also that she gambled away her mother's diamonds one night and had to do unspeakable things to a Swiss banker to get them back. And apparently three very famous sisters have been sharing the same wildly handsome tennis instructor without any of them knowing, only Tippi refuses to confirm names until I see her!'

Grace shook her head. 'No, thank you. I haven't got the stomach for it. The entire place sounds like a zoo.'

'But a beautiful zoo,' Mallory sighed, 'with sun and sand and glorious sea!'

'And far too many wild animals. Be careful, Mal,' she warned. 'Don't let Tippi eat you for lunch!'

Shortly after midday, Monsieur Tissot rang; he'd managed to arrange a meeting with Yvonne Hiver, who'd requested that they meet at the apartment.

Grace decided to walk to the appointment. When she arrived in the courtyard outside the apartment, a large shiny black Daimler was already parked outside; a uniformed driver was leaning against the bonnet, smoking a cigarette as she passed by.

She'd hoped to be the first one here, to have a few moments alone in the apartment again.

The front door was propped open. Someone had been scrubbing the steps; a tin bucket and brush were pushed to one side in the hallway. Mounting the stairs, she heard voices – Monsieur Tissot and a woman; low voices, speaking French.

The door to the flat was open. Grace walked inside to find them standing in the drawing room, facing the wall of windows that overlooked the garden square below.

They turned.

Yvonne Hiver looked younger than she'd expected. Dressed in a very modern tweed sheath dress that hugged her figure, with a Persian lamb scarf, she exuded the air of a woman used to spending her days glowing brightly at the centre of her own, personal solar system. Her matching hat had a thin mesh veil which she had folded back; her hair was brushed away from her face, highlighting her excellent bone structure, and her eyes were accentuated by bold flourishes of black eyeliner. It was the kind of deceptively simple day ensemble that easily cost a fortune.

'I'm afraid,' Grace apologized as she removed her gloves, 'that I must be late.'

'Not at all.' Monsieur Tissot walked over and took her hand. 'Madame Hiver is very prompt. In fact, she was already here when I arrived.'

'The door was open downstairs,' Madame Hiver explained.

Catching Grace's eye, Monsieur Tissot smiled reassuringly. 'May I present Madame Hiver. Madame Hiver, this is Grace Munroe.'

It struck Grace that he had used her first name; as if somehow he were staking a subtle claim to her autonomy.

Yvonne Hiver took a step forward, offering her hand. Grace could see that closer up, she must be easily in her mid-forties. 'Madame Munroe, how kind of you to meet me.' Her voice was a low, rich contralto, and there was a certain bored, drawling out of her vowels; a universal characteristic of the upper classes that Grace recognized even through her heavily accented English. She shook Grace's hand. 'This is good of you,' she added.

'And a pleasure to meet you, Madame Hiver. I understand you have an interest in purchasing this flat, is that correct?' Grace was aware of sounding abrupt but found herself unexpectedly nervous, thrown by Madame Hiver's commanding self-possession.

'That's correct.'

Grace slipped her hands into her pockets. 'And may I ask why?'

'This apartment has been in my husband's family for years. Now that it is empty, I would like to restore it to the Hiver portfolio. And as I'm sure you know, property like this, in a good location, is always an excellent investment.'

'But surely not at twice its estimated value.'

Madame Hiver tilted her head slowly to one side, like an animal sizing up its prey. 'Well, perhaps we could say it's for sentimental reasons.'

'Sentimental?'

Yvonne Hiver took out a gold cigarette case. 'Do you think that's odd?' She removed a cigarette.

Monsieur Tissot leaned in to light it for her.

'*Merci*.' Madame Hiver exhaled, aiming a stream of smoke at the ceiling. 'Let us not be coy,' she suggested, looking straight at Grace. 'You may already be aware that Eva d'Orsey had an arrangement with my late husband – an agreement that spanned many years.'

'Yes.'

'Well, then,' she concluded, with a little shrug. 'We had something in common.'

Grace stared at her, speechless.

To her surprise, Yvonne Hiver laughed. 'You are very easily shocked! It's a charming quality, I assure you. But you see, I bear no ill feelings to Eva d' Orsey. She played a role, a role someone was bound to play, in my husband's life and therefore in mine too. And to her credit, she was clever with it. She kept herself to herself, didn't try to become the second wife. In short, she knew her place.'

'Her place?'

'Yes.' Again, Madame Hiver exhaled. 'Do you have children, Madame Munroe?'

'No.'

'Well, when you do, you will have a nanny. A young woman who will get the children up, dress and feed them, teach them letters and numbers and manners . . . And then when you come home, they cannot wait to see you. You take them to the park and play and they are delightful. The same is true for a mistress. She rolls up her sleeves, tends to the hard labour. She pretends this middle-aged man is fascinating, listens to his woes, massages his ego. She even goes so far as to reassure him physically. But that's all it is. Flattery. And then he returns home, refreshed, grateful . . .' She paused. '. . . repentant. One can proceed with one's own interests knowing that one's spouse is perfectly content.'

Monsieur Tissot looked at Grace.

She looked away, embarrassed. Was this how she was meant to feel about Vanessa? Is this how sophisticated people behaved?

'I seem to be in the habit of shocking you today,' Madame Hiver deduced. 'I apologize. I only wanted to illustrate to you that I appreciated her contribution. She did other things as well. During the war, she entertained all of those men who were so important to keeping our industries open.'

'You mean the Nazis?' Grace asked.

Yvonne exhaled slowly, giving her a look. 'Yes, them. It was necessary, during the occupation. A pragmatic move on our part. But still, one didn't want to dine with them. Luckily, there was always Eva. How do you think she merited such a grand apartment in the first place? And they liked that, I'm told. Being entertained by the mistress.' She was staring at Grace, observing her reactions with a cold curiosity. 'This property has a place in our family history, for good and bad. It's always been part of the Hiver property holdings. And now I wish to own it again.'

Grace turned her father's lighter round and round inside her pocket. She wasn't immune to the disdainful note in Madame Hiver's voice or the subtle insistence of her request. Madame Hiver did her best to downplay her urgency but it was there just the same.

'I appreciate your candour,' Grace said. 'Thank you for taking the time to explain. I've not yet decided exactly what I will do, however I can assure you that I will certainly consider your offer very seriously.'

Madame Hiver's face hardened. She'd obviously hoped for more. But all she said was, 'You're too kind. It means a great deal to me to be able to ensure my son inherits the traditional family estate, intact.' Then, pulling the black net veil over her face, she adjusted it beneath her chin. '*Au revoir, madame.*'

'May I escort you to your car?' Monsieur Tissot offered, opening the door.

'Of course.'

As she reached the doorway, Madame Hiver turned once more. 'All terms are negotiable. If the offer isn't quite what you'd hoped to achieve . . .'

'I can assure you, you are more than generous.'

'How right you are to consider all your options,' Madame Hiver conceded with a terse flash of teeth. 'Although I hope you realize, an offer like this cannot be available indefinitely.' And with a brisk nod of the head, she left.

Grace felt her shoulders relax as soon as Madame Hiver was gone. Suddenly her mouth was dry and she realized she'd been holding her hands in fists by her side. Walking into the kitchen, she leaned over the sink to drink handfuls of cool water from the tap. Groping for a tea towel, she turned.

Then she stopped.

Invisible fingers, like cold wind, brushed against the back of her neck, sending a shiver up her spine.

Each of the cupboards was just slightly ajar, the drawers not quite closed, the closet door off the latch, as if someone had been looking through them; someone in a hurry.

Grace went through to the drawing room, looking out of the window onto the courtyard below.

The chauffeur was climbing back in the front seat, closing the car door, turning on the engine. Then the big black Daimler turned out of the courtyard and sped away.

&

It was late in the afternoon when Grace knocked again on the narrow red door in the alleyway behind Rue Christine.

There was the sound of the dog barking and then the slow descent. The door opened a crack, a black eye appeared.

'Good afternoon, Madame Zed.'

'Good afternoon.' Madame Zed opened the door wider. 'I almost didn't recognize you – you have had your hair done!'

Grace smiled, self-conscious. 'Yes. I have.'

'Well!' Madame took her in, nodding approvingly. 'What an interesting counter-attack!'

'A counter-attack? Against what?'

'Against fate, my dear.' She stepped back and Grace came in, following her upstairs, into the drawing room.

'Are we at war with fate?'

'It's a tango, don't you find? Sometimes dramatic, sometimes quiet, but always with a few good hard slaps thrown in.' Madame Zed gestured for her to sit. 'That's what fashion is, really. A way of renegotiating the terms that life deals you. When a woman changes her hair what she's really saying to fate is, no. I refuse to be defined by those terms.' She settled into her favourite chair. 'You've obviously decided your past no longer serves you.'

'Perhaps,' Grace admitted.

'It's a good thing. A woman who no longer cares about how she looks has given up on more than fashion – she's given up on life.'

There was the high-pitched whistle of a kettle coming to the boil.

'I'm just making tea.' Madame Zed stood up. 'Would you like some?'

'Thank you, that would be lovely,' Grace said, taking off her coat.

After a few minutes, Madame came back again with a tray, setting it on the low table between them. Pouring out a cup, she handed it to Grace, then another one for herself. 'Do you take lemon or milk?' she asked, lifting a slice of lemon into her cup.

'Milk, please.'

'Paris becomes you.' Madame passed her the creamer.

'Thank you. I'm sorry to trouble you.' Grace poured in some milk. 'I know I'm disturbing you. But I still have so many questions. I wondered, you mentioned the other day about some men, who'd broken into the shop downstairs . . . in a black car?'

'Yes?'

'Did they take anything?'

'It's hard to tell. I think I disturbed them before they found what they were looking for.'

'Found what they were looking for?' Grace sat forward. 'What makes you say that?'

'They were searching through the drawers and files. Common thieves would have simply taken as much as they could grab.'

330

'Do you have any idea what they were looking for? Or who they were?'

'It's difficult to say. Though not many burglars can afford to drive to work in expensive motor cars. Your inheritance,' she looked sideways at Grace, 'does it include anything else besides the apartment?'

She'd asked her this before. 'Well, yes, there are shares.'

'But nothing else?' she pressed. 'No letters or correspondence?'

'No. Why?'

'I just wondered. It doesn't surprise me that Eva invested,' she said, sidestepping the question. 'She had a good head for business. Even when she was at her worst, she could always turn a profit.'

Grace lifted her teacup to her lips and was about to take a sip when she noticed a pungent, sour smell. The milk was off. Discreetly, she put the cup down again. 'What do you mean, "her worst"?'

Madame settled back into her chair. 'She drank too much. "There's a piece of glass digging into my brain," she used to say. "And I can't get it out."'

'I wonder if that's what killed her?'

'I wouldn't be surprised. She was one of those people who could be perfectly civilized, though – never slur or stumble, carry on fairly normally even though she was drunk most of the time. But as I said, she was always good at business. Knew how to make money.'

'I'd like to hear more about her.'

Madame took a sip. 'My memory isn't what it used to be.'

'Last time, you told me that Eva had left New York, with Lambert,' Grace prompted. 'And you and Valmont had gone to Morocco.'

Madame put her teacup down. 'Yes,' she nodded, remembering. 'We travelled for some time and lost touch with Eva entirely. But Valmont continued to grow and develop in his art. He seemed to have gained a sense of himself. We travelled around India, gathering rare absolutes. And then I became very ill.' She shifted. 'I had contracted meningitis. Eventually, we returned to Paris. I could no longer work with him and he, well, he was eager to set out on his own. Only,' she sighed, 'Andre wasn't like other people.'

'In what way?'

'He had enormous difficulty being personable. Several times I arranged for him to have an interview at some of Paris's finest perfumers but always his arrogance and pride would get in the way. He didn't mean to be awkward, he simply had no social veneer. All he cared about was work. I gathered what money I had left and invested in this building, so he could open his own business. But even working for himself, he managed to upset people. He simply couldn't get or keep customers. And he had no flair. The shop looked like a medical laboratory. In desperation, I finally sent him to the coast, to the Côte d'Azure, during the height of the season. I was still too weak to accompany him but I tried to impress upon him the importance of making connections with potential clients, of getting in with the right set of people.'

'The whole thing most likely would have been a disaster, if it weren't for Eva. She was travelling with Lambert, though now he went by the name Lamb. His debts kept him moving from place to place, assuming different identities. And like many Englishmen of his class he preferred nicknames; he called her Dorsey, which was, of course, a play on her surname. She'd grown. Filled out, I think is the expression.' She paused, recalling an image from the past; summoning it to the forefront of her mind. 'At that stage in her life, she was magnificent – there wasn't one element about her that didn't capture the erotic imagination. The way she moved, the clothes she wore. But she was the Englishman's girl. His good-luck charm. And he was a hopeless alcoholic. Everyone knew it. She'd surpassed him in every possible way. But she was trapped.'

'Trapped?' Grace leaned forward. 'In what way?'

Madame Zed reached for her cigarette holder, fitting one in, lighting it. She took a deep breath. 'The Englishman had a hold on Eva that went beyond money or loyalty. Or, for that matter, love.'

Hôtel Hermitage, Monte Carlo, 1932

'Good morning, sir.' The doorman bowed his head. 'Welcome to the Hôtel Hermitage.'

'Thank you.' Valmont walked into the enormous golden lobby, bustling with the early morning activity of Monte Carlo society. Guests were checking in and out, flowers were being delivered, and valets were scurrying to procure tickets for luggage and dinner reservations while exquisite women lounged on the rose silk settees, pulling lazily at the fingers of their white gloves and smoking gold-tipped Russian cigarettes behind the veils of their hats.

Standing back, Valmont registered their particular mixture of indolence and petulance with dread. These were the women he'd come to conquer. The moneyed, idle, voracious wives and mistresses of the Paris elite. Monte Carlo was the place to gamble, gossip and sunbathe, exchange an old lover for a newer one, and acquire next season's fashion statement a full three months before the rest of Paris. And now that he had arrived, it would also become the place to purchase yourself the rarest of fashionable distinctions, a personal perfume; one that set you apart from anyone else in the room.

At least, that was the plan.

Valmont took a deep breath and pushed his hands into his pockets, hoping his nerves didn't show.

He loathed these sort of places, almost as much as he loathed the people who frequented them. Here was a club it was almost impossible to get into, even with wealth and breeding. But for someone like him, it was equivalent to jumping off a cliff in the blind hope that he might be able to sprout wings and fly.

It was only out of desperation that he'd come at all. But his new shop in Saint-Germain, as small as it was, was already floundering; he was unable to make any inroads into the clientele he needed to secure a lasting reputation. And he was in debt. If some dramatic steps weren't taken quickly, he'd have failed before he'd even begun.

Coming to Monte Carlo was Madame Zed's idea. Despite her financial backing and considerable connections in Paris, Valmont had failed to make the right impression. Worse, it was his own fault and he knew it.

'Why must you be so rude?' Madame Zed had fretted, to no avail. 'How many times do I have to tell you? You cannot insult someone who is giving you money!'

She was right, of course.

But Valmont was quite unwilling to hide his annoyance for anyone who couldn't immediately appreciate his talent. And if he were honest, his arrogance was nothing more than a defence against the inevitable rejection he felt certain was coming his way. It was easier, if considerably less profitable, to reject clients as being too stupid to comprehend his vision. But in truth, he was terrified. He couldn't seem to find his place in this rarefied world of fashion, style and, most of all, money.

And now he was here, alone. In perhaps the most famous, shallowest pool in all the world.

The bellhop carried his bag over to the front desk and Valmont followed, overwhelmed and irritated by the noise of the cavernous marble lobby. He'd been up well into the early hours of the morning, debating whether to come or not. Although it was not a long journey, he was tired now and eager to get to his room.

He could feel the stares of the other hotel guests burning into his back as he made his way across the lobby. The cut of his suit was dated; the fabric had gone shiny in places from too much pressing and his suitcase was inexpensive and battered. Worse, he could smell the perfumes of his rivals wafting up from the pillow-strewn settees in a noxious cacophony of odours – the orange blossom of *L'Heure Bleue* battling next to the hesperidic top notes and deep jasmine heart of Coty's *Chypre*; both of them drowning in a sickening mixture of *Arpège*'s twisted adelphic cocktail clashing against the lush overstated orientalism of *Mitsouko*. To him, it was as discordant as four orchestras sitting side by side, playing warring symphonies.

It never ceased to amaze him that anyone would be so pedestrian as to wear the same scent as someone else. They might as well be appearing in public in an identical dress. And yet women did it all the time. It also baffled him that they would happily wear the same perfume every day; it was like eating the same meal, day in and day out, for breakfast, luncheon and dinner.

These creatures were idiots! He should turn round, head back to the train station now.

'May I help you?' The receptionist regarded him coolly.

'Yes. I'm Andre Valmont. I've booked with you for a fortnight.'

'Really.' He glanced at the register in front of him. 'Oh, yes, here it is. One of the smaller rooms. Without a sea view.'

Valmont's eyes narrowed. He was on the verge of saying something but just managed to hold his tongue.

'I'll be a moment while I see if your room is ready yet.'

The man left and Valmont sank into despondence, staring blankly into the middle distance. Already he was receding into the familiar, private world of his imagination.

Across the lobby, the lift doors opened and a young woman walked out. Without being entirely conscious of it, Valmont found himself staring at her. At the easy, languid way in which she crossed the floor; of the taut perfection of her figure, which, without being conspicuously on show beneath the soft folds of her white summer dress, was not entirely hidden by it either. It struck him as a calculated statement; both ambiguous and provocative without being obvious. This subtlety pleased him. Although finely boned and petite, she possessed bearing and composure; a certain reckless enjoyment of her own body. And her face was equally striking, with large feline eyes and full lips, poised on the verge of a smile, as if she were recalling a private joke. Her hair was black. It was brushed back from her face and arranged like a soft dusky halo round her head. A little straw handbag dangled from her wrist and she frowned slightly as she made her way up to the front desk.

The receptionist's face lit up when he saw her. 'Mademoiselle, how may I help?'

'Please tell me it's going to rain today, François.'

'Ah!' He smiled. (This was obviously familiar territory.) 'I regret to inform you that the forecast calls for nothing but sunshine.'

'*Relentless* sunshine,' she corrected him.

'Yes, mademoiselle, relentless sunshine.'

She leaned forward and for the first time, Valmont caught a trace of her scent; a distinctive, unique formulation that blended with the natural earthiness of her skin to create an aura of musky, acrid warmth. There was a refinement to it that literally made his mouth water.

'François, I'm longing for it to rain.'

'Yes, mademoiselle.'

'Well, who do I have to speak to about it?'

He thought a moment. 'God, mademoiselle?'

'Oh dear.' She sighed. 'God and I are not on speaking terms.'

'Mademoiselle, every day you ask me the forecast. Every day you want it to rain. Why?'

'Because all this sunshine is uncivilized, François. Great conversations cannot be had by a poolside. I long for the roll of thunder, the darkening sky, the sudden eruption of a cold refreshing shower!'

She sighed again.

'You have a unique view,' François pointed out.

'Also,' she added, 'there is nothing more morbid than being unhappy while the sun shines down on you.' She opened her handbag and took out a pair of sunglasses. 'I require rain, François. Please see what you can do.'

And with that she turned and walked away.

Both Valmont and François watched as she strolled past the doorman and out of the main entrance.

'Who is that young woman?' Valmont asked.

'Mademoiselle Dorsey.' François leaned his chin in his palm. 'She's travelling with an Englishman named Lamb. From London. I believe they have a lot of rain in London.'

'Yes. Yes, they do.'

The receptionist returned, handing a key to the porter. 'Sir, Marcel will take you to your room.'

Valmont followed the porter to the lift.

There was something familiar about Mademoiselle Dorsey. Something in her voice, in her scent.

Valmont began to wonder if it was possible to make a perfume that smelled like a warm summer pavement after a sudden rain shower; both coolly damp and heat-soaked at the same time. It was an interesting proposition. He liked the idea of two

341

opposing temperatures; two contrasting emotional states, rubbing up against one another, pulling in different directions.

They stepped inside the lift and the doors closed, sealing off the din of the lobby.

And suddenly Valmont didn't feel quite as irritable or tired anymore. His imagination was engaged, whirring on various combinations and possibilities. Without ever speaking to him directly, the girl in the lobby had posed an interesting question – one he was determined to answer.

∽∽

It was three days later when he saw her again, after dinner.

Valmont stood a moment at the entrance to the ballroom, observing.

She was sitting at a table with half a dozen other people. The ballroom was crowded. A band was playing, couples were dancing, waiters scrambled to provide a constant supply of champagne and large platters of fresh iced oysters and caviar. She was wearing a simple silver sheath cut within an inch of indecency, curving round her slender shoulders and then falling away to expose the smooth white skin of her back and just a hint of the soft round curve of her breasts. She had on no jewellery, only a pale wash of lipstick, and again the black halo of hair was arranged so that it looked almost wind tossed. Yet her dark tresses shone, framing her face with a soft, unearthly light. Next to the other women at the table, with their diamonds, heavy strands of pearls, and meticulously groomed faces and hair, she seemed feral and bewitching. The impact of her beauty lay in her confidence and her utter lack of self-awareness. In contrast, others appeared to be trying too hard, careful and staid.

She was laughing, speaking in French and English at the same time; making party hats out of the dinner napkins for the French Secretary of the Interior and his wife. A few seats over, a handsome older gentleman watched as she launched into an impromptu rendition of 'For He's a Jolly Good Fellow', which was soon echoed by the tables around them and then accompanied by the band. Valmont concluded it must be the French Secretary's birthday – at least he hoped it was.

Then he stopped one of the waiters and had a word with him, pulling a handkerchief from the breast pocket of his dinner jacket.

The waiter wove his way through the crowded room towards Mademoiselle Dorsey.

She looked up at him as he delivered the handkerchief and indicated whom it had come from.

Valmont took a cigarette case from his pocket, lit one and leaned against the portico.

He watched as she rose, walking slowly towards him, slipping easily through the crowds.

'Sir,' she stopped in front of him; her eyes were a curious shade of grey-green, 'you have given me a hanky.'

He nodded. 'Did you by any chance smell it, mademoiselle?'

She frowned a little, lifting it to her nose. Her face changed. 'Rain!'

He took another drag. 'Actually, summer rain on a warm pavement. But who's arguing?'

She inhaled again. 'You made it rain,' she said softly, delighted.

'Everyone needs a respite from the sun.'

'Yes.'

She stood, looking at him quite boldly, a half-smile on her face. 'Where are the rest of my storm clouds, monsieur?'

'In a bottle upstairs.'

'And what is the ransom for this bottle?'

'Oh, I don't know. All terms are negotiable, Eva.'

She tilted her head. 'I know you, don't I?'

'Am I so easy to forget?'

She took the cigarette gently from his fingers, inhaled, and gave it back to him. 'I would like very much to see the bottle of rain, Monsieur Valmont.'

Valmont's heart skipped a beat. 'What about your companions?'

'My friends can do very well without me.'

He held out his arm and she took it. And he felt his entire body flush with warmth at the proximity of her. Her delicious natural odour was intensified by the warm night; he could detect each layer, each nuance.

Valmont took her to his tiny room. The curtains had been left open; the blazing lights of Monte Carlo below illuminated the shadows, filling the room with a blue glow.

He reached for the light switch but she stopped him. 'No, I prefer it this way.' And without waiting for an invitation, she curled into a corner of the bed, propping the pillows around her.

He pulled over a straight-backed wooden chair and sat across from her, unsure of what to do next.

This wasn't the same little girl he'd met in New York. And beautiful women didn't frequent his bedroom in Paris. She possessed an ease and confidence he could only mimic.

Taking his cigarette case from the breast pocket of his evening jacket, he lit one with as much poise as he could muster. 'I didn't even recognize you at first. I thought, "I know that girl," and yet for ages I couldn't think how.'

She stretched out, smiling to herself. 'I'll take that

as a compliment. And what have you been doing with yourself, besides creating storm clouds for me?'

'I am a perfumer, of course.' He took another drag. 'Easily the best in Paris.'

'Of course!' She laughed. 'How could I doubt it? It's just, I wonder that I haven't heard of you?'

She struck a nerve. He straightened. 'I have my own shop now, in Saint-Germain.'

'Bravo! Is that Madame's idea?'

'Perhaps.'

'How is she? She really was the most incredible creature! And, more importantly, how is business for the best perfumer in Paris?'

'It's been a great success, actually.'

She looked round the tiny room. 'And yet you have such a refreshingly unostentatious style!'

He felt his cheeks flush and was glad of the darkness.

'Have you brought me here to seduce me?' Her voice was low and smooth.

'Of course not!'

'Really?' She sounded disappointed, leaning her cheek on her palm. 'Don't I interest you?'

'Oh, yes. I mean, I didn't mean to imply . . .' He shifted uncomfortably. 'It's just, I . . . I'm a man without much experience in these matters. I've had a business to attend to. A career to build.'

346

'So why am I here?'

He pulled himself up, re-crossed his legs. 'You . . . well, the truth is, I overheard your conversation a few days ago in the lobby and your request for rain inspired me.'

'It's not the first time you've made a perfume for me,' she reminded him.

'No, no, it isn't.'

'Are you hoping I'll buy this from you?'

Her bluntness caught him off guard. He felt transparent, made of cellophane. 'Well . . . that's not quite what I meant . . .'

She cocked her head to one side. 'Why not?'

She was so much more adept at this sort of thing than he was; so unabashed.

Instead, he reverted to what was familiar; he took the small vial of perfume from his travelling case of ingredients. 'Would you like to know how I made it?' He tried to assume an authoritative, professional tone.

'Oh, Andre!' She shook her head. 'You're not quite honest, are you? I understand that. You and I can't afford to be, can we?'

'I'm sorry?' He stared at her, her face illuminated by the city lights like a ghostly apparition.

'But you must tell me the truth. Look, I'll make a deal with you – if you're honest with me, I'll be honest with you. And believe me, there aren't many people in this world I would trust.'

He hesitated. But the temptation to confide in someone was too great.

'My shop is failing,' he blurted out. 'I don't know how to sell things – especially things that I haven't even made yet.' He sank back into his chair. 'In truth, Eva, I loathe people. I always have.'

'Go on.'

'I loathe idle chit-chat. I despise idiots. I can't bear to sit and talk to people.'

'Imagine that!'

He smiled in spite of himself; she could always see right through him. Relaxing further, he took a deep drag. 'To me the most irritating part of the business of making perfume is the client. The truth is, I can only really create my best work when I'm moved by someone, as I am by you. I own a shop but I hate customers. Isn't that mad? And now I'm here, in Monte Carlo, to do little more than prostitute myself to the very people for whom I have the least respect. I am out of money. I am out of time. And now I loathe myself for coming here at all.'

'Oh dear!' She tipped her head back, laughing. 'What a tragic tale!'

Her sarcasm popped his grandiosity like a bubble; he couldn't help but laugh too.

She spread her arms wide. 'Welcome to the brothel, my dear Andre! The difficulty is not that you must prostitute yourself but that you do it so badly. You need these people and whether they know it or not, they need *you*. But if you're going to get paid to swallow, my dear, you'd better learn not to choke.'

Shocked, he coughed and spluttered on the smoke of his cigarette.

'You need to learn the art of seduction,' she continued. 'After all, prostitutes aren't paid for ambivalence. There is only one rule – you can sell me anything as long as you adore me.'

'But I . . . I don't know anything of these matters. I don't even want to. I only know how to make perfume.'

'Yes, but I do. And let me tell you something – your arrogance is justified – you are a genius. With the smallest effort and guidance you could easily be the best perfumer in Paris.'

'Really?' He'd doubted himself; her words were like a balm to his bruised and smarting ego.

'I know all about these people. Their habits and secrets, how they think and feel, every single Achilles heel. And let me tell you, they're not complicated. You must trust me, Andre.'

'Why would you help me?'

'Because,' there was something both tender and melancholy in her tone, 'you made it rain.'

He stared at her, enthralled. 'But tell me, what are you doing here? How did you come to be so, so exquisite?'

She stood up. And with a little shake of her shoulders, her dress slipped to the floor. She was naked except for her silver sandals, which she kicked off as she came closer, stopping in front of him. She was radiant, her skin like white marble in the balmy darkness.

Reaching out, he dared to run his fingers over the smooth arch of her back. 'Eva . . .'

She held up a finger. 'Shhhh!'

Leaning forward, she kissed him. Valmont felt his body warm with the heat of an unfamiliar desire.

Pulling her to him, he closed his eyes, burying his face against her. He breathed her in – each moist hollow, every sumptuous curve – inhaling hungrily the vast, varied landscape of her skin.

～～

She sat in the alcove of the window seat, smoking by the open window.

'So, what are you doing here?' Valmont propped himself up on his elbow, jamming a pillow under his head. 'Who are you travelling with? Please say it's not your husband.'

'No, it's not my husband. It's an associate.'

'Associate?' He pulled the sheet across his bare torso. 'What does that mean?'

She exhaled. 'He's the man I work with, Lambert. Although he goes by Lamb here. The man who taught me my trade.'

Again, the word struck him as odd. 'You have a trade?' He'd assumed she was someone's lover or mistress.

'Do you doubt it?' She looked across at him, challengingly. 'You're not the only one who's come to Monte Carlo for business. This place is full of people on the make – gigolos, prostitutes, salesmen, schemers, social climbers, snobs.'

'You make it sound like a cesspool!'

She gave a little shrug. 'Just the normal entourage of the rich. As for me, I have a number of skills. But mostly I count cards.'

'Pardon?'

'I'm a professional gambler, Andre.'

'A professional gambler!' He wanted to laugh but was too stunned. 'Do people really do that?'

'People certainly gamble all the time. But no, not many have the ability to turn it into a profession.'

'But you do?'

351

She nodded. 'Does that surprise you?'

'Well, yes, frankly.'

'Good! That's the way I like it. But with Lamb, the whole thing works.'

'Really?' Already he was beginning to dislike this Lamb fellow. 'What's so special about him?'

'Well,' she yawned, arching her back, 'if I were to sit down at the tables, play all night and win, I'd probably end up dead or in jail. But with a partner, especially one like Lamb, we provide just the right amount of distraction and plausibility.'

'You're not plausible, then?'

She gave him a look. 'A woman is always conspicuous at a casino, especially if she wins. No, my job is distraction. And I do stick out, in case you hadn't noticed.'

'I had.'

'Whereas Lamb looks as though he belongs at the tables. Knows how to talk to people.'

Valmont folded his arms across his chest. 'So, how exactly does it work, this association with you and Lamb?'

'It varies. We have systems, codes in place. We play them, improvising on the feeling in the room. But the basic principle is simple. Lamb sits at the tables and plays. And drinks. Far too much. By the time I arrive he's always down a great deal of money and too intoxicated to walk let alone cheat. To anyone watching us, I seem as though I'm a pretty little fool and he's a drunkard. No one ever suspects that I'm the one who's in control. In two hands, I can recoup all his losses. In three, I can put us ahead. We rarely stay for four hands but in four . . .' She smiled. 'In four, I'd push us too far and we'd be rumbled. Win little and often, unless you want to spend every night on the road. They call me his good luck charm. No one ever thinks that a girl could be that clever.'

'And is he, Lamb . . . is he also your lover?'

She snorted, laughing. 'You make it sound so romantic!'

Valmont felt his irritation rise; already he felt unreasonably possessive. 'What does that mean?'

'It's not like that. And don't pretend to be jealous. It doesn't suit you.' Standing, she stretched her arms high above her head. 'It's a business arrangement. The truth is, he looked after me when I had nowhere to go. I owe him.'

'How much?'

'I'm sorry?'

'How much? When is your debt paid?' he demanded.

She turned away from him and stubbed her cigarette out in an ashtray. 'That seems to be a matter of debate,' she said quietly.

He watched as she crossed the room, stepping back into her evening dress and pulling it up over her hips. 'I need to get back to the tables. He'll be losing now quite heavily, which is no bad thing.'

'When will I see you?'

'I'll be around. Trust me, you won't be able to miss me.' She slipped on her sandals and picked up her evening bag. 'In the meantime, I don't want you to talk to anyone. Do you understand? No introducing yourself, no idle conversations by the pool, nothing. Allow your natural sullenness to thrive.'

'Sullenness!' He frowned. 'I'm not sullen.'

She smiled. 'But that's precisely what I want you to be.' Sitting down on the end of the bed, she stroked his leg. 'The first thing you need to understand about the wealthy and privileged is that they're like children – they only want what they can't have. If they knew you'd come to sell them something they'd demolish you before breakfast.'

'Then what am I meant to do?'

'Simple. Talk to no one. When someone comes towards you, walk the other way. These people are used to being fawned over – they not only expect it, they rely on it. If there's one thing they can't bear, it's someone who isn't paying them any attention. So, as far as they're concerned, you want nothing more than to be left alone.' She stood up. 'Allow me to do the rest. And we will need to see a tailor. Immediately.'

'No.' He shook his head firmly. 'I don't have the money for a new wardrobe.'

'Andre, the second thing you need to understand is that you're not selling perfume – you're selling yourself. The idea of you as an eccentric genius. You can't afford to blend in – you must look distinctive.' Hands on her hips. 'How can I help you if you don't take my advice?'

Valmont stared at her. She was familiar and yet completely unknown to him. 'You're not the same girl at all.'

Crossing the room, she opened the door. Light from the hallway illuminated her from behind; her face was shadowy, yet her black hair shone as though it was on fire.

'We are none of us the same girl, are we?'

The Grand Casino at Monte Carlo was a triumph of elaborate Belle Époque design, a golden canopy of gleaming gilt and elaborate flourishes. In the evening, under its vast domed ceiling, all of Monte Carlo society could be observed, including one delightful, wayward young woman and her tragically debauched English guardian.

Valmont watched from a remote seat at the bar as Eva worked her charms.

Her role at the tables was just as she had outlined. She seemed to pay little if any attention to Lamb, acting instead like a very sexy, tempestuous child. Occasionally she'd steal a sip from his drink or tap out an impatient little rhythm while he was glowering over his cards. More often she'd flirt, dance, tell rude jokes. Sometimes Lamb would beg her to be quiet or try to get her to leave. But she always ignored him. Only Valmont guessed that her well-timed interruptions were, in fact, carefully orchestrated signals.

Lamb's reputation was crucial to the success of their venture. An alcoholic of heroic proportions, he regularly lost staggering amounts of money on sloppily played hands, ensuring that few devoted gamblers ever took him seriously. But then, after everyone had long written him off, and Eva was begging him to give up, he would place some magnificent bet and the tables would turn.

Shortly afterwards, she would haul him back to the hotel in a stupor.

That night he kept his distance. But Valmont couldn't help but notice a seamless affinity between the two of them, an instinctual rhythm only he was aware of. Eva was so charming, outrageous, and seemingly oblivious of anything but herself. And

Lamb so perfectly dismissive of her; it was almost impossible to imagine that together they were pulling off these nightly coups. And never once did Eva ever do anything that betrayed her level of true concentration and focus.

When next he saw her, he complimented her on her skill.

'You're the only one who knows, Andre,' she sighed. 'But I'm bored with playing the fool. I want a new conquest. Let's make you famous, shall we?'

She was true to her word.

Over the next week, Eva found ways of taking very public notice of Valmont, planting an air of mystery around him. She whispered to her companions as soon as he appeared in the lobby or at dinner and since he was under orders to ignore everyone, he would register her with nothing more than disdain, retiring to a table in the far corner on his own.

She took him to a young tailor in the hills of Monte Carlo who made him a pair of very simply cut, clean-lined black gabardine trousers and two shirts of dark grey silk. 'If you cannot fit into the mould, then you must step out of it.' Eva smiled approvingly, running her fingers along the smooth fabric across his shoulders. The dark colours and simple silhouette made him seem taller, chicer and far more modern. 'Anyone can wear a suit, but casual clothing is the great equalizer. What I adore is that you look as if you're not taking anything too seriously. That makes everyone else appear overdressed.'

In return, he repaid her in the only way he could. 'I want to take you somewhere; to show you something miraculous.' He took her by train one day to the jasmine fields of Grasse. They travelled third class, slipping away in the early morning like two teenagers playing truant.

To Valmont, Grasse was like a sacred shrine.

'I'm going to teach you how to smell,' he told her, as soon as they got on the train. 'Most people judge scents and they avoid looking into the heart of them.' He found seats for them across from a couple of farm workers who were heading to market.

'Inhale the sweat, the dirt, the oil from their unwashed hair,' he whispered in her ear.

She shot him a look. 'Why would I want to do that?' she whispered back.

'Because this is the root of all perfume creation. To change the way we smell. It could be argued that all perfume is born out of shame; a self-consciousness of our natural odour. We want to hide it.'

'Or change it,' she murmured.

'That's right. In that way, fragrance is an aspiration. A goal. Not just a tool of seduction but of power and status. Do you realize how much the ancients used to pay for frankincense or myrrh? Whole empires were built on the trade of these commodities. You see, even then, when life was short and cruel, people wanted to smell differently. To be transported. But these coarse natural odours – filthy hair, pungent skin, unwashed women – they're the root of everything – of our disgrace and desire. That's what I meant by people judge them.'

Eva rested her head on his shoulder. 'And what are we meant to do with them, professor?'

'Observe them. Appreciate them. They have a profound energy, a rich, sexual, animal vibration all their own.'

'You make it sound like music.'

'It *is* like music. An orchestration. And sweat is like silence; the reason why the composer reaches for his pen in the first place.'

When they got out, they walked behind a mule cart down a country road that cut through two fields. 'The smell of the shit is so pure – so absolute! That animal eats nothing but rainwater, grass and hay. If it were a note, it would be played on a cello.'

Near the end of the road, the mule turned one way, they the other. 'Here we are.' Valmont took her hand. They were visiting Philippe Mul whose family had owned jasmine fields for centuries, pressing and distilling the precious flowers into the world's costliest and rarest jasmine absolute. Monsieur Mul had known Madame Zed for years. He took them on a tour of his factory, and demonstrated how the plants were gathered in specially designed baskets, crafted from chestnut splits, that easily fitted around the harvester's waist while allowing the blossoms to breathe without bruising. And then he showed them the fields.

The plants were just beginning to flower; soft, indescribably delicate white blooms, tinged with palest pink. It would be September before they would be ready to harvest but already the air was sweetly scented each time the wind rustled through them.

That day Eva and Valmont sat, for hours, with barely a word between them.

Philippe let them picnic in the groves. Afterwards, they rolled their jackets up under their heads and dozed, the sun warming their faces. The air was luxuriant with the combined fragrance of fresh sea-salt breezes, sun-baked earth and translucent, milky flowers.

'There is nothing like it,' Valmont said, turning over to look at Eva. 'You see, don't you? The world is defined by smells – not words or shapes or sounds. This is the language that makes sense, that everyone understands.'

She nodded, reluctant to fill the air with words or shapes or sounds.

In the silence of fragrance, Eva saw how ambiguous, complex stories could be told. Shifting and mutating, they blossomed, bloomed and faded; their very impermanence was incredibly moving to her. You could be laughing in public yet wear, right on the surface of your skin, a perfume ripe with longing, dripping with regret, shining with hope, all at the same time. It would fade as the day faded, vanishing into gossamer on your skin. And still it had the power to catch you unaware, piercing right through you, when you hung your dress up that night.

'This is my religion,' Valmont sighed, closing his eyes again, completely at ease for the first time in weeks.

And here is my salvation, Eva thought to herself. I will not go mad as long as there is beauty in the world and I can be near it.

They stayed until the light dimmed, and, as they stood in the shadows of the spreading twilight, the blooms exuded their richest, silkiest perfume.

***

Soon, whenever Valmont appeared, heads turned; people began to talk. A telltale hush followed in his wake. He fell into the role that Eva had assigned him with ease; chin in the air, a book tucked under his arm, he ignored everyone. And it was working.

The concierge began to greet him enthusiastically each morning, the maître d' to save a special table for him, off to one side but with an excellent view of the whole dining room; fresh flowers even appeared on his dressing table. Shortly afterwards, he was moved to a room with a sea view courtesy of the management and he extended his stay.

Then the invitations began to arrive.

'"Madame Legrand requests the pleasure of your company at afternoon tea"!' Eva read the invitation aloud, laughing as she tossed the card into the wastepaper basket.

'What are you doing?' Valmont scrambled to get it out again. 'Legrand is rich.'

'What are you doing? You cannot go. You must turn them down.'

'But this could be a client!'

'Are you willing to throw it all away? And when we're so close? Think, Andre. The wrong clients will kill you before you've begun. It's up to you to set the tone. Tea? With Madame Legrand and her lady friends? Are you mad?' She stood up, pacing the room. 'Your perfume should be the magic potion that allows the average person to transform into a god or goddess. The people you create for should be these Olympians!' She turned on him. 'Have you seen Madame Legrand?'

'No, not exactly,' he admitted.

'Well,' she folded her arms across her chest, 'Madame Legrand looks very much like Monsieur Legrand in a dress. Is that worthy of your art?'

He had to smile.

Her passion was invigorating; her vision even more comprehensive than his own. And he loved to hear her talk about his work.

'I leave it to your discretion,' he conceded.

And so Monsieur Valmont respectfully declined. Madame Legrand was in a frenzy.

To make it up to him, the very next evening Eva introduced him to her friend Yvonne Vallée, the beautiful wife of film and cabaret star Maurice Chevalier. Yvonne had a childhood fondness for violets, a romantic memory of the scent that she'd never been able to recapture. Was there any way, she begged, that Valmont might be persuaded to create something based on this simple flower?

Valmont sighed wearily, as if he couldn't imagine anything more tedious.

That very same night he set to work tempering the overwhelming sweetness of the flowers with heavy doses of damp green moss and rosewood, and sensual undertones of old leather, black earth and amber. It took several days, transforming his bathroom into a makeshift workroom; sending Eva to Grasse for supplies.

Yvonne was delighted and amazed with the result.

The perfume became her signature scent, made all the more tantalizing by the fact that Valmont would create it for no one but her.

Soon afterwards, Thelma Furness arrived, the radiant, married paramour of the Prince of Wales. At Eva's urging, Valmont conjured an exotic, narcotic creation of night-blooming jasmine, jonquil, narcissus, tuberose, sandalwood and musk . . . an operatic formulation full of decadence and lust.

She was devoted. Monte Carlo swooned over both her and her scent.

And Paris began to take note.

This was followed by discreet enquiries by the Prince of Wales himself. No matter how vehemently Valmont denied all rumours of the association, his stock skyrocketed overnight. And the French, being besotted with the sex scandals of the English, were quick to equate him with two of the world's greatest aphrodisiacs: exclusivity and illicit sexual desire.

In a very short amount of time, Eva had managed what Valmont couldn't have accomplished in years on his own. Soon he couldn't imagine making a professional decision without discussing it with her first.

In the evenings he stalked her. He didn't mean to, but night after night he found himself in the Grand Casino, watching her from a distance. And he was aware that he wasn't the only one. She had many admirers.

There was the Italian newspaper editor with the curling moustache and cigar, the businessman from Vienna, and the French cabaret star, who kept delaying his departure to Hollywood on the off chance that Mademoiselle Dorsey might return one of his many telephone calls. Valmont observed in silent mortification as notes were exchanged, expensive gifts delivered to her room, 'chance' meetings staged so that they might speak to her.

Somewhere in the background, Lamb presided over the entire drama. His demeanour was relaxed, even amused. He acted like a man in possession of an exceptional racehorse. Drink in hand, he was content to sit back and watch as she sidestepped one man, or flirted with another. But his composure alarmed Valmont. Whatever ties he had to her, they were unthreatened. And while Valmont drifted from one location to the next like a ghost haunting her wake, Lamb let her wander freely, from his room to anyone else's, without so much as the bat of an eye.

He was sure of himself.

This sureness depressed Valmont more than if she'd been wearing a gold wedding ring and pushing a perambulator.

He tried to confront her about it. 'You could have

any man here,' he pointed out, trying to present the argument as an impartial witness. 'Why do you stay with Lamb?'

'One man is very like another,' she answered vaguely.

'That's not true. He's a drunk and a third-rate gambler! He needs you much more than you need him.'

'If only that were true. He has something I want.'

'What can he have that you can't get more easily from someone else?'

Eyes dimmed, she turned away. 'It doesn't matter. You wouldn't understand.'

The conversation was over.

His questions had forced her into a private world he could sense but not penetrate.

One night, very late, he heard Lamb boasting about her in the bar. He was beyond drunk; his tie was undone, his jacket off, and he was badly in need of a shave. The sickly sweet odour of alcohol and sweat oozed from his very pores.

A racing-car driver was quizzing him. 'How is it you have ended up with the most beautiful girl in Monte Carlo? An old man like you!'

'An old man like me!' Lamb took another swig and leaned back. 'I tell you what, I'll do you a deal. You can have her for a small fee.'

'A fee? Are you mad?' The man laughed.

'No, I'm perfectly serious. Ten thousand pounds and she's yours.'

'Ten thousand pounds!' The man whistled. 'That's no small fee.'

'She's worth it.'

'But how can you sell another human being? It's impossible.'

Lamb shook his head. 'If you buy the lead, my dear man, then you can have the dog for free.'

'Dog? Lead? What is this? I don't understand.'

Lamb clapped him on the back, a little too hard. 'Unless you have the money, the rest is unimportant.'

The driver laughed awkwardly, and the conversation changed.

Valmont was incensed. He wanted to strangle him.

He was possessed by a painful, confused longing, charged with possibility. When Eva was close to him, he was satisfied, whole. But his desire to touch her was waning. Her scent was all he needed to satisfy and stimulate him. It filled his dreams, spurring him to new refinements in his art.

He formulated *Auréole Noire*, inspired by the fiery halo that seemed to burn around her that first night she visited him. It was, in fact, a variation on the theme of her own natural scent. An elaborate composition on the central aria of her smell.

Bright, icy clear and yet tender at the same time – built on the original idea of contrasting states that had inspired him with the rain. Top notes of velvety violet leaves, luxurious white flowers and light geranium, warmed to fiery depths, created from amber resins, smoky wood and smouldering dry citrus leaves. Underlying doses of ouhd and ambergris lent it a melting, shifting quality; metamorphosing from an apparition of pure light, to a burning dark core and back again. It was a scent that lacked coyness, made no concessions to charm. Like standing on the edge of a great and terrifying cliff, it was shocking, beautiful, sublime.

Something of Eva's disturbing beauty, slow-burning sensuality and razor-sharp mind was reflected in it.

And yet he doubted himself.

No other perfume smelled even remotely like it. It was too bold, unorthodox, veering from one extreme to another without any mollifying middle notes; it assaulted the senses rather than seduced them. It had an unapologetic grandeur, ancient and iconic, like the hard, symmetrical face and staring unseeing eyes of Greek gods, carved in cold white stone.

Valmont realized with a sickening sense of fear and disgust that suddenly Eva's opinion mattered more to him than his own.

No one, not even Madame Zed, had ever held such power over him.

His muse possessed him, saturated him the way water soaks into a flimsy cloth until the fabric is more liquid than solid.

He hid the perfume from her.

It was his first act of betrayal. And, his first true act of independence.

※

Then the actress Kay Waverley came to spend a fortnight by the sea.

Kay Waverley had flared into stardom seemingly from nowhere. And like many would-be sirens of the silver screen, she was tight-lipped about her origins. The studio claimed she'd been discovered working as a clerk at a Woolworth's in Missouri, backing the story up with a photo spread of her visiting one such store, surrounded by awestruck, young women in uniforms. But here in Europe there were other rumours, rumours that her past was considerably less wholesome – that in fact she'd earned her living as a highly paid prostitute before she acquired the trappings of a Hollywood starlet. But nobody knew for sure either way.

The single fact that everyone agreed on was that she'd been the lover of the German film director

Josef Wiener. He'd launched her career in the bizarre surrealist movie, *Moon Dust*, in which she'd received mixed reviews. Her one universal success had come from her portrayal of Salome in his film of the same name. But then he'd grown tired of her and replaced her with a beautiful young girl from Kentucky. (Some said that she was still a teenager at the time.) Alone and unattended, Waverley's star flickered uncertainly in the Hollywood firmament. She moved from one lover to the next, from leading men to producers to scriptwriters. There were tales of morphine addiction after she'd fallen from her horse filming *The Bandit of the West*. She was replaced.

Now she'd taken up residence in one of the sprawling pale pink villas in the hills that surrounded Monte Carlo. Apparently she needed to rest her nerves. But the sudden presence of the Italian playboy and her former co-star Enzo Gotti made it unlikely that rest was what she was getting.

She appeared at the Grand Casino late one evening, dressed in a gold silk gown, her hair twisted inside a matching turban, escorted by Gotti and a coterie of his friends. She spoke very little French and almost no Italian and as a result seemed sullen in comparison to her companions, smoking steadily, rolling her eyes when autograph seekers approached, scanning the room nervously for more when they disappeared.

It was a sweltering, humid evening. Eva arrived later, after a dance competition that she had entered with an Argentinian polo star. Lamb was doing rather well that evening without her.

Valmont was waiting at a table on his own, watching for her. From where he was seated, off to one side, he had a clear view. He saw Eva enter, pausing at the doorway, surveying the scene.

Her eyes rested on the centre craps table, where Gotti was attempting to impress his new lover by placing higher and higher bets. Eva watched as he urged her to blow on his dice for good luck; Kay Waverley, in all her golden glory, hung from his arm, distracted and bored.

There was something about Eva's face, her level of concentration, that stuck Valmont. Her energy had always been mercurial, uneasy and agitated. But right then, right there, she solidified. Her focus, on Gotti and especially on Kay Waverley, sharpened into a fixed stare. It was as if she'd suddenly spotted something she'd been searching for, for a very long time. He didn't realize it until much later, but in that brief, unguarded moment, Valmont observed a complete shift in Eva's personality. Nothing about her changed outwardly, but internally, a decision had been made. In that moment, she turned away from him, towards a separate, shadowy agenda of her own.

Eva proceeded to the blackjack table and threw an arm around Lamb's shoulder, accidentally bumping into Gotti just as he was about to throw. 'Pardon me. And who is this?' she asked, turning. 'Why, it's Adonis, throwing dice!'

Gotti laughed and gave a little bow. 'Mademoiselle.'

She bowed back. 'Say I'm forgiven. I can't bear to offend.'

'You're too kind. I'm certain you'll only improve my luck.'

'What more luck can the gods bestow on you?'

He laughed again, thrilled by her attention.

Waverley's eyes narrowed.

'But I've disturbed you,' Eva apologized. 'Go on – show your mother how it's done.'

Gotti's friends gasped, twittering to each other in Italian.

Eva pretended not to notice. '*Ah, parli italiano? Fantastico!*'

Valmont watched as she chatted away in Italian to both Gotti and his friends, before announcing to anyone who would listen that she fancied a little skinny dip before dawn.

Completely out of her depth in multilingual society, Kay Waverley was reduced to mute fury.

Some of Gotti's friends decided to race after Eva

onto the beach. Gotti, left behind, looked after her with longing.

But before she left, Eva did something Valmont had never seen her do before. She wrapped her arms around Lamb's neck and gave him half a dozen kisses.

Eva taunted and teased Lamb; everyone knew they shared a suite. But she never displayed any affection for him. Lamb laughed, shrugging her off, but even he looked a bit surprised as he waved them away, into the night.

Kay Waverley slipped her arm through Gotti's, reeling him in closer.

Then she cast a look over her shoulder at Lamb, who'd just tripled his winnings.

He was buying a round of drinks for everyone. For one shining moment, he was the most successful man in Monte Carlo; handsome, urbane, gracious.

And above that, clearly the man this little fool Dorsey adored.

Her face softened into a half-smile.

But Valmont couldn't help but notice that something in her too had suddenly sharpened; the bored distracted look was gone. She looked at Lamb several more times as the evening progressed.

He wasn't sure why, but suddenly Valmont felt uneasy.

Kay Waverley knew how to charm when she wanted to. And she'd launched a charm offensive now. She appeared, magnificent and toned, sunbathing by the hotel pool one late afternoon, even though she had a private pool of her own in her villa. Young men seemed to collect by her side, ready with drinks and conversation. She tanned quickly and easily, her delicate limbs oiled and gleaming. In the evening, she made the most of her new tan in low-cut clinging evening dresses in white or black. And suddenly the Grand Casino was her favourite haunt. Gotti had been dismissed, sent abruptly back to Rome. Instead, she began arriving alone in the evenings, late, sitting at the tables, a whisky glass in hand. In addition to her good looks, her other great natural talent was that she knew how to drink.

Kay Waverley drank like a man, matching anyone shot for shot. She became neither tipsy nor morbid; she never giggled, slurred or swayed. Instead, she eased herself into a drunk, like falling, weightless, into an old lover's arms. She had a finely honed appreciation for the irony and ridiculousness of the human condition which shot out as wry little asides. She could savour pathos without becoming pathetic;

she could intimate that she was one of the boys without sacrificing any of her sex appeal.

Men tended to look after her. She tended not to stop them.

Kay made a point of sitting next to Lamb one evening. It didn't take long before they were sharing a bottle and a joke.

Eva became visibly distraught at this new alliance. It was excruciating for Valmont to see the way she tried to drag Lamb away or interject herself between them. This was no longer an act, he was sure. Suddenly Eva circled the tables like a gadfly; hung on Lamb's arm, tried to lure him onto the dance floor or into another room.

The tension between them was palpable. One evening Valmont heard them arguing in hushed, angry whispers on the terrace before supper.

'You promised!' Eva's tone was vehement.

'I never said I was willing to go that far. Never!'

'She likes you. It will be easy.'

'And what about me? What if I don't like her?'

'Do I have to remind you how far I've gone for you?' Her voice turned vicious. 'How much I sacrificed? Don't tell me you can't remember!'

'Dorsey, don't!'

'There are only two people I hate in this world. And she's one of them!'

There was a taut silence. 'I did what was best. It was best for all concerned. Eva, please . . .'

Her voice caught. 'Don't touch me! And don't fail me! And don't ever pretend to know what is best again. I've kept my side of the bargain and it's time you kept yours.'

She ran in through the open French doors, eyes blinded with tears, past the entrance to the dining room which was filling up for the last dinner service.

When Lamb came in to supper, he looked tired and visibly shaken.

He drank more than usual that night.

Only he didn't do it alone.

Dorsey was out of her league. When a woman like Kay Waverley took you on over a man, you were done for. It was the scandal of the season and all of Monte Carlo agreed; poor little Dorsey wasn't handling it well.

One night, right in the middle of the piazza in front of the Grand Casino, she confronted Lamb as he escorted Waverley to her car.

'What do you think you're doing?' She grabbed his arm.

'Dorsey, stop it!' He pulled away. 'Go back to the hotel, for Christ's sake.'

'Not without you.'

Kay had stepped aside. She knew when to play the star and when to slip into a supporting role. 'I can make my own way.' She waved to the valet. 'After all, I don't need a babysitter.'

'I said go back to the hotel!' Lamb hissed to Eva.

Kay's silver Bentley pulled up and Kay slid into the driver's seat.

'Not without you!' Dorsey's voice had reached fever pitch. She was pathetic, clinging to him.

'Damn it! Leave me alone.' He gave her a shove.

She stumbled backward, almost falling.

'Don't! I'm warning you,' she threatened.

A small crowd was gathering, clusters of well-dressed patrons, spilling out of the casino, eager to watch the drama unfold.

'Stop making a scene.' Lamb regarded her with unveiled disdain.

Kay rolled down the window. 'Hey, sailor, can I drop you somewhere?'

'Yes,' he decided firmly, 'as a matter of fact, you can.'

Kay opened the door and moved over into the passenger seat. 'In that case, you can drive. A man's place is behind the wheel.'

Lamb climbed in and she curled up next to him, leaning her head on his shoulder. 'Maybe we should do some skinny dipping of our own. What do you think?'

She laughed as the car pulled off, making its way up the winding streets to the villa on the hillside.

And Dorsey, humiliated and sobbing, ran off alone into the dark narrow streets.

―◆◆―

'Didn't you hear? She made the most ridiculous scene last night.'

Valmont was sitting at breakfast across from the Lyonesse Sisters. Both widows in their seventies, they came to Monte Carlo every year at the same time; a permanent feature of the social hierarchy. Their father had owned the Lyon Sugar factory and so they were known by their maiden name and considerable fortune.

'She's a pretty girl.'

'A very pretty girl,' the other agreed.

'But she's out of her depth.'

'Completely.'

'Kay Waverley is a woman of the world. And so is Lord Lambert.'

'Lord?' Valmont looked up, surprised. 'I didn't know he was titled.'

'He never uses it. But we know all about him – we know his father, in fact. But young Dorsey made such a scene.' The old woman sighed, stirring an extra lump of her family's sugar into her coffee. 'And that will never do.'

'Not the way to impress a man like Lamb,' her sister surmised. 'Shouting, grabbing at him.'

'Like some sort of fishwife. Right in the middle of the courtyard.'

'I almost felt sorry for Kay. And for Lord Lambert.'

'I suppose they're in love.' Leaning forward, she lowered her voice. 'I hear he hasn't been back to the hotel yet.'

'That young girl has no mother,' the other concluded. 'A mother would have instructed her in how to handle the situation. One should never give the other woman the satisfaction.'

'It's best to simply ignore it,' her sister agreed. 'And of course to find a lover of your own.'

(They were both old campaigners and had survived many marital skirmishes in their time.)

'Yes,' the old woman chuckled, reaching for another slice of fresh brioche, 'men can only focus on one lover – either yours or theirs. And after they've made their conquest, yours becomes considerably more interesting.'

Valmont sipped his coffee too, but inside he felt lacerated by the strength of Eva's feeling for Lamb. Ever since Kay Waverley had arrived in Monte Carlo, she'd been distracted and elusive. The woman who was once his keenest advocate could barely spare him a few words. The conversation moved on, but he sat miserably.

After they'd parted company, he tried to send a message to Eva's room but was informed that Mademoiselle Dorsey had left the hotel that morning, without leaving a forwarding address.

Valmont sat on his bed, staring out at his newly acquired sea view.

She was gone. And it had never even occurred to her to let him know.

His hatred of Lamb hardened into a knife in his heart. He found himself searching the casino and bars for him, unsure of what he would do when he found him, only that it would be as violent as he was capable of making it. But with no luck.

Lamb had not emerged from the pink villa in the hills.

In fact, Valmont never saw him again.

Two days later he received a telegram from Paris.

*YOUR SHOP INTERIOR IS HIDEOUS STOP
ARE YOU PLANNING TO SELL PERFUME
OR RAW MEAT STOP*

Within the hour, he was on a train.

———✂———

It was months later that Valmont read, quite by chance, of the death of an Englishman in the South of France. The body of Viscount Charles Lamb, aka Charles Alexander Haveston Lambert, only son of the Earl of Royce, and the recipient of the British Victory Medal for his service in the Great War, was discovered early one morning reclining in a deckchair on the beach at Cap Ferrat, staring out towards the sea. The coroner concluded that he'd gone there deliberately to overdose, which he'd accomplished with a substantial amount of morphine, to which he'd been addicted ever since he'd suffered a serious leg injury in the war.

He'd just won 20,000 francs at roulette a few hours earlier. The money was nowhere to be found. Theft was ruled out when it was discovered that he'd posted a letter in the early hours of that morning, a fact that had been noted by the night receptionist at the hotel.

During the post-mortem that took place in Cap Ferrat shortly afterwards, when the medical examiner was asked if he suspected any foul play, he surprised the court by answering an unequivocal 'no'. When pressed as to what reason Lord Lambert might have had for taking his own life, he paused, looking around the crowded courtroom, before he answered.

'I'm afraid that the man known as Charles Lamb was very seriously ill, Your Honour.'

'Really?' The Coroner adjusted his glasses. 'Can you elaborate? What was the nature of his illness?'

Again, the medical examiner hesitated. Then, clearing his throat, he continued. 'Mr Lamb, or rather, Lord Lambert, suffered from an advanced case of syphilis. His liver was already inflamed, indicating hepatitis, peritonitis, and possible kidney disease. His prognosis would not have been good. And he probably suffered a great deal of pain. Further manifestations would most likely include seizure, meningitis, dementia, not to mention horrendous pains in the lower extremities and possible deformity.'

And so the case was concluded.

The money and the letter were never traced.

Lambert's family refused to collect the body or pay his outstanding bills and so the local people gave him a burial at sea as a civic kindness.

Sitting in the dining room of his Paris apartment, Valmont read the story over and over.

He thought of Eva's face the first night she'd seen Kay Waverley and the argument she'd had with Lamb on the terrace.

'She likes you. It will be easy.' Her words resounded in Valmont's head.

Without knowing why, he had the sickening feeling that Eva had manipulated the situation to her own particular ends. Had her jealous hysterics been just another deftly played con – one that even he had fallen for?

He considered asking her about it but recoiled from phrasing the questions out loud. Part of him suspected she wouldn't answer him truthfully; that in all probability she would claim complete ignorance. And he couldn't bear to have her lie to him.

Shortly afterwards, he heard through the Parisian gossip that the actress Kay Waverley no longer presided at the pink villa hidden in the hills of Monte Carlo.

Apparently there had been a minor motorcar accident in the early hours on one of the steep winding roads. The driver had emerged unscathed but Kay had been thrown forward into the windscreen, suffering damage to the right side of her face. Some said that the scars left behind from the accident never fully disappeared, despite the expertise of some of Europe's finest surgeons.

She never resurfaced in the world of films.

In fact, she ended her days, some say prematurely, in a remote house on a dairy farm in Minnesota.

Paris, Spring, 1955

Madame Zed lifted the stopper off the second bottle, marked *Auréole Noire*, and passed it to Grace.

'This is Andre's second great tribute to Eva. *Black Halo*,' she translated.

Grace held it up. The scent rose like an otherworldly incense, full of light and fire, with hypnotic lush white top notes and then a searing drop to intense woody depths. It had a volatile yet enveloping quality; unsettling and overwhelming.

'It's extraordinary,' she murmured.

'But . . .?'

'But unsteady,' Grace decided, surprised by her own assessment. 'It's not a comfortable beauty.'

'No,' Madame Zed admitted, looking at her sharply. 'You're really quite perceptive.'

Grace passed it back to her.

'You don't like it,' Madame guessed.

'I don't know why, but it makes me sad. And a

little frightened.' Grace sat back in her chair. 'It has no net.'

'I'm sorry?'

'Most things,' Grace searched for the right words, 'most things that are meant to be beautiful have a familiar structure – a beginning, middle and end – that acts like a net. You can only fall so far. This perfume doesn't have that.'

Again, Madame nodded. 'Yes. You don't know quite where you're going to end up. Personally, I admire that.'

'Do you still have the other perfume? The one that he made for her that smelled like a storm?'

'Oh, that?' She thought a moment. 'No, I've never seen it. Perhaps it developed into one of his larger accords, I'm not sure.'

Of all the scents Madame had described, that had been the most intriguing.

'Eva had an excellent eye,' Madame continued. 'She transformed his little shop. The mirrored ceiling, the silk walls . . . that was all her. The wealthy are fascinated by their reflections. "Give them something new to look at," she used to say, "even if it's the tops of their heads, and they will stare at it for hours!"'

'Was Valmont in love with her?'

'In his own way, perhaps.'

'Why didn't they marry?'

'The situation was more complex than that. Andre's real passion was always his work.'

'So,' Grace frowned, 'he wasn't in love with her?'

Madame Zed thought a moment. 'He was in love with aspects of her. Andre wasn't capable of expressing himself like other people. He dreamed in smells, he heard music in colours. In many ways I believe he was a true genius. But he was extremely protective of his way of seeing the world. The smallest thing could distract him and throw him off for days. He wanted Eva's approval but resented his dependence on her. And they argued over the direction the business should take.'

'Why?'

'Eva wanted him to create mass-produced scents as well as personal commissions. But Andre didn't believe in it. They had bitter disagreements about it.'

'Yes,' Grace conceded, 'but how can a perfumer not believe in selling perfume?'

Madame stiffened. 'He didn't believe in selling everyone the *same* perfume. She got her way in the end, though.'

'What do you mean?'

'She sold one of his formulations to Hiver during the war. She betrayed everything Andre believed in.'

Grace thought back to what the shop assistant had told them in the Galeries Lafayette: the Hiver perfume created by a small outside house during the war, a formula that couldn't be reproduced . . . 'Are you talking about *Ce Soir*?'

She nodded. 'Even the name is common.'

Grace sat forward. 'But why would she do such a thing?'

Madame Zed shook her head, her face suddenly drained of colour. 'During the occupation, Andre was arrested, taken to Drancy concentration camp. Eva got it into her head that she could persuade Hiver to use his influence with the Third Reich to have Andre released. But she needed to make it worth his while, to prove that Andre could be indispensable to Hiver's business. Only Hiver was a stupid, shallow man. He took the formula but Andre died in Dachau.'

Grace struggled to take it all in. 'And yet Eva continued to stay with Hiver after the war?'

Madame flashed her a look. 'Now you know why we didn't speak. But Eva had no willpower. By then, she was nothing more than a drunk. You see, for Andre, meeting Eva again in Monte Carlo was a turning point, the beginning of his success. But, for her, it was already too late.'

'Too late for what?'

'By the time Andre met her again she'd already been ruined. Even though she was still so young, she'd developed ways of surviving that made her hard. She and Lamb lived far beyond their means. They always had. For years, Eva had tried to put money aside but Lamb drank most of it, gambled the rest. The dresses she wore were remodelled a thousand times. The illusion they presented was just that. They stayed at the finest hotels, placed the biggest bets, knew all the right people. But at a tremendous cost. Though, I believe,' she added, 'that for all his faults, Lamb truly cared for her. In fact, I know he did.'

'What makes you say that?'

'He did for her something no one else could do.' Madame eased back into her chair. 'Love is self-serving – we do all sorts of things for our own comfort and call it love. But revenge is an intimate thing, don't you think? Would you be willing to enact another person's vengeance?'

It was a disturbing manifestation of devotion; one that seeded itself uncomfortably in Grace's imagination.

'Please don't misunderstand me,' Madame continued. 'He owed her that much. And for once in his life, he made good on his debts.'

Crawley, West London, 1928

It had been raining all week without respite. Cold, unrelenting rain, all day and night. He'd walked to the hospital from the flat they were renting. He would've liked to have taken the bus but he'd lost a great deal on the horses yesterday and money was tight. If he could just hold out until tomorrow, there was a poker game in a club in Soho he had high hopes for. And his luck might finally change.

When he arrived on the ward he was drenched, shaking the water from his raincoat the way a dog shakes out after a swim, raindrops rolling round the brim of his hat.

The nurse on duty was young; a plain, solid girl with a round, doughy face. She stared up at him with wide eyes. He looked like Douglas Fairbanks. When he spoke, it was clear he was a gentleman.

'How is she?' he asked.

'She's still recovering, sir.'

'How long until she'll be able to come home?'

'Perhaps a week. She lost a great deal of blood.'

'And the baby?'

'A girl, sir. A lovely healthy girl.'

'I see.' He frowned, staring at the floor.

The nurse had seen this reaction before. Men who'd wanted sons. But Mr Lamb seemed particularly disappointed.

'Would you like to see your daughter?' she offered brightly. As soon as they saw them, their feelings often changed.

'My daughter?' He looked up at her with surprise, as if she'd just slapped his face. Then he paused, remembering himself. 'Ah, perhaps later. I'd like to see . . . to see my wife first.'

'Certainly, sir.'

The nurse led him down to the far end of the maternity ward, bustling in front of him with a proprietorial air. She wanted to appear efficient; to impress him with her expertise.

But as it happened, he wasn't looking at her.

It was visiting hour; there were clusters of family groups gathered round several of the other women's bedsides, cooing over newborns. The new mothers had made an effort; they were sitting up, wearing bed jackets knitted in soft candy colours for just this occasion, their hair freshly combed, wearing lipstick, with proud, beaming faces. There was a celebratory, party atmosphere around them.

Lamb watched as they passed the babies from one pair of hands to another.

Eva's bed, however, was at the end of the row, nearest to the nurse's station; separated from the others. The curtain was drawn; the blind on the window pulled down, shutting out the grey sky. The nurse quietly drew back the curtain.

Eva was sleeping. Her face looked drawn and pale, her arms thin. And he was struck again by the fact that she was only a child; a girl at best.

He turned to the nurse, his voice suddenly accusatory. 'She doesn't look well.'

The girl blinked. 'As I said, she lost a lot of blood. It was a very difficult labour,' she explained.

'I want her to be taken care of,' he insisted, suddenly frightened for her. 'Properly taken care of!'

'Of course, sir. We're doing everything we can.'

He glared at her and she backed away.

Pulling up a chair by the side of the bed, he sat down. He took off his hat, turning it nervously around in his hands.

He didn't want to be here; hated that she was so fragile and small. If only he'd won yesterday . . .

Her cheeks were flushed, her hair matted from sweat. She smelled of iodine and blood. They should have given her a wash. Couldn't these people do anything right? He forced his fingers through his hair.

He would speak to them later.

Around and around he turned his hat.

Around and around and around. Outside the rain beat against the windowpane.

After a while, Eva's eyes fluttered, then opened. 'Where is she?' Her voice was raw, just above a whisper, as if she hadn't spoken in days.

'She's fine. Everything's fine.' He patted her shoulder reassuringly.

'I want to see her,' she insisted.

'And so you shall. But we have matters to discuss first. You and I have an arrangement, remember?'

She nodded weakly.

'I've looked after you, haven't I? Months, without anything in return. But it's cost me.'

Eva tried to sit up but it was too much effort. 'Have you seen her? Does she have hair? What does she look like?'

'It's cost me,' he said again, firmly.

She slumped back down. 'Yes. I know. I'll make it up to you. I'll get a job.'

He laughed, a dry, coughing sound. 'You have a job, my dear. You just haven't been able to perform it yet.'

'I know. But if I get someone to look after her . . .'

He gave her a look and her voice trailed off.

'We've spoken about this,' he reminded her. 'That wasn't the deal. You have a special talent. We can make money, big money. But we can't do it here. Not in England. We need to go abroad. And I'm not toting some baby with us, understand?'

She pressed her eyes closed, tears running down her cheeks.

He shook his head, turned his hat around and around.

He hated this; it was easier to leave a lover than to do this.

Rummaging in his coat pocket, he took out a packet of cigarettes and lit one. 'Look, I've always been straight with you, Dorsey. And now you owe me, quite a bit.'

'But it's different now. She's here now.'

He leaned in. 'How are you going to look after a baby on your own? Think about it. Once you get past the romance of it, what's it going to be like day to day? Where are you going to live? How are you going to make ends meet? Who do you think is going to hire an unmarried girl with a baby in tow?' He exhaled a long stream of smoke. 'Do you want to die in poverty and have your little girl do the same?'

'Stop it!' She turned her face away. 'It doesn't have to be that way.'

'No, it doesn't. Listen to me – I have a sister.

Lovely, accomplished. Kind. Married to a good man, a war hero. They have no children. But they do have a large house, money, and social position – something money can't buy.'

'Please!' She took his hand. 'Give me some time.'

'We haven't got time.' He shook her off. 'How do you think we've been living up till now? For God's sake! If I don't win tomorrow, we'll get kicked out – I can't even pay the rent.' He closed his eyes, took a deep breath.

'You don't have to give her up forever,' he pointed out, calmer now. 'Just until you've got yourself back on your feet. You come to Europe with me and we make some real money. The casinos there are sagging with millionaires. And when we've had enough, we come back.'

He stroked her hair, pushing it gently back from her face. 'And you, my dear, will have enough money to buy your own house with a garden, pay for good schools and beautiful frocks. You'll be a rich woman, able to give her anything she needs or wants. But nothing is free, Dorsey. You know that. Besides, she's only a baby. She won't remember who looked after her when she was tiny.'

'I will.'

'Maybe, but you owe me. I've looked after you for quite a while now.'

'What about your family? Couldn't you speak to your father?'

His face hardened. 'No. I told you, I'm dead to him and he to me. I wouldn't take anything from him even if he offered, which, believe me, he won't.'

'We . . . we could get married . . . for real.'

'Jesus! She's not even mine!'

She was being unreasonable; making it much harder than it needed to be.

He tried again. 'I'm not marrying anyone. Besides, let's not pretend, you and I. Let's do each other that small kindness.'

He stared down at the hat in his hands. 'I have an illness – a little gift from the war. I can't take a lovely young wife. At least not without risking her contamination too. And I'd rather kill myself than let it take me slowly. I made up my mind about that a long time ago.'

'Is that why—'

'Yes,' he cut her off. 'That's why you have nothing to fear from me. But let's be clear – I'm not your Prince Charming. I live by my wits, such as they are, and I intend to die that way too. Face it,' he took another drag, 'we're both in a pickle, you and I, with not a lot to offer anyone.'

She said nothing.

'Let me do this. This baby doesn't belong with

us. Not now. Let my sister help us. The child will be safe, well looked after.' He jerked his head in the direction of the nursery. 'That poor child deserves better than this, don't you think?'

'Maybe. I don't know.'

His voice softened. 'But one thing's for certain – of all the people I could drag around Europe with me, I'm glad I chose you.'

Another tear worked its way down. 'Why?'

'You're smarter than anyone I've ever known. Truth is, I'm in awe of you. Not that I believe in God, but if I did, you'd be on the list of things that proves his existence.'

It was as close to a compliment as he'd ever come.

Her head throbbed; the room was shifting, the edges around things smudging. She closed her eyes, trying to make it stop. 'It wouldn't be for long, would it?'

'No. The faster we get on with it, the shorter it will be.'

'And your sister, she'd give her back to me, wouldn't she? You'd explain it all to her?'

'I'll arrange everything.' He stood up.

She tried to sit up again but her arms felt shaky and weak. 'Where are you going?'

'Eva, trust me.' He pressed his hand to her cheek, then frowned. 'You're hot. Too hot. I'm going to speak to the doctor. I'll be back.'

She sank down once more, drifting in and out of sleep. After a while, she couldn't tell how long, the nurse came back and took her temperature; her face lined with concern. 'You have a fever, Mrs Lamb.'

'Where did . . . where did he go?'

'Your husband? He's gone, dear.'

'Gone?'

The nurse adjusted her pillows. 'I'm going to give you an injection. It will prick a bit.' She took out a needle.

'It's cold,' Eva shivered. 'I feel so cold.'

'Be still now. Don't move.' Eva winced as she injected the morphine into her arm.

'When can I see my baby?' she murmured. 'I haven't seen her yet. I want to look at her.'

'Well, just as soon as you go home, dear. She'll be there waiting for you. Here,' the nurse laid an extra blanket over her. 'You have an infection, you need to rest.'

Eva took her hand. 'But I want to see her now.'

'My dear, your husband took her. It's for the best. You don't want her to be ill too now, do you?' She gently but firmly extracted Eva's hand. 'Besides, you cannot look after the baby when you're ill. She's in good hands. Sleep now. She'll be back in your arms in no time.'

Paris, Spring, 1955

Madame Zed looked across at Grace, 'You do understand, don't you?'

Grace opened her mouth to speak but stopped. The knot tightened in her stomach, as if someone were pulling, playing tug-of-war with her insides. 'What do you mean?' she asked numbly.

Instead of answering, Madame reached over, pulled open the drawer of a small end table next to her and took out a photograph.

'Have you ever seen a picture of Eva?'

Grace shook her head.

She passed it to Grace. 'That was taken many years ago.'

It was an old black-and-white photograph, taken in a studio. The girl in the picture was very young; she had a heart-shaped face, radiant clear eyes. Her hair was a shining black helmet, her skin pale. The Cupid's bow lips were curved into a knowing half-smile. The eyes, lined in thick charcoal, looked challengingly into the very centre of the camera lens, daring it to blink before she did. A kind of sexual heat radiated from her, a sultry, defiant sophistication.

Madame Zed had taken out a silver cigarette case. 'She's beautiful, don't you think?'

Grace nodded, unable to stop staring.

This wasn't the woman she'd expected. Nothing like her at all. She tried to match the picture with Monsieur Tissot's description of a woman whose face was changed by pain; with the sharp, sophisticated perfume that lingered in the apartment.

But the girl in the photograph was so surprising in her immediacy, and so terribly young.

Madame Zed opened the silver cigarette case, took the last one. 'Here.' She passed Grace the empty case.

Grace didn't understand. 'I'm sorry?'

'Go on,' she nodded to it. 'Look.'

Slowly, Grace lifted it up. Her face reflected back at her in its smooth surface.

'Do you know why you are here, Mrs Munroe? In Paris?'

Grace struggled to see what was before her eyes.

Here was the same heart-shaped face, the same clear, grey-green eyes.

'My mother . . . my mother was Lady Catherine Maudley,' she heard herself say.

'Of course.' Madame struck a match, the flame flared to life as she lit her cigarette. 'Only, whom do people usually bequeath their property to?'

Grace swallowed hard, tears pricking at the backs of her eyes.

'My mother died in the Blitz,' she said, stupidly.

Madame Zed didn't bother to respond. Instead she got up, went to the sideboard, poured a glass of cognac, and handed it to her. 'Go on. Drink.'

The sweet amber liquid burned down the back of Grace's throat; the alcohol seeped slowly into her limbs. She took another drink, draining the glass.

Madame sat down. 'You can't have come all this way and not at least have had the thought cross your mind.'

Grace put the glass down. 'You don't absolutely know for certain . . . do you?'

She looked at Grace, not unkindly, then got up and filled the glass again.

Grace drank it, staring at the photograph yet unable to see it clearly anymore. 'How do you know?' she asked, after a while.

'You were born when Eva was just a teenager.'

Grace pressed her eyes closed. 'But *how* do you know?'

'Because, drinkers talk too much.'

The dog twitched in his sleep, whimpering a little.

A shaft of sunlight shifted, moving almost imperceptibly across the floor.

'I think I'd better go.' Grace stood up, her legs oddly shaky underneath her.

'Where?'

She stared at the old woman blankly. 'I don't know.'

Madame Zed looked up at her with those large black eyes. 'You have nowhere else to go.'

She was right.

Grace sat down again, her body leaden and numb. 'Why didn't she try to contact me?'

Madame shook her head.

'She knew where I lived and how to get in touch with me after her death!' Grace heard her voice rising, like the panic inside her. 'Why didn't she bother to do it while she was alive?'

'You're angry.'

'Why shouldn't I be angry? What is the appropriate response when you discover your entire life has been built upon a lie?'

Madame Zed looked at her but said nothing.

Grace reached for another drink of cognac. 'Why did she include me in her will?'

'Because she was connected to you. Because even despite her absence, she existed and you existed. You are a fact in each other's lives in the same way that the sea exists even if you never go to the seaside.'

Grace pushed her glass across the table. 'I'd like some more.'

'I think you've had enough.'

'You're wrong.'

Madame Zed got up and poured her a third.

Throwing her head back, she downed it in one.

'Who is my father? Lambert?' She spat the name out.

Taking a deep drag, Madame shook her head. 'No.'

'Then who?'

'I don't know his name. She never told me. Besides, I don't think it's important.'

'Oh really?' Grace laughed bitterly. 'Apparently I'm not something important!'

'Your mother—'

'My mother? Don't you dare call her that!' Grace snapped angrily, surprised by her own strength of feeling. 'You have no right to call her that! A mother is someone who is there – who stays.' The words felt strangled in her throat. 'Not someone who simply abandons you!'

Madame Zed inhaled slowly on her cigarette. 'That wasn't her intention.'

'So what happened? Did it slip her mind? I don't care who this woman is – Catherine Maudley is my real mother. Do you understand?'

Madame got up. 'I think perhaps you're right – maybe you should go back to the hotel now.'

Grace stood too; she felt unreal, as though she was floating, grounded only by her anger and rising fear. 'I'm sorry I trespassed, madame. And I'm sorry I came back. In fact, I'm sorry I came to Paris at all.'

'Allow me to help you find a taxi,' she offered, holding Grace's coat open for her; showing her to the door.

Grace yanked the belt of her coat tight round her waist and pulled on her hat. 'I want to walk.'

'I don't think that's safe.'

'I'm tired of being safe.' She opened the door and headed down the narrow stairs to the street below.

Madame Zed watched as she made her way outside. A gust of cold wind blew in, racing up to the landing, hurling itself against her like an angry, invisible fist before the door slammed shut.

Edouard Tissot's secretary had already left for the day and the office was quiet as the afternoon drew to a close. He was working late, jacket off, sleeves rolled up, papers covering his entire desk, concentrating hard on the details of a complicated settlement proposal. Then suddenly she was there, standing in the doorway.

He didn't know what made him look up; she appeared without a sound. The lights in the outer office were turned off; the sky outside had darkened to a deepening mauve. She seemed shadowy and unreal, especially the way she was standing, so quiet and still.

'Madame Munroe?' He got up. 'I didn't hear you come in. Please, sit down.' He gestured to a chair opposite him.

But she didn't move.

There was something different about her; about the hard set of her jawline, her eyes that seemed to stare past him, the flat line of her lips, drawn tight.

She shook her head, forced her fists deep into her raincoat pockets. 'I'm sorry to disturb you, Monsieur Tissot, and to come without an appointment. But I thought you should know that I'm ready now, to sign any papers you need to complete the sale of the property to Yvonne Hiver.'

'I see.' He looked at her in surprise. 'Please, won't you have a seat? And we can discuss it.'

But again, she didn't move.

'Forgive me,' he continued, trying to discern what had changed about her since this morning, 'but I was under the impression that you hadn't completely made up your mind yet.'

'Well, you have convinced me.' Her tone was

brusque and detached. 'Will it take long to draw up the papers?'

'No. I shouldn't think so . . .'

'Good. I'm eager to finish this business as quickly as possible.'

He came closer. 'I realize that women enjoy the privilege of capriciousness but this is quite sudden. Has something happened?'

She looked past him rather than at him. 'No. I want to go home. And you're right – there's no reason for me to stay here, when I already have an offer from a wealthy buyer.'

'Nothing scares me more than when a woman tells me I was right all along,' he joked.

Only she didn't laugh.

He tried again. 'Don't you even want to advertise the property? See what it's worth on the open market?'

'I'm sure it's not necessary. Madame Hiver's offer is more than generous. Will the papers take long, Monsieur Tissot?' she asked again.

'No. I can have them ready for you later tonight.'

'Fine. I'll be in all evening.'

'Madame Munroe,' he took a step closer, 'Grace . . .'

Her eyes flashed, stopping him in his tracks.

'Why don't you tell me what has happened?' he suggested.

The look on her face was fierce, almost frightened; her tone one of uncharacteristic hardness. 'Nothing has happened. I'm the same as I've always been.'

Then she left.

Gone as suddenly as she'd appeared.

<hr />

It was after nine when he had finally finished preparing the documents and later still by the time he arrived at the Hôtel Raphael. Still, he was surprised to be told by the receptionist that Madame Munroe wasn't in her room, but waiting for him in the hotel bar.

It was a Friday evening. The bar was filled with people, a jazz pianist was playing and the air was dense with smoke and laughter. He paused at the doorway, searching the crowded room for her.

She was sitting alone at one of the side tables, smoking; a whisky in front of her. And she was wearing a black dress that would've been simple if it weren't for the absolute perfection with which it framed her pale shoulders and highlighted her slender curves.

It was a garment of such modern elegance that it demanded a certain worldly sophistication from the woman who wore it. Tonight, with her deep red lipstick and wide-set, dark-lined eyes, Madame Munroe was almost unrecognizable: coolly chic, aloof. This was not the same young woman who had balked at eating an oyster or dragged him through a junk shop. However, the magnificent armour of her appearance made her seem all the more fragile to him. And as he made his way through the people towards her, he couldn't help but wonder, with a thrill of adrenalin, if this effort had been made on his behalf.

'Madame Munroe . . .' He stopped in front of her. 'You look very beautiful tonight.'

His compliment seemed not to register. She raised her eyes slowly. 'Please,' she motioned to the seat across from her.

Almost immediately a waiter appeared; she seemed to excite special attention tonight, even in this busy place. 'Would you like something to drink?'

He took off his coat, sat down. 'What are you having?'

'Scotch.'

'I'll have the same.'

She pointed to his briefcase. 'Are those the papers?'

'Yes.' He took this as a cue and got them out, passing them across the table to her.

'And where am I to sign?'

She certainly wasn't wasting any time.

He indicated the spaces at the bottom of the pages. 'I have marked the places with an X.'

She took a quick drag of her cigarette, balancing it in the ashtray. 'Do you have a pen, by any chance?'

'Would you like me to go over the terms of the agreement?' He took a pen out of his breast pocket and passed it her. 'I'd be more than happy to talk you through it.'

She scrawled her signature across the bottom of several pages. 'No, thank you.'

'Don't you even want to know how much money it is selling for?'

Again, she scribbled her signature. 'Whatever it is, it's bound to be considerably more than I had when I arrived, isn't it?' She flashed him a terse smile and handed his pen back to him. '*Voilà*, Monsieur Tissot.' She pushed the papers back across the table. 'We are done.'

The waiter arrived with his drink.

'Madame Munroe,' he began, slipping the documents back into his briefcase, 'I cannot help but feel that something has happened . . .'

'Please, Monsieur Tissot,' she took a final drag of her cigarette, stubbed it out in the ashtray as she rose, 'I want to thank you for all of your assistance here in Paris. Your services have been excellent.' She held out her hand.

He stood too, suddenly affronted. 'My services?'

'Yes. Your dedication to your profession is

admirable and I'm extremely grateful for the time you've given me. I'm aware that you've gone above and beyond to accommodate me. I want to thank you and wish you luck in the future.'

He stared at her, his face inadvertently flushing with anger. 'Are you dismissing me? Do you think my time with you was based solely upon professional courtesy?'

She stiffened, withdrew her hand. Somewhere behind the thick black mascara he could see in her eyes that he'd hit his mark. 'You wanted me to sign the papers, didn't you?'

'Yes but I . . . I was trying . . .' He stopped, thrown back on himself. 'I was simply trying to advise you, in a professional capacity, on the most reasonable course of action.'

'And so you have.' She picked up her handbag from the table. 'Your responsibilities to me are finally ended.'

She slid past him, through the busy bar.

He grabbed his briefcase and coat, heading after her into the foyer.

'I don't understand. What has happened to you?' he demanded, catching her up.

'Nothing.' She made her way down the main corridor to the lift at the end. The doors opened and she stepped inside. He got in too.

'What are you doing?'

The doors closed.

'I'm following you.'

'Why?'

Suddenly, he stopped, sniffed the air. 'Are you wearing perfume?'

'Why not? All women like perfume,' she said, matter-of-factly.

'Not you. You don't. What is that anyway?'

She kept her eyes trained straight ahead, on the lift doors. 'Something my friend bought me. From Hiver.' She gave a hard little laugh. 'Appropriate, don't you think?'

The doors opened and she got off. Again, he kept pace with her.

In the middle of the corridor she stopped, turned on him. 'What are you planning to do? Follow me to my room?'

'Why are you wearing perfume? Where did you get this dress?'

Her eyes narrowed. 'You don't like the way I look?'

'I liked the way you looked before!'

'Oh really?' She turned away, her pace quickening. 'I find that hard to believe.'

'Besides, that's not the point.'

'What is the point?' She took out her key, unlocked the door to her room.

'Something's happened and you're not telling me what it is.' He reached out, grabbed her arm.

'What difference does it make to you? Oh I know!' Suddenly she laughed. 'You think I'm broken and you want to fix me – that's right, isn't it?'

Her words stung him, but still he held fast. 'You're not yourself tonight.'

She stopped laughing. 'Now there's a concept. No, monsieur, I am most definitely not myself.' She tried to pull away but he wouldn't let her go.

'Why?'

Suddenly she stopped resisting, relaxed back against the door frame. 'You don't like the way I look?' she asked again, looking at him challengingly.

His eyes met hers. 'I always like the way you look,' he answered truthfully.

'Do you?'

He nodded, let go of her arm. 'It has little to do with what dress you're wearing, or the style of your hair.'

She moved closer, until he could feel the warmth of her breath on his cheek. 'What does it have to do with?'

'It has to do with who you are.'

He let his briefcase and coat fall to the floor. Reaching out, he took her face in his hands.

She closed her eyes. 'And who am I?'

Leaning in, he grazed his lips ever so lightly over hers. 'Surely you're the creature who's been sent to drive me mad,' he whispered.

He pulled her closer and kissed her. Her mouth was soft, tender. She yielded, responding slowly, teasingly. The smooth contours of her body softened against his. The strange perfume clung to her hair, her neck; it blended into her skin, lent her an earthy, green freshness. He kissed her harder now, running his hands down her back, along the swell of her breast, over the curve of her hips.

Then suddenly she pulled away.

He reached for her again but she stepped back; eyes now wide and frightened.

'Forgive me. I'm not myself tonight.'

Before he could respond, she had slipped inside the room and shut the door.

———✦———

'Darling, it's me!' Someone was knocking on her door. 'Let me in. It's me, Mallory.'

Opening her eyes, Grace could see the bright sunshine slicing through the break in the curtains, a beam of white light on the carpet.

Getting up, she staggered across the room, unlocking the door.

'Oh!' Mallory looked at her in surprise. 'You're not even dressed. I thought you wanted to go sightseeing. Are you all right?'

'I'm a little hungover,' Grace lied. 'I need some more sleep. Can you manage without me?'

'Of course. Can I get you anything? Some aspirin, or perhaps,' she grinned slyly, 'a pick-me-up? You know, I might be persuaded to join you.'

'No,' Grace shook her head. 'I can't bear the thought.'

'Spoilsport! I suppose I have that French lawyer to blame for getting you drunk.' She took out her gloves from her handbag. 'I'll go to Notre Dame and Montmartre but I'll save the Eiffel Tower for when you feel better, all right?'

Mallory headed off and Grace closed the door.

Somewhere around four, she awoke again. The air in the room was warm; the weather had turned almost summery. But her head hurt. There was a tenderness, like an ache, across her chest.

Feeling shaky, she rang down for something to eat – in the end deciding upon *tarte au citron* and tea. She had no real appetite but wanted something sweet.

When room service delivered her food, she found an envelope on the floor that had been slipped under the door. It contained the signed documents along with a note.

I recommend that you reconsider. Please, at least meet me before you leave.

E. Tissot

Grace left the letter on the table and pulled back the curtains.

She didn't want to talk to him today. She didn't want to talk to anyone.

She just wanted silence.

Whatever it was that she'd thought of as herself had shattered. In its wake was only emptiness. It was as if her parents had died all over again; only this time, all the memories she had were eradicated too. Suddenly every single one of them was tainted.

Eva d'Orsey hadn't given her anything.

Instead she'd taken away the only life she'd ever known.

The hollowness inside Grace deepened into a dull, senseless exhaustion.

She left the tea and tart untouched and closed the curtains.

And fell once more into a heavy, deep sleep.

———✸———

She had been dreaming.

The room was dark. It was night now.

His arms enfolded her warm skin; his jacket smelled of wet wool, as if he'd been caught in a sudden shower. 'Come to your senses.' His lips on her neck, fingers slipping through her hair. 'Come.'

Grace rolled over.

There was a knocking at the door. Not Mallory again.

But she wouldn't go away.

The knocking persisted.

Grace sat up.

It was pitch-black. She staggered across the room, fumbling with the latch.

The door opened, the glare of lights from the hallway flooding in, blinding her.

'Good God!' She stepped back, blinking. 'Roger?'

'Well it's about time,' he said. 'I'd nearly given up on you.'

'What are you doing here?'

'I wanted to see you. After all, I am your husband.' He smiled. Roger had a charming smile, one that illuminated his whole face; wrinkling his nose, crinkling the skin around his hazel eyes. 'My God!' He laughed. 'Whatever in the world have you done to your hair? Never mind – I suppose it will grow back.'

Tossing his overcoat over the back of the desk chair, he settled into the settee, took out his cigarettes.

Grace remained standing, still stunned; arms folded protectively across her chest over her white cotton nightdress.

'Come on, now!' He laughed at her sternness, tilting his head sideways. 'Are you really going to tell me you're not even a little bit pleased to see me?' He pushed his fingers through his sandy-blond hair. 'I've come all this way. Want one?' He held out a packet of Chesterfields.

'No, thank you.'

She watched as he lit one, easing back into the settee. Already he was at home. He had the talent of annexing any space he entered, claiming it for his own.

'But what are you doing here?' she asked again, holding her ground.

His eyes softened. 'I've come to bring you back to London, Grace. I've been going mad without you. The truth is, I've been stupid and selfish.' He sat forward, elbows on knees. The smoke from his cigarette wound upwards around his fair head. 'You need to know, nothing happened with Vanessa. She just happened to be in Edinburgh, at the same hotel. We saw a film together but that's all. I swear it.'

'Then why did you lie?'

'I don't know.' Sighing, he shook his head. 'I was angry, I suppose. Frightened. And she can be very sympathetic.' He looked up at her again; straight into her eyes. 'We've had such a dreadful go of it, you and I, haven't we?' he said softly. 'And I'm sorry, Gracie, but I didn't handle it very well.'

Grace opened her mouth to speak but didn't know where to begin, the words sticking in her throat. 'You . . . I don't understand . . .'

'Please, darling.' He got up. 'Forgive me. You've married a fool. But I'm *your* fool, I promise.' Wrapping his arms around her, he pulled her close.

He was so tall, she slipped in easily, just under his chin. She could feel his heart beating, smell the familiar soapy aftershave he wore. She stood very still, her cheek against his chest, until he took a step back.

He was smiling, handsome, relieved.

'God, I'm shattered! What a journey.'

Tucking his cigarette into the corner of his mouth, he lifted his case up, setting it on the luggage rack. He unsnapped the locks and took out his shaving kit.

She watched as he untied his shoelaces, slipped off his shoes, hung up his suit jacket. 'Is that the loo?'

She nodded.

Roger padded past her into the bathroom and locked the door. She could hear the water running.

Grace sat down on the side of the bed.

He was back. All the way from London.

And Vanessa . . . apparently little more than a misunderstanding. If she believed him.

It had taken all of five minutes. He'd come in, made his apology and now he was in the bathroom – *her* bathroom.

So why didn't she feel anything?

Running her hand over her forehead, Grace pressed her fingers deep into her skin. Yes, she could feel them. But why was she so numb inside?

After a while, Roger came out again.

Without saying anything, Grace turned off the light and he finished undressing in the dark. She stretched out along the far side of the bed with her back to him and he crawled in next to her.

It had been such a long time since he'd been this close; her heart pounded so loudly in her head she thought he might hear it.

But when he reached across to touch her, she moved away.

'No.'

When Grace woke up the next morning, Roger was already fully dressed, sitting at the writing desk. He was looking over some papers, his reading glasses low on his nose.

Still groggy, Grace propped herself up on her elbows. 'What time is it?'

He didn't bother to look over. 'I'm not sure.' He turned the page. 'There's a time difference, isn't there?'

Grace rubbed her eyes. 'What are you doing?'

Taking off the glasses, he turned, holding up the papers. 'Do you have any idea what a valuable share portfolio this is?'

Grace sat up, fully awake now. 'Those papers belong to me, Roger!'

'You're my wife, Grace. They belong to both of us now.'

'Why were you even looking at them?' She swung her legs out. 'Who gave you permission?'

He looked at her, his upper lip curling slightly, as if she were mad. 'They were here on the desk, for anyone to see. Besides, Mallory told me you were having difficulty with some business matters. I know how to read contracts, Grace. I do it all day long. You should have shown them to me as soon as they came in the door.'

'Mallory?' They'd been discussing her behind her back? 'What has she got to do with anything?'

'Nothing. My God, you're touchy!' He turned

round in his chair to face her. 'I rang her, all right? I wanted to know that you were safe.'

'Then why didn't you ring me?'

'Because,' he stood up, 'you weren't listening to me! Were accusing me of having an affair. What is wrong with you this morning?'

Grace turned her back on him. It felt as though her head was going to explode. He was too big, too loud; took up all the space in the room. No sooner had he arrived than he was going through her papers, telling her what to do, ringing her friends. Grabbing a dress from the wardrobe, she marched into the bathroom.

When she came out, Roger was going through the documents she'd signed with Monsieur Tissot. 'We absolutely need to have these translated properly. And I'm going to ring this Edouard Tissot and get him to meet me here this afternoon. I'm telling you, this is negligence,' he insisted, shaking his head. 'I cannot believe that you would sign anything without consulting me first, Grace. This could be a serious mistake. Have you any idea what the going rate of property is in this area? You're lucky I found them in time.'

Grace picked up her handbag and coat. Put on her hat.

Roger took off his glasses. 'Where are you going?'

'I need some fresh air.'

'You can't leave now, Grace. You need to tell me exactly what you've done here. We have to go through these. Don't you understand? This affects both of us. Who is this Eva d'Orsey, anyway?'

She opened the door. 'I don't want to talk about it. And these are my affairs, Roger. They do not concern you.'

The first place she went was to Mallory's room but there was no answer.

After scanning the dining room and terrace, Grace eventually found her sitting in one of the corner sofas in the drawing room, writing postcards.

Mallory smiled. 'Hello, stranger. Feeling better?'

Grace threw herself into one of the armchairs across from her. 'Roger is here.'

'He's *here*?' Mallory looked up, shocked. 'In Paris?'

Grace leaned in close. 'Why did you tell him about the inheritance?'

Mallory put down her pen. 'You mean you haven't?'

Grace ran her fingers over her eyes. It was as if the walls were closing in around her. Paris, where she'd felt so autonomous and free, had overnight become as suffocating as London. 'He's into all my papers now, Mal. He's ringing the lawyer, he's going to have the contracts translated.'

'Well,' she said, frowning, 'isn't that rather a good thing?'

'No, Mallory. It isn't.'

'You don't think he might be useful?'

'This is my affair,' Grace insisted. It had never struck her before how crucial it was that she figure out these questions on her own; how deeply her autonomy mattered to her.

Mallory's brow furrowed; she bit her lower lip. 'I'm sorry, Grace. I thought you were, well, out of your depth. When he rang the other night, he sounded genuinely concerned. He told me he just wanted to know that you were all right. I had no idea you hadn't told him. And I certainly didn't know that he was going to turn up. Honestly, darling,' she put her hand over Grace's, 'I just wanted to do what was best for you.'

Grace stood up. 'This isn't it.'

'How can you be sure?'

Grace looked at her. 'I . . . I don't know,' she floundered, taken aback. Mallory had hit a nerve; Grace was normally the confused one, the one floating aimlessly, stumbling in the dark.

'Well,' Mallory sighed, 'what *is* best then?'

Grace pulled her coat on. Even Mallory doubted her. 'I don't know.'

'Where are you going?' Mallory got up too.

'I need to be alone.'

'Wait!' Mallory took her arm. 'Did Roger apologize? Tell me, what did he say?'

Mallory's face was so intent.

Grace stared at her, trying to yank her mind back into focus. But it wouldn't go. For some reason the whole question of Roger, of what he said or did, didn't matter as much as something else – something she couldn't quite define. It hovered just out of reach of her awareness, like a shadow.

Mallory was waiting. Grace's brain spun. She could hardly remember the details of last night's conversation; only that Roger had arrived, swallowed up all the air, taken up all the space. And after months of wishing he would touch her, now she was the one pushing him away.

In contrast, the guilty memory of Edouard Tissot's mouth on hers ricocheted through her entire body.

'I don't know. I'm not sure . . . I suppose so.' Her voice was flat, lifeless. 'He said everything I wanted to hear. Told me it was all . . . all a lie. Only, now I don't want to hear it anymore.'

———— ✺ ————

She was sitting in the park across the street, with her back to the playground, looking out across the river. Her dog, the ageing terrier with his watery eyes and moulting fur, was crouched in a neat little ball underneath the bench, hiding from the screaming children.

It was easy to spot her – the long black coat, the wool felt turban-style hat. Even from behind, her stiff bearing gave her an imperious air.

Grace didn't want to be here; with all her heart she didn't want to speak to Madame Zed ever again. But here she was, just the same.

When she first left the hotel, she'd gone to the Louvre. It was so enormous; her plan was to lose herself in the miles of galleries. Spend the whole day or at least until her head quietened down. But no sooner had she gone inside than the sheer scale of the palace overwhelmed her. The pale marble walls and high columns echoed with voices chattering in half a dozen languages; the incredible opulence of the gilded walls and ceiling of the Apollo Gallery dazzled too brightly; all around her on the canvases, bodies writhed, wars raged, heroic actions prevailed. The grandeur jarred rather than soothed.

So she left; wandered the streets, bought a coffee she didn't drink. Walking into a bookshop, she stood, staring, unseeing, at the titles on the shelves.

A gentleman in glasses approached. '*Comment puis-je vous aider?*'

'*Pardon?*'

'*Comment puis-je vous aider?*' he repeated slowly.

It took Grace a moment to realize she was staring

at a row of anatomy journals; this was an academic bookshop.

'Non. Non, merci.'

Soon it became clear that no place would offer the refuge she sought. Her mind stumbled and careered, tripping and falling again and again into the same unanswerable voids. One moment the taste, feel and smell of Edouard Tissot seemed to have taken over her body and then, equally as intense, the horrendous truth blinded her – that she could no longer trust herself; that everything she thought she was, was a lie.

Now she was back, on the Left Bank. Searching for the person who had cracked her life open like an egg.

Grace stopped in front of the bench. Hands in her pockets, she gripped her father's old lighter, holding it tightly in the palm of her hand. 'You must really hate me.'

Madame Zed looked up at her, surprised. Then, taking in Grace's expression and demeanour, she shook her head. 'No, I don't hate you. I don't even know you.' Her lips hardened into a thin, taut line. 'But I loathed her.'

Grace stared at her in shock. 'Why?'

'Why not?' she shot back, her black eyes fierce. 'He was mine. I discovered him, I trained him! My money bought him the business. He was my whole world – the child I never bore, the husband I never married, the companion I never found. And then she arrived, out of nowhere!' She leaned forward. 'Do you know what was so devastating about her? She truly had a unique talent. She knew how to catch the flavour of the times, how to distil it into the perfect atmosphere. She was good at it. And more than anyone else, she knew how to make him listen.' She gripped the terrier's lead tightly, winding it round her boney hand. 'When I spoke, my voice disappeared like the wind. Eva knew how to bring out the best in him. When she made a suggestion, he took note. It was obviously right. Do you realize how galling that was? I was reduced to an onlooker – an antiquity from another age.' She stared out across the choppy grey water for some time. When she spoke again, she sounded empty, hollow. 'Even when she left, he'd become so cocksure, so indepen-dent, he didn't need me anymore.'

Grace shook her head. 'That's not even true! What about the correspondence I found? The letter with those strange accords you were creating with him – wet wool, hair and so on?'

Madame wound the lead even tighter. 'That wasn't Valmont.'

'Then who was it?' she demanded. 'Who else would want your help to create a perfume?'

'Who indeed.' She turned, locking Grace in with her unfathomable black gaze. 'She only made one formula. I cannot believe it, even to this day. To have such success with one's first real attempt.' She shook her head, laughing bitterly. 'Unheard of!'

Grace sat down on the edge of the bench. 'What are you talking about?'

'The formula she sold Hiver – Eva created it.'

'But you told me she'd betrayed Valmont! That it was his!'

'It had his name on it. But no. She'd been working on it for a while, on her own. It was a private obsession.'

'How could you do that?' She stared at her in dismay. 'Did you lie about anything else?'

'Some day you will have a nemesis,' Madame warned bitterly. 'It's not easy, you know. Someone who has the ability to do everything you wish you could, but with greater ease, style, success.'

Grace folded her arms across her chest. 'I already have a nemesis, thank you.'

'You're too young to understand what it's like to be dismissed from someone's life – someone you love.'

Grace glowered at her. 'I could write a book about it.'

They sat a while.

Then Madame Zed spoke again. 'I've known her so many years, hated her for so long, she's like a part of me. A limb. When you told me she had died, I actually felt bereft. Sometimes I wonder if we don't hold our hatreds closer than our loves. Then you, of all people, came to me for answers.'

'And you saw the chance to get your own back.'

'No, that wasn't my intention at all.' She turned on Grace, suddenly indignant. 'Do you think I want to be petty? That I'm not repulsed by my own jealousy and resentment? I wanted to be fair.'

'But you weren't.'

'No, no I wasn't,' she agreed. For a while, she sat very still. 'I lost my ability,' she said at last.

Grace shook her head. 'I don't know what you mean.'

'In India I contracted meningitis. I never fully recovered. Over time, it eroded my sense of smell.'

'But what about the perfumes you showed me . . .'

'They were recounted from memory. But I can no longer make anything. I became useless.'

Grace thought back to the spoiled milk, the burning supper.

'It's true that I should not have agreed to talk to you.' Madame admitted. 'But in the end, I think Eva and I had more in common than I realized. She lost what mattered most to her too.'

'Lost!' Grace shook her head in disbelief. 'You make it sound as though I was misplaced.'

'Don't you want to know where you came from?'

'Is that how you justify it to yourself? That you're helping me? Explaining to me how my entire life is a fraud?'

Madame Zed kept her eyes trained on the ground between her feet. Deep creases cut across her brow. 'No. I can't justify my actions. I suppose I did want you to hate her,' she said quietly.

'Well, you've succeeded. And all it's done is tear me to pieces.' Against her will, there were tears. 'Made me think less of the entire human race.'

'Well, now. We can't have that.'

Madame Zed rose, the little terrier scurrying to his feet too. The afternoon was clouding over, the wind gathering strength. Gusts battered against her thin frame, threatening to topple her. 'Come with me.'

'Why?' Grace looked up at her. 'Why would I ever come with you again?'

Even when she was wrong, Madame managed a superior tone. 'Because I have one last perfume to show you.'

⁂

Madame Zed picked up the simple chemist's vial with the peeling label. But before she opened it, she said, 'Let me tell you what happened.'

'You've already lied to me once. Why should I believe what you say?'

'Why don't you hear what I have to say first?' she countered, evenly.

'Fine.'

Madame Zed sat down and Grace took a seat opposite her.

'When Eva was just a young girl, working as a maid in New York, she became pregnant,' Madame began. 'Charles Lambert, or Lamb as he was known, brought her with him to England. But it was agreed between them that Eva would pay for her fare and Lamb's protection by working with him, after the baby was born, in the large gambling casinos of Europe. That's what he was relying on and why he agreed to help her. She had a rare, extremely rare, gift for numbers.'

Grace was unimpressed. 'You've already told me that.'

Madame Zed took her rudeness in her stride.

'Eva was fifteen, maybe sixteen when you were born,' she went on, 'without friends or family, in a strange country. Lambert convinced her that he should take the child to live with his sister, Catherine. That she would be able to look after you better than anyone else. Catherine was married to a man named Maudley, a soldier who'd been badly injured in France. They never thought they would have children. So when Lambert came to them one day with the baby of an unmarried young girl, it seemed like a godsend.'

Grace's heart speeded up. 'You're talking about my parents.'

Madame Zed nodded.

A memory flashed into Grace's mind; her mother's lips pressed to her forehead as she tucked her into bed at night. 'Goodnight, my darling girl.'

Instinctively she touched her fingers to her brow.

'Eva didn't want to let you go,' Madame continued. 'But Lambert insisted. He promised her that when she'd repaid her debt, he would write to his sister and arrange a meeting; that Eva would be able to have you back. Time passed. Eva did everything Lambert asked of her. But it was never enough. He was a raging alcoholic. Even her skill couldn't prevent him from digging them deeper and deeper into debt.'

'What was meant to be a temporary solution became a permanent one. Lambert kept his sister's name and address from Eva. He said she would only ruin things if she tried to contact her on her own, but in truth it gave him power over Eva. However, the night he took his life, Lambert wrote to her, finally giving her the details. He also confessed that his attempts at negotiating the child away from his sister had failed – Catherine had become too attached to the little girl. She wasn't prepared to give her up without a battle. You see, Lambert had given his sister not just the child but the birth certificate too. Eva had no proof that you were hers.' Madame looked across at her. 'But Eva refused to give up.'

Grace felt her insides twist and knot. 'Go on.'

'Catherine and her husband didn't live in the main household of her father's estate. Instead, they chose one of the smaller private houses on the grounds. They didn't have much in the way of help. Then one summer,' Madame continued, 'Catherine Maudley began writing a book. They decided to hire a nanny. In fact, the girl they employed was initially taken on as a housemaid and cook. She'd appeared quite out of the blue one spring, asking the village pastor if he would help her find a position. But her devotion to the little girl was so instant and touching, that in addition to cooking and cleaning for the Maudleys, she gradually assumed greater responsibilities, taking charge of the child's entertainment and care while her mother worked. The girl Catherine Maudley hired was French. She was called Céline.'

Grace felt the bottom of her stomach disappear.

The name triggered something. Out of the dark shadows in her memory, a face emerged.

'Lena,' she murmured.

The crack opened wide, images tumbling to the forefront of her consciousness.

Lena had been small, with dark brown hair and a soft, pleasing voice. And for a time, she'd been everywhere, in the kitchen baking, out on the lawn hanging up the washing, up on the landing calling her into her bath . . .

'Lena! Lena!' Grace could remember the feeling of her name in her mouth, on her tongue; running in through the back door of the house, calling out, 'Lena!' She wasn't so much a nanny as a playmate, a constant conspirator in fun. 'Lena!'

And she'd smelled of something familiar, something so natural, so elemental that forever afterwards and for reasons she could never quite place, Grace would associate the sudden drop in temperature, the darkening of the sky and the low growl of thunder, with peace and comfort.

She'd smelled of rain.

West Challow, Oxfordshire, England, 1935

It was an unusually warm afternoon in early March.

Grace had been playing in the back garden with the dog, Fry.

The back door to the kitchen was propped open. The smell of roasting chicken, rich and savoury, wafted out into the garden, making her mouth water, drawing her in.

Grace walked into the kitchen. Everything was clean, organized; pots boiled on the stove, the floor was freshly scrubbed; it felt good, right.

Lena was sitting at the kitchen table in her apron, with a pen and paper. Her head was bent down.

'What are you doing?'

'I'm writing a letter, darling,' Lena answered, without looking up. But Grace knew that even ordinary things became special with Lena.

'May I watch?' Grace asked.

Lena looked up at her, smiled. 'Watch me write a letter?'

Grace nodded.

Then she dared to ask something she would never have asked of her mother; had never asked of anyone before. 'May I sit on your lap, please?'

Lena's smile widened. 'Of course!'

Pushing her chair back, Lena held out her arms and Grace climbed onto her lap. She leaned her head against Lena's chest, could feel her heart beating softly underneath her dress. She smelled so different from anyone else in the world; it was a fresh, earthy smell, a smell that promised safety. 'Who are you writing to?'

Lena smoothed Grace's hair down, kissed her forehead. 'A friend of mine. In Paris.'

'Is he your husband?'

'No. I don't have a husband.'

'Why not?'

'Oh, sometimes that's just the way things work out.'

'Yes,' Grace agreed solemnly, although she didn't really understand. 'I suppose so.' She snuggled deeper. 'Where's Mummy?'

'She's not home yet. Now, you must be quiet or I shall not be able to write.'

'But she will be home soon?' (In truth, Grace didn't care when her mother came back. She just wanted to stay on Lena's lap. But she'd never done it before; didn't know what was expected. So she talked about what she always talked about, which was her mother, so that Lena would let her stay.)

'Yes, she will be home soon. And then there's roast chicken for supper and you shall have the wishbone. What do you think of that?'

Grace smiled, looking up at Lena, hoping she would kiss her forehead again. 'I shall wish a husband for you,' she promised, tugging gently at Lena's long hair.

Lena picked up the pen, pausing a moment, her brow creasing. Finally, she began.

Dear Andre,

Please forgive me for not writing sooner. I know we parted on poor terms, for which I am truly sorry. I should not have left so suddenly. As you can tell from the postmark, I have gone to England after all. I know you believe my actions are folly, however, I have met with success. I have been hired as a cook and housemaid in the very same home where my darling one lives. She is with me now, in fact, on my knee as I write.

At first she was shy. You can imagine how difficult it was not to gather her up in my arms and hold her close, but soon her courage grew. After a week, we were fast friends. And she is so clever and delightful!

If you could see me now, I know you would understand. I finally feel as if I can walk with my head held high and I am happy – yes, even scrubbing dishes and sweeping floors! My only regret is that you and I . . .

Lena stopped again. Her frown deepened.

Then she folded the letter in half and slipped it into her apron pocket. 'I will finish this later. Come on, darling. What shall we do now?'

Grace shrugged, snuggling in closer to her chest. Everything Lena did was fascinating to Grace.

She brought order and peace; called her 'darling' and 'dear'. Grace liked to follow her around and see what she was up to next. Sometimes she would find her changing the bed sheets or dusting; one day she'd discovered Lena outside with one of the hallway carpets flung over two chairs, holding a broom.

'What are you doing with that?'

'I'm beating the carpets, dear. Here.' Lena handed her the broom. 'Would you like to try?'

Grace had liked that. She walloped the carpet with all her might and a big cloud of dust came out.

'Look at how strong you are!' Lena laughed and Grace had taken another swing and another, just to prove she was right.

Or after supper she could be found washing the

dishes. Lena showed Grace how to press a fork deep into the soap and blow bubbles by dipping it into a glass of water. Soon the kitchen was filled with glassy bubbles. The dog had gone mad trying to chase them, barking hysterically.

Later on they played cards together. Lena knew a game that no one else could work out. But Grace was quick to learn.

'You're a very clever girl, do you know that?' Lena stroked Grace's cheek softly. 'You must never forget that. Now, what would you do here? Think before you answer.'

Grace concentrated hard. She wanted to please Lena. And the game was both fun and difficult, which made it the best sort of game.

Sometimes, Lena and Grace went for a walk in the woods at the back of the house to gather petals. There was, in a small, sheltered grove, an unexpected patch of wild narcissus, or paperwhites as the English called them. Tiny, delicate white blooms, they gave off an intensely sweet fragrance.

Together, they harvested the freshest flowers and, back in the kitchen, Lena showed Grace how to make perfume from them. Taking two old panes of glass from the conservatory, she washed them clean and spread a thin layer of rendered tallow on each one. Then they laid out the blossoms one by one on the first pane, carefully placing the other pane of glass on top. Afterwards they stored them high on a shelf in the cool, dark pantry.

'It's called *enfleurage*,' Lena explained. 'We will gently extract the perfume oil from the blooms by pressing them into the tallow. But we must change the petals regularly and add new ones. Then we can make it into a pomade.'

'Did your mummy teach you this?'

'No. A friend taught me.'

They found a few more glass panes and experimented with different types of foliage – moss, grass, mint leaves from the herb garden.

One day they bought a lemon in the village. At home, Lena gleefully put together yet another glass press, making the most remarkable, fresh scent from only a few slices. (The rest they had with their fish that night.)

'Can you make perfume from anything?' Grace asked.

'Anything!' Lena asserted.

'What about wood?' Grace challenged. 'Or a piece of wool.' She giggled.

'Well, let's try.'

That afternoon they searched for the richest, dampest piece of tree bark they could find. It was difficult to shave it down to bits that could be effectively pressed but eventually they were able to extract a very subtle hint of wood. As part of the same experiment, Lena unravelled the sleeve of one of Grace's old cardigans and pressed the wool as well.

'This one is very tricky,' she conceded, with a frown. 'It's not a strong smell to begin with.'

'Why did you have to undo one of my cardies?' Grace complained, examining the unravelled sleeve. Even though it was too small, she still liked it.

'Because part of the smell of the wool is your smell too. They mix. And I, for one, want both – though, to be honest,' she sighed, 'we may end up pressing this old wool for months before we get anything.' She caught Grace's eye and grinned. 'You know what I would like to try? A bit of your hair.'

'My hair!' Grace thought this was hysterical. 'Hair perfume!' she cried, dancing around the room with excitement. 'That's mad!'

However, the paperwhites were easily Grace's favourite. She loved wandering through the grove gathering their blooms, piling them into Lena's basket. They were, after all, her favourite flower.

'You may have this perfume when we've finished. It shall be your birthday present,' Lena promised.

But today Lena had another idea. 'I know,' she suggested after a moment, 'would you like to help me make some biscuits?'

Grace looked up from her lap. 'What kind of biscuits?'

'Black.' Lena gave her a squeeze.

'Black biscuits?' Grace sat up.

'That's right. Made with charcoal, for your father.'

Grace made a face. 'Why does Daddy eat charcoal? Do I have to eat charcoal?'

'No, *mon ange*. Daddy needs it because his tummy is unwell. In the war, they sprayed a gas into the air that made all the soldiers sick. Your father has a pain in his tummy but these black biscuits help.'

'Does the pain ever go away?'

'I'm not sure.'

Grace took this in. 'Is that why he's cross?'

'Cross?'

'Yes. He's angry with me.'

Lena stroked Grace's hair again. 'Your father is not cross, darling. But he is . . .' she stopped, searching for the right words, 'he is not comfortable.'

Grace looked down at her feet, dangling in the air. She wondered if she should tell Lena the truth; that her father had never liked her, that she'd clearly done something to upset him, although she couldn't think what it was. That was why he didn't speak to her; why he scowled all the time.

But if she said it out loud, Lena might not like her anymore either.

Grace gnawed nervously at her thumbnail.

'So,' Lena put Grace down and stood up. 'Shall we start baking?'

'Yes, please.'

'Then let's get you an apron.' Lena took a spare off the hook by the back door.

———

'Hello? Hello!' Catherine Maudley strode into the front hallway upstairs, her heels clicking against the wooden floorboards. 'Hello! Grace? Lena?'

Instantly Eva felt her back go rigid.

Catherine was walking downstairs now; she strode into the kitchen, hat in hand, pulling off her white gloves. 'There you two are.'

Instinctively, Eva averted her eyes, focusing instead on tying the apron around Grace's waist.

Lady Catherine was an attractive woman, older than Eva, with a natural hauteur and authority. Her voice was slightly breathy, giving her a rather harried, uncertain energy, and her accent snapped with the crisp consonants and flatly drawled vowels of the upper classes. Her fine auburn hair was styled away from her face and her features echoed Lambert's with disarming accuracy; her brother's ghost could be seen in the same wide forehead and startling azure eyes.

442

'What a journey! The station was packed,' Catherine complained. 'What are you doing?'

'We're making black biscuits for Daddy,' Grace announced.

'Black biscuits!' Catherine tossed an evening edition of the newspaper down on the table, along with her gloves. 'Is this a joke?'

She looked over at Eva, who forced the corners of her mouth up into a smile. 'No, ma'am. They have a small amount of charcoal in them, which aids digestion and gives them their colour. They are very popular in France.'

'Oh dear!' Catherine shook her head. 'What will they think of next?' She reached out and stroked the head of the family dog, Fry, a mixed breed of wolfhound and retriever. 'And where is your father?'

'Daddy's in the greenhouse, of course,' Grace offered, as Lena pulled up a stool for her to stand on.

'Yes, of course,' Catherine sighed.

Jonathan Maudley was, in fact, rarely out of the greenhouse. Though it was nearly the size of the main house already, he'd built an extension onto it recently which housed a laboratory and office, from which he conducted his research for a major pharmaceutical company. It was one of the reasons they didn't live in the Great Hall. He could be found there, often before sunrise until late in the evening, deeply involved in experiments, piled in notes. His considerable collection of plant specimens was fastidiously attended to by him alone and kept under lock and key. It was his private domain, strictly off limits.

'I wonder why I bother asking,' Catherine added, wandering over to the back door and looking out of the window. 'Lena, don't let that washing sit too long on the line. I don't want my blue dress bleached out by the sun.'

'Yes, ma'am.'

She turned. 'I take it we're having chicken for supper?'

Eva nodded.

'Lovely. Can you make ordinary boiled potatoes, please? That last dish you made . . .' she paused, searching for the name.

'*Le gratin?*'

'Yes. Very nice but I swear, Lena, it had garlic in it.' Catherine shot her a reproachful look. 'One cannot go about in public places smelling like a foreign sailor. I was mortified in case someone sat next to me on the train or in the library. Has the post arrived? I'm waiting for a letter from a publisher.'

'It's on the table in the front hallway, ma'am.'

'Good. Well, my darling,' she turned to Grace, 'I was going to ask you if you wanted to walk the dog with me.'

Grace hesitated.

'Darling,' Lady Catherine's smile faded, 'you don't want me to go by myself, do you?'

'No, Mummy. It's just—'

'Lena can make the biscuits.' She held out her hand. 'God knows, you've spent all day together!' She snapped her fingers impatiently. 'Now, come along!'

Climbing off the stool, Grace tugged at the apron ties; it slid down to the floor.

'Of course, Mummy.' She took her mother's hand.

'Lena, have a look at those gloves, please, will you? The fingertips are quite filthy from the train. White gloves really ought to be white, don't you think?' Catherine gave her daughter's palm a squeeze. 'Let's run some fat off this old boy, shall we? We'll be back before supper,' she called as they climbed the stairs, Fry at their heels.

~~~

Eva stood, very still, in the empty kitchen.

Then she picked up the apron from the floor and hung it back again on the hook by the back door.

Moving mechanically, she took out the flour and sugar from the pantry; butter, salt, a mixing bowl.

She tossed some flour onto the counter and spread it smooth, took out the rolling pin.

Reaching deep into one of the kitchen drawers for a biscuit cutter, she found one in the shape of a small oval, made of tin.

She stopped . . . ran her finger along the sharp, delicately serrated metal edge.

Eva put the cutter down on the counter and pressed her palm into it, hard.

The sensation was exquisite and excruciating. Feeling flooded in. And the pressure valve in her head loosened, easing just the tiniest bit.

She closed her eyes.

There was a whole vocabulary of suffering, eloquent in its wordlessness, which gave voice to all the things she couldn't do or say.

Opening her eyes, she forced her hand into a fist, stretching out her fingers again and again. Then she turned to get the milk.

Jonathan Maudley was standing, watching in the doorway.

He leaned awkwardly against the door frame.

Tall and very thin it was clear that at one time he'd been handsome. With large blue eyes, a high, intelligent forehead and a firm jaw, he might have been the very model of well-bred English manhood. Only now his eyes were ringed with deep bluey circles, the result of years of nightmares and fragmented sleep; his sandy-blond hair had thinned, his cheeks were hollowed and his lips drawn. His large hands were expressive and elegant. They should have been the hands of a gentleman or a diplomat, only now the long tapered fingers were stained with nicotine from too many cheap roll-ups, a habit he'd acquired in the trenches and failed to give up, and the fingernails rimmed with black soil.

Upstairs the front door closed; Catherine and Grace had left.

Down here, the low ceiling of the kitchen pressed in on them, trapping the heat of the oven, the air warm and moist. A cloud passed over the sun; the room fell into shadow.

Eva reached for the milk. The pain that a minute ago had been a release was now an obstacle. She poured a little into the bowl, mixing the ingredients together, methodically.

She felt his eyes following her movements.

'You've hurt yourself,' he said.

Eva looked up.

The veil dropped from his features; gone was the public face of a distracted intellectual. Suddenly she saw in him a comprehension of loss that was terrible to behold.

Unnerved, she turned away.

When next she looked round, he was gone.

There had been no plan. The idea had begun with a simple wish; just to see her daughter.

Three years earlier, after Lambert's death, a letter had arrived. And for the first time, Eva knew where her daughter lived; knew her name.

But when she looked up the address Lambert had given her, her hopes plummeted. The Great Hall, West Challow, Oxfordshire, was no ordinary home. In fact, she found an etching of it in a library book entitled *The Stately Homes of England*. Her child was living on an estate, surrounded by thousands of acres, the legal daughter of landed aristocracy. Eva wouldn't be able to even gain access to the grounds, let alone her little girl.

Still, she paid a considerable amount to see a well-known lawyer, hoping he could offer advice. Instead, he dismissed her claim completely. 'You have no proof,' he interrupted her, halfway through her explanation. 'If you are the child's mother,' he gave her a look that made it clear he seriously doubted it, 'then why would you remove her from a life of privilege and opportunity? From what you've told me, she'll have a social position, possibly an inheritance. . . . am I mistaken? What kind of parent would wish to destroy their child's chances in this world simply to satisfy their curiosity?'

Folding his hands in front of him on the desk, he waited for her to respond. When Eva didn't, he shook his head. 'What did you say your position was again?'

'I'm a manageress, that is, a clerk. A sales girl in a store,' she answered, meekly.

'No,' he corrected her. 'You're an *unmarried* sales girl. Let me be frank, mademoiselle. Do you honestly believe that your daughter would want to even know that you exist? Consider this carefully,' he cautioned. 'Once the information, such as it is, is revealed, she can never return to her former ignorance. You will have tainted her by your history and your inferior circumstances.' He looked at her hard. 'In my professional opinion, you would be stealing from her a life of infinitely greater possibility. And you would have nothing to offer in its stead.'

Her attempts to convince Andre fared no better. He'd taken the news of her child badly. Now he wanted to pretend she didn't exist.

'You see, I have the address now,' she explained over supper one day to him. 'Perhaps we might go together to visit the village. It's of a reasonable size – right near Oxford. Anyone might go there as a tourist!' she added excitedly.

He put his fork down. 'What are you going to do

when you arrive – knock on the front door? Hide in the bushes until she appears?'

His sarcasm stung her. 'This isn't a joke, Andre.'

'And I'm not treating it as one.' He pushed his plate away. 'You have a life. Your place is here with me. Our work is what matters. That . . . that girl is fine without you.'

'You don't understand.'

Sighing, he leaned back in his chair. 'Then explain it to me.'

He waited, crossed his legs, smoothing down the wool fabric of his trousers with his hand. He was savvy now, having fully adopted the character she'd created for him – the avant-garde virtuoso of scent. He was taking Paris by storm, while she stood by him, beautifully dressed, endlessly encouraging.

Explain what? she thought. What could be more obvious than the desire to see your own child?

Still, Eva tried. 'Andre, she's the only person in this world connected to me, who is truly mine.'

'I'm connected to you. Doesn't that matter?' He ran his hand over his eyes. 'Eva, who is to say that seeing her might not be worse than never seeing her? You cannot simply run up and grab her! This is a dream. An illusion. You must wake up now.'

She'd imagined that he would come with her, as her husband, perhaps accompanying her to the authorities to advocate her case. But instead he thought her deluded, capable of hiding in bushes and snatching the child like a madwoman.

Andre reached for her hand. 'I need you. Your place is here. You need to face the truth; you were never meant to be a mother. You haven't got it in you. That child is better off without you.'

She pulled away. 'How do you know? Who's to say I haven't got it in me? And what does that leave me with, Andre? A job as your sales girl? A life with a man who will not touch me?'

He looked away.

He'd ceased to be her lover a while ago, a rejection they never spoke of, that left her embarrassed and confused. Talk of an engagement had faded too. More and more the relationship assumed a purely businesslike focus. His business. His focus.

'Is that all that matters to you?' he asked. 'Do you think that's all love is? A crude groping in the dark?'

'You tell me what love is, Andre!' she shot back.

He picked up a teaspoon and twirled it impatiently in his fingers, glaring down at the table.

Eva hadn't forgotten the body in his bed in New York or the new friends, attractive young men, who occupied his evenings now.

'So, you think you're just a sales girl?' he surmised quietly, shaking his head. 'That if I'm not grabbing at you and thrusting, you have no place in my life?'

'What place do I have? What do you need me for?' The floor seemed to disappear beneath Eva's feet. The world she'd invested in was false, built on little more than wishful thinking. She was falling now, into an unseen abyss. 'What place do I really have anywhere?'

Across from her, Andre sat silently, spinning the spoon round and round.

He wouldn't even look at her.

'You don't love me.' Pushing her chair back from the table, she stood up. Her head was reeling; the very tips of her fingers throbbed, so acute was her sense of betrayal. 'In fact, I don't think you're capable of love!'

He didn't stop her as she walked away.

That was the last time they ever spoke about it.

But in spite of these disappointments or perhaps because of them, a foolish improbable dream took hold, rooting itself deep in Eva's heart. She refused to believe that there was no way to make contact with her child without compromising her; she obsessed, turning the problem round in her head, gnawing round its edges day and night. She enjoyed a life of independence and excitement. Almost every evening she was out, as part of a set of bohemian artists, designers and thinkers – dining in cafés, going to the theatre, dancing in the many nightclubs that made Paris famous. But even then or when she was overseeing a client in the perfumery, her mind never stopped. How could she penetrate the invisible barrier that separated her from her child? In what way might she slip through the fence posts of breeding and class to gain even the smallest glimpse of her little girl?

She cradled this hope, nurtured it, fed it for three years.

And then one day, quite accidently, the answer came to her.

It was an autumn afternoon. A woman entered the shop, accompanied by a small boy. It was clear from her dress that she was in service and when she addressed Eva, she stumbled and started, unused to being in such an exclusive establishment.

'I'm sorry, madame, pardon me. But I am here . . .' She opened her pocketbook, took out a piece of paper, which she passed across the counter to Eva. 'I am here to collect an order for my mistress.'

'Certainly.' Eva collected the parcel from the black Chinese cabinet and looked across to where the little boy was climbing on top of the leopard ottoman.

'Charles, get down!' the woman hissed, grabbing his arm and yanking him off.

'That's all right.' Eva smiled.

'I apologize,' the woman said stiffly, putting the package into a basket on her arm. 'We have been given some errands to do and he's not yet been to the park. But I can assure you, his mother will hear of this when we return home.'

With that, she took the little boy's hand and dragged him out of the shop.

Eva leaned her elbows of the counter, watching as they rounded the corner and disappeared from view.

The girl was the child's nanny.

A domestic servant, who spent more hours of the day with her charge than the mother did.

Suddenly the puzzle cracked wide open.

～～～

A week later, Eva visited a pawn shop in Montmartre and sold anything she had of value. Instead, she purchased simple, functional clothes – shapeless cotton dresses, a pair of sturdy second-hand shoes. Off came the dark red nail varnish and matching lipstick; she combed her hair back from her face, arranged it in a heavy net. Any spare money she stitched into the lining of her brassiere. She exchanged her luggage for an inexpensive travel case, her reputation for forged references.

And then she left, without telling anyone.

Her first stop in West Challow, Oxfordshire, was at the local church. She was an experienced, diligent girl, looking for employment, willing to do anything . . . could they help? Did they know of anyone? Her English was good and she could cook.

The Revd Johns thought she might try the Hall – he knew the housekeeper, Mrs Dunnan. He would be happy to put in a good word. Also, he thought there might be some work to be had at Ivy House. It was part of the estate . . . they were a young couple and needed an extra hand.

Of course, Eva already knew the Hall and, more importantly, Ivy House – the red-brick Queen Anne house, set back on the grounds, behind a high garden wall covered in ivy and moss. She'd walked past it a dozen times since her arrival, hoping against hope for a glimpse of her little girl.

The interview at Ivy House had been terrifying; exhilarating. Catherine Maudley had fallen upon her like a starving man at a banquet. 'At last! I can really work!' she declared, barely glancing at the references in front of her. 'When can you start?'

Now, as Eva pressed her head to her pillow at night, with her cheek against the cool linen, she listened, waiting until the house fell quiet. Then she got out of bed, crept soundlessly down the steps from her room in the attic and stole, undetected, into the nursery.

Crouching down by the side of her bed, she watched as Grace's chest rose and fell in an even, sighing rhythm.

Sometimes she stayed there half the night.

Leaning over, she inhaled the fragrance of Grace's matted hair; an intoxicating blend of warm sweat and tender, young skin. It was a smell that went to her very core; feeding a hunger that could never be satisfied.

Reaching out, Eva ran her fingers gently along the curve of Grace's round little cheek.

Whatever her sins were, God must have forgiven them.

Here was heaven; here was redemption.

Here was her place on earth.

Folding the morning paper, Catherine Maudley took another sip of her tea, then held out her cup for Eva to refill. 'Take Mr Maudley something to eat, Lena, will you?' She stirred some milk into her cup. 'He's been up half the night and has locked himself away in that office of his again.'

Eva hesitated. The greenhouse was normally off limits. 'What shall I take him, ma'am?'

'Tea and toast,' Catherine decided, opening one of her many notebooks and slipping on her reading glasses. 'Or whatever. I shouldn't think it matters. I don't suppose he'll actually eat it, but one tries, doesn't one?'

'Yes, ma'am.' Eva nodded, heading back down into the kitchen. She wasn't keen to go on her own.

Grace was sitting at the table, making a drawing with some colouring pencils, swinging her feet to and fro.

'Darling,' Eva turned to her, 'would you like to give your father some of those black biscuits?'

Grace slid off her chair. 'Yes, please!'

Eva arranged a tray with a pot of tea, a jug of milk, and some sliced apple and cheese, along with the charcoal biscuits on a pretty little plate. (No one wanted to eat cold toast.) She gave the plate to Grace to carry and together they walked over to the green-house and knocked on the door.

After a while, Jonathan Maudley unlocked the door, dressed in a laboratory coat. He looked from one to the other. 'What's this?'

'We brought you something to eat.' Grace held up the plate eagerly. 'These will help your tummy! We made them, only Lena made them mostly . . .' she corrected herself.

'They have charcoal in them, sir. But only a small

amount. They aid the digestion,' Eva explained quietly.

'Do they?' He gave an uncertain smile, then took a step back. 'Well, then, you'd better come in.'

They followed him through the main body of the greenhouse, past the laboratory and into his office at the back. Plants were lined and labelled in meticulous rows; the air was humid, thick with the damp ripe scent of greenery mixed with rich, black soil. There were pots and troughs, and neatly arranged species in various stages of growth; the laboratory was lined with small glass Petri dishes and vials, a large microscope, charts and notebooks. The office itself was small, housing mostly a large writing desk and an old settee, pushed up against one wall. It was clear from the way the pillows were arranged at one end that it often served as a bed.

Eva placed the tray down on the desk.

Grace stood tightly clutching the plate of biscuits. The thrill of being a guest of her father's was almost too overwhelming.

Eva was about to go when Jonathan Maudley crouched down in front of Grace. 'May I?' he asked, taking one of the biscuits.

Grace's eyes widened. 'Yes, Daddy.' She held the plate up higher.

He took one and bit into it. 'Not bad,' he decided.

'I think I feel better already.'

'Really?' Grace stepped forward, the biscuits sliding perilously close to the edge of the plate.

'Careful, *mon ange*,' Eva intervened, steadying her hand.

Jonathan Maudley was looking at her, at the mark on her palm.

She let go. 'We should let your father get back to his work,' she said briskly, laying a hand gently on Grace's shoulder. 'He is a busy man.'

But Grace didn't want to leave. She'd never been allowed inside the greenhouse before. 'What are you doing, Daddy? May I watch?'

Jonathan hesitated. Then he took the plate from her and set it on the desk. 'Come with me.' He held out his hand and she slipped her palm into his. It was large and warm and calloused.

He led her into the laboratory where almost a dozen small plants were lined up in identical pots, each numbered and labelled.

'I am studying this common plant, called belladonna,' he explained. 'It grows wild all around Great Britain and has many possible medicinal properties but it's also highly toxic.'

Grace stared at him.

'It can be made into medicine,' Eva interjected gently, 'only it is also very poisonous.'

'But how can poison be medicine?' Grace asked.

Jonathan smiled. 'That's a clever question. Many medicines can be helpful in small doses but if you have too much, they will make you extremely ill.'

'Like sugar,' Grace added, eager to prove she understood what he meant.

'A little like sugar,' he agreed, 'only much more serious. For example, aspirin, which you take when you have a fever, is made from willow bark. If you were ill and didn't have any aspirin, you could brew yourself some willow bark tea instead. Nature is miraculous that way. But you can't do that with belladonna.' He pointed to the row of tiny plants. 'My job is to see if I can breed a form of this species that has the good qualities without the harmful ones. But, in the wild, you must remember that they have terribly poisonous berries and you must never eat them. Promise?'

Grace nodded solemnly. 'I won't ever!'

Eva looked around her, at the fragrant heat and greenery. It reminded her of Andre's workshop – the long wooden table lined with notebooks, the various vials; a private world of creation.

'We should leave your father now.' Again, she tried to move Grace towards the door.

Grace pulled away. 'But we haven't finished yet, have we?'

'We shall see your father at supper,' Eva reminded

her. 'But we must allow him time to work.'

Jonathan reached out, laid his hand gently upon the top of Grace's head. 'Perhaps another time.'

'But supper's ages away!' All of sudden Grace felt panicked. She'd only just arrived; who knew when she would have another chance?

She wrapped her arms around her father's legs, tight. 'Don't make me go, please! Let me stay with you. I promise I'll be good, please, Daddy. Please!'

Jonathan Maudley went rigid.

'Please, Daddy. Let me, please!'

'Grace!' The look on Jonathan's face was one of blank horror.

'Please, Daddy!' Her voice rose to a hysterical pitch. 'Please! Please!'

'Don't, Grace . . . you must stop!' He tried to pull her hands off but she held on even tighter, pressing into him. 'I cannot . . .' He looked desperately at Eva. 'Take her, damn it! Just take her away!'

Prising Grace's fingers off, Eva hauled the screaming child up over her shoulder.

She carried her out of the greenhouse, just as Catherine Maudley came running down the path.

'What is going on here?' she demanded furiously. 'Grace! Stop that at once!'

But Grace couldn't stop. 'I want to go back, please, Mummy! Please!'

Eva put her down and before she could do anything to settle Grace, Catherine had grabbed her by the shoulders. 'Just stop it now!' She turned to Eva. 'What in God's name were you doing in there anyway?'

'We . . . we just took him his tea.'

'I told *you* to take it to him. What were you thinking of? Stop it!' She shook the child. 'Stop it! Do you hear me? No more of that noise! Your father must have quiet. Do you understand? You're hurting him!' She slapped Grace across the face, hard. 'Do you want to hurt him?'

Grace stopped, too shocked and frightened to make another sound.

Catherine stood up. 'I won't have this sort of thing, do you understand, Lena? The greenhouse is off limits for a reason. Don't take her there again.'

Turning abruptly on her heel, she marched back to the house.

~~~

Jonathan Maudley sat at his desk, staring into nothingness. Outside, the cool spring day softened. But he was far away, in another time and place.

'Please don't make me go! Please!'

'Help me! Please!'

He closed his eyes. But the voices persisted.

Opening his desk drawer, he reached for a bottle of whisky. Struggled to get the top off. Tipping his head back, he took a long swallow. Then he pulled a roll-up from his shirt pocket and lit it.

He inhaled hard, holding on to the lighter, pressing it into the palm of his hand. He ran his thumb along the inscription. *Always and Evermore*, it read – a gift from Catherine when he'd joined up. But still the memories unfolded like an unstoppable newsreel in his head.

Here was an open field, a gentle green hillock. The expanse of brilliant blue sky above. Dawn had risen over the valley of the Somme as gently, gracefully as on a page from Genesis, unfolding into a beautiful morning, cloudless, hot.

And young men, passing cigarettes and flasks, joking; laughing at their own nerves.

Then it began, out of nowhere.

Someone shouted an order; others followed.

Shells whistled through the air . . . there were the cartwheels – horizontal, with machine guns . . . swinging round, a belt of fire on the hill, filling the air with black smoke and noise.

Jonathan took another swig.

Here were the faces he didn't want to see.

Men twisting, dancing, arms outstretched – body

parts exploding in mid-air, showering down in sprays of guts, sinew and bone. The ground beneath them turned greasy, slippery with blood.

And the roar. The unholy, ceaseless sound of terror.

'Please! Please!'

The dying dangled in the sea of barbed wire, caught mid-air. Like men praying, falling to their knees, only the wire wouldn't let them.

They just hung there.

'Please! Please, sir! Don't leave me, please!'

Jonathan staggered past them, half-blind, deafened; his right arm shattered open.

'Help me, sir! Please!'

Half a man's face was gone, an eye swinging from its socket, yet his mouth still moved.

Jonathan shot him with trembling hands. His own man.

The boy slumped forward, a marionette, strings cut.

'Fall back! Move! Move, you bastard! Move!'

Someone was waving, shouting; hauling him up by the collar of his jacket.

Looking over his shoulder, he saw the long lines of Germans sweeping along the brow of the hillock, four hundred yards away. They were marching slowly, shoulder to shoulder; a solid grey wall of men and ammunition.

He managed to make it back to the third line and

there, in a state of delirium, manned one of the machine guns until he fell unconscious from loss of blood.

So many years had passed now.

But that day would never end.

<hr />

It was late, almost ten in the evening, when Eva went back to collect the tea tray from Jonathan Maudley's desk. He hadn't come in to supper, as she'd promised Grace. Instead, Grace had eaten alone with her mother. Some time after seven, Eva had heard the sound of the motor starting, heading down the drive. Probably to the pub. And not long afterwards, Catherine retired to her bedroom for the night.

The greenhouse had no electricity. So Eva took a lantern with her, illuminated by a stubby, low candle. Pulling her cardigan around her against the cold, she made her way down the garden path. The moon was bright and high; shadows shifted in the darkness, wind rustling through the leaves. She knocked on the door. No reply.

Pushing it open, she went through to the office.

There, on his desk, untouched, was the tea tray. But as she went to lift it, she noticed there were also a number of papers that hadn't been there before, a small collection of old newspaper clippings.

Lifting the lamp higher, Eva picked one up.

Local Hero to be Honoured in Memorial Ceremony, it read.

Another one contained a photograph of him in uniform, *Capt Maudley Receives Military Cross for Bravery*.

Suddenly she heard the crunch of gravel under the wheels of a car. Putting the clippings back where she had found them, Eva picked up the tray and, moving as quickly as possible, made her way out of the greenhouse.

From the safety of the kitchen, she could just make out the outline of a figure, staggering and reeling towards the house.

That night, in bed, Eva thought about how handsome and young he had looked in the newspaper clippings.

And how different, unrecognizable, he was now.

     ———

Grace was lying on her stomach on the floor, stacking wooden blocks into a precarious structure with great concentration. Her little brow was knit, her tongue pressed hard into the corner of her mouth.

Eva sat down on the chair near the fireplace. 'What are you building?'

'A fortress,' she answered, without looking up.

'You never like to play with dolls, do you?' Eva noted.

Grace shook her head. 'I'm going to make things. Like Daddy.'

'Not a mummy with a baby?'

'A mummy with a baby and a maker,' she determined, balancing another block.

'Lena!' Catherine was calling from the kitchen. 'Lena! Come here, please.'

Both of them hurried downstairs. Catherine was standing in the kitchen, arms folded in front of her. Her face was serious.

'I'd like an explanation, Lena.' She pointed to the greasy panes of glass, with bits of dead flowers smashed between them, lined up on the kitchen counter top. 'I went into the pantry to compile a shopping list and I found these.' Her upper lip curled in disgust. 'What are they? Please don't say that we're meant to eat them!'

'They are flower presses, ma'am. To make perfume.'

'Perfume?' Catherine was at a loss. 'But why?'

'Well, I . . . it's just . . .' Eva blinked. 'I thought it would be something to do, ma'am. As a project for Grace.'

'Little girls don't need projects. And if they do,

you can teach them how to knit or sew – something useful!' Gingerly she picked at the side of one of the glass panes, recoiling from the greasy edge. 'What is that anyway? Lard?'

'Tallow, ma'am.'

'Good God!' Catherine shuddered, wiping her fingertips off on a tea towel. 'And what's this?' She pointed to another.

Eva looked down at the floor. 'Hair, ma'am. And a bit of wool.'

'I have honestly never seen anything so disgusting in my life! And in the kitchen of all places! Really, Lena. I don't understand – you're normally so clean. Get rid of them. It's bound to be rancid by now.'

'But it isn't, Mummy,' Grace interjected. 'And this one,' she pointed out the panes with the paperwhites, 'this one is going to be mine when it's ready!'

'*Yours?* Are you mad?' Catherine looked at her incredulously. 'In the first place, little girls don't wear scent and in the second, I won't have you running about smeared with beef fat!'

Grace reached out, took her mother's hand. 'But I want to smell like flowers. Don't you?'

Catherine pulled her hand away. 'Darling, that is not scent. That is a greasy mess! And no, I have no desire to reek like the floor of a cheap florist's stall – it's vulgar. Get rid of them, Lena.' Catherine eyed

468

them both fiercely. 'And please, restrain yourselves. Teach her French, instead. She doesn't know a word and at this rate, she never will.' Catherine ran her hand across her eyes. 'I have a searing headache today. Have you taken anything in yet to Mr Maudley?'

'No, ma'am.'

'Please, Lena,' Lady Catherine pleaded, 'I need your help. Just take him some tea. I have the shopping to do and a deadline to meet.'

She heaved a great sigh and picked up her list.

***

For luncheon they had cheese sandwiches. Eva had a way of making them, of putting them in the top oven so that the cheese melted, forming a gooey crust on top of the bread. Then she cut them into little strips and fanned them out on the plate around thin slices of apple.

Then it was Grace's nap time. Eva took off her shoes and dress, pulled the curtain across. She sat on the edge of the bed, ran her fingers through the child's hair.

Grace closed her eyes.

Her breathing slowed to a regular rhythm.

The window was open; soft fingers of wind gathered the gauzy net curtain up then released it, slowly.

Outside, a hazy warm stillness settled over the afternoon. There was nowhere to go, nothing to do. Only time, unfolding gracefully from one moment to the next.

Eva pressed her lips to the top of Grace's head, then went back downstairs to the kitchen and put the kettle on. Arranging a tea tray with milk and a slice of yellow cake, Eva carried it outside to the greenhouse.

She looked up at the sky. The air had suddenly gone still, the sky a flat shade of grey. Rain was coming.

Fry, the dog, wove between her legs, yapping excitedly. 'What's wrong?' She rubbed his head. 'Calm down! Do you want to play?'

She knocked on the door of the greenhouse.

There was no reply.

After a minute, she pushed the door open with her back. 'Hello? Sir? Anyone here?'

It was so quiet.

Walking through to the office, she saw his back at the desk.

'Just leave it, please,' he said without turning round.

Eva left the tray on the corner of the laboratory table and left. Back in the kitchen, she began slicing vegetables for stew.

470

The dog was restless, barking at the window.

'What can you see? A squirrel?' Eva went over, looked out.

The gate at the bottom of the garden was ajar. The wind was rising; the gate banged against the latch again and again. It led out onto a field of high wild grass and then to some woods.

Eva thought she caught sight of something moving in among the trees, a fleeting shape. But it was gone now.

'Rest easy boy, there's nothing there.'

She went back to peeling carrots.

Just after three, she went upstairs to wake Grace.

Pushing open the door, she moved quietly to the side of the bed. 'Darling? *Mon ange?*'

Eva pushed back the mound of covers.

The bed was empty.

'Grace? Grace! This isn't funny!' she called, looking under the beds, inside the laundry hamper, behind the settee.

Eva searched the house, the garden. She even went back through to the greenhouse. The door was unlocked. The tea had been poured, the cup on the desk still warm.

But no one was there.

The clouds darkened. The air was still.

The birds had stopped singing.

Fry was standing by the gate at the end of the garden, barking wildly. He turned to look at her, tail down, ears flat.

Eva followed him into the field and broke into a run.

<hr />

The sky was a vast rolling sea of navy and black; the temperature had dropped and everything looked unreal, as if it were pasted on a flat grey background and lit from within.

Eva ran through the high grass, lurching and stumbling across the uneven ground. Only the distance seemed to expand rather than contract, as if she were wading through water. Finally, she reached the woods.

It was darker here; light gave way to flickering shadows. She forced her way through the undergrowth, the thick green leaves and low-reaching branches pulling at her hair, thorns scraping her legs, hidden roots pitching her forward. The dry forest floor crunched beneath her feet.

'Grace!' she shouted. 'Grace!'

Her voice seemed to be swallowed up by the thick, heavy air like a vacuum. Every second she couldn't see her little girl seemed like an hour; her heart pounded so loudly she thought her head would explode.

High above, the wind blew. A flock of ravens, huge and black, swooped down, screeching loudly, before cutting back up across the sky.

Then suddenly she spotted a fluttering bit of white in the distance – thin, filmy cotton.

She ran faster, staggering into a clearing; the clearing of paperwhites.

Grace was in her nightdress, crouched on the ground. She was holding something small, golden. Coming closer, Eva saw that it was a lighter, with a mother-of-pearl inlay. 'Where have you been?' She reached out to her. 'I've been searching everywhere!'

Grace stared at Eva blankly, turning the object round and round in her little hands. Then she pointed to something, a few yards away. 'I can't wake him up.'

Jonathan Maudley was lying on his back in a ditch. Eyes wide open, motionless; staring unblinkingly at the dark rolling sky.

His lips were tinged a dark, almost navy-blue grey; from the sickly, sweet berries of the belladonna plant.

'You asked to see me, sir?' Eva stood in the doorway of the drawing room.

The man by the window turned. He was in his seventies, with very straight military bearing, a meticulously trimmed silver moustache and fierce blue eyes. His features were familiar, the stern template of both his children.

He took a few steps forward, indicating a spot on the settee. 'Please sit down.'

Eva did as she was told, folding her hands on her lap.

It hadn't taken long for Catherine's father, Lord Royce, to take over after Jonathan Maudley's death. He'd arrived the day afterwards from London, where he'd been convening with the House of Lords; making arrangements, overseeing his son-in-law's funeral, dictating word for word the obituary that appeared in *The Times*; the terrible accidental death of a war hero and promising scientist.

Catherine was naturally distraught. Unable to sleep or eat, she'd barely managed to say two words to Eva since her husband's body was recovered. During the day, she slept. But Eva could hear her moving about at night, pacing, back and forth in her room, until dawn. The house was cloaked in silence; even the dog was sombre. But Eva had heard the hushed tones of urgent conversations behind closed doors;

there were private phone calls and telegrams delivered at odd hours.

And now Lord Royce wished to speak to her.

Looking out the window, Eva watched Grace, playing outside in the front garden. She had two dolls her grandfather had bought her; expensive china dolls with real human hair. She was making beds for them in the leaves underneath the chestnut tree, burying them in dirt. Her face was so intent; so serious. Eva could tell from the way her mouth was moving that she was making up different voices for each of them.

Settling behind the writing desk, Lord Royce took a deep breath. 'Let me begin by saying, how grateful my daughter is for everything you've done to help her through this terrible time. As you know, she is very distressed and unable to manage these affairs. However, she wished me to convey her gratitude.'

'Thank you, your lordship.'

'Naturally, this event has meant that changes have to be made. Now is a time when my daughter needs the support of her family. This little experiment,' he looked around at the modest drawing room, 'in independence is over. She will be moving back to the main house with all possible speed.'

Eva swallowed. 'I should be pleased to continue to serve them and you, sir, wherever they go.'

'How accommodating. However, all my kitchen and cleaning staff requirements are already met. I'm sure you understand.'

He slid an envelope out from behind the blotter on the desk. 'I think you will find my daughter has been extremely generous in both her severance and her letter of recommendation.'

He held the envelope out.

Eva stared at it.

'I would be happy to work in any capacity. For example, I have looked after little Grace for some months now. I would be so . . . so very pleased to continue . . .'

The look on his face was a mixture of both irritation and disdain.

'My granddaughter will, of course, have a proper nanny,' he clarified pointedly. 'A professional qualified to educate a young lady of her class.' Rising, he held the envelope out again. 'Arrangements have already been made. Your services are no longer required.'

Eva took the envelope. She could neither see nor hear clearly.

'I can do anything, your lordship,' her voice was just above a whisper, 'anything, at all . . . I will work in the kitchens or laundry . . .'

'Why?' His expression changed. He came closer. Eva looked up. 'I'm sorry, sir?'

'Why?' he repeated. 'You have money, references. Oxford has many opportunities. Why do want to stay here so badly?'

'You . . . you misunderstand me, sir.'

'Do I?' His voice was icy. 'Your eyes are a very unusual colour.

'Sir?'

'I've only seen eyes like that once before. They are almost exactly the same colour as Grace's.'

Eva felt her body go rigid. She tried to say something but her mouth just opened, gaping soundlessly.

'You're not who you pretend to be, are you?' His face hardened. 'I always knew that some day there'd be trouble. I expected blackmail. But I didn't expect anything like this.'

Again, Eva tried to swallow, her throat tightening like a fist, but made no reply.

'If I were to ring the Home Office, I believe I should have no difficulty in verifying your true identity. What is it you call yourself? Celine? Do you realize the seriousness of traveling on forged papers? You could be arrested as a spy, or simply deported.'

'I . . . I don't know what you're talking about, sir,' she managed.

'Don't you? Would you care to bring your papers to me for examination?'

Tears stung the backs of her eyes; Eva bit her lower lip hard, to hold them back, and shook her head 'no'.

'I didn't think so. You have two days to leave this country. After that, I shall notify the authorities. And please don't misunderstand me, there are no lengths I won't go to remove you if you defy me.'

He moved towards the window again, his back to her, watching Grace playing on the front lawn.

There was a movement just outside the drawing room door. Then the faint sound of footfall on the stairs.

'I had a son once.' He spat the words out, edged with bitterness and hatred. 'He died too. Of drunkenness, debauchery and disease. The only decent thing he ever did was for his sister. Do you really think that I'm going to allow some cheap French tart to destroy my daughter's last remaining happiness?'

Paris, Spring, 1955

'Madame Munroe? Madame Munroe?'

Grace blinked, looking up into Madame Zed's face.

Madame Zed got up, went into the kitchen and poured her a glass of water. Then she set it on the table next to her.

Grace stared at the glass. She could see it, but it was as if she couldn't place its purpose.

'What happened to her?' she asked after a while.

'She was dismissed. Do you remember that?'

Grace shook her head. 'I remember vaguely being at my grandparents' home. That we seemed to stay there forever. A woman named Mrs Press looked after me. She was older, with thick white hands. I used to think they were made of lard. My mother always told me my father died of a heart attack.'

'Well, what else could she say?'

'Yes,' Grace agreed numbly.

Madame Zed passed her the final vial. *Choses Perdus*, she said. 'It means "Lost things". This is the accord Eva was obsessed with – the heart of the fragrance Hiver can't reproduce.'

Grace took it, held it up.

Suddenly the gap in her senses closed. The air became tighter, more compressed. Her eyes filled with tears.

'I have never been able to smell it.' Madame sat forward. 'Please, will you describe it to me?'

Grace nodded. 'It's the smell of wool, paperwhites, wood . . . and hair . . . my hair.'

The letter was delivered by Jacques Hiver's driver, in the early afternoon.

It had been a quiet day. Eva had been dusting the shelves for the second time that week, taking the bottles down, carefully wiping each one with a damp cloth, when she saw the black Daimler crawling slowly up the street. It was surrounded by a crowd of neighbourhood children, running after it, shouting and banging against the windows. With strict petrol rationing, non-military vehicles were increasingly rare. Only the very rich or important could afford such a luxury. Eva watched as the driver shooed them away, before he came into the shop.

The note was a typically brief communication, just a location and a time scribbled in Jacques's spidery, perpendicular handwriting. The only thing that set it apart from the other notes he regularly sent was that this time the location was a private address rather than a hotel.

Eva folded it back up, put it into the pocket of her skirt.

'Who was that?' Andre called from the back room. 'A customer?'

'No.' Customers had been few and far between. 'Nothing important.'

'Oh. One of your admirers,' he said.

They both knew the term 'admirer' wasn't quite accurate. And they both refrained from saying so.

Ever since Eva had returned to Paris seven years ago, she and Andre had reached a kind of unspoken agreement. After her abrupt departure, he had struggled on without her, at first angry and hurt, then torn between regret and self-loathing. When, months later, he arrived one morning to find her standing, waiting on the front doorstep of the shop, he was overwhelmed with gratitude and relief.

But as he unlocked the door, he said only, 'Are you back?'

'Yes,' she answered.

She walked in and, without another word, set about rearranging the counter display.

He never asked her to explain and she never did.

Things were different now, expectations gone.

Neither of them had the reserves for strong emotional gales. A respectful distance protected both of them. Kindnesses were rendered, trespasses ignored, narrow spaces negotiated in a state of amicable reserve.

Pushing back the thick velvet curtain that separated the shop from the storeroom, Eva leaned against the door frame. Andre was balanced on top of a ladder, reaching for a sealed jar of ambergris tucked away on one of the high shelves. He was thin, very thin. Everyone in Paris had lost weight with the strict rations but often Andre was too distracted to eat even his modest share. He subsisted on a diet mostly of cigarettes, white bean stew and weak 'coffee' made from chicory and barley. With the decline in commissions, he channelled his considerable energies into the reorganization of his entire collection. Already he'd managed to categorize and cross-categorize his existing perfumes to a remarkable, almost pathological degree, creating occasionally bizarre, whimsical classifications, which he labelled underneath each vial. Eva knew he was simply trying to steady himself, to keep his mind from the looming shadow of the future.

'Why don't we take a break?' she said. 'Let's lock up the shop for half an hour and step out for a breath of fresh air?'

Climbing down, he put the jar on the counter. 'There's nothing fresh about the air in Paris anymore.

Besides,' he scratched at an angry red patch of eczema that had developed, spreading across the back of his right hand, 'I'm in the middle of something.'

Eva didn't press the point. She knew he hated to be seen in public, wearing the barbaric yellow star stitched onto his lapel. He only really felt comfortable now in the shop. The beautifully tailored suits he once wore hung untouched and undefiled in his wardrobe. He'd capitulated only once, stitching the badge onto his least favourite suit jacket, which he wore every day. He no longer frequented cafés or bothered to meet with friends.

In fact, he was becoming a recluse, hardly leaving the workroom, working away in the basement, after curfew, well into the night. And the fruits of his obsessive labours could be found on the now-crowded shop shelves, vials upon vials of new formulations, sometimes two or three in a single night. It was beyond prolific; it was like a kind of brilliant possession. Andre was at the height of his powers, creating subtle, daring, elegant compositions. Frequently he spent hours showing her his notebooks, taking her through each detail of the process, as if he both doubted himself and wanted a witness to carry on his legacy. Some afternoons, he would make her test twenty different variations of the same formula, only to discount them all. Other times, he was emphatic, dictatorial, chain-smoking heavily, proclaiming amidst a fog of thick smoke that he was the only real nose left in Paris.

Eva found this frenzied outpouring both moving and painful to witness. He was racing, running himself out. Part of her sensed that he wasn't afraid for himself, so much as for his own talent; terrified that something uniquely beautiful might not be realized unless he coaxed it into being.

She came, stood beside him. 'What are you working on?'

'I want to do a Greek series.' Glancing up, he gave her an awkward smile. 'I long for archetypes.'

'Well, I may step out for a while. That is, if you don't mind.'

She knew the chance of anyone coming in was slim, but knew also that Andre shrank from dealing with customers.

Today he just shrugged. 'Do what you like. But turn the sign around, will you? I don't want any uninvited guests.'

He was talking about the Germans. The only people left in Paris with the money for luxury goods.

Eva set out walking down the thronging Boulevard Saint-Germain. Since the invasion, it seemed that more people spent time milling in the streets, rubbing up against one another, looking to each other for clues as to what was happening. During the day, the streets teemed with people standing in line for rations, bartering with makeshift stallholders selling black market goods, spilling out from the cafés to smoke, argue and talk. At night, the same streets were eerily silent.

She crossed the river at the Pont de Sully. The banks of the Seine were lined with fishermen, both men and women, waiting patiently, hoping to supplement their rations by any means possible. As she headed into the 4th arrondissement, the atmosphere changed. Here the wide boulevards were quieter, the streets devoid of the many teeming bicycles and rickshaws that crowded Saint-Germain. Suspended from the roofs of government buildings, enormous swastika flags fluttered soundlessly in the breeze. Suddenly, Eva caught sight of a flock of birds, circling above. There were almost no pigeons left in Paris, most had been caught and cooked.

Finally arriving through the narrow cobbled entrance, Eva stepped into the wide expanse of the Place des Vosges, with its stately central square. The trees were all but bare now, a few golden leaves clinging in defiance. Some children were huddled in a circle, shooting marbles in the dirt. An older man was sweeping the rest of the fallen leaves into high piles, aided by his wife, a small, stocky woman, wrapped in a knitted shawl. The four large fountains were dry; the playground equipment dismantled long ago. They all seemed to be moving like nurses around the bed of a sleeping patient, cautious and quiet.

Checking the address again, Eva made her way to the far end. A group of German soldiers were sitting on bench, smoking. They laughed, shouting and whistling as she passed.

The concierge, a rather frightened, dour young woman, was waiting for her outside of one of the buildings. She led Eva up a set of marble stairs to an apartment on the first floor. She unlocked the door and disappeared back downstairs before Eva could ask her anything.

'Hello?' Eva stepped inside.

It was empty, unfurnished.

'Hello, is anyone here?' she called again.

Her voice echoed off the bare walls and floor. Was this some sort of joke? What was he playing at?

She was drawn to the wall of windows, overlooking the city. It was a remarkable vantage point, a sprawling panorama stretching in all directions for miles.

'Do you like it?'

Eva turned.

A striking woman was standing in the doorway. She was only a few years older than herself, with an elegant, lithe figure and strong features. She was wearing a simple day dress and flat shoes, as if she'd been out shopping or running errands; two activities it was impossible to believe. She looked Eva up and down, regarding her as if she were a cut of meat dangling in a butcher's window.

'I'm sorry?' Eva scoured her memory. 'I don't believe we've met.'

'No,' the woman answered. She untied the silk headscarf she was wearing, revealing a mass of dark curls, rearranging it so it draped loosely around her neck. 'And we never will. Do you mind if I smoke?' she asked, taking a gold cigarette case out of her handbag.

She lit one, not bothering to wait for Eva's reply.

'So, do you like it?' the woman asked again, shooting a stream of smoke at the ceiling. 'It has an exceptional view, don't you agree?'

Coming over, she stopped in front of the window. 'I think it will do nicely. Don't worry about furnishings. I'll send over some pieces later on in the week. I mean,' she laughed a little, smoke streaming from her nose, 'I'm sure your taste is more than adequate. But you'll appreciate that these additions are special.'

Now Eva knew who she was.

She slid her hands into her coat pockets. 'I'm not sure that will be necessary, Madame Hiver.'

Something flickered in Yvonne Hiver's dark eyes. 'Well, it's up to you of course,' she said lightly. 'You work in the little perfume shop, don't you? What's the name of that place?'

Eva didn't answer.

Yvonne tilted her chin down, watching Eva's face carefully. 'You're not the only one, you know. There are others.'

'I presume you're referring to other women.'

'Naturally.' Yvonne took another drag. 'My husband's quite sentimental. Some girls he's held on to since we were engaged. Sweet, I suppose.'

'Or lazy.'

Yvonne exhaled slowly. 'How did you meet him, anyway?'

Eva nodded to the cigarette she was smoking. 'Do you have another one?'

Yvonne frowned, irritated. Nevertheless, she took out the gold case again. 'I suppose rationing has made beggars of us all.'

Eva took one and, leaning forward, lit it from Yvonne's. 'I have plenty, thank you. I simply prefer yours.'

Yvonne stared at her then smiled. 'You were about to tell me how you met.'

'At the Casino de Paris. He followed me out one night. I'd left my winnings behind. He was under the impression it was a mistake and wanted to return them to me.'

Yvonne eyed her carefully. 'But it wasn't a mistake?'

'I didn't care about the money. I only go to play cards.'

'So he gave you your money and bought you a drink, no doubt.'

Eva exhaled. 'Actually I told him to fuck off. But he took the money back to the casino, and had the cashier hold it for me in chips for the next night. When I came back, he was there, waiting.'

Yvonne took a moment to register this information. Clearly, it didn't fit her imaginings. 'Do you often go to casinos on your own?' she asked, as if she were making conversation at a party.

'Yes,' Eva answered truthfully. 'I find it soothing.' She gestured to the empty apartment. 'Is this your idea?'

'Yes.'

'Why?'

Instead of answering, Yvonne opened the French doors, stepping out onto the terrace. 'You know, no one is going to have any money to buy perfume anymore. Not while there's a war on. But then I'm sure you already know that. I'm amazed that little shop hasn't shut down already.'

Eva followed.

Below them, the garden square was like most of the city, relatively untouched by the Germans. It was easy, seductive even, to make believe that nothing was happening. Of all the disturbing aspects of the occupation, Eva found the veil of normalcy the most sinister. Was any wound more painful than the one no one else could see?

'I've done a little research on you, Mademoiselle d'Orsey,' Yvonne confessed. 'I know that you have a running tab at the Café Flore that you never quite manage to pay off. I also know that they like to seat you in the back because you drink too much. I'm already aware that you enjoy spending your evenings gambling, in dubious company. And that your business partner, Andre Valmont, is a Jew. I also know that my husband is fond of rescuing things – frightened kittens, wounded sparrows, women who've misplaced their morals.'

Eva took a long drag. 'And that's why you're offering me an apartment?'

Yvonne leaned forward, resting her elbows on the railing. 'It occurs to me that you have very little to lose and a great deal to gain. All I want you to do is continue to entertain Jacques and a few of his new friends. Only naturally, I'd like you to be able to do it in fitting style.'

'And would these new friends by any chance be wearing grey uniforms and jackboots?'

Yvonne stubbed out the half-finished cigarette, tossing the butt over the side of the balcony. 'None of us has anything to gain by watching Hiver Cosmetics go under. We must cooperate.'

'Or rather, *I* must cooperate,' Eva corrected her. 'You will keep your distance.'

'We have never met, mademoiselle. And we never will.'

'Why are you making these arrangements? Why not Jacques?'

'I don't trust him.' Yvonne seemed to find this amusing. 'Imagine that?' she laughed. 'But some matters are too important, too delicate to leave to his judgement.'

Eva's head hurt, hunger gnawed at her stomach. She turned, gazing out over the landscape of Paris. She was unused to seeing it from this height, of viewing it spread out in its entirety. Suddenly she felt angry, betrayed. Paris was as beautiful as ever. There was something duplicitous, deeply wrong with this beauty.

She looked down. The soldiers were still there.

The whole of Paris was crawling with them; theatres and galleries, restaurants and nightclubs – wall-to-wall with Nazi uniforms, the air punctuated with guttural German sounds. They strolled in the parks, ordered beer in cafés, stood frowning in front of Matisse's paintings with art catalogues in their hands. There were women, French women, who laughed at their stories, hung on their arms, allowed them to buy them drinks. Eva found them pathetic and desperate, avoided looking them in the eye. She knew what she would find there – fear and despair dressed up in childish bravado and defiance.

'I'm not that fond of your husband,' she said after a while.

Yvonne shifted, sighed, like someone forced to wait for a bus when they wanted a cab. 'What you will get in return is this apartment, and a generous, regular stipend.'

'I prefer stocks.'

Frowning, she pursed her lips. 'As you wish. Do we understand each other?'

Eva turned to face her. 'So you want me to do you a favour?'

'A favour?' Yvonne's eyes flared.

'What price is your husband's company or your reputation, Madame Hiver?' She smiled softly. 'I'll consider it, on one condition. I want you to do something for me.'

'And what's that?'

'Andre Valmont. I want Hiver to hire him. I want

493

you to ensure he's protected and classified as essential wartime personnel to the company.'

Yvonne's eyes narrowed. She folded her arms across her chest. 'We're not hiring anyone. Especially not Jews.'

'He's a world-class perfumer. A genius. Just the kind of visionary Hiver needs.'

'I don't know what you expect me to do.'

'What if he created a perfume for Hiver?' Eva persisted. 'One that was sold exclusively under the Hiver name. Then it would prove he was essential to the future of the company.'

'The Nazis have taken over our factories,' Yvonne explained, exasperated. 'We're not producing cosmetics right now. We're making nylon for parachutes and God knows what else!'

'We could make it, Andre and I – in the shop. We still have supplies. We could produce the formulation in small batches. Your products are still being sold.'

'It's old stock. And it's running out fast. The longer this war lasts the more precarious our position becomes.'

'Yes, but what if, during France's darkest hour, Hiver delivers, against all odds, a new perfume. Can you imagine what it would mean to an ordinary woman, at a time like this? Just that something beautiful is being created, that it exists – something

494

uniquely French. What's more quintessentially French than perfume? Do you think that hope has a fragrance? Allegiance? Loyalty? And the very fact that you were producing it without factories, in spite of the Germans, would spark the imagination. It would seem like an exquisite act of patriotism.'

Yvonne pursed her lips again, said nothing.

Thinking aloud, Eva continued. 'The bottle should have a picture of the Eiffel Tower on it.'

'And what will you call it?'

'*Mon Coeur*. Now, always, forever.'

Yvonne snorted, shaking her head. 'It's ridiculous! And dangerous.'

'Acts of courage require daring – that's why they're admired. It's perfume, not politics.'

'Everything is politics. We can't afford scandal.'

'Scandal is the best form of advertising.'

'You don't bite the hand that feeds you.'

'And you don't lick the one that rubs your nose in the dirt and beats you!' Eva snapped back.

'We're aiming not to get beaten, mademoiselle,' Yvonne pointed out smoothly. 'We're striving to survive intact. Though now I can see why Jacques finds you so fascinating.'

'Don't be fooled,' Eva looked at her sideways 'He doesn't. He finds himself fascinating. But only when there's an audience.'

'That's not very flattering to you.'

'I'm nothing more than a shiny little shard of glass, madame. He looks to see his own face, not mine.'

Some shadow of recognition moved across her features. 'I wonder that you're satisfied with so little,' she said, quietly.

'The important thing,' Eva changed the subject, 'is that the perfume have the Hiver name and that its creator, Andre Valmont, be identified as essential personnel to Hiver Cosmetics.'

'There are no guarantees.'

'But you will try,' Eva pressed.

Yvonne nodded slowly. 'You know, I think,' she reflected, 'that maybe the bottle could have a picture of the Eiffel Tower, but that the name should be something more neutral. Perhaps something like *Ce Soir.*'

Eva frowned. '*Ce Soir* doesn't mean anything.'

'I know.' She smiled. 'But products that carry the Hiver name don't need anything else. Go on. Why not look around?' she suggested, with a wave of her hand.

Eva walked back inside. Yvonne trailed in after her.

Eva inspected the apartment, moving slowly from room to room. When she came to the bedroom, she stopped. 'What's this?'

'It's a bed of course.'

'It's a little vulgar.'

Yvonne folded her arms across her chest defensively. 'It's a family heirloom.'

Eva shrugged.

When they were done, Yvonne Hiver took up her headscarf, re-tied it around her head. 'You know,' she admitted, 'there was a time when everyone was talking about that little shop of yours, about Andre Valmont. I was really quite envious. But now I wonder, is this Jew of yours really as talented as you say he is? Or has he lost his way?' Reaching the doorway, she turned. 'Only, for all the fuss, I thought you would smell better than you do.'

Paris, Spring, 1955

Grace walked into the empty apartment. Going to the window, she looked out over the Place des Vosges. An uninterrupted view of the Paris skyline was spread out before her, like a giant landscape painting rendered in shades of bluey-grey, charcoal and purple-tinted umber; the dreamy palette of shifting shadows at twilight.

The blue hour.

Lightly, she pressed her fingertips against the cold window pane.

Le droit de choisir.

Freedom.

Eva d'Orsey had wanted her to have, above all, the ability to choose the kind of life she wanted for herself.

Behind her, she could hear footsteps, coming closer, stopping in the doorway.

'It's you, isn't it?' Roger said.

Grace turned. 'What are you doing here? How did you find it?'

'I was looking for you.' He turned on the switch. A cold white light filled the room. 'That's better. Also, I met with that French lawyer this afternoon. He drove me here. I wanted to see this place for myself.'

Grace looked down into the courtyard below. Standing in the widening glow of the street lamp, Edouard Tissot was waiting, leaning against his car.

She turned back, suddenly self-conscious. Her heart sped up and her hands felt numb.

Roger was walking from room to room. 'This place is enormous!' he shouted from the bathroom. 'It's bound to be worth more than he's letting on.'

'She was my mother,' Grace blurted out, unable to contain the information anymore.

Roger came back into the drawing room. He looked at her carefully. 'I'm sorry, what did you say?'

'Eva d'Orsey. The woman who left me all this.' Her voice caught, her heart thundering in her chest. 'I'm adopted, Roger.'

Roger stood very still for a moment, thinking. Then he came closer, took Grace firmly by the shoulders. 'I'm glad you told me. That's an end of it, do you understand?' He pulled her to him, held her close. 'No one ever needs to know.'

Without warning, Grace found that she was crying, sobbing. Her shoulders shook and she struggled to catch her breath between sobs. Roger stroked her hair tenderly, kissed the top of her head. 'We can sell all this in a heartbeat,' he assured her. 'We can buy a house in Belgravia now. I promise you, this will all disappear, darling, like a bad dream. I'll take care of it from now on. And we shall never speak of that woman again.'

After a while, when Grace had cried herself out, Roger handed her a handkerchief from his coat pocket. She blew her nose.

'Now go and splash a little water on that face.' He smiled. 'Your nose is all red.'

Grace dutifully went into the bathroom and splashed her face with cool water. Only, looking at her reflection in the mirror, a different face stared back at her, one she couldn't un-see. It was Eva's face.

When she walked back into the drawing room, Roger was pacing the room, counting out the approximate square footage. She stood in the corner, watching him.

'Why did you say we would never mention her again?' Grace asked.

He was calculating in his head and held up his hand, signalling for her to wait. 'I'd say it's easily thirty-five feet by twenty,' he decided, taking a small notebook out of his breast pocket and making a notation.

Grace went back to the window.

Edouard was still there.

'Why did you say we would never mention Eva d'Orsey?' she asked again, wondering if Edouard would look up and see her.

'Why would we? The less we say about the whole affair, the better,' Roger decided. 'Imagine if one of us slipped and it came out in public.'

Grace turned back to him. 'But you don't even know anything about her.'

'That's not the point. You have a family, a very important family, Grace. That's all that matters. Anything else just complicates things.'

'But my family,' she stopped, searching for the right words, 'that's not real. That's not the whole story.'

'Look,' he sighed, 'the truth only matters if it's useful.'

'But don't you even want to know about who she was?'

'If you want to tell me, then I'll listen. But these stories, well,' he sighed, 'they tend to be a bit pathetic.' Suddenly, his face changed. 'She didn't have any other family, did she? Any who could contest the will?'

Grace shook her head. 'No.'

He relaxed. 'What a stroke of luck! Honestly, darling, I don't think this could've worked out better. She lives in another country, has no family; no one in England will have ever heard of her. You know, considering what you've just told me, I have to say, I'm impressed with the way this woman's handled the whole thing.'

'Eva,' she interjected.

'What?'

'Her name is Eva.'

'Yes, well, Eva. She's been extremely generous and also incredibly discreet. She obviously understood what was best.'

Grace slid her hands into her pockets, began to fidget with her father's old lighter. 'I suppose.'

'We can say you received the money from an old friend of your father's.'

'You think we should lie? I mean, not just omit the details, but actually lie?'

'I'm only suggesting we get our story straight in case someone asks. Listen, who gains by us broadcasting her existence? No one. Imagine trying to explain it to our friends.'

'Do you really believe that it would matter that much?'

'Grace,' he looked at her indulgently, 'as much as I adore you, I can't believe you're even asking that.'

Roger began counting out paces in the bedroom. Grace walked over to the window again.

'You haven't got a light by any chance, have you?' she called.

'Not on me.'

'I'm going downstairs. Monsieur Tissot will have one I'm sure.'

As Grace crossed the darkening courtyard, Edouard straightened, instead of leaning on the car. She stopped in front of him and he gave a little nod. 'Madame Munroe.'

'Hello. I . . . I've been wanting to speak to you.' She paused unsure of how to begin.

He waited.

'Eva d'Orsey was my mother,' she said. 'Did you know that?'

His expression changed to one of concern. 'No, I didn't. How did you find out?'

'Madame Zed told me. Showed me a photograph . . .' Her voice trailed off.

'It must be a little disorientating.'

'I feel very bizarre. Like I don't know myself anymore.'

They stood a while. She had wanted so badly to

503

see him again, to speak to him. Now she didn't know what to say. The wind had picked up, cold gusts pushing up from the river. Grace turned the lighter round and round in her pocket.

'My husband is measuring the floor plan,' she said stupidly.

He nodded again. 'How very thorough your husband is.'

'I behaved very badly the other night,' she blundered.

'Really? Well,' he frowned, looking down at the pavement, 'I suppose everyone does things they regret.'

Her heart tightened. 'Do you regret it?'

He looked up at her, his face suddenly stony. 'What would you have me say?'

'You're angry at me.'

'Yes. No.' He sighed. 'I'm angry with myself.' He shifted, took a deep breath. 'In any case, this is probably the last time that we will see each other. Your husband prefers to have this matter handled by an English firm.'

She shook her head. 'This isn't what I want.'

'What do you want, Grace?'

Roger came out of the building, paused on the steps, still jotting notes in his notebook.

Grace glanced over her shoulder then turned back

to Edouard. 'I want to go to a café and sit with you. I want you to order something I've never eaten before and then tease me about it. And I want to walk, anywhere, nowhere in particular, and for us to disagree.'

His eyes softened. 'Are you sure? What if the food has too much flavour?'

She nodded. 'I want too much flavour. From now on that's all I want.'

Roger stopped in front of them. He looked from one to the other and smiled. 'I'm done. Shall we go back to the hotel?'

'I'm so sorry.' Grace touched Roger's hand lightly. 'I'm afraid I won't be coming with you.'

A week later, Grace unlocked the door and Mallory walked inside.

'So, this is it!' Mallory strolled into the empty drawing room. 'You weren't joking, were you?' She whistled. 'It's huge! Now I can see why you want to keep it.' She held up the cardboard box she was carrying. 'Where shall I put this?'

'Oh, anywhere.' Grace lugged her suitcase in.

'I hate to be the one to point it out, but you have no furniture.'

'Yes, I had noticed that.' Grace opened up the

French doors. A warm breeze wafted in, tousled the girls' hair.

They walked out onto the balcony.

'I have a whole speech prepared, you know.' Mallory leaned her elbows on the railing. 'About how you really ought to reconsider. Think of your family, your friends. That's me by the way.'

'Yes.'

'But the truth is,' she sighed, 'I envy you, Grace.'

'Really? I don't know what I'm doing, Mal. Or how I'm going to manage.'

'You'll manage just fine. I'm not worried about you.' She looked across at her friend. 'But what am I going to do in London without you?'

Grace reached out, took Mallory's hand. 'I'll probably be back in two weeks, with my tail between my legs.'

'Then I'll march you right back to the airport and put you on the plane again. I want you to be happy, really I do. I just wish you didn't have to do it so far away.'

'You can come and stay.'

'Don't think I won't. And just for the record,' Mallory wiped a tear from her eye, 'I have a real bone to pick with this Eva d'Orsey. How dare she leave you a fortune!'

Grace smiled, gave her hand a squeeze.

'So, seeing as I'm here,' Mallory walked back inside and opened the cardboard box, 'let me help you unpack.' She unwrapped the tissue paper from the little china figures, lining them in a row on the wooden floor. 'My God!' She laughed, shaking her head. 'They're even more ghastly than I remembered! What are you going to do with them?'

'I don't know.' Grace picked one up. A shepherdess with a lamb, sitting on a tree stump covered in ivy. 'They sort of grow on you, don't you think?'

'No.' Mallory passed her another one – a little girl with long blonde hair, picking daffodils. 'I can't believe she went out of her way to make sure you got these.'

Grace looked over at her. 'What did you say?'

'Well, it's just so odd that she saved these for you, gave them to the concierge, put your name on the box. You would've thought it was the family jewels, for God's sake!'

The family jewels.

Of course . . .

Grace picked another one up. The tree stump was wood, the lamb was wool, the daffodils were paper-whites . . .

'My God, Mallory! You're a genius!'

'Really? I've never been accused of that before.'

Grace turned the figure over. It had a hole at the

bottom; the figures were hollow inside. She poked her fingers into the recess.

Nothing.

She turned over the shepherdess.

Empty.

But when she looked in the bottom of the woman with the veil and fan, lounging on a chair with her cheek in her hand, she found it. A tightly rolled scroll of paper, tucked deep inside.

'What is that?' Mallory peered over her shoulder.

Grace unravelled it. The paper was covered with very fine writing; a long list of chemical ingredients, very specific measurements.

'It's the family jewels.' Grace passed it to her.

Mallory's eyes widened.

La Formule Originale de Ce Soir, it read.

Paris, Winter, 1954

She was standing in his office, by the window over-looking the Louvre, when he came in that morning.

'I'm sorry,' his secretary whispered, taking his briefcase and coat by the door, 'but she was early. I didn't know what to do with her, so I showed her in.'

'It's fine,' he told her, though slightly irritated to be caught off guard. He walked in, positioning himself behind his desk. 'Madame d'Orsey?'

The woman turned to face him. She was attractive, perhaps in her early forties, with dark greying hair and rather surprising pale green eyes. She was wearing a deep navy suit, a hat and gloves, and on the desk, lying across her handbag was a small Latin prayer book. When she crossed to greet him she moved slowly, carefully, as if with some effort. And he could see, as she came closer, that her skin was sallow; her remarkable eyes ringed with bluey circles. Removing her gloves, she held out her hand.

'Monsieur Tissot, how kind of you to meet with me so early.'

'My pleasure,' he assured her, indicating a chair opposite. 'What may I do for you?'

Sitting down across from him, she opened her handbag and took out an envelope. 'I am here today to draw up a will.' She passed it to him. 'I have included a list of my assests and the name and address of the recipient. And I have chosen you, because I'm assured you have an excellent grasp of English.'

'Thank you.'

He opened it. Inside was a letter, outlining the sale of a property and a considerable amount of equity retained in shares by an investment firm in Les Halles. On a second sheet, there was the name and address of a woman in England.

Madame d'Orsey opened her handbag, took out a cigarette case. 'Do you mind if I smoke?'

'Please.'

Opening the case, she took one out and lit it. Then, exhaling, she leaned back in her chair. 'I want you to help her. The beneficiary, I mean.' She nodded to the paper in his hand. 'She's not from this country and will need advice.'

She was speaking as if her demise was imminent – not years in the future but months.

'Of course,' he agreed.

'And promise me you'll meet with her alone. If anyone else comes with her, ask them to please wait outside. I want . . .' She paused a moment. 'I want the bequest to be read privately.'

He nodded, made a note on a pad in front of him. 'As you wish.'

Her shoulders relaxed, the tensions in her face eased. 'Good, then.' She sighed, taking another drag. 'Oh, and this might help you.' Reaching forward, she opened the prayer book. Inside there was a newspaper clipping folded into the front cover. She took it out and handed it to him.

It was obviously some years old, cut out from an English publication. It showed a photograph of three young debutantes, standing on a grand marble stairway, dressed in white gowns. Looking at the caption, Edouard matched the face of the first young woman with the name on the bequest. 'Is this her?' She was so much younger than he anticipated. 'A lovely girl,' he added, looking up. 'Is she a relative of yours?'

Madame d'Orsey was quiet for a moment. 'I don't think that matters,' she decided.

Suddenly, a smile spread across her face, softening her features, banishing the pain in her eyes. And when she spoke, he caught the warmth of something confident and sure, like pride, in her voice.

'The past is over,' she decided.

Her shoulders fell, as if a great weight had dissolved.

'What matters now, all that matters now, is what Grace Munroe chooses to do next.'

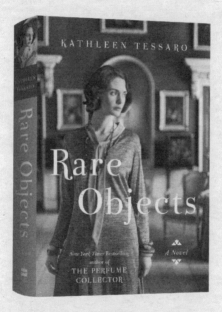